WAKING DANGER

Ryan stared at her with warlike intensity. "It isn't wise to wake the ghosts of the past, Miss Lancaster. Especially those that have taken so long to rest, as it is."

Abby heard the note of warning in his voice. An infinitesimal recoiling of courage stopped her for a moment. She steeled herself, refusing to let him intimidate her. "What's that supposed to mean?"

"Are you familiar with the phrase, 'Let sleeping dogs lie'?"

"Yes."

He eyed her steadily. "Then I suggest you heed it."

"You won't be offended if I ignore your advice, I hope?"

"Not at all," he said. "Just as long as you're not offended by what you learn as a result of your nosiness."

"I'd hardly call exploring my mother's past 'nosy,' thank you very much."

Ryan's eyes narrowed. "Leave. Go home. This isn't the place for you, just like it wasn't the place for your mother before you. No one wants you here. And if you're not careful, you'll wind up getting exactly what you wish for."

SARAH ABBOT

Destiny Bay

LOVE SPELL NEW YORK CITY

For Rose Moses-Wilson, beloved grandmother,
who always celebrated imagination.
I'll love you forever.
And for Andrew,
with all my heart.

LOVE SPELL®

September 2008

Published by

Dorchester Publishing Co., Inc.
200 Madison Avenue
New York, NY 10016

ISBN 10: 0-505-52774-X
ISBN 13: 978-0-505-52774-5

The name "Love Spell" and its logo are trademarks of Dorchester Publishing Co., Inc.

Printed in the United States of America.

10 9 8 7 6 5 4 3 2 1

Visit us on the web at www.dorchesterpub.com.

ACKNOWLEDGMENTS

I've always enjoyed reading authors' acknowledgements, as it gives me a peek into the world of the writer I'm presently enjoying.

If you were to look into my world, the first person you'd see is my husband, Andrew. Andrew, thank you for your unwavering faith in me. Thank you for making "daddy time" such an unequalled delight for our children, and for giving them lots of it so that I could write this book. Thank you for saving this manuscript every time I accidentally sent it spiraling to its cyberdeath. Tina Turner got it right: you're simply the best.

My sincere and heartfelt thanks go out to Natasha Kern, my brilliant literary agent. Thank you for your endless patience, for your encouragement, and for being as dedicated to developing great writers as you are to selling books. Thank you for believing in the dreams of others, and for making them come true.

To Carol Craig, thank you for your insight and guidance. I loved working with you.

Thank you to Alicia Condon and to everyone at Dorchester that made this experience so enjoyable. Alicia, it has been a pleasure working (and laughing) with you.

To my fantastic, wonderful, inspiring friends, thank you for reading, cheering, and telling me that I was on the right track. For countless dinners, unforgettable girls' trips, and for being there when I needed you, thank you Christy, Karen, Laureene, Maria, Nancy, Dawn, and of course, Marni—my ever-true pal since grade school.

Dad, you always told me I could do anything I set my mind to. I never forgot it. Thank you. Mom, thanks for teaching me to love books.

And last but not least, very special thanks to Robert Pembroke. The trajectory of my life changed when I met you. Thank you for being the first person who told me I ought to be a writer, and for saying it with such conviction that I actually believed you.

Destiny Bay

Prologue

Tuesday.

Glorious Tuesday. Magnificent Tuesday. *Fat Tuesday.*

His own, personal, Mardi Gras.

The Lover licked his lips, breathless with the revelations of the day.

He had heard the news at precisely 11:45 A.M.—a moment that would live forever in his imagination; the moment in which fate, at long last, had smiled upon him once more.

The Lover curled into the depths of his shabby armchair, reliving the glorious moment, the magnificent moment, the *fat* moment that he had heard what he *couldn't* have heard, but somehow had . . . *she was coming!*

He'd been gathering his mail at O'Donnell's Post and Petrol when Mavis O'Donnell mentioned the interesting tidbit she'd heard from her husband, Franklin: Abrielle Lancaster, daughter of Celeste Rutherford, was coming to Destiny Bay—a quest, of sorts, to learn about her long-dead mother.

Oh, the things he could tell her!

A veil of perspiration had sprung into instant being when he'd heard the words. Breath had caught in his throat. Mavis had taken one look at him, and said: "My, but you're pale!"

He'd dropped his mail, raced to his car, and—when at last he could—put the vehicle in gear and drove home, mouth watering the entire drive as he glutted himself on memories that made his throat squeeze with their richness.

He felt the memories surge anew within him, as if awakened by the summons of his thoughts. Memories were like that—languishing until resurrected by the dreamer's invitation to dance across the stage of the mind, ripe for the transforming touch of dark imagination.

He remembered *everything* about his lovely Celeste: how she walked, how she looked, the scent of her hair . . . even after all these years, she was still with him in memory, still with him in spirit.

Even though his lovely Celeste was long dead, there could be no denying such love as they shared. Not even death could deny what love insisted upon. In the great scheme of things, love was the impetuous, enchanting child, whose desire had only to be voiced to be fulfilled . . . and death was but the weary disciplinarian, unable to stand firm against love's unrelenting insistence.

The Lover drew his finger over the silky feathers of his parakeet, Amore. *How long has it been?* he asked himself, as if he didn't know *exactly* how long it had been since his lovely Celeste left Artist's Cottage, left Destiny Bay . . . left him. As if every moment of every day without her hadn't etched a line upon his heart.

The deepest of those lines—the one that sometimes gaped so suddenly it made him weak—had come on the blackest day of his life: the night Celeste died.

He closed his eyes, squeezing away the tears that threatened. He couldn't go back to that night—to the needless loss of his beloved Celeste.

At her funeral, he had drifted silently amongst the somber knot of mourners, calm in the face of the terrible pain within him, eyes fixed upon the polished casket as it was lowered into the loamy mouth of Cresthaven Cemetery.

That was when he'd looked up and seen her: a tiny, fighting baby, swaddled in a pink blanket, struggling against the grasp of her father as he, too, watched Celeste disappear into the earth.

Celeste's baby. The last, living testament of her flesh. And anyone with eyes could see that Celeste was strong in her.

Now, Celeste's daughter was all grown up, and she was coming to Destiny Bay.

There could be no doubt that this was Celeste's sweet magic at work. She was fulfilling her destiny the only way she could—through her daughter, Abrielle . . . and he would risk anything to claim her.

Oh, yes. He would court her, would lure her with his matchless love until at last, she remembered who she was—remembered who *he* was. Until she released herself to him, and the essence of her would purr in the palm of his hand, as lovely and pliable as memory.

But memories were obedient in a way few people were. It bothered him that there were variables over which he had little or no control, such as the innate character of a woman. Women could be willfully rebellious and utterly foolish . . . even about things that would bring them nothing but joy. Hadn't Celeste proved that to him? Hadn't his mother?

He stroked Amore with the back of his finger, frowning at the thought.

In all these years, Amore had been his one consolation, the only soft spot in his soul.

Like his mother before him, he loved birds. Mother had been able to coax chickadees from the trees to perch on her fingers and feast on the oily black sunflower seeds in the palm of her hand. With her other hand, she would toy absently with his hair, all the while fixated upon the birds, and say, quietly, "See, lovey? All it takes is patience. Good things come to those who wait."

But the thought of his mother always made him heartsick, so to distract himself he looked down at the box that lay open on the arm of his chair.

Reaching within, he lifted the bound strands of Celeste's long, red hair—so like his mother's—and inhaled deeply. They draped over his palm, awakened thoughts of *other* treasures he had carefully gathered so very long ago.

Looking at Celeste's hair, it occurred to him that perhaps he had more control than he'd originally thought.

The Lover smiled. *These will be the instruments of her awakening*, he thought, the well of satisfaction within him filling up, running over with bounty. *These treasures will help Abrielle realize that she was born to be mine . . . and that I was born to be The Lover.*

Chapter One

Abrielle Lancaster pulled her rental car onto the gravel shoulder, frowning at the tangled convergence of roads that bloomed in front of her. The fact that this was her third time at this very spot wasn't exactly reassuring.

"Who are you kidding, Abby?" she whispered to herself. "*Reassuring* was a lifetime ago."

Or at least a few months ago, before her grandmother died and willed her the house in which six generations of Rutherfords had passed their lives. Tears welled in her eyes at the thought of the gray-haired matriarch of the Rutherford family—the woman who'd shouldered the unexpected task of raising Abby from infancy after the death of her only child, Celeste.

And now, the house that was always meant to pass to Celeste had passed to Abby.

Many people would sell their souls for an address within the exclusive, old-moneyed enclave of Regency Park, but Abby wasn't one of them. It wasn't that she was *ungrateful* for the house—it was just that she'd never really *liked* the house. In fact (though she'd never told her grandmother), she *hated* the house—hated how the stench of loss seemed to penetrate the very wood. Hated how she had inhaled it into her childhood dreams at night, how it pooled in the hollows of her footprints, scattering a trail of murky puddles upon the green path of privilege that was her past. Hated how it had come to be known as the house of The Accident, The Tragedy, The-Terrible-Thing-That-Happened-To-The-Rutherford-Lancaster-Family. People had many names for it, and in the twenty-eight years since the incident, she was quite certain she'd heard them all.

Abby closed her eyes, remembered the standard reply to her childhood questions about her mother: *"She's in heaven."* That had been all she'd needed to hear . . . until she overheard a neighbor whispering that shortly after Abby was born, Celeste Rutherford had jumped to her death from the attic window on the fourth floor. Her broken body had lain on the flagstone terrace until morning, when the cook discovered her, fair and moist with the dew of a new day.

Abby shuddered. The horror of learning the truth was still as vivid to her as it had been twenty years ago, when she was just eight.

Her grandparents, when asked, were tight-lipped, and would say only that Celeste had always been "fragile." Her father—who had been so wounded by Celeste's death that he held Abby at arm's length for the rest of his life— refused to discuss the matter at all, and continued refusing right up until his death of a heart attack two years ago.

Now her father and grandparents had passed on, and all she'd had left of her mother was the striking resemblance she bore to her and the knowledge that her birth hadn't been enough to keep Celeste here on earth.

That was all she thought she'd ever have, until the day she decided to clear out her grandmother's closet. Hidden behind the Chanel suits and Hermès bags, she'd found a painting of her mother, and it was *nothing* like the formal portrait of her that hung in the library.

She could still feel the subtle give of the canvas beneath her fingertips; could still envision the light shift delicately over the peaks and valleys of paint that evidenced the artist's brushstrokes. She could still feel the awe that had swept through her when her eyes met those of her mother's, staring out of the canvas with such naked longing as to make her bare flesh appear demure, by comparison. And demure, it wasn't.

Ample, rounded breasts caught the dappled sunlight, a petal rested in the hollow of her navel. Her thighs were young and strong, rippled with muscle that seemed tense enough to grasp the painter in an unrelenting knot.

Something about that painting had made Abby feel as if she knew her mother—not the prim, practiced society matron in training that others had professed her to be, but the real woman, whose blood rushed through Abby's own veins.

What had brought her mother to this tiny island off the coast of Maine? Who was Douglas McAllister, the artist whose signature was scrawled across the bottom of the portrait? And what *was* it about this painting that seemed to make Abby's heart stand still in her chest?

She'd risked too much to waste a minute, including her job. The three-month leave of absence she'd finally talked Henry Davidson, the CEO of the Pursuits Network, into approving was already four days gone.

"Do you know what you're risking?" Henry had asked, as if she didn't realize every waking minute that no less than three people were breathing down her neck for her job. When he finally realized she wouldn't be dissuaded, he'd grudgingly relented, saying, *"Corinna Williams will assume your responsibilities while you're gone."*

Abby had no doubt he'd chosen Corinna because he

knew exactly how much she wanted to front *Write Away*, Abby's own brainchild.

Every week, *Write Away* featured a different novel, and whenever possible, its author. Abby worked painstakingly to re-create the mood and tone of the featured work as her viewers were led on a tour of the locales featured in the novel (or that had inspired the work). Even the music was carefully chosen to reflect the unique flavor of each area. Abby had hosted the show since its inception over three years ago, and was revealed to be a gifted and insightful interviewer.

"*I think you're making a big mistake, Abby,*" Henry had said as she'd left his office. "*I've never known you to be impulsive.*"

He was right, of course—she'd never been impulsive. Abby swallowed a lump of distress. A pang of remorse followed close on its heels. How many times had she wished she was otherwise? More impulsive, more carefree, more *anything*.

Well, she'd officially made the leap.

Her reputation as a woman of sound judgment and good sense had gone up in smoke. Her friends thought she'd lost her mind. Running off to a tiny island off the coast of Maine in search of a secret that might or might not exist was not something a cautious and sensible woman like Abrielle Lancaster did. A week ago, she would have agreed with them . . . but that was before she found the painting— and before she experienced the unmistakable certainty that she'd found it for a reason. Somehow it felt good to get away from the competitiveness of her career, the emptiness of her personal life. Like it or not, the painting had led her here, staring at a maze of dirt roads.

Abby squinted to better read the road names that ran the length of the sign-festooned pole rising in front of her. Pegleg Lane, Miller's Pass, Brigantine Way, and right at the bottom: Cragan Cliff Road. She checked her directions.

Yup, Cragan Cliff Road was the route to Abandon Bluff—the place her mother had once lived with the artist who'd painted the mysterious painting.

She turned down the bumpy road, anticipation filling her chest. The wind from the open window felt fresh with promise, and she breathed it in, letting the briny breeze blow away her sadness. This was a new beginning for her, and it *wasn't* about sorrow.

Cragan Cliff Road wound along the top of the cliffs like a ribbon of gray. Looking down, Abby saw miles of golden sand mediating the space between the sea and the wall of sandstone that was the cliffs, and just beyond the shore, a colony of seabirds took flight from the skeletal remains of a scuttled ship.

To her left, gnarled pines clutched meager scraps of earth, crippled by buffeting winds that were their constant companion. She turned with the road—the trees seeming to part before her—and was struck with the impression that an unseen jeweler had lifted a cloth enshrouding the town below, which resembled nothing so much as a gemstone necklace, flung onto the arced bosom of the island.

A smile tugged at her lips as she saw homes painted violet, tangerine, turquoise, lime and sunny yellow. The town sparkled through the dissolving mist of morning. No wonder her mother had lived here—it was beautiful!

Was this what had ignited her mother's true spirit and allowed the artist to captured it to perfection, or was there something more? Something that might still be there, on the shores she had lain upon?

That was what Abby had come to Destiny Bay to find: that *something* that made her mother alive. And perhaps, if she looked hard enough, she might even find the something that led her mother to the east-facing window that terrible night. What was it about this place that made Abby feel secrets were hidden here?

The portrait was the key, somehow she just knew it. She was more determined than ever to find out what had happened to her mother. Only then could she unlock her own heart—and she was so very tired of looking for that key.

"I'm coming to find you, Mom," she whispered, and hit the gas harder, almost feeling her mother's spirit drifting on the wind. The cottage she'd rented couldn't be far, now. Feeling suddenly lighter, she flicked on the radio and sang along at the top of her voice. " 'Life is a highway, I'm gonna ride it all night long!' "

She couldn't take it in fast enough—the color, the light, the diamond sparkle of the sea. She let her gaze flit like a butterfly, landing on a tangle of wildflowers, a deer peeking through the trees, and a hand-painted sign declaring: WORLD'S BEST CLAMS!

Then her eyes caught a sudden movement—a discordant spring of bracken just off the roadway. She squinted into the velvet green of the roadside forest and gasped.

A face stared out at her, wild-eyed and grotesque, twisted like the crippled trees that lined the cliffs. The man was looking directly at her, holding her gaze with a malevolent stare that made her blood run cold.

Abby, his mouth said, grinning wickedly.

Abby tried to stifle the scream that clawed to escape her throat. When she looked back at the road, the cliff edge was right in front of her—there was no way she could make the switchback turn in time.

She cried out, grabbing at the wheel, images of the cliff's edge flashing in her mind. Instinctively, she hit the brake. The car spun out of control, twirling sickeningly as it skidded ever closer to the edge of the cliff. She pawed the wheel, too terrified to breathe. The back tires skidded off the gravel road, tearing up grass.

By the time it stopped, the car had come to a rest in the ditch opposite the cliff.

Abby's heart galloped in her chest; spots danced before

her eyes. She rested her head on the steering wheel and simply breathed. *She was alive!*

Surf thundered at the bottom of the cliff, an ominous suggestion of what might have been had she not been lucky.

She straightened slowly, grasped the steering wheel and pressed the gas. The wheels spun uselessly. "Oh no," she whispered.

A quick peek at her cell phone told her she was in a dead zone—no service whatsoever.

Abby peered in the rearview mirror. No one. She looked out of each window. As far as she could tell, she was alone.

Cautiously, she stepped out of the car to survey the damage. There appeared to be none, but the rear tires were a good three inches off the ground. If she wanted to get out of the ditch, she'd need traction.

With her back to the car, she looked into the woods. She had no choice but to gather branches to jam under the tires. No way was she staying out here until another car happened along—not with that maniac in the woods!

She scurried into the brush and started gathering branches to push under the tires.

Why hadn't she seen a sign warning of that deadly turn in the road? And what kind of maniac lurks around in the bushes?

A snapping of twigs made her heart stop.

Very carefully, she inched backward, eyes darting from tree to tree as she made her way back to the safety of her car. Her heel hit something solid and she toppled over, landing hard on her rump.

"What on earth . . ."

Abby looked down at the stump that had once been a road sign. Near it, the top half of the sign lay in a tuft of grass. It read: REDUCE SPEED, 20 MPH. SHARP TURN AHEAD. The sign had been sawed off near the base—and recently, if the sawdust and woody smell were any indication.

"Bloody kids could have killed someone!" she muttered, righting herself and wanting very much to believe that the sawed-off sign was the product of teenage mischief.

Quickly, she jammed the brush under the back wheels. It was just enough.

A chill snaked down her spine as she jumped back into the car and locked the doors, eyes scanning the road, the trees, anywhere a person could hide.

She stared into the woods. No sign of the face that had snagged her attention at such a crucial and dangerous bend in the road. As unlikely as it seemed that someone would be out here in the middle of nowhere, just staring at cars drive by, Abby knew she hadn't imagined it.

She needed to get out of here. Fortunately, the branches beneath her tires did the trick. A gentle nudge of the gas pedal had her back on the road.

Immediately, her thoughts went to the painting in the trunk. If the jostling she'd heard in the slow-motion terror ride was any indication, her things had been tossed around and good.

What if she'd come all this way, risked everything she had to follow the clues in a painting, and she'd gone and ruined it before even reaching her destination?

She shook her head at the thought. The painting had to be fine . . . it just *had* to be.

And Abby—the least superstitious woman around—began to wonder if landing her rental car in the ditch before she even found the cottage could possibly be a bad omen.

Chapter Two

Ryan Brannigan had never liked surprises. Surprises, by their very nature, robbed a person of control in any given situation, and above all, Ryan Brannigan was determined to be in control.

Slowly, he inhaled through his teeth. "Tell me you're joking."

His mother looked at him over the rim of her glasses, as if allowing him a moment in which to rephrase the demand, if not withdraw it altogether. "I beg your pardon?" she asked, brows all but disappearing into her hairline.

"I said, *'Tell me you're joking.'* Tell me that you didn't rent the cottage to Celeste Rutherford's daughter."

Cora Brannigan's eyes narrowed menacingly.

Ryan was undaunted.

"I'll do no such thing," she said with characteristic brusqueness as she bustled around him. "I've never been known as a tease, much less a liar."

She swept into the back office, and Ryan followed, a gust of sea breeze at his heels as the door of Brannigan's General Store swung open to admit another patron.

He turned a baleful eye on the unabashedly curious stares of the staff and customers alike. Faces lowered, one by one, as Ryan closed the office door behind him. He was more than accustomed to being the topic of conversation in Destiny Bay, but that didn't mean he liked it.

"Can you at least tell me why I had to hear this news from Gerald Blake, and not from you?"

Cora smiled pleasantly. "Perhaps for the same reason I learned that you and Jennifer were getting a divorce from your Auntie Joan, and not from you."

Ryan blinked—an infinitesimal break in the poker face that he immediately rectified. "That was four years ago. And stop trying to change the subject—I'm not interested in discussing the past."

"Oh, you're not interested in the past, is it?" She closed the ledger that sat in front of her with a thud. "If that's true, you'll leave this business about Abrielle Lancaster be—what's done is done, and neither you nor I can change it, son."

"Abrielle Lancaster is not welcome here, any more than her mother was before her."

Cora shot him a gaze fit to render any other man incapable of further comment. He'd seen it strike other men speechless. Unlike other men, however, he'd spent the better part of his misspent youth building up resistance to that very glare.

"Not welcome?" said Cora. "Says who? I'll wager her money is as good as anyone else's, and the cottage has been vacant for close to a year."

"*I'll* rent it." He snatched his wallet from a back pocket, spread the supple leather, and began thumbing through the bills. "I'll double the damage deposit, and pay you an extra fifty a month."

His mother threw her head back and laughed. "Why, I've never heard of anything so foolish. Vengeance doesn't become you."

"Make it one hundred." He held a fan of bills out for her inspection.

"Put your money away, son. I'll not break my word with the girl, and I'm offended you'd suggest it."

He brought his hand down hard on the desk where she was seated. "*I'm* offended you'd rent to her in the first place!"

Cora lifted a warning finger. "I'll not have you berate me in my own store, Ryan Brannigan. I raised you better, and well you know it. As for the cottage rental, might I remind you that Franklin O'Donnell gave her my number because I own seventy-five percent of the rental units in this town, and you own the other twenty-five percent. Who else was he going to refer her to, might I ask? When Franklin found out who she was, he thought it would be nice for her to stay in the cottage her mother lived in. She jumped at the chance."

Cora leaned back in her chair, her tone guarded. "It's time you moved on, son. Time you took a risk and dared to live and love in spite of the blows life dealt us all those years ago."

Ryan's blood began to boil. "Move on? *Move on?* Remembering is what makes me strong."

"No, son. Remembering makes you less than you could be." She rounded the table and smiled gently at him. "Let it go, Ryan. You weren't born to be shackled."

His jaw flexed beneath burnished skin; his eyes fixed on the horizon beyond the window. "I'm not going to let it go. Ever."

Cora smiled sadly. "Keep hold of some things, yes. Keep hold of what made us who we are today. I'm a self-made woman and you're a well-educated, self-made man. We'll never want for anything. Not ever again." She placed her hand on top of his.

"Hardship brings its own blessings, my boy. Just think, Ryan . . . without them, I'd never have become a fighter, a survivor! I would have never had the strength to pull myself out of my poverty. And you, well, you would have never had such a fire in your belly." Cora patted his hand. "But fires burn hot, son. Hot enough to destroy."

Ryan rubbed along the length of his jaw. "And hot enough to temper steel. *This* fire only makes me stronger." He rose from the corner of the desk and strode toward the door. "I don't want her here, Mom. Mark my words, no one will."

He slammed the door in his wake.

Ryan strode past the gaping customers, glaring at any

who dared make eye contact and, at the same time, scorning the cowards who began digging in purses and industriously studying the labels of soup cans, instead.

He would be fodder for the gossip mill—of that, there could be no doubt. Among the faces that had gawked up at him, he had seen both Winnie Small and her meddling cousin, Geraldine.

He slipped on his sunglasses, grateful for the iota of disguise they afforded his emotions, and strode out of the store.

In the growing light of morning, the sound of burgeoning engines filled the air, mingled with the lonely call of seagulls wheeling above the trap-laden decks of lobster boats.

Ryan quickened his pace as he caught the first whiff of sea-touched air, heard the beckoning hiss of surf upon sand.

Before him, the harbor basin cradled the liquid silver of the sea, offering the quiet magnificence of its wind-ruffled surface to any who would accept its gift. The morning sun was golden, yet somehow purest white as it tripped over wavelets and fell headlong into the ocean.

Another glorious day in Destiny Bay, and he had fouled it up royally.

There was no way around it. His mother deserved an apology. *Not* his strong suit, to say the least—and if it were anyone other than Cora, the offended would have had better luck coaxing a prison guard into a tutu.

Too forgiving for her own good, she might be, but Cora Brannigan deserved much in this life, not the least of which was kindness and respect from the boy she had single-handedly raised to manhood.

What he needed was to cool down.

He rethought his intention of completing some paperwork and made a sharp left onto Brigantine Way, heeding the call of the sea that sang in his veins.

He rounded the corner of the restored saltbox that

served as office and packing facility of Brannigan Fisheries—
a company he had built from scratch with nothing but
determination and the winnings from a lucky hand of
poker.

The building had cost Ryan a small fortune to restore and
convert, but such was the price of conducting business on
the historic waterfront. Even the tattoo parlor had not been
spared the relentless mandate of the Historical Society, and
had grudgingly set up shop in a prim little Cape Cod.

Ryan shook his head at the incongruous sight of tangled
rosebushes, picket fence, and garish neon sign that read:
BODY ART AND PIERCING. "Only in Destiny Bay," he
muttered under his breath as he pushed through the gate
leading to Brannigan Fisheries' private dock.

The sea surged rhythmically, placid as a summer's sigh
as it rose up the length of barnacle-encrusted pylons beneath the dock, then hissed in retreat. Ancient-looking
ropes draped the underside of the weathered wood, lifted on
the current and heaved mussel-bound, glistening tentacles
into the sunlight, their backs as smoothly humped as an
emerging pod of whales.

Ryan surveyed the scene, glanced at the vessels
moored at Brannigan Fisheries, and spied the decidedly
unsophisticated-looking *Carrie-Rose*—a lobster boat with
an unparalleled knack for plowing through nor'easters.
She lifted and beckoned seductively on the swelling breast
of the sea, and without a split second's thought, he leapt
from the dock and landed in a neat squat on her deck.

A flock of gulls took flight, squawking their protest into
the wind, but the sturdy *Carrie-Rose* barely registered a
shudder in response.

A head peeked over the stern of the trawler *Fish Tale*,
brow ruffled at the commotion. "Ryan, I didn't expect you
today. You needin' something, man?"

"Yes. Keys." He lifted both empty palms, smiling
crookedly. "Do you have a set?"

Terry Friars, captain of the Brannigan Fleet, looked curiously at his employer. He ran his hands over the sides of his coveralls, fished into a bulging pocket, and withdrew a jangling set of keys. They skittered across the deck of the *Carrie-Rose* and landed at Ryan's feet.

"Thanks. I'll be back in an hour or so."

The man nodded and turned back to the engine of the *Fish Tale*.

Ryan hardly spared him a thought. Didn't so much as indulge the realization that for some unknown reason, his finest lobster boat wasn't at sea, filling her bowels with the flapping green-backed treasure of Destiny Bay. Right now, he was content that she was there, like the perfect lover: ready, willing and able to provide an escape.

He steered her carefully around the sandbars, through the north passage that led into the undulating Atlantic, and pressed her engines forward as he plowed into an oncoming wave.

Before him, the ocean glistened; a jewel of countless, shifting facets and immeasurable bounty—the only woman who had ever caught him, hook, line, and proverbial sinker.

She had lapped at his feet in playful childhood, had raged with him in the anger of his youth, had washed over his flesh when he made love on her shore.

It was the sea that breathed a wisp of silent remembrance, sent tendrils of mist from her foaming crests to lure him out of himself and beckon him home from sterile, inland cities that reeked of diesel and concrete.

He eased the engines to a halt a few hundred feet from shore, drew the salty air past the constriction of anger in his throat, felt the involuntary flex of his jaw.

Of all people to rent the cottage, why *her*?

Ryan furrowed his brow, wondering if there was anything to the laws of karma, and if so, cursing the misstep that had brought this specter from his past to the island.

Not that it was much of a stretch to begin with. Destiny Bay was a quiet town, where the voice of the past was *always* heard. One voice, in particular, resonated like no other—that of an artist's muse; a young woman of such rare beauty as to make the very landscape envious, if rumors were to be believed.

Often, Ryan had imagined her, this woman that people still spoke of. Whatever happened to the artist's woman?

That was what irked him the most about Destiny Bay. People never forgot a bloody thing.

To their credit, they never forgot one of their own, either, and Ryan had been raised and nurtured by a village who considered him one of theirs.

That's not to say that he didn't have his share of run-ins with his elders—his infamous youth was the stuff of legends, even still. And he had had the dubious distinction of being escorted to Cora's door by more fathers, farmers and fishermen than he cared to recall, *and* warned to stay away from their daughters in no uncertain terms. Still, they had been patient, and when they whispered behind his back that the lad could hardly help himself with the father that he had, he had done his level best to keep from taking swings at the men, even as his blood raged in his veins, revolted at the very mention of his father's name.

The folks of Destiny Bay loved him, of that there could be no doubt. And more than a few of the very fathers who had warned him off their daughters now seemed eager to offer them up on a silver platter.

As if to quell the rising indignation he felt, he breathed slowly and deliberately, focusing his thoughts on the swells that surged beneath the heaving deck.

There.

Like magic, the sea worked like an elixir on his rankled soul.

He opened his eyes at the precise moment the sun

caught Abandon Bluff in a wash of amber light—gilded heather and stone touched rolling earth with strokes of violet. On the far horizon, a pale, reluctant moon paused and dangled like a pearl on the morning sky's gray bosom. Artist's Cottage was not visible from this vantage point.

The uncultivated beauty of the place was breathtaking. *Even to a jaded soul like me*, Ryan thought silently.

He stared as if he'd never before witnessed the particular shade of light unique to Destiny Bay at midmorning; as if he'd never before seen the colors of sand and sea and sky enshrouded in an illusion of gauzy whiteness.

A gentle gust of wind fluttered the pages of the captain's logbook, catching his attention. Ryan scowled at the curled and dog-eared corners, pulled his eyes away, and did his level best to ignore it.

The wind grew, rattling the weighted cover, refusing to be ignored.

An indrawn breath all but exploded from his lips in exasperation. He yanked the cover open and ripped a sheet of paper from its binding. A quick rummage produced a serviceable—if rather gnawed—pencil, and, ignoring every instinct of the islander he was, Ryan turned his back on the ocean, faced the town perched on the edge of the Atlantic, and began to sketch.

With the swiftness of one who knows his subject thoroughly, he drew the village across the bay. It was perched on the edge of an island shaped like a sliver of moon; a village that had thrived in spite of gale, loss of fathers, sons, and livelihoods; a town that had been built from the sea-soaked wood of scuttled ships. He drew streets that followed the shore, and some that soared up the vast hills of Destiny Bay, drew brightly colored homes that wore the leftover paint of boats with names like *Siren's Song* and *Lucky Lady*.

He drew quickly, almost frantically, sketching in the

bench in front of Brannigan's General Store, as well as a few of the ancient fishermen who polished it to a shine with their rumps.

Ryan looked down at the sketch he had created and couldn't deny the quality he saw.

He clutched the drawing in a ruthless grip. Then he hurled the sketch into the sea, watching as the salty water saturated the paper and at last, swallowed the picture into its briny mouth.

Ryan swore under his breath.

Why her? Why now?

He, along with the rest of the populace, had been shocked to find out exactly who Abrielle Lancaster of *Write Away* fame was—though many were the claims that they would have recognized the daughter of Celeste Rutherford anywhere.

Before Johnny Mackenzie, brewmaster and womanizer extraordinaire, had informed him of Abrielle Lancaster's parentage, he had actually thought the woman a knockout when he'd occasionally caught her on TV. Anyone would be hard-pressed to get him to admit it, now.

Well, she wasn't welcome here, any more than her mother before her.

Ryan Brannigan swore by the sea; swore by the fish that gave rise to the town he loved, by the salt, the sand, and every sacred oath known to fishermen and their sons that Abrielle Lancaster would regret her choice to come here.

She might have come, but if *he* had anything to say about it, she wouldn't stay.

Chapter Three

Abby hauled her luggage down the length of the verandah. A quick rummage in her purse produced the key she had sought—incongruously flimsy in comparison to the thick, weathered door that stood before her.

She swiped a tangle of windswept hair from her eyes and entered the main room of the cottage.

It was beyond charming, with low-beamed ceilings, slip-covered furniture, and souvenir plates hanging on the wall. Chintz and gingham winked at her through the dimly lit room, and a bank of glowing embers crackled in protest of the brisk draft that entered at her back. She closed the door quickly, enveloping herself in the faint, musty aroma of the unoccupied cottage.

She walked through the kitchen and into the living area, ran her hand over the thick, oak mantle that crested the fieldstone fireplace, wondered if her mother had touched it, wondered if she had stood just here, warming herself by the flames.

To her left, a huge window occupied much of the wall and looked out over the heaving Atlantic Ocean.

Smiling, she started tugging her bags up the little stairway. The upper landing opened to another room—the bedroom—which featured a waist-high bed piled with quilts, a washstand and a gorgeous antique dresser.

Her mother had been happy here—she could just feel it.

She wanted to settle right in, unpack, have a shower, and find a bite to eat. After that, she intended to make a list of questions regarding her mother. When she encountered people who had known her, she wanted to be prepared.

First order of business, however, was a shower.

She headed downstairs. Now, where was the washroom?

A sudden, sinking feeling swept through her chest. *Where was the washroom?*

"Oh, no." Abby raced back up the stairs of the tiny cottage for the second time. This time, she didn't waste a moment admiring the charming little place or wondering if her mother had touched this or that. This time, she was on a mission.

She yanked open the one other door she could find on the second floor. A closet. "Oh, no!"

Back downstairs.

She yanked open the odd little door that was tucked beneath the stairs, eyes searching frantically.

All she saw in the awkward space was a few shelves and a large, metal tub.

"Oh . . . no." Cautiously, she walked to the back wall and lifted a lace curtain at the window. Her heart plummeted. There, tucked beneath a stately oak, was a small wooden building, maybe four feet wide and seven feet tall. The turquoise paint was peeling from the walls, and the yellow door—which featured a crescent moon cutout— was hanging on what appeared to be one, rusty hinge.

And wouldn't you know it? She had to go.

"Horrid cottage," she muttered, stomping through the dewy grass. "Stinking outhouse!" She swatted a low-hanging branch from her face, breathing through her mouth in an ill-conceived attempt at avoiding the stench of the outhouse . . . only now she swore she could *taste* it.

An outhouse! And *she'd* used it! And *what* was that metal tub she'd seen in the closet? Was *that* what she was meant to bathe in? And was she supposed to fill it with water *by hand?*

This was going from bad to worse.

Abby emerged from the clump of trees that surrounded the outhouse and walked between the trunks of two pristinely white birch trees to the beach below. Abby felt the scowl melt from her face, felt a tingling surge wash through her being.

There—about two hundred feet away—standing on the deck of a lobster boat, stood a man. Not just any man. Abby felt washed in a tide of unmistakable familiarity. She *knew* this man.

She inhaled sharply, her skin prickling. *But that's not possible!*

The man was young, tall, lean, and moved with the grace of a born athlete. He looked at the ocean, and as he did so an extraordinary expression came over his face.

Abby felt it mirrored on her own face—felt as if everything but this moment was draining away from her consciousness.

The man seemed as though he had absorbed some of the primitive mystique of the island; some of its gold and its light, some of its secret darkness. She watched his bronze skin, saw the rhythmic surge of smooth, corded muscle beneath; envisioned the strong bone that kept him balanced on the deck—as silent and deadly as a predator, as beautiful as its prey.

There was something purely magnetic about the man— something feral and charged that she felt instantly. The feeling intensified as he moved toward the wheel, grew in thrumming presence, until he turned that icy stare directly upon *her*.

Abby gasped—more at the instinctive internal recoil of her inner being than at the unhidden hatred in his eyes.

Her cheeks pricked with heat. As impossible as it seemed, it was as if he knew she'd be standing just *there*, as if he had summoned the darkest memories of his life and visually spewed them at her.

She turned quickly, wanting nothing more than to be far, far away from that person. She definitely did *not* know him!

The ground was uneven, and Abby cried out as she tripped and tumbled to the grass. She glanced over her shoulder and glared at the massive swell of tree root over which she had tripped in her haste to escape the man's threatening gaze. She heard the thrum of a motor as the lobster boat departed.

She let her head fall back on the green, sheltered grass, which was soft and cool and mercifully upwind from the dreaded outhouse.

Who *was* that man? Why on earth had he seemed familiar? Abby squeezed her eyes shut, hoping he wasn't a close neighbor. If it turned out that he was, he might just replace the outhouse as reason number one why she was moving out of this cottage ASAP.

Every ounce of surety that she had felt about coming here evaporated. "What a disaster," she said, thinking that perhaps she *hadn't* been led to the painting for some great, cosmic reason. Thinking that perhaps it was a bad sign that she was talking to herself so much.

I blame the outhouse, she said silently, deciding it wasn't so bad to talk to herself as long as she did it in her head.

If she were lucky, she'd be able to find her way back in to town. If she were even luckier, there would be a nice little apartment, complete with a fully functioning bathroom, ready for immediate occupancy.

"Hello? Anyone home?"

Abby almost swallowed her tongue at the unexpected voice. It had come from the other side of a neglected-looking boathouse. She scrambled to her feet. "Hello," she called back, dusting bits of grass and twigs from her behind. "I'm over here."

A woman—scarcely larger than a child—emerged from around the corner, chin resting on the neatly folded stack of linen she carried. She looked at Abby and stopped dead in her tracks, her face turning pale. Just as quickly, she recovered. "I brought you some towels," she said with an unmistakable tremor in her voice. She extended a hand in greeting. Abby shook it, yet couldn't help feeling that she had startled the woman, even frightened her by her presence.

"I noticed the other day that the ones I had in the linen cupboard were looking a bit threadbare," she said with contrived brightness—or had Abby imagined that? "You must be Miss Lancaster. I'll be Cora Brannigan. I thought I'd come by and meet you. So sorry I couldn't be here to greet you proper. Did my best to ready the place for you though—it having been empty for nigh on a year—and it's a good thing I did! A fine mess, it was, but that's what I get for renting to bachelors—three tenants running, no less."

"Thank you, Mrs. Brannigan. How kind of you."

"Mrs. Brannigan's me mum, dear," she said, the tremor nearly gone. She tilted her head to better see into Abby's eyes, and the strange expression was there again. Abby couldn't quite decipher what it meant. "We don't bother much with the Mr. and Mrs. bit 'round here—unless of course it's a fine lady like yourself."

"Oh, please," she said with a wave of her hand. "Call me Abby. I love your accent. Do you mind me asking where you're from?"

Cora chuckled. "I'm from right here, deary! Saint Cecelia Island was settled by Irish, Scottish, French—and anyone else who happened to wash up on our shores. We're isolated, see, so the accents mingled and stuck. You should hear the folks on the north side of the island— they've got the French up there, aye? You can't understand a blessed word they say!" Everything about the woman gave the impression of movement—from her hurried yet graceful stride to the large blue eyes that seemed to take in everything around her at a single glance. Abby felt thoroughly sized-up—albeit benevolently.

"And listen to me, babbling away while your poor self stands looking so lost!" Cora looked in dismay at Abby's disheveled clothing. "Had a tumble, did you?"

"As a matter of fact, I did." She loped up behind Cora, who was already making her way down the verandah. Abby didn't take her eyes off the planks she walked upon. The verandah was suspended over the heaving Atlantic on the most precarious-looking stilts she'd ever seen, and if those stilts had any intention of giving way, she wanted to be the first to know about it.

She rounded the corner, which offered her a view of the rocky coast. The lobster boat was no longer there. Abby shivered as she recalled its captain.

"Cora, just before you arrived I saw a fisherman." She pointed to where the boat had been. "Just out there. I'd guess he was in his thirties, he was tall and . . ." Abby paused, realizing she had no vocabulary to describe him, realizing that her reaction had been so immediate and so visceral that she could barely recall his physical features. "I was just wondering if you know who he might be."

Cora turned to face her, looked up the coast as if to discern by the air currents that stirred in his wake the identity of the stranger on the boat.

"I only ask because he seemed incredibly angry."

Cora's expression was guarded, but her voice was cheerful. Too cheerful, perhaps. "Oh, well it could have been most anyone, I s'pose. Now, let's get you settled."

"Uh, there's another thing," Abby said, plunging forward before the unsettled feeling she was getting from Cora distracted her. "About the outhouse . . . I didn't realize there was no plumbing at the cottage. I've been thinking that I really ought to reconsider our lease agreement."

"No plumbing?" Cora said, looking at her askance. "There's running water in the kitchen."

"Well, yes, but there's no actual *bathroom*, Cora. A bathroom's a pretty vital part of plumbing, at least where I come from."

Cora chuckled. "Why, you're lucky to have electricity. We only ran it up to Artist's Cottage last spring."

Abby looked at her expectantly . . . surely she was joking? "Well, be that as it may—"

"And besides the outhouse, there's a chamber pot for cold nights. I thought sure I'd mentioned it to you."

"I—I'm certain I'd have remembered."

Cora Brannigan was chuckling again as she led a stammering Abby into the low-ceilinged main room of the cottage. "Ah, you'll get used to it. It's a small price to pay for life in paradise, says I." She rattled the embers in the grate. "I must remember to thank Simon Gorham for startin' this fire for you. It'll get a mite chilly come evening if there's been no fire through the day. Now the least I can do is help get you settled after your difficult day. I feel sorry, Abby, if I forgot to mention the, uh, rustic nature of the place—but it *is* a cottage, aye? I must have gotten distracted when I learned who you were and why you wanted to rent it in the first place." There was an unmistakable undercurrent in her voice, as if each word—no matter how cheerfully spoken—was tethered to something bottomless and immovable within her. "Imagine, after all these years, Celeste's daughter, come to Artist's Cottage!" When she stood and faced Abby, her smile seemed genuine, albeit sad.

She knew my mother. It was all Abby could do to fight the urge to pepper Cora with questions. Something about the woman's demeanor told her to resist . . . for now.

Abby smiled tremulously in return. She felt as if she'd stepped into very deep water. As if she had been swept into a societal riptide that was hopelessly beyond her ability to understand, much less extricate herself from. She couldn't help believing it had something to do with her mother's past here on this island.

"When I found out that my mother had stayed here, it seemed the obvious choice."

"Of course," Cora said, gathering her stack of linen and making her way to the stairs.

Abby followed her up, where Cora placed the towels in the small linen cupboard.

"I heard the sad news of your mother, rest her soul. And your father, rest him, too. Poor lamb that you are! You've come to a nice place for healing a weary heart, though." She caught her breath as though realizing she'd revealed too much, as if she understood all too well about weary hearts. She turned back to the towels, straightening them industriously.

"Did you know my mother?" Abby asked, deciding against informing Cora that both of her parents had died some time ago. And how had Cora heard of their deaths in the first place? She felt at a definite disadvantage, as if she had arrived on an island peopled by folk who knew all about her, while she knew nothing about them. "Did you have the chance to meet her?"

A dangling silence slithered into the small landing, swayed between them before dropping to the floor and coiling, snakelike, upon the woven rug. "I did meet her, yes," she said at last. "But I didn't know her as well as did some. Now then," she said, her voice clipped and bright again, "let's unpack this pile of luggage."

Cora appeared dismayed at the jumble of bags around the room. She grabbed a handle and started heaving. "Oh, what 'ave you got in here, deary? Stones?" She plunked the largest of the bags on the waist-high bed.

Abby rushed over, slapping a hand down on the suitcase. "I can unpack myself, really, Cora. What I mean to say is that I won't be staying, anyway."

Her landlady frowned. "Why ever not?"

"Well—" How best to phrase it? How best to tell your landlady that though you had just met her and genuinely liked her, you knew there was something strange going on between the two of you? And that you really didn't want to encounter that man on the boat again? And that there was no way you were going to use that nightmare of an outhouse or set foot onto a verandah that gave way to a churning, hungry sea? "It's just not what I expected, Cora."

"I thought you wanted to be here because your mother had lived here."

"I did, I mean, I *do*." She was feeling guilty already.

"There, there," soothed Cora, patting her arm. "These things always seem clearer on a good night's sleep. Let's unpack just what you need, and if you still decide that you'd like to leave by tomorrow morning, I'll help you repack *and* rent you an apartment in town."

Abby's shoulders fell. Cora might be small, but this woman's will had the momentum of a fast-moving freight train. "I'll stay on for the night," she agreed at last. "But I can guarantee I'll be moving come morning."

"Well," Cora said, opening a suitcase, "at least you'll be able to say you spent one night at Artist's Cottage with our famous White Lady!"

"What famous White Lady?"

"Our resident ghost," she said, flicking the light switch experimentally and nodding as the bulb flooded the room with light, then just as quickly bathed the room in darkness. Cora frowned, then flicked the switch a few more times until light returned.

"Your . . . your ghost?" Abby stammered. "Here, in *this* cottage?"

"Oh, aye. She's quite helpful, too. She pops up now and then. A sighting of the lady is supposed to warn of coming danger." Cora drew the last word out until it gained a life of its own, sent a wave of apprehension crashing down over Abby. Unzipping Abby's luggage, Cora handed her a neatly folded stack of shirts from within. "Why, not three months ago Winnie Small saw the White Lady glide across the road, right in front of her car, no less! She knew from talk 'round the village that a sighting of the Lady means you ought to be on your guard. Had she not been driving very slowly, heeding the omen of the White Lady, she would have driven clear off Cragan Cliff Road—which, unbeknownst to her, had been washed out in a nor'easter just the night before! She'd have gone headlong into the Atlantic, she would have. Headlong!"

Abby grasped the handful of shirts Cora passed her, staring disbelievingly at her new landlady. Ominous strangers? An outhouse? *Ghosts?* The cottage had officially lost all vestiges of charm. The image of the man appeared before her mind's eye. Impossibly, this man whom she had seen only once and for only seconds was infinitely more unsettling than the other problems combined. Why could she not shake the chill she was feeling? The chill that had everything to do with that man?

"There's a dresser behind you, luv," Cora said, eyeing her peculiarly. "Just go on and put them in."

"Oh, yes, thank you." Abby opened the drawer and shoved in the shirts. "You know, I really can unpack myself."

Cora narrowed her eyes skeptically. "Mmm. Well, perhaps I should stay anyway. You've just put your clothes into the chamber pot, deary."

"I what?" Abby looked behind her. Sure enough . . . "And you're certain this White Lady lives *here?*" she asked, removing her shirts from the porcelain oddity that indeed occupied much of the top drawer, and placing them in the drawer beneath.

"Oh, aye." She handed Abby a bundle of lingerie, not even blinking at the intimacy of what she was holding. Abby did her best not to snatch it.

"Who is she?"

"The cottage is over two hundred years old, you see; she could be most anyone. A whaler's wife, a sailor's fiancée, a smuggler's lady. All I know for sure is that the White

Lady—whoever she may be—met with great misfortune during her lifetime. Perhaps even tragedy. You never hear of a happy ghost, aye?"

A chill snaked down her spine. "I suppose not," Abby said, shrugging as nonchalantly as possible. "But you take for granted the possibility that I actually *believe* in ghosts in the first place. I can assure you that I don't."

Cora looked pointedly at Abby's fingers as they drummed apprehensively against her thigh. "You do a fine imitation of someone who does."

She stilled her fingers self-consciously, curling them into a fist. "I'm from the city. We don't believe in ghosts."

"Oh, my guess is that you will," Cora said, her confidence enough to undermine Abby's substantially. "Trust me on that."

The wind rose around the cottage as Cora spoke, as if the White Lady was assuring Abby that indeed, they *would* meet. Abby shivered and shook off the ridiculous notion. "Say you're right, just for a minute," she said, folding her arms over her chest. "What if I don't want her here?"

Cora's answering laugh filled the quiet cottage. "Why ever wouldn't you? She's helpful, as I've said. She warns people when danger's a-comin'."

"And who," Abby asked, brow lifted eloquently, "warns people when the *White Lady's* 'a-comin'?' "

"No warning there, I'm afraid. Don't worry, you'll come to appreciate her, Abby."

"Strangely, I don't find that reassuring in the least." She tucked the last of her clothing into a drawer. "So tell me, Cora, have you ever seen her? The White Lady, that is."

Cora tilted her head, eyes shadowed. She stared at the wall behind Abby, as if conjuring the ghost from her memory. "Aye, long ago. She was floating over Briggs' field, just before I was about to take a shortcut through so that I might get home early. I took the long way," she said, her tone suggesting that any fool would have done the same. "Can't imagine what would have happened if I'd gone through the field, but I'm glad I didn't just the same."

"What did she look like?"

Cora froze. "Beg your pardon?"

"The White Lady." Abby was suddenly breathless. "What did she look like?"

Cora blanched, as if she were seeing the ghost all over again. "Why, she looked a bit like . . . oh, who can say? It was dark, aye?"

A sudden chill cooled the room. A trail of goose bumps prickled along Abby's skin, as if an unseen presence had brushed against her. Abby felt an inner tension, as though strangely, impossibly, the end of Cora's sentence was going to be: *she looked a bit like you.*

If she could have, Abby would have given herself a good shake. She was clearly exhausted, and not dealing well with it at all.

"Right, then," said Cora, dusting her hands as if to rid them of excess flour. "You're all set. Come see me to the door, and we'll have a chat about this lease, just in case you decide you'd like to move out after all. I'm thinking perhaps you'd be more comfortable in one of my apartments downtown. I have a lovely one—fresh painted and all— that looks right over the bay. A very pretty view, to be sure."

"It sounds great." Abby's stomach growled loudly, as if to inform her that she hadn't eaten since early morning. "Cora, if you'd be so kind as to recommend a restaurant, I'd be indebted. I'll need a place to have dinner. You know, I recall seeing a place called Rum Runner's on my way here. How's the food?"

Cora's eyes bulged. "Oh! You don't want to be goin' there, dear!" She led Abby down the stairs, where she rummaged in her purse for pen and paper. "The Surfside is where you want to go. The food is tasty, and—" Cora's cheeks reddened. She lowered her face hastily, as if to concentrate on the directions she was writing for Abby. "Your mother once worked there as a waitress. You know, when she was living with Dougla—with the artist. She, uh, did a fine job, if I remember rightly."

A thrill bloomed within Abby, thoroughly eclipsing Abby's questions regarding Cora's peculiar demeanor. "Oh, Cora, thank you!" She accepted the hastily scrawled directions to the Surfside, held them over her heart and swiped her suddenly tearing eyes. "I'm sorry, I'm a mess. This is all so overwhelming."

"Aye, that it would be," Cora said, her tone gentle.

Abby followed her into the late afternoon light that flooded the verandah. She took one look and stopped dead in her tracks.

It took her precisely half a second to come to the realization that a sunny day in Destiny Bay was just this side of magical.

She stood for a peaceful moment, letting the auburn light unfold around and within her.

Late summer was thick in the air, and evergreens seemed to stretch and yawn to the late-afternoon sounds of nature. Their shadows fell beyond the cool expanse of sand, dabbling their skinny tips in the hissing surf.

Abby inhaled a lusty portion of sweet, ocean air, deciding, as she did so, that if she could figure out a way to bottle the stuff, she'd be in the running for a Nobel Prize.

Between the weathered planks she stood upon, Abby could see tangles of vegetation and the gray boulders that supported the house—so similar in color to the sun-washed, silvery wood beneath her feet. Beyond the polished banks of stone, the surging ocean was a dither of sapphire and diamond.

A flood of impossible remembrance filled her thoughts. It was as if she had been here before, had waded through the water and trailed her fingers through the surf, rippling its surface with her passage.

Perhaps her mother had been so moved by this place that it had changed her in some way, had interwoven itself in the double helix of her DNA. And now, it was in Abby. Thumping with her heart and blood.

Abby closed her eyes against the swell of emotion that engulfed her. Her mother had lived here, had loved here, had breathed this air and swum in this ocean. She had slept beneath the very roof of this apple red cottage—and somehow it all seemed so much more intimate a connection with her than the house in Regency Park had ever been.

Abby looked at Cora, who was smiling knowingly. "I think maybe I'll stay on. Just for a bit."

"Aye. I thought you might," said the woman. Her mouth lifted at the corners, eyes gone soft with the knowledge of what it meant to be swept up in the spell of Destiny Bay. "Most of our settlers landed here because of shipwreck—in other words, completely by accident. I always thought it interesting that they all chose to stay."

"Perhaps they had no means of getting off the island once they got here."

"Oh, it had nothing to do with that," Cora said wisely. "There's a reason it's called Destiny Bay, aye? Folks have always said that the island chooses who comes here and who doesn't. The island drew my folks' ship off course over a hundred and fifty years ago. I'm here because I'm meant to be." She patted Abby's hand. Abby felt a subtle yet definite kinship arise between them, as delicate as a spider's web, and every bit as tenacious. "And like it or not, my dear, so are you."

Chapter Four

Abby shut the door of her car, trying to ignore the loud rumbling in her stomach. The tea she'd consumed after a short rest at the cottage had done nothing to appease her hunger. She'd amazed herself by finding her way back into town, which was nothing shy of a miracle considering her distracted state.

Her brow furrowed as she recalled Cora's flushed face, the way she had dipped her head when she'd mentioned that Celeste had worked at The Surfside. *Why had Cora reacted that way?*

In fact, many of Cora's reactions were downright confusing. She seemed to be a lovely woman—warm, welcoming, cheerful and generous. And yet, there was something undeniably enigmatic about her. It was as if a constant undercurrent of loss and secrecy eddied and pooled around her, leaving Abby feeling completely perplexed.

Was it a natural distrust of strangers? The island *was* isolated. Did that make islanders suspicious of strangers, no matter how innocent the motives behind their visit?

She sighed quietly, hoping that she was wrong. If they were mistrusting of newcomers, her quest would be thwarted before it began.

It's nothing a little kindness and determination won't overcome, she assured herself, forcing her mind to her present goal of finding something to eat at the restaurant her mother had worked in, and perhaps even a person who might remember her.

She amazed herself a second time by making it across the impossibly narrow cobbled street without losing the heels of her Jimmy Choos. She looked up and felt her jaw drop.

The timbers of the building were old, and were stained black. The front bay window looked as if it had been snatched from a sea captain's cabin of yesteryear, and a crow's nest soared from the roof. An amply endowed figurehead held a sign over the door that waved on rusty hinges, and her bulging eyes seemed to look down at the curlicue script that read: THE SURFSIDE RESTAURANT.

Warmth and music spilled into the street as people exited the building. A delectable aroma wafted toward her, along with the sound of laughter and a faint ribbon of smoke. She picked up her pace with designs on whatever menu selection was responsible for the marvelous smell now purling over the cobblestones . . . as long as it wasn't *that*. Her eyes locked on the chalkboard placard declaring the chef's special: SEAL FLIPPER PIE.

Abby stifled a gasp. *They were kidding, right?*

Another group of patrons passed by her, all of whom paused on the large front step. A thunderous volley of stomps and a chorus of "*A curse on you, Jack!*" filled the still, evening air.

Abby stared, dumbfounded.

"Well, give it a stomp!"

She looked up at the man holding the door for her. He nodded encouragingly.

"Right," she said, utterly confused. "A stomp."

Abby rose gingerly onto the front step and stomped.

"Oh," he said, a look of disgust on his thin face. "You can do better than *that*."

She stomped again and looked up expectantly.

"That'll do, I suppose," he said with a shrug. "You'll have to try a mite bit harder, though, if you don't want Black Jack giving you nightmares tonight."

"I'll, uh, keep that in mind," she said, even though she had no idea what he was talking about. She followed him through the door and blinked, knee-deep in unfeigned amazement.

"Oh, I hardly heard you come in," said the hostess, who stood, menus in hand, at the front door. She was tall, stout, and crowned with the thickest mane of bluish white hair Abby had ever seen. "You'd best practice that stomp. Bit tentative, it was." The woman handed her a menu and tossed her head to the left. "There's a table over by the helm. I'll be with you in a minute."

The helm?

Abby spied a slightly raised platform, complete with wheel. She made her way toward it, gazing around the interior of the building—the bulk of which, she suspected, had known its heyday in the grand old age of sail. Menus printed on aged parchment and floorboards that bore the warp and stain of seawater only added to her initial suspicion.

A haze of smoke swooned beneath the lazy turning of ceiling fans, and the sounds of camaraderie, clinking glass and accordion music filled the air.

Abby seated herself and unrolled her menu.

"You're not from around here, are you?" The hostess had returned, breadbasket in hand.

Abby looked up into extraordinary eyes, green as ocean glass. They reminded her of two marbles that had been pushed into a dried apple, and she wondered how she'd failed to notice them earlier. "No, I'm not. I just arrived today, in fact."

"I thought as much. I'd remember a fine-looking woman like yourself. Gotta keep my eye on the competition," the woman said with a wink. "Your waitress will be Ronnie Morgan, owner of the Surfside. She doesn't usually wait tables, but thanks to Marie-Claire's second hangover this month, she's slogging away with the rest of us," she said merrily.

"Oh . . . how nice. I mean, about having the owner as a waitress, not about Marie-Claire's hangover," Abby said, deciding once and for all that this was undoubtedly the most peculiar place her travels had ever brought her.

"Would you like to hear about our specials?"

"I noticed them as I came in," Abby said cautiously. "That pie isn't really made of seal flippers, is it?"

The woman—whose name tag read Rose—cocked her hip. "Well, what else would it be made of? And a right fine job chef has done on it, too. Shall I ask Ronnie to order you a piece?"

"No! No, thank you," Abby said quickly.

"The cod tongues and cheeks are nice."

Abby bit the inside of her cheek. And her tongue—pitying the cods that had given up theirs for the Surfside. She glanced hurriedly at the menu. "Um, how's the cedar-planked salmon?"

"Dreamy, m'dear. I highly recommend it."

"Heavens be thanked," she said under her breath. "I'll have that."

"Oh, a fine choice. I'll tell Ronnie—where has that girl got herself to, for mercy's sake?" Rose asked, glaring around the dining room.

"Uh, Rose? May I ask you one more thing?" Abby's pulse was suddenly galloping in her chest. "Have you been working here long?"

"Oh, aye—since Miss Morgan's folks owned the place. Celebrated my fortieth anniversary last month!"

Abby's spirits rose a little. So did the corners of her mouth. "Oh, congratulations!"

"Thank you kindly. Ronnie and her parents got me a right lovely watch and a full week in Boston! I saw a play, threw a crate of tea into the harbor. Oh, I had me a fine time, indeed."

"I'm sure you deserved it." Abby smiled, wiping her hands down the length of her pants. "There's just one more thing. Uh, I was wondering if you might happen to remember a woman who worked here a long time ago. Her name was Celeste Rutherford."

Rose's face changed from open welcome to barely concealed hostility. "Oh aye, I remember her. You'd be wise not to go remindin' folks of *that* business." She patted her heavily sprayed bouffant hairstyle primly. "Why are you even asking, if you don't mind the question?" She looked at Abby through narrowed eyes that suddenly widened with recognition. "Why, you must be her . . ."

"Her daughter," Abby said icily. She wanted to shout at the woman, but nothing could move past the tightness in her throat. Beneath the tablecloth, her hands fisted.

"Oh, I hadn't thought . . . that is to say . . . I must get this order to the kitchen!" Rose babbled at last.

Abby let out the breath she didn't realize she'd been holding. How dare that woman behave so rudely, and how dare she refer to her mother as *that business*? What on earth was that supposed to mean?

She glanced around the dining room in search of the owner. She had half a mind to complain about Rose to this Ronnie woman.

Heads lowered quickly throughout the dining room. Abby caught the gaze of at least four other patrons, and all had been staring at her with mingled fascination and disdain.

She forced herself to nod in greeting though her mouth quivered and her stomach heaved within her. Her legs twitched with the desire to escape the suddenly claustrophobic room. Something very strange was going on here, and Abby knew that it had everything to do with her mother.

Kindness and determination, she reminded herself.

Abby gritted her teeth and smiled.

"Here you are, miss."

Abby looked up at her waitress—a tall, willowy woman with soft brown eyes and hair that could only be described as burgundy. She placed the mouthwatering plate of salmon, grilled vegetables, and rice pilaf in front of Abby with a flourish.

"I took the liberty of bringin' along a nice carafe of wine. I'm Ronnie Morgan, by the way," she said, holding out her hand and revealing long, polished nails. She was a striking woman, who carried off her quirky outfit of the plaid miniskirt, white, tight-fitting blouse, and black army boots to perfection.

"Thank you," Abby said, shaking Ronnie's hand and suddenly remembering how famished she was. "I'm Abby." Should she say something about Rose? She decided against it. If Ronnie Morgan and her parents had treated the obnoxious woman to a week in Boston, they likely thought she hung the moon.

"*More mozzarella sticks?*" A thunderous voice, followed by a stream of obscenities, floated from the kitchen.

Abby sank in her seat, though a quick glance at the unruffled patrons led her to believe that shouting and swearing were not such an uncommon occurrence here at the Surfside. She hoisted herself upward, deciding that it wasn't all that far removed from stomping and cursing pirates.

"Don't mind Chef," Ronnie said with a dismissive wave of her hand. "People order the mozza sticks just to give him a fit. He thinks he's too good to prepare common fare. Bit arrogant, but he's earned a few braggin' rights, talent that he is. I was a genius to hire him," she said, surprising Abby by sitting down opposite her.

Abby's mouth watered at the enticing aroma wafting from her plate. She popped a morsel of salmon into her mouth, completely at a loss as to what the dictates of etiquette demanded in the event that a waitress seats herself at your table. At present, she was hungry enough not to care. "You *are* a genius!" Abby said. "And so is your chef. This is the finest salmon I've ever tasted."

"Of course it is," Ronnie remarked offhandedly. "Just caught this morning, he was. Gave Uncle Ned a wicked fight, at that. Landed him flat on 'is arse! Old codger charged me extra for that. Imagine!"

Abby blinked. "Is that so?"

Ronnie leaned forward, filling Abby's glass. "'Tis. Old Ned's as slippery as a fish, himself. I only buy from him to keep Aunty Jane in bingo cards, bless her soul. That's his wife, aye?"

Abby nodded, as if she had a clue who on earth Uncle Ned and Aunty Jane were. "Would you care for a drink?" she asked, carafe poised over the glass in front of Ronnie.

Ronnie chuckled delightedly. "Ah, you'll fit in 'round here just fine, Abby. I'll let Chef know you like the salmon. According to him, it's *'Fit for ze gods, cheri! Ze mere fact zat I offer zis ambrosia to mademoiselle and not ze Pope has assured me a place in purgatory!'*"

Abby grinned. "He's probably right, you know."

"Aye, that's true. I must say, it's a relief to find you so friendly, especially with you being a TV personality and all. None of us knew quite what to expect."

"None of us?"

"Oh, the town," she said, as if there were nothing out of the ordinary in being expected by an entire town. She selected a breadstick and bit off a healthy portion. "Now, here's what I don't get: why did you come anyway? Oh, I've heard the rumors. You're here to find a long-lost family heirloom; you're writing a book; you're the artist's love child . . ."

Abby felt in sudden danger of choking, despite the fact that she hadn't placed a single thing in her mouth. "Love child?"

"That's right," Ronnie said, leaning forward just a bit. "So, is it true?"

"Uh, no." Abby dabbed her mouth. "I'm a Lancaster, through and through."

"Ah, that's too bad. My Auntie Jane's put money on it, along with half the folks down at the pub."

As no words seemed forthcoming, Abby simply blinked.

"Tell me about the long-lost family heirloom angle," she managed at last.

"Oh, that. Well, folks say that your mother lost a valuable piece of jewelry. Some say it was stolen, others say it was simply misplaced. Heaven knows if you lost a piece of jewelry in the woods by the cottage, you'd never find it again."

"Do you know what kind of jewelry it was?"

Ronnie shrugged. "Necklace, perhaps? It would be easy to snag the chain, aye?"

"Hmm." Abby made a mental note to jot down this bit of information. "It would be easy, I guess."

"Will you look at that?" Ronnie asked, nodding toward the window. "Look who's standin' out there, just glaring into my restaurant?"

Abby turned. As if drawn by a magnetic force, her eyes fell upon those of the man on the boat. Her jaw dropped, breath caught in her throat. Quickly, she turned back to the table, hoping her face was not as flaming red as it felt.

"Ryan Brannigan," Ronnie announced. "Resident heartbreaker and finest guitar player this side of I-don't-know-where."

"I see."

"Steel yourself, Abby. Mark my words: one look at that man and you'll be smitten."

"I don't 'smite' easily," she said, recalling the fierce anger she'd seen in those eyes. She shivered despite herself.

"Oh, there's nothing easy about Ryan Brannigan." Ronnie sipped her wine, looked thoughtfully into the glass. "I learned *that* the hard way when I tried getting over him."

Abby thought it best to steer the conversation in another, less sensitive direction. "Brannigan . . . is he any relation to Cora Brannigan?"

"He's her son. You'll meet him soon enough, I'm guessing."

"Her *son?*" *That boorish man was Cora's son?* A few curious patrons turned at Abby's outburst. She smiled nervously, shrinking in her seat. "Well," she said quietly, "considering that I rented Artist's Cottage from his mother, I daresay you're right." Though the realization was anything but welcome.

Ronnie sidled her chair closer to Abby, the chains on her army boots rattling. "He's considered quite a catch around these parts, aye? He runs himself a right fine group of businesses, too. Cottage rentals, a fishing fleet. Spends most of his time at Rum Runner's, though—that's the pub he opened when he first moved back here."

Abby's appetite suddenly turned. She couldn't even look at her salmon, let alone eat it. "Sounds as if you're the local expert on the man," she said, her lips tight.

"I like to think so. I'm hoping I still have a chance with him, but if I bat my lashes much more, my eyelids will wind up in traction."

"I wouldn't waste your time." Abby couldn't help the acid tone that crept into her voice. "There's something seriously wrong with him."

"Why on earth would you say that?" Ronnie asked peevishly. "You don't even know him!"

"I may not know him, but I've encountered him twice now since I've arrived, and both times he was positively emanating hostility. If I didn't know better, I'd say he was following me."

"Maybe he's here to see me. Or maybe he's here to eat? Did that ever occur to you?"

Abby bit her lip. She'd said too much and she'd offended Ronnie. She forced a chuckle. "Of course, you're right. How silly of me! Now, why don't you tell me about this building?" she asked a tad too brightly. "I'm guessing it was a ship, at one time."

"It was." Ronnie leaned in, her anger slowly dissipating. "This building was constructed from the most notorious sailing ship ever to run aground in the history of Destiny Bay, and that's saying something, believe you me.

"We've a right proper fleet of war ships, galleons—even a ghost ship or two—just off the coast, there," she said, tossing her head in the vague direction of the ocean. "Saint Cecelia's Shoal is a wicked dangerous place for a ship. Been known as the graveyard of the Atlantic for well over two hundred years."

"Really?" Abby said, suddenly conscious that she, too, had leaned in closer.

"Really," Ronnie said, eyes narrowing just enough to suggest something sinister. "The ship that was used to build this place was called the *Defiant*. A pirate ship, she was, and filled to the brim with the worst sort of fiends you could imagine."

"You've told this story before, haven't you?" Abby asked, grinning in relief when she noticed that Ryan had gone.

"Told it? M'dear, folks here have been *raised* on it. Mainlanders may have their boogey-man," she said, voice barely over a whisper, "but we've got our Black Jack."

Abby lurched in her chair as another thunderous round of thumps sounded outside the front door. "And what's the stomping all about?"

"Oh, that. Well, that's a tradition that's been around since long before you and I were born. You might have noticed that trees are a rare commodity around here, so lumber's precious scarce. Folks 'round here have been salvaging the hulks of scuttled ships for lumber since settling this place."

"Priceless," Abby said, shaking her head.

"Free, actually. Just how we like it," she commented, spearing a morsel of Abby's salmon and popping it into her mouth—a gesture that seemed entirely appropriate, considering . . . well, considering everything.

"The *Defiant*, as I've told you, was a pirate ship. The crew members survived, and wreaked the worst kind of havoc imaginable all over the island before they were stopped and hanged."

"How awful," Abby said, secretly intrigued by this tidbit of Destiny Bay history.

"As you can imagine, our upstanding forefathers didn't particularly want to use the wicked pirate lumber, but we're a thrifty sort. Unfortunately, we're superstitious, too.

"To make a long story short, the good folks of Destiny Bay threw their principles to the wind, salvaged every scrap they could, and settled their unease by cursing the captain of the *Defiant* whenever they crossed the threshold." Ronnie shook her head, defeated. "I lose more doorsteps that way."

It was too much. Abby gaped at her hostess. "Tell me, please, how on earth has this place stayed a secret for so long?"

"Haven't you figured that out?" Ronnie asked, grinning. "We're descended from pirates, m'dear. There's nothing a pirate does better than guard his treasure."

"That's an amazing story."

"And true, every word," said Ronnie. "There's even a festival to celebrate our pirate ancestors—Marauder's Return. It's coming up in a couple of weeks."

"Can I ask you just one more thing?"

"Shoot."

"I understand your parents owned this place before you did. Do you think they'd be willing to speak with me about my mother, Celeste Rutherford? She worked here years ago, and—"

"Ah, so that's why you're here!" Ronnie leaned back in her seat, frowning slightly. "I'll ask, sure, but I can pretty much guarantee they'll say no. It's the way of the island to let sleeping dogs lie. Way back, after the *Defiant*, there was a phrase coined that says: *to speak it is to call it*. It's how people deal with things they can't undo—they pretend it never happened, and they do their best to prevent it happening again."

"I don't understand," Abby said, trying to keep the irritation from her voice. "What harm would it do to talk to me about my own mother?"

Ronnie's gaze was sympathetic. "None that I can see, but as I don't know anything about her, I can't help you." She patted Abby's hand. "I'll ask. Could be that I'm wrong."

Again, the needling thought that this was not going to be as easy as she'd expected occurred to Abby. She rose and gathered her purse. "I'd appreciate that. Thank you for a delicious meal and the delightful chat."

"Oh, it was my pleasure, Abby."

Abby tossed her sweater over her shoulders. "Where should I pay for my meal?"

"Pay?" Ronnie gaped at her. "Why, it's on the house, Abby. We're friends, now."

"Oh, I couldn't . . . you paid extra for that salmon!"

"I insist." Ronnie snatched a bill from her pocket— presumably Abby's—and tore it to bits.

Abby frowned at the tattered shreds of paper that littered the floor. "Would you settle for a fat tip?"

Ronnie's answering smile was angelic. "Oh, only if you think it necessary."

Abby dug into her purse, laughing, and pulled out several generous bills.

Ronnie tucked them into her pocket, eyes a-glitter. "I'll see you again soon, now, will I? I'm hosting a small gathering tomorrow night that I call the Chef's Table. We'll close up shop and eat 'til our buttons pop. Would you like to come?"

"It sounds great!" Abby said, grinning. "Just so long as I don't have to eat seal flipper pie."

"Don't know what you're missing, m'dear." Ronnie steered Abby toward the door, arm linked in hers in the practiced way of old friends. "I'll find out what I can about your ma and get back to you. Now, don't forget to give that doorstep a good thump, or I'll not be held responsible for what befalls you in your dreams—and, repeat after me: a curse on you, Jack!"

Resistance was futile. Abby knew that, now. She stepped onto the front step, felt a brisk wind buffeting her cheeks as she did so. "A curse on you, Jack!" she bellowed, and followed it with a volley of stomps fit to trounce the wicked pirate another few feet under.

"That's the spirit!" Ronnie called, arm raised in farewell.

Abby cuddled into her sweater. It was surprisingly cool for this time of year, and she wondered if she would get to see snow before she went back home in three months.

Three months wasn't long, especially if people decided to maintain this bizarre code of silence they seemed intent upon preserving.

Ronnie's words sounded in her head. *We're descended from pirates. There's nothing a pirate does better than guard his treasure.* Did they guard the past as well?

She arrived at her car and frowned at a small rectangle of white paper that fluttered beneath her wiper. She tugged it out and read, her fingers beginning to tremble and her breath coming quickly. She looked around the street, but saw no one.

The note screamed out to her in the silence.

Abrielle Lancaster,
Go home!

Chapter Five

For two hours The Lover had sat, still as the yearnings he had trained into submission, still as the unwavering memory of her face, still as her bones, laid low in the earth.

Waiting.

His body trembled in protest, quivered with anticipation—like an animal awaiting its prey.

Still, he commanded silently, turning a searching eye inward and watching the building tumult within his soul. *The time is not yet.*

The problem was, nothing within him was still, anymore. Not since the whisperings had begun. Not since he heard that dreamed-of unimaginable: *her daughter is coming.*

That day seemed forever ago, and yet so close he could still smell the sudden wetness that had bloomed on his skin like a fever; he could still hear the riotous, internal *Amen!* that was both an end to his heart's benediction, and its thunderous awakening.

He remembered that moment—the fulcrum upon which his life now seemed to balance—as so profoundly pivotal that every moment leading up to it was before, and every moment following it was after.

Before had once been sweet, then—for far too long—had been bitter.

After would be filled with moments fit to make his memories fade with their brilliance. He would see to that; yes, he would.

He knew, from sweet experience, that good things came to those who waited, but he didn't wish to be kept waiting for another moment. Abrielle had been gone too long, and though he tried to be patient, as his mother had taught him, it was not a virtue that came naturally to him.

Unbidden, his thoughts spiraled back to his childhood, to the days when his patience had first been tried. Nights of crying for his mother's tender care, of pleading with her to come back to him, and always the same entreaty from her lips: *good things come to those who wait.*

But he had been a child—too young to understand that a man must use his time of patiently waiting to nudge along the fates. He must form his *own* destiny.

And Abrielle Lancaster was his destiny.

He crept from his hiding place in the bracken and walked the length of the balcony, as quietly as a ghost. If he stood just there, behind the huge tangle of honeysuckle, she wouldn't even see him. He would be inches from her, and she wouldn't even know! Unless light caught the reflective material that was stitched onto both his jacket and pants.

As if in confirmation, the bright glare of headlights swept around the corner, illuminating the reflective stripes on his clothing. His heart lurched, but the lights continued their sweeping arc uninterrupted.

He breathed deeply, calmed himself with assurances of the love that slumbered deep in Abrielle's heart. He calmed himself with imaginings of awakening that love, bit by precious bit.

Calmness always helped him to think more clearly. Yes, he had been foolish to wear the running suit, but there was a solution to every problem, wasn't there?

A slow, delighted smile spread over his face. After taking something from the pocket, he unzipped his jacket and removed it, folding it carefully and dropping it over the side of the verandah, where it fell onto a smooth gray boulder. He unbuttoned his shirt, removed it, folded it carefully and dropped it on top of his jacket. His pants followed, as did the remainder of his clothing, until he stood naked—the truth of him bare before the very heavens that had brought his love back to him.

The soft wind buffeted his bare flesh, winding around him like a veil. He felt it and knew that it was the caress of Celeste's spirit.

Sweet anticipation filled his chest.

He picked up the locksmith set he'd taken from his pocket. Within seconds, the locked door yielded willingly beneath his ministrations. He smiled to himself. He had a way with his hands.

The cottage filled with sea air as he pushed open the door. He stepped into the main room, barely able to suppress his excitement.

The bedroom, he knew, was at the top of the stairs, and he wasted no time getting there.

Her scent was all around him in the tiny room. He lifted a bottle of perfume and removed the lid. Champs Elysees by Guerlain. He looked down at the rumpled bed and smiled, his eyelids heavy with longing, yet he forced himself to look critically upon the room.

Already, he could discern the skeleton of habits beginning to form. For instance, he could see from the angle of the abandoned pillows that she likely slept on the right side of the bed with a pillow sandwiched between her knees. He could tell by the tea bag that sat in a lonely puddle at the bottom of the trash can that she drank Earl Grey. He could tell by looking at the very few dog-eared corners of her book that she read far too late into the night, and she'd probably finish a book in a night or two.

He opened the bedside drawer and saw a Burberry purse, Lancôme lipsticks, Mac nail polish and three kinds of chocolate.

He smiled, satisfied.

This was his entitlement as the alpha male—to know such things of his chosen, to observe with an eye toward possession. This was the courtship primeval—a solitary practice, in which he was well versed.

But for now, it was time to leave the cottage.

As he turned to go he noticed, for the first time, that a portrait was hanging opposite the bed. His breath caught in his throat as he slowly approached—memories exploding in his mind with every step.

Yes! It was the portrait he had watched being painted!

He reached up and touched the lovely white breast that seemed thrust forward just for him, his mouth filling with saliva. His heart squeezed with longing. Oh how he missed her! He missed her scent and the softness of her skin. He missed the sound of her breath in his ear, her coy little resistances to him—the lovers' game they'd played. He even missed crouching in the bushes for hours on end as she lay naked in the sunlight, letting that foolish artist paint her, letting him believe she loved him.

Yes, even the sun had loved Celeste, touching her with light and making her golden. He should have known that something as exquisite as she could not be meant for this earth, but that's exactly where she'd ended up, wasn't it?

It was time to put such aching thoughts to rest, and so he crept downstairs and through the door and grasped a lush branch of honeysuckle that clung to the verandah post. He lifted the vine, maneuvered himself behind it, and let the tender branches drape and enfold him.

For what seemed like an eternity.

Until headlights crested the hill, turned into the driveway, dimmed with the extinguishing of the engine.

Abrielle emerged from the car, looking tired and worn, looking ripe for the love he could offer. Would Abrielle be coy, as her mother had been?

The Lover leaned forward, eager to rush to her, grasp her to his chest, to reveal to her the secret purpose of her coming—that Celeste had brought her back to him as he'd always known she would. Yet, he resisted.

The Lover knew—from sweet experience—that good things come to those who wait.

Chapter Six

Abby yawned hugely. She stretched in the morning light, lifting her arms and letting the breeze whisper though the snug white tee shirt she had slept in.

She had slept like the dead, despite the fact that countless questions swirled in her mind. Although she hadn't learned anything new about her mother while at the restaurant, she had gained a friend and ally. And maybe, just maybe, Ronnie's parents would agree to speak with her.

But had she also gained an enemy?

She thought back to the first time she'd seen Ryan Brannigan on the lobster boat, thought about the second time she saw him—at the restaurant. Both times he had emanated pure hostility. *Why?* And then there had been Cora's wide-eyed insistence that she not eat at Rum Runner's—her own son's restaurant! *Why?* And who else but him could have left that note on her car?

To let it unnerve her would be to let him win—and it would be a cold day in hell before she let a man with a groundless grudge intimidate her. She couldn't imagine what she had done to anger him, but she planned to find out.

Topping her list of priorities at the moment, however, was clean clothing. With no washer or dryer on the premises, Abby had been forced to wash by hand the blouse and undergarments she'd worn the previous day. She even washed a few articles of clean clothing, just to give herself the practice. The washing part she had licked, but the drying part left her feeling a little less confident.

In yet another experiment in country living, she had resolved to follow the example of Destiny Bay folk and peg her clothing on the clothesline. With a wish on the brisk morning breeze, she grabbed the laundry basket and headed for the backyard.

Thirty minutes later, she stood back, admiring the graduating sizes of clothing and the pretty rainbow of color they made as bras, undies and blouses snapped in the wind in congratulatory salute.

It was ridiculous to feel this proud of herself. She knew it was. She didn't care. "A fine job, Lancaster," she said, as she grabbed the empty basket and turned toward the cottage.

A gust of wind rounded the cottage, bending the flowers that grew around it. They parted just so, leaning forward and right, revealing a muddied patch of soil at their base.

Abby walked over, brow furrowed. She parted the flowers again, peering down at the soil.

Another breeze, this one cooler, swept off the sea.

There, directly beneath her bedroom window, was the unmistakable imprint of shoes. Large, utility-soled, definitely male.

A prickle of unease spread over her suddenly chilled flesh.

Abby turned slowly, scanning the property behind her, peering into the sun-dappled woods. Someone had been here . . . worse, someone had been looking into her window.

And because of the slope of the land, anyone who cared to do so would be able to see into her bedroom window from the backyard.

She rubbed her arms briskly, trying in vain to warm the goose bumps that were her body's response to this unsettling discovery.

Carefully, so as not to disturb the imprint of the shoes,

she placed a foot on either side of the muddy indentations. Her heart thumped again—this time, more fiercely—as she looked through the window, hands white-knuckled on the sill.

She knew what she would see. Still, actually *seeing* it was something quite different.

Abby looked directly down onto her bed, specifically, onto the feather pillow her head had lain upon.

Her gasp mingled with the forest sounds of chattering wildlife, birdsong and shifting branches, interrupting the delicate web of peace they wove.

Abby lurched out of the soil, paint chips clinging to the palms of her hands, body trembling. She stared at the window, at the trampled flowers.

"Think, Abby," she whispered. The command filled her with a quiet burgeoning of determination. When she looked again, it was with new purpose. Her eyes searched the wooded area, intent on discovering the who, the why, the when.

The who . . . well, it might have been Simon Gorham, the neighbor who'd started the fire for her before she arrived and who periodically checked the cottage for Cora. It might have been a curious kid, for all she knew. Or it could have been Cora's son, Ryan Brannigan.

The why . . . if it was Simon, his purposes were obvious. If it was a kid, he might have been wondering what TV personalities wear to bed. Abby shuddered at the thought. It wasn't usually much, in her case. If it was Ryan Brannigan, well, Abby couldn't even begin to imagine what that meant—nor did she want to.

As for the when . . . well, it hadn't rained since she'd arrived. Those footprints could have been made long before she even got here.

Yes, of course, that was it.

"I'm just being paranoid," she whispered under her breath, making her way back to the deck. She flatly refused to be frightened by a couple of footprints that probably had an all-too-logical explanation. Abby chuckled at herself. It seemed that glaring men, ghost stories and pirate legends had gotten the better of her.

She grasped the deck chair she'd been eyeing since arriving yesterday. A riot of honeysuckles had all but engulfed a long-forgotten trellis, and had since embarked upon an enthusiastic coup of the chair. Abby plucked away the largest of the vines and began inching the chair from its niche, letting tumble a bower of honeysuckle that had lazed over its arched back. She frowned at a slip of paper that seemed to fall from the vine.

Picking it up, she saw that it was a receipt for duct tape, tie wraps, and a box cutter, purchased a few days earlier at Lawson's Hardware.

Abby stared at the list, her mind spiraling back to a *20/20* episode she'd seen in which the contents of a suspect's so-called rape kit had been emblazoned across the screen. Hadn't it contained all of these items? Her mind jumped forward, to the hostility she'd seen in Ryan Brannigan's face both times he'd looked at her. And then there were those footprints . . .

"For heaven's sake, Abby, this isn't the city, and it's *certainly* not *20/20*."

Yes, if she'd seen this particular list of items on a receipt back home, she might be more justified in jumping to the conclusion that someone was concocting a rape kit. But here? More likely, Cora—who had been here just the day before—had dropped it.

In an effort to calm her racing mind, she quickly entered the kitchen and grabbed her notepad. Late the previous evening, she'd begun to compile a list of questions about her mother to ask the people who'd known Celeste. She might meet some at Ronnie's gathering tonight, and she had an appointment to see the O'Donnells tomorrow.

On the phone, he and his wife had seemed very friendly, and more than willing to speak with her about her mother.

She scanned the list.

What was she like?

Did you know her personally?

Did she seem happy?

How long was she here?

Did something happen to her here?

Why did she leave?

This day had seemed forever in coming, but now that it was here, Abby felt a thousand butterflies take flight in her belly. What if her whole trip had been for nothing? What if all they could tell her about her mother was the color of her hair, the shade of her eyes? What if all they could give her was what she already had—a fragmented assortment of snapshots, utterly lacking the essential glue of a person, the rhyme and reason that threaded past and present together in a way that created a sum greater than its component parts?

Abby wrapped her arms around herself, shifting slightly inside her nightshirt.

A cool breeze lifted from the sea, redolent with salt and briny with moisture. It clung to her, filmed her with a sudden chill that brought her senses to high alert.

There, on the periphery of her vision, was a fleeting glimpse of white.

Unease prickled over her flesh, an acute awareness that magnified every sound and movement. Abby turned her head slowly.

Her heart lurched in her chest, sent the alarm call to every extremity. Abby swallowed thickly, braced her body, her muscles poised for instant flight.

Heart hammered in her chest as she stared into the trees.

She had seen something moving, a discordant, springlike

release of evergreen boughs—thoroughly unequal to the soft breeze that ruffled the honeysuckle leaves.

She stood perfectly still, staring into the bracken and boughs, narrowing her eyes for intensified focus.

"Is somebody there?"

Silence.

It could have been an animal. It probably *was* an animal. Still, she felt incapable of shrugging off the chill that seeped deeper and deeper into her bones.

Someone had been watching her.

Abby gathered her belongings and walked toward the door, eyes scanning left and right with every step.

Her heart thumped in her chest with the sharpness of a snare drum, then, in an instant, felt as if it stopped. In disbelieving silence, she stared at the stones that lined the shore; stared at the pale figure who moved across them, looking out to sea.

Abby's notebook dropped at her feet, pages flipping in the breeze. Her pencil slipped through a crack on the deck.

It was the White Lady.

A scream lodged in her throat, strangled her need to breathe as she saw the woman dissolve into the mist of the Atlantic morning.

Abby grabbed at the door handle, charged into the cottage and slammed the door.

"I'm seeing things," she said, sliding down the length of the door and landing at its base in a heap. "That's all it is. I'm seeing things."

Seeing things indeed. Seeing a White Lady, a harbinger of doom.

But that hadn't been all. Before she had seen the lady, she had seen trees and branches moving, on the *other* side of the house. And there had been that feeling of instant alert. That flood of awareness that told her she was being watched.

She closed her eyes and breathed with slow deliberateness, forcing her heart rate to halt its mad gallop through her chest. When she was able, she rose on legs that surged with the painful aftereffects of adrenaline. The deadbolt closed with a satisfying snap.

Then, from the corner of her eye, she saw another movement through the window.

She felt frozen to the spot as her gaze met the crazed, menacing glare of the blackest eyes she had ever seen. A shock of white, grizzled hair flung itself out from beneath the edges of a woolen hat; deeply etched lines rimmed eyes, mouth and forehead. A hooked nose protruded over a wide mouth that seemed drawn back in a perpetual sneer.

Abby . . . she watched in horror as his mouth shaped her name.

A scream clawed at her throat, then finally broke free.

As if the sound had released them both from a spell, Abby darted to her purse and grabbed her phone, and the face seemed to vanish into the woods.

"Nine-one-one, what is your emergency?" a voice inquired.

"There's a man outside my house! He's been watching me, and I need help!"

"What is your location?"

Abby rattled off her address, sinking into a tiny ball at the base of a wall. "Come quickly," she said pleadingly, her chest heaving.

She scrambled to the kitchen and pulled open a drawer, grasping the biggest knife she could lay her hands on, all the while staying on the line as the operator insisted.

She stared down at the knife in her trembling hand. Would she have to use it?

"Come quickly," she said again, her eyes riveted on the window, praying that the horrible face wouldn't appear there again.

But just when she thought that perhaps it wouldn't, the face emerged into full, horrifying being, staring in at her with a wicked grin.

Chapter Seven

Abby screamed at the top of her voice, flinging the telephone and running headlong toward the stairs.

Above the sound of her scream, she heard the distant wail of sirens. "Hurry!" she cried, knowing that no one but the madman outside her window could hear, wondering if he enjoyed the sound of her terror.

She thudded up the stairs and raced to her bedroom, slamming the door.

The moment she did so, she was gripped with another fear: she had cornered herself. If the man found his way into the cottage and got to her before the police, she had nowhere else to run.

The siren was getting closer.

Someone was thumping on the front door.

"Police!"

Abby burst into tears of sheer relief. She rose on trembling legs, and inched around the bed. She gripped the wall as she made her way toward the stairs.

"Police! Open up!"

"I'm coming," she called, knowing she dared not go any faster for fear her legs wouldn't hold her up.

She reached the door at last and unfastened the deadbolt.

The door burst open, and through it rushed the sweetest sight she'd ever seen: a man in blue, with his gun drawn.

Abby sank to the floor, weak with relief.

The officer barely spared her a glance. "You alone, miss?"

"Yes. He didn't get in."

He kicked the door shut and continued into the house, peering around corners as he went.

He ascended the stairs, and Abby felt that she could breathe at last.

When he came back down, he had holstered his gun. "Are you okay, miss?" he asked, crouching beside her. He grasped her arm and helped her rise.

"I'm fine," she said, though she didn't quite believe herself. "I'm Abrielle Lancaster. I'm renting this place from Cora Brannigan."

"Have a seat, Miss Lancaster," he said. He turned his back to her and radioed the station. "This is Officer Flynn. Subject is safe. Immediate area secured. We do not require an ambulance."

"Do you still require backup?" came a grainy voice.

"Yes. We need to secure the wooded area behind the cottage."

Abby was shivering now.

"Hey," said the officer, whom Abby put at about fifty. He didn't wait for her to respond. Instead, he pulled a quilt from the back of the couch and threw it over her shoulders.

It was a comforting gesture, and Abby felt her shoulders relax just a bit.

Officer Flynn pulled up a chair and sat opposite her. He had a strong jaw, blue eyes, and salt-and-pepper hair. Abby guessed that he'd been quite a handsome man, back in the day.

"My name is Connor Flynn," he said levelly, his voice soothing. "Why don't you tell me what you saw?"

Abby took a deep breath. "I saw a man, and this isn't the first time I've seen him. The first time, I was driving down Cragan Cliff Road. I saw this crazed-looking man, staring at me so intently that it gave me chills. I almost drove off the road."

He flipped open his notebook and started writing. "And you haven't seen him again until today?"

Abby nodded. "That's right. I had a funny feeling, like I

was being watched. I came inside and that's when I saw his face through the window."

"Can you describe this man?" he asked gently.

Abby squeezed her eyes shut. "I'll never forget that face. He was about fifty or so, with weathered skin and wild black eyes. He had on a woolen hat. His nose was long and hooked." She opened her eyes, and saw that Officer Flynn was regarding her strangely.

"What is it?"

"Well," he said thoughtfully, "I don't want to jump to conclusions, but it sounds to me like you're describing Bartholomew Briggs."

"Who?"

Officer Flynn chuckled under his breath. "The village drunk. He's harmless enough, but he has been known to scare a few ladies. Likes to pop up in their windows and such."

Abby glared. She didn't know which she was more angry with—the village drunk, or Officer Flynn. "I don't find this funny in the least, Officer—harmless or not, the man is a menace!" She rubbed her temples. "Okay, I know that made no sense whatsoever, but . . ."

Flynn jumped at the sound of tires kicking up loose gravel. His hand was back on his gun as he ran to the back window. "Bloody Johnny and his scanner!" he hissed. He looked at Abby. "Just you wait here, Miss Lancaster. I'll deal with this."

Abby stood and looked through the back window, where a tall, dark-haired man was getting out of his truck. The passenger door opened, and another man emerged. Abby gasped. It was the man from the lobster boat—Ryan Brannigan!

She crouched back near the edge of the window, wishing it were open so she could hear what was being said. If the flinging arms and angry faces were to be believed, the two men were determined to know what was going on, and Officer Flynn was just as determined to keep them in the dark. Just then, two more cruisers pulled onto the shoulder.

The two men got back into the truck at last, and pulled away in a cloud of dust. "What was that about?" she wondered aloud.

"Miss?"

Abby whirled around to see Officer Flynn behind her. "Oh, you frightened me! I didn't even hear you come in!"

His smile was reassuring. "Sorry. You don't need to worry about those two. They were heading back to town from some kind of trade show when they heard the call go out over Johnny's scanner. They had no business coming up here, even if one of them thinks he owns this place."

"Whatever you say," she replied dubiously.

"All I need you to concentrate on is getting yourself ready to go down to the station. I've got a few pictures I'd like you to look over. I'll even take you there by way of the scenic route—show you around our little town."

"Uh, that would be great," she said, taken aback only slightly. She was beginning to figure out the rhythm of this place, and accept the fact that most people were friendly to a fault—Ryan Brannigan excluded.

Officer Flynn disappeared from the threshold, and Abby sighed. Here, in this seaside oasis, she'd had more opportunity to fear for her life than she'd ever had in the crime-riddled city.

"Life's just full of surprises," she muttered under her breath, wondering if the same would be true of this evening's gathering at the Surfside. She went upstairs to dress, second-guessing her decision to come to Destiny Bay with every step.

"So, what did you think of Chef's prime rib?"

"Delicious. And if you tell me the steer that gave up his ribs for our meal landed your Uncle Ned on his arse before he caught him, I swear I'll never believe another word you say."

Ronnie chuckled delightedly and slid a shooter across the bar. "Oh, you're a fine one, Abby. See what you think of this shooter. I call it 'The Panty Dropper.'"

"I'm quite pleased with my panties where they are, thanks," Abby said, eying the drink suspiciously. She'd already had two glasses of wine with dinner.

"Your loss." Ronnie winked, tossed her head back and downed the drink in one gulp.

"I'll watch for your drawers. If you hear me whistle, you'll know they've dropped."

"You're a friend, and true, Abby."

"Well, you know what they say," Abby said, grinning, "friends don't let friends drink and drop."

"Shall I get you another glass of wine, then?"

"Only if I'm guaranteed that my underwear will stay in place."

"I think my granny might have a bottle of that particular vintage tucked away," Ronnie replied sweetly, "but we don't sell that poison 'round here."

"How responsible of you. Which reminds me, did you have a chance to speak with your parents?" She had been disappointed that they hadn't come to Ronnie's dinner.

"I did," Ronnie said, wiping a cloth over the bar. "It was very strange, I must say."

"In what way?" Abby asked, leaning forward.

"Well, they got all tight-lipped and huffy. Said I shouldn't be dredging up the past and that a lot of people were hurt in those days. They refused to say one word about her."

Abby slumped back on her stool. "Why am I not surprised?" she asked, raking her fingers through her hair. "I loved meeting your friends tonight, Ronnie, but no one seems to want to talk about her. I have to figure out *why*."

"Oh, there's nothing I like better than a mystery. Why don't you let me do some digging on my own, see what I can find out? Folks might be more inclined to talk to me about it, as I've lived here all my life."

"Would you do that for me?" she asked, her hopes inching back up. "I'd be so grateful."

"I'm on the job," Ronnie said with a wink. Then she paused, sighing deeply. Two bottles dangled, as if forgotten, in her hands.

"Ronnie?"

"It's Ryan. He's just come in. Go ahead and turn. He'll never know we're talking about him. Men are oblivious that way."

Abby turned and looked . . . then turned back quickly, but not before his image was seemingly seared upon her retinas.

A tumble of deep blond hair grew slightly too long, and curled around his collar. Eyes of the most extraordinary tiger-pelt topaz stared out from under his slightly shaggy bangs. A five o'clock shadow intensified his air of ruggedness, though his clothes did anything but. Fine clothing, Abby knew. Apparently, Ryan Brannigan did as well.

"He's certainly handsome," Abby said, rubbing her arms brusquely in a vain attempt to smooth the goose bumps that had sprung up.

"Handsome? That's an understatement." Ronnie looked at her watch, her lips pursing tightly. "Late. Well, that's the last time I save the lion's share of prime rib for *him*. Now that you've had a good look at him, tell me you've ever seen his equal," she challenged.

"I mustn't have. I'd have remembered." Abby glanced at the hearth, longing for the flames of a warming fire to flare into being. The night was warm, but Abby was suddenly chilled.

As if time came to a sluggish stop in the chill of the moment, she watched Ryan turn slowly. She was riveted to his gaze, and an unmistakable bolt of recognition coursed through her, thrilling her, *terrifying* her.

Her cheeks were flaming with heat, her skin prickling with cold. When she thought she might never be able to look away, Ryan turned, shattering her entranced stare.

Abby trembled. She felt branded.

Ronnie leaned across the bar. "I've been crazy about him since grade school. Let me call him over to introduce you."

"Um, uh, the . . ." Abby stammered, blushing furiously at Ronnie's comic expression.

"Rendered you speechless, 'as he? Ah, well, it happens to the best of us."

"What I mean to say is no, I don't want to meet him."

Ronnie looked at her, grinning. "Are you daft, girl? He doesn't bite. Least not until he knows you a bit better. Ryan!" She waved spiritedly.

"No! I said no, Ronnie!" Abby squeaked, grabbing Ronnie's arm.

It was too late.

The man in question turned slowly, lifted his glass in silent acknowledgment toward Ronnie, then turned pointedly away.

Ronnie stared at his wide back, perplexed. "Now what do you suppose has gotten into him?"

Abby felt desperately uncomfortable, knowing that it was *her* that had gotten into him.

Ronnie shrugged. "Ah, well, he's prone to dark moods, you know. He's a Scorpio, see. Get a load of that Scorpio passion, though, and you're more than willing to put up with the drawbacks. What are you, a Libra?"

Home, home, home—it was all she could think. "Cancer," she said absently, placing a splayed hand on her stomach. The meal she had eaten with such relish began to heave within her protesting belly.

She couldn't understand this stranger's effect on her; it was beyond unsettling. Perhaps she was ill?

"Really? That surprises me," Ronnie said, totally oblivious to Abby's distress. "You're very 'girly,' if you don't mind me saying. That jibes fine with Cancer, but you seem a bit . . . well, how should I word it? A bit cautious—like you weigh things out 'til the cows come home. That would be the scales at work. Perhaps you've got Libra ascending?"

"What on earth are you going on about, Ronnie?" Abby asked, pressing her fingertips to her jugular. Her pulse was fast, blood pushing against the walls of her vein as if racing against an unseen enemy.

"The stars, Abby, the stars!" Ronnie said, arms raised toward them in case Abby had forgotten exactly where stars were located. "Now, get yourself up. I'm going to introduce you to our Scorpio friend, and I'll have none of his moodiness, believe you me."

Before Abby could protest, Ronnie had swooped around the bar like a bird of prey, snatched her by the elbow, and was tugging her in her wake.

Abby resisted Ronnie's grip, feeling certain that she was on a collision course with disaster, but to no avail.

"Ryan, you handsome devil, I'd like you to meet my new pal, Abby Lancaster." And with that, Ronnie deftly maneuvered her directly in front of that same hostile gaze she'd witnessed her first day in Destiny Bay.

She felt the blood drain from her face. His eyes were like embers, and seemed to burn into her with equal intensity. His jaw was rigid, his shoulders held stiffly beneath his shirt. All she wanted to do was run. Instead, she mustered her courage.

"H-hello," she said, her voice squeaking as she held out her hand.

Ryan ignored it. Instead, he looked directly past her at Ronnie. He drew her near and kissed her cheek lightly. "Hey, Ron. Good to see you."

Abby's jaw dropped. A few people in the immediate vicinity shifted awkwardly.

"Good to see you, too," Ronnie said, frowning. "This is Abby," she repeated with a helpful shove.

Abby tried not to trip over her feet, and extended her hand once more.

This time, he took it—squeezing instead of shaking—and there was nothing welcoming in his grasp whatsoever. It was an unmistakable warning, made all the more menacing by his narrowed eyes and very quiet voice.

"No introduction necessary."

Instinctively, she slowly drew back. "Nice to meet you," she said lamely, tugging on her hand but finding it held fast.

Ryan leaned down, almost brushing her skin as he whispered in her ear, "You're not welcome here."

Abby stared up at him, wide-eyed, as he let her hand fall.

Ronnie glanced back and forth between the two of them, looking utterly perplexed. She scowled at Ryan and scooped Abby under the shelter of her arm, skillfully diverting her from Ryan's gaze.

"Are you all right, Abby?" Ronnie asked. "What did he whisper to you? Not that it's my business, but if he upset you . . . You know, you don't look well, girl, and trust me, that's saying something."

Abby closed her eyes tightly, amazed yet again by this stranger's effect on her. "I have to go," was all she could say, and she ran into the welcoming darkness of the night.

Chapter Eight

The following afternoon, Abby pulled her hair into a clip and fastened it at the nape of her neck. A touch of lipstick, a brush of mascara, and she was ready for her meeting with the O'Donnells. She smoothed her hands down the length of her ivory silk pants and surveyed her appearance—such as it was—in the warped reflection offered by the living room window.

"Note to self," she said quietly as she pulled a few strands of hair from the clip, "purchase mirror."

After her disturbing meeting with Ryan Brannigan, she'd woken up this morning with every intention of leaving. But something inexplicable held her back: something of the fine salt mist that settled in her bones like a haunting, of dawn's sleepy silence, pierced by a gull's joyless cry. Something in the feeling of a mother's timeless longing—beckoning with outstretched, weathered fingers.

Much as it surprised her, Abby was falling in love with Abandon Bluff, the romantic name given to the slice of land that was mainly occupied by cottages—hers included. Somehow, the cottage seemed so much closer a connection to her mother than the house she had grown up in.

She couldn't seem to stop her mind from racing, and the one point it kept hurtling back to was that Destiny Bay was a treasure more people needed to know about, and why shouldn't she be the one to tell them? The town was filled with glorious old captains' houses—why not turn one into an inn? Why not add a spa? Why not get out of the city, get out of the cutthroat industry she was mired in, and live in this beautiful place for the rest of her life? Why not rescue city-weary folk, much in the same way she was now feeling rescued? Without even thinking, she could count at least forty people who would love to vacation here—who knows what she could accomplish if she actually put her marketing education to good use?

If she were honest with herself, she'd have to admit that she was tired of the television industry. Perhaps that was why she'd been so eager to come to Destiny Bay in the first place.

But of course there was more than just logistics to consider. There were the frightening instances of the footprints, the White Lady, and that feeling of being watched. For now, she was content to believe that her city paranoia had gotten the best of her, and had made perfectly explainable occurrences seem ominous.

The footprints? Simon Gorham, of course, and they'd been there since before she arrived.

The White Lady? The outward manifestation of her complete exhaustion. In other words, she'd imagined her.

The feeling of being watched? Well, the police were about to put a stop to that particular situation.

The only thing that was still troubling was Ryan Brannigan.

It was his eyes that she couldn't forget: utterly still, yet somehow calculating; wounded, yet predatory. Right now, as she looked toward the heaving Atlantic, she saw depths equally as treacherous, but perhaps less cold. She shook her head, perplexed by both the man and her intense reaction to him. And what on earth was *his* problem with *her*? As for what to do about him, well, she could only hope to figure it out soon. In a town this small, avoidance seemed an unlikely option. She had no choice but to face him, and to do it with as much dignity as possible.

The bell above Abby's head jangled as the door of O'Donnell's Post and Petrol closed behind her. She lifted the sunglasses from her eyes and peered around the post office.

A wooden-topped counter dominated the space, behind which was pinned a countless array of stamp books, envelopes and fishing licenses. Franklin O'Donnell had explained on the phone that he'd closed the framing part of his business years before.

Abby wandered over to the counter, where glass jars filled with pickled eggs, candy sticks and organic-looking objects (the origins of which she dared not speculate upon) were set out for sale. A display case filled with homemade fudge towered to her left, brimming with flavors such as cherry cordial, pralines and cream, and . . .

"Be still my heart," she whispered, all but pressing her nose to the glass. "Triple chocolate explosion!"

"Can I get you a piece, deary?"

Abby spun around. "Oh! Hello."

The woman's eyes widened. Her ruddy complexion deepened as she stared unabashedly at Abby, hand pressed to her chest. "Saints preserve us," she said. "My, but you're like her. I'd heard so, mind, but to see the resemblance in person!" The woman maneuvered her considerable girth around the corner of the counter. A helmet of teased, graying hair tipped this way and that, along with her head. "It's like looking back through time, it is."

Abby shifted beneath the unrelenting stare. "You must be Mrs. O'Donnell." She extended her hand in greeting and felt the absent grasp of Mavis O'Donnell's in hers. "Mrs. O'Donnell?" she asked again, this time slightly louder.

The woman shook her head as if awakening, and quickly flapped away the formality. "Mavis, please. And you . . . mercy, I'd have known you anywhere, m'dear." She turned toward the doorway from which she had come, shouting, "Franklin? Get you here, man! You'll not believe who I've got by the hand!"

Abby grew slightly more aware of the hand in question, enveloped as it was, by the warm, meaty ones of Mavis O'Donnell.

"Come into the kitchen and sit you down, deary," she said, bustling around the counter and drawing Abby toward the door behind it.

Abby followed as if pulled into the woman's wake, eyes taking in the aged black-and-white linoleum and cherry-sprigged wallpaper.

Mavis reached into the depths of a yellow-painted cupboard and emerged with three teacups.

"I've tea on to brew," she said, smoothing her hands self-consciously down the length of her floral apron, "and a plate of the finest scones you'll ever have tasted, if I say so myself. Cora'd tell you otherwise, but don't be believin'it."

She reached into another cupboard and pulled out a container, placing it on the table in front of Abby. "I saw you eyeing my homemade fudge. Help yourself to a piece."

"How kind of you, Mavis." Abby glanced around the homey room. "You really shouldn't have gone to such trouble."

"Nonsense!" A plate full of piping hot, flakey scones, the color of fresh butter, were placed before her, along with a cut-glass dish of preserves and its twin, filled with thick cream.

"Well, and where have *you* been, laddie? It's a fine gentleman keeps a lady waiting, says I. Abrielle Lancaster, this is my husband, Franklin," she said, turning her attention to her shuffling husband. "Oh, I know you'll curse your poor, weary eyes when I say this, Franklin, but if this Abby isn't the image of her mother, God rest her." She turned back to Abby, whispering under her breath, "Legally blind."

Franklin looked in the vague direction of the door frame, smiled and nodded obediently. He was smaller than Mavis by a good three inches and fifty pounds, but had a pleasant, intelligent face with a tired handsomeness that put her in mind of tweed jackets and fine tobacco.

Abby liked him instantly, felt filled with gratitude for this unassuming man who had first told her about her mother's sojourn in Destiny Bay.

"*She shacked up in Artist's Cottage with that crazy fool who painted her naked six ways from Sunday,*" he'd explained when she called the number of the framing shop on the back of the portrait.

Abby had been shocked at the news. Naked paintings and crazy artists fit nowhere within the parameters of what she'd thought she knew about her mother—the prim, fragile society woman who had leapt to her death without even leaving a note.

"*You're lucky to have that painting, miss. As far as I knew, Douglas McAllister destroyed every painting he'd ever made of your ma after she gave him the boot. Went right out of his mind, he did, tossing paintings into the bay, drunk eight days of the week . . . aye, old Douglas was a proper nut.*"

Now she reached out to shake Franklin's extended hand. "It's good to meet you in person, Mr. O'Donnell. I can't tell you how much it means to me that you're willing to help me."

"Oh, it's nothing, really," he said, as Mavis maneuvered a chair beneath his rump and he lowered himself upon it with the help of his cane. "I'll be as helpful as I can."

Mavis sat beside her husband. "Now, what would you like to know about your mother?"

Abby exhaled loudly. What *wouldn't* she like to know? "Well, first of all, tell me about this man she lived with . . . Douglas McAllister."

Both O'Donnells shifted in their seats. "Well," Mavis said, folding her arms over the shelf of her bosom, "he wasn't well liked, I can tell you *that* much. Had an eye for the ladies, which caused the men to dislike him, and a habit of throwing the lasses over the moment a prettier girl came along, which caused the women to dislike him."

Franklin grunted his agreement. "He was an odd bird.

Paint up a storm for weeks, he would, then wind up cross-eyed drunk and throw the better part of them into the sea! Can you imagine?" he asked, in a tone suggestive of a man who'd suffered through the blight of one-too-many artists.

"Okay," Abby said, "that's . . . interesting. What was he like when my mother lived with him?"

"Foolish," Mavis spouted. "Tripping over himself, he was. What was it he called her, Franklin?" she asked him with a nudge.

"His muse."

"Right. His muse." She snorted derisively. "He was daft over your mother, rest her soul. Not that it would have been difficult, mind. She was easy on the eyes." Mavis crossed herself, and Abby felt certain that if wishes were enough, her mother was indeed quite restful.

"Okay, can you tell me what you remember about my mother . . . about Celeste?"

Both O'Donnells hesitated. Abby searched faces that seemed suddenly guarded. She turned her attention to Franklin. "I expect you didn't know her well, Franklin, but anything you could tell me about her would be appreciated."

Did Mavis's grip on his hand tighten, or did she imagine that?

"Well," Franklin said cautiously, "I guess you could say that she was . . . out of her element here. She rallied well, mind, despite the hardships of living with Douglas and being scorned on every front."

"Scorned?" Abby said, sitting bolt upright. "What do you mean by that?"

Again, the hesitation.

Mavis braced herself as if preparing to jump into very cold water. "In the beginning, your mother was not exactly welcomed here, Abby."

The words hit her like a kick in the stomach. She felt her insides tighten. Abby looked from one to the other, searching their faces. She saw no reprieve. "Why?" she asked, the word coming through her teeth. "Why was my mother not welcomed? Why was she 'scorned'?"

Mavis shrugged, sighed as if held breath were being expelled. "Well, 'tis best you know the truth of it, I suppose." She rose and topped off all three teacups and sat again with a sudden weariness. "She came to live with McAllister—that much you know. But what you may not know is that he was engaged to marry another woman when he brought your mother here. A woman who was dearly loved by the entire community. This woman also happened to be well advanced in a pregnancy of *his* making. I suppose it would be safe to say that your mother was looked upon as something of a—"

Now it was Franklin's turn to nudge—hard. "Watch yourself, Mavis."

"A home wrecker?" Abby finished, red-faced. She turned her attention to Franklin, emotions seething. "And what did you think of her, Franklin?"

Franklin was quiet, now. The entire room was quiet.

"Well?" she asked, mindful of the edge in her voice but helpless to temper it.

"I resented her as much as we all did, I'm sorry to admit."

Abby closed her eyes, willing the stinging moisture away. She needed these people, as rotten luck would have it; needed them to help her piece together a lost segment of her mother's life. To think, only moments ago she had thought them gracious to a fault.

She steeled her resolve. To alienate the O'Donnells now would be to foil her own purposes. She swallowed the lump of defensiveness that swelled in her throat, promising herself a good cry when she got home.

"Was no one kind to her?" Abby asked, feeling a catch in her throat that she hoped was not translated in her voice.

"Well, we were civil," Mavis said. "It's only that we didn't welcome her into the bosom of our society, so to speak. You must understand, Abby, that we all detested McAllister—being the source of such heartbreak to his fiancée. Looking back, I can see that we painted your mother with the same brush. I can also see that your mother never knew about the woman he left behind," she added quietly.

Abby straightened in her seat. "Where is the woman now?" She could have sworn Franklin's eyesight returned— if only for long enough to shoot a warning glance at his wife.

Mavis shifted uneasily. "Oh, she's long gone, m'dear. Too many bad memories, I imagine. Douglas couldn't have been easy to love, and then to be jilted by him with a babe on the way . . . oh, it rankles the very essence of decency, it does."

Why won't Mavis meet my eyes?

Lie-dar her grandmother used to call it—a play on the word radar. When Abby was a troublesome teenager, Gran would use the term whenever she felt that Abby was lying to her, and she was almost always right.

Abby decided then and there that she'd inherited Gran's lie-dar, and that Mavis O'Donnell was definitely lying. *But why lie about where this woman is now? What does it matter?*

A weighty silence settled around them. Abby placed her teacup upon its saucer. "She must have found it difficult," she said, gritting her teeth at the admission. Had anyone wondered if *her* mother found life on this island difficult?

"She did indeed," Mavis said. "And I'm sure your mother did, as well, rest her soul. I'm sorry for it."

Their eyes met over the cluttered surface of the Formica table. Abby saw the apology clearly in the hazel eyes that stared back at her. "Thank you."

"Now, if memory serves me correctly," Franklin said,

seemingly eager to be on with the purpose of Abby's visit, "your mother didn't stay on longer than a year. Surprised us all by lastin' that long, truth be told."

"Do you know why she left?"

"There was some trouble, if I recall correctly. Seems to me she was harassed by some character—never did find out who."

"Harassed?" The more Abby learned about her mother's experience, the more she, too, was surprised the "fragile" woman she'd been told about had lasted so long.

"The proper term is 'stalked,' Franklin," Mavis said. "It's against the law now."

"Hmph," he said. "Shoulda been then, too. The police weren't much help, I'm afraid to say. Never had that sort of a thing 'round here before. Then when she was robbed, well—"

"She was robbed? What was taken?"

"Seems to me she lost some jewelry. I remember she posted reward signs. Shame, it was."

Jewelry. She remembered Ronnie's suggestion that she had come to Destiny Bay in search of a family heirloom. Could the piece of jewelry be the heirloom in question? "Is there anything else you can tell me, Franklin?"

"Well, I remember a few things. It's likely a waste of breath to say she was a rare beauty. You know that already. But, I do remember a soft look she'd get in her eyes whenever she looked at old Douglas. She loved him, against all reason, mind, but love him she did. There could be no disputing that."

"You know, there's *something* else," said Mavis, the light of sudden remembrance illuminating her face. She sat up straighter, resting her chin on her hand. "Funny how I'm only just recallin' this now. It seems to me that when your mother first arrived here, she was *one* way, and when she left, she was another."

Mavis had Abby's full attention. "Can you elaborate on that, Mavis?"

"Oh, to be sure. I remember your mother being a lovely-tempered girl, kind of soft, like. When she first got here, she was smitten with old Douglas—though I can't imagine why—so she *was* a bit dreamy-like." Mavis dropped a lump of sugar in Franklin's teacup and stirred, handing it to her husband. "And even months after her difficulties in the community, the robbery, the business with the stalker, she was still sweet, still eager to be part of us. Gradually, we started lettin' her in. We couldn't blame the girl for Douglas's indiscretion forever, now could we? It was awful difficult to, at any rate. She was a nice person, any way you cut it."

Abby felt her eyes well up, felt her heart surge with relief. "Go on," she said, blinking away a threatening tear.

Mavis leaned back in her chair, rubbing her chin thoughtfully. "Then, she changed."

"In what way?"

"She just *changed*. She was like a ghost of herself; like the sweetness drained away and left her hollow inside. Oh, Douglas was beside himself, he was."

"Yes, he was," Franklin said, nodding at the memory that shadowed his face.

"She drifted around so quiet, you wouldn't even see her. Like I said, she was like a ghost."

Abby swallowed, almost sickened by the omen of her mother's ghostlike transformation. Was that when it had happened? Was that when her mother had lost her way?

"We all thought she'd seen through Douglas at last, but he was fair daft over it, as well, buying her gifts, painting her portrait . . . but now that I think on it, I've never seen a person just fade away over a lover's spat before."

Just fade away . . . like the ghost on the rocks, her mother had faded away. A living ghost, fading and fading, surging once in a while with the brilliance of a shooting star, leaving every witness to her momentary brightness mourning its loss forever after.

Abby cleared her throat. "And then?" she asked hoarsely.

Mavis shrugged, returned to the present with a quick tilt of the head. "And then, one day we all woke up and she was gone."

Yes, she thought silently. *That happened to my family, too.*

"After she left, McAllister drank himself into a yearlong stupor. Couldn't even drag himself out of his self-centered misery long enough to introduce himself to his wee son. A fine man, he was," Franklin said bitterly.

"I thought you said the woman who had his baby left the island?"

"Oh, she did," said Mavis quickly, her cheeks coloring. "Eventually. But she hadn't left yet."

Lie-dar. What was this woman hiding?

"I see." Abby felt a swell of sadness so acute that she wanted nothing more than to be alone in the place her mother had lived, had loved, had breathed.

She looked at the O'Donnells. Their faces seemed tempered by a similar sadness.

Age often brings reason, and looking at them, she had no doubt they regretted their part in closing the ranks of Destiny Bay.

And as beautiful as this island was, Abby had no doubt whatsoever that it could sometimes grow very, very cold.

Chapter Nine

Flowers. A true gentleman began a courtship with flowers—
no exceptions. His mother had taught him that. Yes, she
had raised him to be a gentleman, and he would do her
proud.

He could hardly wait for Abrielle to come home and
find his floral offering. What would her facial expression
reveal? Joy? Excitement? *What?* Oh, the very thought
made him weak.

The Lover smiled gently at Amore as she danced
around in her cage. His impatient little one. She wanted
to be petted, stroked, but he was preoccupied.

He looked down at the pink silk panties he had taken
from Abby's clothesline. The soapy fragrance that unfurled
as he rubbed them made him dizzy, made him drunk. He
clasped the scrap of fabric in his hand and stroked his
cheek, let it slide over the stubble that felt vibrantly,
painfully alive.

He placed the underwear back in his secret box,
reached for a bra. It was mauve, lacy, and hinted at small,
lovely breasts. This much he knew. He had watched her
last night as she bathed in the small, metal tub that
mercifully left nothing to his imagination. He'd watched
her slick a bar of soap over one breast, then the other. Had
stared at them as they glistened with suds, then with the
stream of water she wrung from a cloth.

Lovely.

Yes, the courtship had begun.

With due ceremony, he had opened this new chapter of
his life, going to the secret place—the *sacred* place—and
unearthing one of his treasures: a tiny box of Celeste's

hair, silently gathered from a brush one night as she slept, unknowing, in her bed, not six feet away from where he had stood.

It had thrilled him—to be so close, and yet still not to touch. It hadn't been time.

He smiled in remembrance. Of course, the time *had* come eventually. Ah, yes . . . good things come to those who wait.

He had taken the hairs, those precious, few strands, and braided them together with care. He had placed Celeste's hair in the box beside a lock of his mother's hair, which he had snipped from her lifeless body as she lay in her casket so many years ago.

It had been easy to linger at the funeral parlor after his relatives had meandered into the foyer, heads bowed and voices hushed. It had been easy to lift the lid of her closed casket.

It had not been easy, however, to look at her once beautiful face. They had done their best to cover the bruising, the collapsed facial bones, the deep gashes above her eyes, but there was no disguising the ugly facts of her death.

Foolish woman. Dear, beautiful foolish woman.

He thought of his mother's folly and how closely it paralleled Celeste's. Both women had spurned his offering of love. Both women had wantonly followed the lure of a man far beneath themselves. Both women had ended tragically.

But it would not be so for his Abrielle, oh no. He would see to that. He would end this cycle of needless loss, and he would make her his. This he vowed as he wove the strands of Celeste's hair around an offering for his Abrielle: a bouquet of rosemary for remembrance, forget-me-nots and honeysuckle.

Ah, honeysuckle. He remembered how the artist had sprinkled petals of honeysuckle over Celeste's body as he painted her there on the rocks, how she had smiled as they landed on her flesh.

McAllister, the artist, had stood knee-deep in the frigid water, ogling her, caressing her whenever he could, not even imagining that it was The Lover for whom she lay naked and inviting. The Lover for whom she posed.

And now, at long last, Celeste had come back to him in the form of her child, Abrielle Lancaster.

Of course, Abrielle did not recognize him yet.

That would take time, courtship. Her remembrance would come during the slow dance of seduction that The Lover would choreograph—indeed, *had* been choreographing.

And Abrielle's conscious entrance into the dance would begin the instant her eyes fell upon the offering. Forget-me-nots, honeysuckle, rosemary, hair the color of fire.

Oh, how he hoped she would love the flowers!

He smiled at the thought of her, his lovely girl. Abrielle, he was forced to concede, lacked the natural grace of Celeste, but there was time. Under his patient tutelage, he knew she would blossom as had her mother.

Yes, he thought, a new sort of satisfaction purling through him. He would mold her—would train her—in so many things.

In the art of grace, the art of love . . . oh, yes, the art of love indeed. He would drink the delicacy of her into his soul, and there she would live.

This, he thought silently, *is my calling. To save her from the folly of the women who went before her.*

I am The Lover. The courtship has begun.

Abby had spent an hour sitting on the beach below Abandon Bluff, just thinking. What had happened to her mother here? She was no closer to finding the answer than when she'd first arrived.

Was it possible the mystery had something to do with

Ryan Brannigan's hostility toward her? First chance she got, she was going to confront the man. She had enough to deal with on this island without adding an enemy to the list. Finding out the simplest fact about her mother was proving to be far more difficult than she'd imagined, and she needed all her concentration and energy focused on her reason for coming here.

The sun was sinking now, and she was exhausted as she returned to Artist's Cottage. What she needed before she confronted anyone was a good night's sleep.

Abby paused on the deck, startled by the realization that she had just thought of this place as home. She thought of the house she had been raised in—all of its sprawl and elegance—and realized, with another surprise, that she'd *never* really thought of it as home.

But here, now, standing so close to the sea, Abby felt the possibility of *home* more strongly than ever.

She gazed in awed appreciation at the play of color and light that lay before her eyes. In spite of its lack of creature comforts, this place almost felt like it *could* be home. There was something of her mother here. She felt it, as surely as she felt the breeze against her flesh. Something of Celeste Rutherford had imprinted itself upon the stones, the sand, the twisted pine.

She'd been told that bagpipes had played at her mother's funeral, had serenaded her coffin's slow descent into the earth.

Ever since, when she heard bagpipes, she imagined the music finding her mother's wandering spirit, taking her to the clouds, taking her to a magical place where her soul could finally be at rest.

Now, seeing the sea glow translucent beneath frothy curls of surf, the setting sun catching every undulation in gold, Abby had the unmistakable feeling that the music had brought her mother *here*. That *this* was the home she had found, at long last.

She stared at the scene, for once not wondering why her mother had originally come to Destiny Bay, had secreted away the painting that reminded her of this glorious place.

A subtle smile played on her lips. *What if I actually stayed here?*

Of course, it was impossible. She had too many ties back home . . .

But, what if her life could be just this simple? This elemental? What if she could leave her empty life behind and find a real purpose here?

She grinned at her own whimsy, digging in her purse for her key.

"What on earth . . ."

Abby placed her purse on the bench, crouched and reached for the small bundle that was hanging from the doorknob: a posy of forget-me-nots, rosemary and a delicate blossom of honeysuckle. She lifted the bouquet and sniffed, twirling it in her fingers as she looked for a note.

Something about the small token bothered her.

Abby looked more closely, moving her fingers to examine the knot that enclosed the posy. It was tied in something braided, something reddish gold. She drew her fingertips over it and a feeling of revulsion swept through her.

The flowers were tied in braided strands of long, red hair; human hair. In fact, it looked exactly like the color of her mother's hair.

A strangled-sounding cry tore from her throat. She dropped the flowers as if they were aflame, staring at them in disbelief.

"Rosemary for remembrance," she whispered, "forget-me-nots. Honeysuckle—just like in the portrait." And the red hair was a direct allusion to her mother.

Was Bartholomew Briggs responsible for this sick joke? Well, if he thought that a pitiful tangle of plants would bother her, he could think again!

Abby looked up, felt a shiver over her flesh, a call of warning from her heart.

Again, an ominous chill crept its way over her prickling flesh, as if someone were watching her. Abby scanned the trees, the stones, but saw no one. The feeling persisted.

This time, there was no doubt in her mind.

Abby knew she was being watched.

She tried to put her emotions into perspective as she stared into the green darkness of the woods.

Nothing stirred; nothing interrupted the tranquility of the forest. She felt the bouquet wilt in her grasp, felt its green, living liquid seep from its leaves and mingle with the sweat on her palm. With calmness she was determined to possess, she walked at an unhurried pace into the kitchen.

The feel of the dead bolt in her hand was as soothing as a lullaby, and she clicked it soundly.

Her calm evaporated as she lurched into action, double-checking all the locks and windows. She raced into the kitchen, twisted the broom head from its pole and broke the stick cleanly over her knee. The resultant halves found new homes wedged against sliding windows, and—she was gratified to learn—prevented the opening of them quite effectively. As long as no one decided to smash the glass.

She made another judgment call while she was at it. As long as someone was lurking around her home, she would not be trudging to the outhouse.

Abby gathered her purse and raked her fingers through her hair.

A visit to Cora Brannigan was in order, as was a trip to the Home Sweet Home boutique. Curtains were a definite priority, as was a bathroom.

She punched Cora's number into her cell phone and sighed with relief when she answered. "Cora, hi. Abby Lancaster here. I know it's a bit late, but I was wondering if I could stop by for a quick visit. I have something I need to discuss with you about the cottage."

"Oh, Abby dear, I'm on my way out the door. Mary Hopkins's grandbaby has finally decided to be born—ten days late, mind—and I'm on my way down to the hospital with a gift. Can it wait?"

Could it wait? A voice in her heart told her it couldn't. "It really is important, I'm afraid. Perhaps I could stop by when you get home from the hospital?"

Cora paused almost painfully, or did Abby imagine that? "If it's that important, I suppose you could stop by Rum Runner's. My son Ryan is the owner, and he's generally quite accommodating to my tenants." Her voice seemed to quaver at the suggestion, and Abby had the distinct impression that Cora hoped she wouldn't take her up on that offer.

Abby smiled. Why not kill two birds with one stone? "Thank you, Cora. I think I will stop by Rum Runner's. Have a nice visit at the hospital."

She hung up the phone with a satisfied smile. She could discuss her idea of a bathroom addition with Ryan, and at the same time gauge his attitude toward her. If it still seemed unreasonably hostile, she would confront him. There was nothing she liked better than getting to the bottom of things.

But first, it appeared another call to Destiny Bay's finest was in order.

Chapter Ten

Ryan Brannigan swiped a cloth over the surface of the bar. It soothed him to be back at Rum Runner's. Spending a little time behind the bar always gave him the lift he needed. Though Brannigan Fisheries was infinitely more lucrative than Rum Runner's, it was here that he felt most at home, surrounded by solid wood and familiar faces.

He had always enjoyed Ronnie's Chef's Table, and it irked him that Abrielle Lancaster had been there last night. Just his luck. That woman seemed to turn up everywhere!

"Johnny," he said, scowling at the head on the ale he poured, "you were due behind the bar fifteen minutes ago. Watch the breaks, eh?"

"Sorry, man." Johnny tied an apron around his middle and nodded at Sheriff Flynn, who sat in his usual spot at the bar.

Flynn belched into his fist and leaned his elbow on the bar. "Now, Johnny, you're a fine judge of women. Tell me what you think of this Abrielle Lancaster."

Johnny's grin bordered on leering. "I'd tell you what I think, Sheriff, but it's kind of hard to do, what with the blood rushing away from my brain every time I lay eyes on her."

Both men chuckled.

Ryan slammed the glass he had poured on the bar. "You mind checking the pressure on the tanks, Johnny?"

His head bartender looked at him oddly. The tanks didn't need checking and both men knew it, but the last thing Ryan wanted to hear was more talk about Abrielle Lancaster.

"Sure, boss." Johnny turned and sauntered into the back room, tossing a cloth over his shoulder as he went.

"Can I get you something else, Sheriff?"

Sheriff Flynn hitched his foot on the brass rail that ran the lower length of the bar, then leaned in a bit closer. "Another beer will do, Ryan. So, what do you think about all this fuss? I'll tell you what *I* think—I got my eye on this Abrielle Lancaster, that's what. She'd best not be thinking she's gonna waltz in here and stir up the same pile of trouble her mother did. According to Connor, she's already been trying to spook out old Bart."

"Trouble is what her kind does best, Sheriff." Ryan slid the drink across the bar, eyeing the paunchy man with interest, wondering if he'd found an unlikely ally in the sheriff . . . *and* wondering how Abrielle Lancaster could possibly "spook out" grizzled old Bart. In his experience, it was generally Bart who did the spooking.

"You met her yet?"

"Not yet, but I'm thinking it's inevitable. This is a small town."

Sheriff Flynn nodded, squinting as he swallowed the last of his beer. "If I were you, I'd keep clear of that one, Ryan. Her kind of history doesn't bear repeating." He shoved a bill across the bar and knocked the wood twice—loudly, arrogantly. "You take care now."

Ryan nodded at Flynn, watched the door close behind him. In his opinion, Flynn had no more business being sheriff than Bartholomew Briggs. He had the job because his father had been mayor for years, as had his grandfather. Flynn had appointed his younger brother Connor as deputy, and every other relative sat on the town council. The Flynns had run this town for too long, and Ryan would dearly love to see the end of that particular dynasty.

Ryan gritted his teeth. That wasn't the only thing he'd like to see the end of. Ever since that blue-blooded society princess had set foot on his island, it seemed he couldn't go anywhere without hearing people talk about her . . . not even his own bar!

There were Abby sightings, Abby encounters, and Abby speculations, and fate seemed determined to make certain Ryan heard each and every one of them.

"Ohhh no, you don't," he said under his breath, watching through narrowed eyes as the one and only Abrielle Lancaster came striding down the road toward his bar, grasped the door handle and . . .

Abby was still shaken by the flowers that had been left for her, and when she'd spoken with Officer Flynn, who had given her his direct line, he'd assured her that she was right to be concerned. Even Bartholomew didn't tend to get this overt with his crush of the moment. Flynn had suggested that she bring the flowers by the station the following day. Meanwhile, she wasn't about to twiddle her thumbs. She still had the issue of Ryan Brannigan to deal with.

She strode into the semidarkness of the pub. A hazy swirl of smoke meandered around the blades of ceiling fans along with the gravelly voice of Joe Cocker.

Ryan is here. Impossibly, unimaginably she *felt* him—felt his every nuance of movement as though the sticky air were water, and the current he stirred washed over her again and again.

How is that possible? she wondered, her mouth dry.

At her sides, her hands began to tremble. She felt like Daniel stepping into the lion's den—though sadly bereft of angels. Who would stop the devouring jaws that waited only feet away?

Just walk over there and introduce yourself, she thought, forcing away her unease, doing her level best to convince herself that all this foolishness with Ryan Brannigan had been in her imagination; that the visceral reaction she had experienced when she first encountered him was due more to jet lag than to any sort of groundless animosity on his part.

That sort of hatred—the kind capable of reaching from someone's psyche and rattling someone else's—took history, and she and Ryan shared none.

There, she said silently. *I'm just being silly.* Now, if only she could believe it.

Abby forced one foot in front of the other and at last seated herself on a bar stool. First, she would take Cora's suggestion and speak with him about the bathroom. If he acted horribly, she would confront him about his behavior. If not, well, she was content to believe it had all been her imagination.

But before any of that could take place, he'd have to turn around. Abby waited. And waited.

Ryan stood at the other end of the bar, idly wiping the rim of a glass with a white cloth. He had seen her. There was no doubt about that. There was also no doubt that he was outright ignoring her.

Two more customers arrived and were served.

"Excuse me," Abby called, leaning forward just for good measure.

Another man slipped behind the bar. He was older than Ryan, with jet-black curls, an angular, weathered face, and deep-set, chocolatey eyes. The lids were lowered almost sleepily as he approached her. A lewd smile teased the corners of his mouth. A cloth was tossed carelessly over his shoulder. The man wore a name tag that read JOHNNY MAC.

"Well, if you ain't the spittin' image of your beautiful mama," he said softly, eyes raking over her. "You know, she and I used to be friends."

Abby felt instantly chilled. No way was this man a friend of her mother's. She didn't like him, and it went deeper than his suggestive smirk. There was something cold and calculating within him, and it seemed to ooze out like tentacles toward her. She shuddered involuntarily.

"What can I get for you, darlin'?"

A can of mace. Great big Doberman on the side. "I'm here to speak to Ryan," she said, loudly enough for the man in question to hear. "I'd appreciate it if you could let him know."

"You sure you wouldn't rather deal with me, miss?" He leaned across the bar suggestively, enveloping Abby in the musky scent of his cologne. "Bet you'd find me friendlier."

Yeah, I'll bet. "No, thank you. I'll wait."

Johnny lifted his brows and exhaled long and slow. "Hey, Ryan," he called, only taking his eyes from Abby's face long enough to let his gaze trace the shape of her breasts. "There's a lady here who's requiring your services." He turned away with a wink, dragging a damp cloth over the bar as he left. "You just call if you need me, miss."

Ryan paused a moment too long before turning to face her. Tigerlike eyes stared into the very heart of her, pinning her to the seat. "Yes?"

"I'll have a glass of . . ." She stopped short, the request for wine frozen on her tongue. Her mouth felt cottony— too dry to speak. "What-whatever you have on tap."

His pace was measured, almost belligerent. Ryan Brannigan poured her a drink, never for an instant taking his icy stare from her face.

Abby squirmed in her seat. Nope, she hadn't imagined his anger. It was there in all its hostile glory. "Thank you. Ryan, right?" *Like she didn't know.* "I'm Abby. I saw you at Ronnie's." Her extended hand was ignored. She withdrew the offer, practically wilting in the acidity of his gaze. "I was hoping to speak to you about the cottage."

He leaned forward on the bar, arms braced on either side of him. "If the cottage was any of my concern, you can bet it would be empty as we speak." He turned his back, picked up pen and paper, and began recording the inventory of bottles stacked in neat rows behind him.

Abby gulped—a little too loudly—and couldn't help

wondering exactly *when* her esophagus had gotten so small. "I realize that Cora owns the cottage, but she said that I could speak to you . . ." Her voice trailed away into a sheepish silence.

Ryan turned around, arms folded over his chest, as if challenging her to speak. "And what could you possibly have to speak to me about, Miss Lancaster?"

"I, uh, the—" She cleared her throat self-consciously. "I'd like to discuss an addition to the cottage. A bathroom specifically. It's unreasonable to ask tenants to use an outhouse in this day and age, and—" Her words poured out like the waters of a dam, unleashed. Abby drew a long, dramatic breath into her aching lungs. "What I mean to say is that I need a bathroom, and I'd like to have one added as soon as possible."

"No." He turned abruptly and began to serve another customer.

Abby recoiled as if slapped.

She slid down another seat. Surely he wouldn't be so rude with another patron nearby? "Mr. Brannigan, if you could just hear me out—a new addition would only add to the property value, and—"

She jumped at the crack of glass against the polished bar as another drink was served.

"I said, *no*."

Abby felt her jaw drop. *This* was Cora Brannigan's son? She'd be quicker to believe the man had been raised by baboons. She glanced toward the other customers at the bar. Several had simply averted their gazes. One, in particular, shrugged, offering her a sympathetic smile.

"Well, perhaps I'll wait and speak to Cora about this matter, after all. Something tells me she'll feel different."

Ryan braced his hands on either side of the bar, jaw working as he gritted his teeth. "There will be no addition of *any* kind to the cottage, Miss Lancaster."

Abby stared at the man. Regardless of what she had said to every other person she'd met, she *would* let this man call her Miss. "With all due respect, Mr. Brannigan—"

"I don't want your respect, we don't need an addition, and the property value is none of your business." He strode away, leaving her gaping in his wake.

Abby gathered her wits and purse, scurried down the length of the bar, and dug in her heels. "Mr. Brannigan," she said through her teeth, "I must inform you that at no time during my initial discussion with Cora was I informed of the state of plumbing at the cottage. Such a glaring deficiency is at least worth mentioning, don't you agree?"

"Cora Brannigan didn't get to be the businesswoman she is today by forgetting to mention—what was it? *Glaring deficiencies?*"

"Are you suggesting that I simply *forgot* the fact that there's no plumbing?"

"You're the one who rented a cottage with no plumbing. Who's to say what goes through your head?"

"Wanna guess what's going through my head right now?" The muscles in his jaw worked beneath the bristly skin. "No addition."

"Oh, I'll have that addition if I have to pay for it *myself*!" she said, a crimson stain burning her face. Fury blossomed in her belly. Her pulse chanted with it. A million curses on the man! "You just watch and see, Ryan Brannigan. I'll have that bathroom and I'll take you on a guided bloody tour of it if I have to drag you by the ear!"

"We'll see about that!" Ryan thundered, storming through a doorway behind the bar.

"Don't you walk away, you, you . . ." She couldn't think of anything rotten enough to call him. How dare he try to humiliate her in front of the patrons of his horrid little bar. She glared around at the gawking faces, daring anyone to meet her gaze. The few who did appeared torn between shock and downright amusement. Well, if it was a show they wanted, she'd be more than happy to oblige them.

"Get him back here!" she said to the older barman, motioning at the door through which Ryan had disappeared.

Johnny Mac's smile melted. "Uh, that might not be such a good idea."

"Well, I'm not leaving until I speak with him, so you might as well pour me another drink," she said, throwing back her shoulders and lifting her chin.

As if summoned by her voice, Ryan Brannigan reappeared in the doorway behind the bar. Instantly, his expression hardened. "Ready to take me on your bathroom tour already?"

A few nervous chuckles sounded around the bar. "Fasten your seat belt," came the muttered suggestion from a ruddy-faced fellow two seats down.

If she'd *had* a seat belt, she *would* have fastened it. "No," she said, feigning a brightness she didn't feel, "but it'll be worth the wait. I have my eye on a faucet that's to die for." She seated herself on a bar stool, squelching the instinct to run, ignoring the gaping jaws and riveted attention of every other patron in the bar. "You've been a jerk since the first time you laid eyes on me, and I want to know why."

A disbelieving silence reached out, clutching the room in a merciless grip.

Please, somebody drop a pin. Anything to shatter the airless quality that lay heavily upon the bar.

Ryan stared at her with warlike intensity. "It isn't wise to wake the ghosts of the past, Miss Lancaster. Especially those that have taken so long to rest, as it is."

Abby heard the note of warning in his voice. An infinitesimal recoiling of courage stopped her for a moment. She steeled herself, refusing to let him intimidate her. "What's *that* supposed to mean?"

"Are you familiar with the phrase, 'Let sleeping dogs lie'?"

"Yes."

He eyed her steadily. "Then I suggest you heed it."

"You won't be offended if I ignore your advice, I hope?"

"Not at all," he said. "Just as long as you're not offended by what you learn as a result of your nosiness."

"I'd hardly call exploring my mother's past 'nosy,' thank you very much."

Ryan's eyes narrowed. "Leave. Go home. This isn't the place for you, just like it wasn't the place for your mother before you. No one wants you here. And if you're not careful, you'll wind up getting exactly what you wish for."

"I don't care for your cryptic warnings, Ryan Brannigan, nor do I care to be brushed off. If you haven't the courage to speak plainly, then don't waste my time."

He circled the bar as easily as a shark. "Don't question my courage. Ever."

"Don't question my determination. *Ever*."

They were nose to nose, unmoving and surrounded only by the breathless silence of their rapt audience.

"Why did you come?" he asked, his voice quiet with rage.

Abby folded her arms, lifted her chin. She was suddenly more nervous than angry, suddenly more afraid than she cared to admit, but there was no way she was going to let him know that. "You know why I'm here. I want to find out everything I can about my mother, and I won't leave until I do."

Ryan's face flushed. "I'll tell you the only thing you need to know about your mother, Abrielle. Celeste Rutherford was nothing but a common tramp."

The words shot out and snatched the breath from her, prowled around her in a wicked dance that left her head spinning, her heart racing. She blinked away the swath of tears that filmed her eyes, drew back her hand, and slapped his face with a ferocity that exploded from the pit of her soul. "You liar! How dare you talk about my mother that way! You didn't even know her!"

Ryan glared at her. He touched his cheek, looked at the hand he withdrew from the mottled flesh, as if expecting a streak of red to stain it. "I know all that matters. Now, so do you."

Abby snatched her purse and burst through the doors of the bar. Her tear-blind eyes darted left and right, and at last settled on the road directly ahead. The road Cora Brannigan lived on. Surely she'd put to rest her son's horrible lies.

She started running as if the words were nipping at her heels. *It can't be true! It just can't!*

She heard other feet then. Someone was right behind her, his breath in her ears, his anger unfurling around her like a noxious cloud.

Ryan grabbed her arm, turned her to face him. He was breathless. Sweat beaded his brow as he glared down at her. "You have no right being offended. You came here to find the truth about your mother, and I just gave it to you."

"Get your hands off me!" She shook free of him, breathless herself. "You're a liar!"

"Am I?" He stared into her eyes unrelentingly. There was no hint of dishonesty in their depths, but there *was* something else.

The rage in her heart stilled as she saw a flicker of something unimaginable. Hurt. Vulnerability. The truth was right there in his eyes, and there was nothing angry about it.

"Do you know that some nights I can still feel the hard floor beneath me, because my mother couldn't afford child care, and I'd have to sleep behind the cash register while she worked nights at the grocery store? Do you know it took years for her hands to recover from cleaning other people's toilets? Or that to this day I can remember the taste of cold, canned spaghetti, because heating the stuff over a candle was damn near impossible and the electricity had been cut off *again*—and why? Because the man who should have stepped up to the plate and looked after us was so enthralled by another woman, he forgot he had a family to feed!"

"Wh-what?"

"Do you have any idea what it's like to be whispered about behind your back? To be expected to fail because of who you are and who you came from? Do you know what it's like to endure shame for being the bastard of a man who never wanted you?"

Abby's heart caught as she remembered the whispers about her mother's suicide, the shame she felt in the knowledge that her mother hadn't loved her enough to go on living, the abject loneliness. Only moments before, she had slapped him. Now, unimaginably, she wanted to reach out and touch him, to forgive him for his rage and tell him, *I understand.* Because she *did* understand. She'd been there.

"Ryan?" she asked softly, her fury draining away from the tender parts of her soul, uncloaking the compassion that only another abandoned child could know.

Ryan's mask reappeared. He was stony again, though lit by the red haze of resentment. "Your mother snatched Douglas McAllister and left my mother without a dime to put food on our table," he said through clenched teeth. "I was born a bastard, and don't think for a moment that I don't know where blame ought to be placed."

Where has he gone? The real, feeling Ryan Brannigan I just witnessed?

"I don't know what you're talking about," she said, taking a step back, feeling bruised and dizzy from the ricocheting emotions that pummeled her insides.

"I'm talking about the legendary Celeste Rutherford," he shouted. "I'm talking about the woman who waltzed into town and stole my mother's chance to give her son his father's name, who stole her dignity."

Cora! The woman Douglas threw over was Cora!

Abby froze, felt the blood in her veins do the same as it seemingly slowed to a labored halt. *Can it be true?* What had Franklin O'Donnell said? That the artist had thrown over another woman for her mother; that people had called her names.

And all this time Cora had held her silence, had welcomed her kindly and even assisted her in her quest!

Abby grasped at her midsection, feeling suddenly ill. "I . . . I—" Her voice caught, she swallowed, squeezing her eyes tightly closed. She wouldn't, *couldn't* let him see her cry. When she opened them at last, she caught a flicker of something in his eyes, something she had never seen there before.

Was it pity? Did he actually pity her?

Well, she wouldn't give him the opportunity. The last thing she needed was his pity.

She deliberately paced her breathing. She wouldn't reveal her distress to him; she couldn't. To give him that satisfaction would be completely unthinkable.

"Is there anything else you'd like to know?" he asked quietly.

"Yes," she said, blinking tears from her eyes. "I'd like to know how on earth you were raised by a woman like Cora Brannigan, because right now, you bear absolutely no resemblance to her. And if I were you, I wouldn't worry too much about the lack of a name. I'd be willing to bet that you're your father's son, through and through!" Abby turned her back to him and started to run.

Chapter Eleven

All she could think about was escape. All she wanted to do was pack her bags and follow Ryan Brannigan's suggestion to the letter.

Abby ran around the corner of a warehouse, leaned on the mustard-colored wall, then slid down its length. The rosebushes she settled between were mercifully bereft of thorns, and the mulch beneath her smelled of forests.

Abby shook her head, marveling at the wicked twist of fate that revealed Cora as the woman her mother had replaced. She caught her head in her hands and concentrated very hard on breathing in and out.

When at last she could, she rose, rounded the corner of Suffolk Lane and skirted the village, eyes intent upon locating Cora Brannigan's house in the twilight darkness.

She passed stately homes once owned by sea captains and the sturdy, simple abodes of long-dead whalers, and at last huffed up and found the periwinkle blue colonial that Cora had described to her.

By the light of the rising moon, she could make out shutters the color of goldenrod and a bevy of petunias fluttering in window boxes.

Abby placed her hand on the glowing white wood of the gate, hesitating as the smallest of movements caused the gate to squeak on its hinges.

A head poked around the corner.

"Abby! You're here. Come round the back, love. I've just got home, myself."

Abby flushed with apprehension, felt a sudden slickness beneath her palms. She wiped them against her thighs and strode through the gate, hoping she looked better than she felt. The last thing she needed was to have Cora coddling her.

She walked around the house, saw the garden looking mysterious in the moonlight, and felt her stomach wince with a surge of acid. "Why didn't you tell me?"

"Tell you what, dear?"

"About my mother and Douglas McAllister. About *you* and my mother and Douglas McAllister."

Cora looked at Abby, hands falling to her sides. "Who told you?"

Abby ascended the steps, head at a thoughtful angle. "The artist's son."

"Ryan, Ryan, Ryan," Cora said, rummaging for her keys. The hinges of the screen door squealed as she pulled it open. "I told him to leave well enough alone."

Abby's hands were trembling almost as badly as her stomach. She felt ill at having relied upon Cora as a landlady. All the while, Cora had never let on—not for a moment—that she had regarded Celeste Rutherford as anything but a friendly acquaintance. "You should have told me."

Cora's face softened with concern. "Come in, dear."

Abby allowed herself to be steered into the kitchen and seated in a captain's chair.

"Tea?"

"No, thank you." She folded then unfolded her hands. "Why didn't you tell me?"

"I saw no need for it," Cora said, her tone gentle. Pretense seemed to fall away from her, every hint of discomfort vanished. Abby felt—for the first time since meeting her—that Cora was being 100 percent truthful.

"My son's the one who can't stop dwelling on the past, not I."

"Tell me," Abby said. "Tell me everything. Don't worry about hurting me or offending me. Don't worry if I cry." She leaned forward, her expression raw with need. "Cora,

I only want the truth—every bit of it, no matter how much it hurts. Celeste Rutherford was my mother, and all I've ever been told is half-truths. Tell me. *Please.*"

Cora gazed down at the woodgrain that swirled over the tabletop, hands nestled around a piping cup of tea. She was silent for so long, Abby wondered if Cora had forgotten she was there.

"It took me six long months to convince him to marry me," she said at last. "Six months of groveling—I disguised it as reminders of his Christian duty, honor and love, mind—but it was groveling, nonetheless.

"I was nineteen, pregnant, unmarried and terrified."

Abby stared at her thoughtfully. "It's hard to imagine you terrified by anything."

"Oh, trust me on this." She placed a cup in front of Abby and stirred in a splash of milk. "When he finally agreed to marry me, I was so overjoyed I convinced myself that he would grow to love me the same way I loved him—and I did love him something fierce. Heaven only knows why.

"I loved him regardless of his faults—and believe you me, they were many; not the least of which was a roving eye. Ah, the more fool I, for believing it was harmless." Cora stared into the depths of her teacup, as if drawing a faraway memory into focus. "Douglas was poor, and too proud to fish. Fancied himself better than all the rest of us, I guess. He'd sit on the corner of Hyde Street and Brigantine Way, paintings propped around him, trying to sell his wares to the folks with money . . . the *fishermen,*" she said, smiling sadly at the irony.

"At last, he accepted a summer job teaching at a college in New York. For me, he said. Me and the baby." Cora stared into space. "He sent a few checks back to me. I rented a tiny apartment, painted a nursery blue and hoped for a boy. Then the letters stopped. It wasn't long after that he came home with the young art student he'd met. Brought her home to Destiny Bay. His muse."

Abby bit her lip. "My mother."

Cora nodded. She patted her hair, tucked a strand behind her ear, and smiled sadly. "I could hardly blame Douglas for loving her. Celeste Rutherford was the most beautiful woman I had ever clapped eyes upon—and lovely, too—kind, like. How could I blame any man for falling head over heels?"

Abby lifted her shoulders and let them drop. "I feel . . . guilty, somehow."

Cora wafted the suggestion away with a wave of her hand. "I forgave them both, long before you were even thought of, dear. Life's too short to hold grudges."

But not long enough to forget a broken heart. Not completely. "I doubt your son agrees with you."

The open face clouded significantly. "Ah, now there's a horse of a different color." Cora refilled her cup. "Ryan is a sort who feels things deeply, you know?"

"No need to convince me on that point."

"Douglas was a miserable father, but Ryan always hoped that he'd come 'round. The fact that he never did was unforgivable to Ryan."

"I think I understand how he felt, in a way. My mother took my father from me, too."

Cora looked startled. "In what way?"

"He loved her so much that when she died, so did he. In every way that matters, anyway. Just left his body here to mourn her loss. I was raised by my grandmother, who was wonderful . . . but I still wished I'd had a mother and a father who still had love to give."

"It seems Celeste Rutherford was unforgettable to many," Cora said quietly.

"And I'm the only one who can't remember her."

"Oh, surely you remember her, love?"

Abby shrugged. "I was a baby when she . . ." *No need to sugarcoat it, Abby.* "When she killed herself."

Cora stiffened. "Oh, Abby. I had no idea."

Abby felt the fight drain out of her. "My grandmother never touched her room. It's still the same to this day. That's where I used to go to talk to her."

Cora placed her hand on Abby's. "I'm sure she heard you, lass."

Abby wanted so much to believe she had. "I found this old bottle of perfume. It was thick and rancid by the time I discovered it, but I could tell it once smelled like gardenias. I still have that bottle." She ran a finger beneath her eye, caught a ripe tear on its tip. "I wore her scarves, I cuddled her winter coats. They all smelled like gardenia, at first."

"Why?" Cora asked, her brow furrowed. "Why would she do such a thing?"

"No one knows. That's why I'm here, to find out anything I can. I can't leave any clue unsearched. It's my own heart at stake, Cora. This is for me as much as it's for her."

Cora nodded slowly. "My son was rude, but only because he struggles with a cross of his own. I know he wouldn't have hurt you like he did if he knew your story. Forgive him his anger, will you? You don't need to carry the weight of that along with what you already shoulder."

Abby shook her head. "I don't know if I can. You didn't hear the things he said."

"I can only imagine. He's a passionate person, aye?" She smiled sadly, picked a cookie from the plate and stared at its crinkled surface. "Serves him well in some respects, but it fires up his anger something fierce. I'd never tell him so, but he's inherited his father's temperament every whit."

"I'll *try* to forgive him, but only because he's your son, and you love him."

"Like nothing you could imagine," Cora said, a hint of her own passion rising. She smiled gently, patted Abby's hand. "You just leave this business with Ryan to me, aye? I have a way of making him see reason."

Abby was skeptical, but she smiled and nodded. "If you can do that, you're either a miracle worker or a wizard."

"I'd have to say wizard, since my ways depend upon my own secret alchemy."

Wizardry indeed—Abby's anger was slowly dissolving in a mist of curiosity, and Cora had dispelled it with her soothing voice and her mysterious promise. "What kind of alchemy?" she asked cautiously.

"Like I said, you just leave that to me."

Ryan Brannigan slid down the frame of his mother's door, landing with a dull thud at its base.

He had come here with the intention of heading Abby off, of forbidding her to go to his mother and discuss what he had just revealed to her. The last thing Cora needed was to be reminded of that painful phase of her life.

But he had been too late.

Because he'd gone to the wharf to breathe, regroup, collect his scattered emotions, he had given Abby precious time to get to Cora. By the time the thought occurred to him that Abby would likely go to her in order to verify his story, it was too late. She was in there, talking about Celeste Rutherford . . . to his mother.

What else should I expect, he had seethed silently. *Since when do society princesses have a clue how to fight fair?*

His blood was on the verge of boiling when he'd heard the timbre in her voice, the tremulous query about her mother, then the admissions that followed: Celeste's suicide, a coat to cuddle, a beloved fragrance, turned rancid with time.

Ryan felt a hitch in his heart as he remembered another child, other questions. *I saw Dad at the market today, Mom. He said I was getting real tall. Do you think he'd come to my birthday if I invited him?* And: *See what I drew, Mom? Do you think Dad would like it?* And, later: *No. I don't want to go to his funeral. I'm just glad he's dead.*

A volley of memories thudded within him, pounded against the surface of his mind with a howling, internal commotion that had made his hands tremble on his knees.

Left behind. Just like him.

He could see her hands through the screen—all that was visible from his vantage point. Delicate fingers twisting and knotting a tissue. The sight of it stirred something visceral within him, something that found its home in his soul . . . that same twisting and knotting was within *him*, now.

This woman, his enemy, was suddenly *not*.

Pure understanding thundered through his being. They were not so different, he and she, except for the fact that what he had seen as weakness and despised, she had seen as need, and accepted. Where he had felt hatred, she had felt longing, and all at once, he understood the heart of her, understood why she had come to his cloistered oasis in the Atlantic, and it had nothing to do with destroying his carefully ordered peace.

Much as he still despised her mother, he had no choice but to acknowledge that Abby *wasn't* her mother.

Not once in his entire life had anyone in the village of Destiny Bay compared him to the man who fathered him. Not in his wild childhood, his rebellious youth, the heart-breaker years that followed—not once had anyone said the waited-for: *You're just like your father.* That was a measuring stick he'd never desired to be held to, and yet, it could have easily been done, as Abby had pointed out.

His head started to pound. Realizing he'd been wrong always affected him adversely.

A comforting surge of anger curled through his veins.

So he'd been wrong to paint the daughter with the same brush as he had her mother—that didn't mean he had to get chummy with Abby. She was still a spoiled society brat, and he'd been smart to give her a wide berth.

And besides, if people didn't learn from the past, they were doomed to repeat its mistakes, right?

Well, *he* wouldn't repeat them, and Abby could take that to the bank.

Chapter Twelve

Abrielle had not reacted to his gift of flowers as he'd hoped. The flowers were meant to be received in gratitude, yet she had been repulsed by them. It was another subtle reminder that Abrielle was not the lady her mother had been. But she would progress under his patient tutelage.

Patience. That was the key.

Though Abrielle was apparently unschooled in the dictates of polite courtship, *he* was not. He would patiently continue along the prescribed path of romance. After flowers came jewelry.

There would be no shopping at a jewelry store for him, oh no. He had something infinitely more precious to offer his darling Abrielle, and it was hidden here, in the graveyard.

The Lover looked up at the polished marble angel, saliva filling his mouth with longing, hands trembling only slightly as they rested on his bent knees.

He was alone in the cemetery—the one place that he never felt entirely lonely.

How many years, he asked himself, *how many years have I come to this very place?* As if each day of every year had not added a leaf of pain to the burgeoning growth that now threatened his very existence.

If he could grasp it within his hands—the agony that had twined around him for so long—if he could peel back the layers like the rippled skin of forbidden fruit, he would find Celeste within the layers, and his darling mother at the core, with her long red hair so like Celeste's, wrapped around the fertile center of his pain.

The pain throbbed with renewed energy. It fed on every thought; it mutated into something so gargantuan, so excruciating, that he marveled at the love and the agony his ever-expanding heart was able to bear.

He squeezed his hands into fists—felt the scabbed palm of his left hand crack in protest. *This* was a pain he could endure . . . indeed, it was a joy to endure it.

Carefully, he lifted the gauze that wrapped his hand and began unwinding it—the wound beneath becoming less obscured with every lifting layer. The bandage slithered to the earth, forgotten, as he looked at his palm—now freshly pocked with blood—and smiled at the wound that was a tribute to his love. There, in the cup of his palm, he cradled the symbol of her—the graceful shape of a letter A.

He had carved it there the night before, so that he could wear the badge of her on his flesh as surely as he wore it on his heart.

The Lover looked up at the angel. Elizabeth's angel, they called her, in honor of the woman who lay in eternal slumber beneath the sheltering canopy of her marble wings, but The Lover knew better, as did the angel.

It was said that she had been modeled after the beloved wife of Captain Josiah Watson in 1893. If that was the case, she had been lovely, indeed. It was also said that the captain had turned two previous statues away, saying that they couldn't possibly compare to Elizabeth.

Josiah Watson was a man who demanded perfection, and it appeared that he'd gotten it.

In this, the good captain and The Lover were kindred spirits.

He sat on the marble bench at the foot of Elizabeth Watson's grave, staring up at her—this monument to devotion and love—and looked at her face with a critical eye.

There was no denying it. Captain Watson's wife had been beautiful, indeed. But not as beautiful as *his* love; not as beautiful as his mother or his lovely Celeste.

Now they, too, had lain their bones down to rest . . . had been buried far from him, far from the love they had shared.

Secretly, he had renamed the angel. Celeste, he called her. And it was *her* bones he imagined lying here; *her* bones to which he paid homage.

For years that seemed like eternity, this was as close as he'd imagined he could come to her; until he greeted her on the other side.

Until now.

Now, he believed in miracles.

The Lover looked up at her, and he saw it: that same, wondrous light he had seen so many years ago, falling across the angel's face in wordless confirmation . . . the light that had brought him to her feet in the first place!

The Lover had seen that light but few times, and each time was engraved upon his heart. He had come to realize that the light was a heavenly message from his mother—her way of doing penance. His mother sent the glowing light, crowning the chosen one in ethereal gold, telling him that this was the woman he was meant to love, the woman who could heal all the wounds she, his mother, had left him with.

Once, he had seen it cast its prophetic glow upon the face of Celeste. Later, after her death, it had come to rest upon the face of Elizabeth's angel, and he began to believe that he'd never have a flesh-and-blood woman he could adore. Most recently, he had seen the golden tracery of love's light illuminate the face of Abrielle Lancaster.

Yes, it was a sign.

His mother had sent Celeste to him, but she had failed him. Now Celeste was on the other side along with his mother, and fully able to see the error of her ways. Celeste, too, was doing penance, and in so doing had sent her daughter to him. It was what was right, after all. A heart for a heart.

But it seemed he would be battling fate for the soul of a woman yet again.

Suddenly, he squinted his eyes shut against the burgeoning rage he felt in his belly; remembered the jolt of disbelief he'd experienced when he saw the artist's bastard looking at his Abrielle. The Lover saw the way Ryan Brannigan's eyes caught, how his face filled with something unutterable.

Just like so long ago, when his lovely Celeste had misguidedly loved the artist—or *thought* she loved him.

As he'd known it would be, after one taste of his love, she had left the artist.

That's all it would take now. One taste of him—her heart's destiny—and Abrielle would love him as had her mother so long ago.

The Lover dropped to his knees. Gently, he pressed his lips to the angel's feet, stroked them with a tenderness that spoke of his broken heart, and his longing to have it mended.

No woman has ever been loved this way, he thought. *Not even the beloved Elizabeth Watson.*

As his mouth moved over the slick coldness of the granite angel, he thought of Abrielle, his destiny; thought how she would relish his kisses, his touch; thought how the angel was surely glowing beneath his ministrations.

He was The Lover. There was none quite like him—no man could love as deeply, as purely.

His heart squeezed in his chest, threatened to burst with the thought of what was so very near.

At last, he let go of the angel's feet and started digging at her base, fingers raking away the grass, clawing away layers of earth, until he had scrabbled down six inches.

There, exactly where he had left it, was his offering to his angel, Celeste.

He withdrew the mud-caked box, gently brushed the earth from its surface, and looked inside. Still there.

Yes, this was the key to unlock his destiny.

Schooling his fingers against the frantic need they felt to uncover the treasure, he opened the box gently.

There, beneath the moonlight, glittered the ring.

He would give it to her, and she would love him. And he would call her "Abrielle," her given name, not the common-sounding "Abby." Hardly a name fitting for the child of a woman called Celeste—a woman whose only place could be among the stars.

Then, another thought struck him.

He could call her by a different name; another, more suitable name.

She was the image of her mother, was she not? She was the very incarnation of her. Yes! He would call her Celeste.

The moon above him shone down upon the ring, upon him, child of destiny. Celeste had come back to him, the only way she could, and she would be his again, as she was always meant to be.

Chapter Thirteen

Cora lifted the bread pudding from the oven, held the piping dish beneath her nose, and inhaled lustily.

Perfect.

She had honed the recipe over the course of countless nights as she sat awaiting her errant son, praying for his safe return . . . then, for the grace required to spare his life after she got her hands on the lad.

If she had a dime for every bread pudding she'd made, she'd have been rich long ago.

To say there had been many would be an understatement. After all, *this* was the pudding that had lured that boy of hers through a teenaged rebellion so spectacular, it had become the stuff of legends.

His shenanigans had even outshone *hers*, and her days of running wild and loving the artist had raised more than their share of eyebrows.

After all these years, young men still tried to equal his status on the island . . . none of them anticipating that without Ryan's devastating smile, it was next to impossible to carry off mischief with any measure of panache; or that before you attempt to *pull a Brannigan*, you ought to at least confirm that you have the agility of a cat, the tongue of a politician, and the speed of a comet (when you're stone-cold sober, let alone three sheets to the wind). Needless to say, none of the pretenders had yet managed to duplicate Ryan's signature mix of brawler, Casanova and brooding rebel.

Who would have thought he'd turn out so well?

Cora shook her head in remembrance, realizing that even *she* had foreseen disaster in his future.

But then, it had been hard to imagine much else when all she ever saw were notes from teachers (marveling over his fine grades even as they bemoaned his inattentive nature and surliness) and seething fathers (Clark Murphy came to mind; as did his pretty young daughter, who had been escorted to the prom by Ryan and returned to her frantic parents the next day—at lunchtime).

There had been underage driving, underage smoking, and underage drinking, and always that charming smile, used most often on her, the mother with the endless patience and the best bread pudding on earth.

Now that he had grown into such a fine man, she could hardly deny a secret pride in his youth. Oh, it was good for a laugh now that it was all said and done.

If only *he* could get over the hurts of his youth as easily.

She shook her head and uttered a silent prayer for her son's peace.

Ryan Brannigan was a man among men, even if she did say so herself. The type of man who never forgets.

She frowned to herself as she ran a knife around the rim of a cheese soufflé.

The shadow of resolve cast itself long across her heart. Cora stared into the foamy depths of her soufflé, knowing that in some vital way, she had failed him.

For the first time in her life, she wondered if she'd be able to win him over to the side of reason. She wondered when he had gotten as old as he had, and if, by chance, he could have developed a disturbing resistance to her cooking. She hoped not, because to come right out and demand that he desist in his vendetta against Abby would be to cause him to dig his heels ever deeper into the fertile earth of his determination.

He was a hard man. Too hard. Not even a beautiful face could sway him—and more than a few had tried.

Heaven help Abrielle Lancaster.

Cora had seen it clear enough. Seen it in his eyes the moment he heard that Abby was coming to town. He'd set his cap for the unsuspecting woman, and not in a good way.

The girl was as good as gone if something wasn't done to derail this runaway train.

Forbidding was not the way—but, how to make the boy see reason?

It was a question that had perplexed her most of her adult life. She fussed over the table, looked at the clock, and smoothed the cotton apron that was tied around her midsection.

Well, if her son wouldn't listen to reason, it was time to

bring out the big guns. She inhaled unabashedly, feeling her mouth water.

It was time for bread pudding.

He hadn't eaten since the previous day—when he had overheard his mother speaking with Abby about Celeste. Not surprisingly, the entire episode had made him lose his previously unconquerable appetite, but the aromas wafting throughout Cora's house provided the cure. He was starving.

Ryan's mouth watered as he looked at the lush array of food set out on his mother's table for their Sunday lunch.

Starving or not, it made him nervous.

For her to slave away over a meal of this caliber could mean only one of two things: she had found yet another candidate for the position of daughter-in-law, or she was luring him in for a proper tongue-lashing.

Since there was no potential wife in sight and there were only two plates set at the table, that could only mean he was in trouble.

Well, fine. He'd choose trouble over a woman hands down. Women—one, in particular—were their own brand of trouble, and he'd had his fill of it.

Unbidden, the image of Abrielle swam into focus in his mind. He could almost hear the timbre in her voice as she spoke to Cora about her mother. It tugged at his heart . . . which made him even more nervous than the delectable meal set out before him. So nervous, in fact, that he started shifting on his feet.

Oh, this can't be good.

It was time to wipe the thought of Abrielle from his mind, time to strike her name from his vocabulary. He didn't want to even *discuss* that woman again.

"What have I done, Mom?" he asked, jamming his hands in his pockets and suddenly feeling all of sixteen years old.

Cora smiled sweetly. *Too* sweetly. "Whatever do you mean, Ryan? Come sit you down, tell me about your day."

Hmm. That was too easy. But he allowed himself to be bustled into the dining room, smiling softly to himself as she directed him to a chair. Just as pointedly, he grasped her elbow, escorted her to her chair, and seated her.

She chuckled. "Why, thank you, sir. Sit down, help yourself."

The table was laden with salad, rolls, a tureen of seafood casserole and Cora's famous cheese soufflé. Ryan inhaled lustily and froze midway between sitting and standing. He smelled bread pudding.

He cringed. Bread pudding meant serious trouble, not just the garden variety, and he'd been in enough scrapes in the past to know the difference.

"Looks great, Mom," he said, lowering himself onto the chair as cautiously as if he were about to sit on a grenade. "Now, you mind telling me what this is all about?"

"Does a mother need an excuse to cook for her son?"

"I smell bread pudding," he said warily.

Cora selected a roll, still warm from the oven, and pressed her thumbs into it, breaking it down the middle. "There's something we need to discuss, Ryan."

"Ah, the truth comes out at last. You know," he said, nodding toward the lavish spread, "if you wanted to have a word with me, you only had to say so."

She lifted a brow. "Says you."

"What do you want to talk about?"

"Abrielle Lancaster."

Ryan heaved himself out of his seat. "I'm leaving."

"You'll do no such thing."

With jaws clenched tight, he stared at his mother. Abby was the last person he wanted to talk about.

He'd resented Abby and Celeste for so long, it had become part of who he was, as in: *Age:* 35. *Height:* 6'2". *Occupation:* businessman. *Likes:* hockey, German beer,

and (heaven help him) bread pudding. *Hates*: Rutherford/
Lancaster women.

What would happen to the "who" of who he was if any
one of those few certainties were to crumble and fall? It
was crazy, he knew, to even wonder . . . but somehow, he
couldn't help it. Because something inside him was
changing, and had been changing since that damnable
moment he'd sat outside Cora's door and listened to Abby
talk. It was like an internal metamorphosis over which he
had no control, and above all, Ryan was always, *always* in
control.

He regarded his mother a moment, then sat grudgingly.

Cora nodded. "It has to stop."

"What are you talking about?"

"Don't play innocent with me, Ryan Brannigan. You're
hell-bent on trouncing the girl out of town, and it's not
right."

"Says who?" he demanded.

"Says I."

Ryan's words caught in his throat. He closed his eyes,
searched around his soul for the familiar rage that always
overtook him when he thought of Celeste, Abby, his father
and the suffering of his mother.

It wasn't there.

Deliberately, he remembered the nights he'd heard his
mother crying herself to sleep; forced the memories of his
hungry belly and threadbare clothing to the forefront of
his mind, and still, the anger slept.

Ryan leaned back in his chair, raked his hands through
his hair and closed his eyes at the low rumble that vibrated
in his throat. It wasn't, in fact, far off from a growl.

Slamming his chair back on all fours, he rested his
weary head in the cradle of his hands.

For the first time in his life, he was tired of it: the
constant hatred he carried.

His mind spiraled back to the moment he'd overheard

Abby's admissions—admissions that had made her human. Admissions that made it clear to him she hadn't come to destroy his peace. She had come to find her own.

Why did he so begrudge her that? Why couldn't he let it go?

In the heart of him, he wanted to, but he didn't know how to admit the fact that he knew there was something deep and seething and black within him—wasn't even sure if he was *ready* to. "I can't talk about this right now, Mom."

"Well, you're going to have to!" Cora said, hitting the table with her palm. "Enough is enough, Ryan. Can't you leave the past where it belongs? Both Celeste and Douglas are dead, son. Won't you let them go? Won't you let Abby find what she's looking for? Your choice to remain wounded by your history shouldn't prevent her from being healed!"

Cora's voice collided with the internal racket of his soul. Some sort of shift had occurred, an earthquake of the heart that left him gaping and vulnerable and utterly unprepared for what was happening to him. The walls that cloistered his indignation were crumbling, leaving him exposed to the truth he should have seen long ago.

He had no right to rob her of her peace. He had no right.

Cora's voice sliced through the haze of disbelief that was smothering him, choking him.

"No son of mine could be so blind to reason!"

Ryan drew in a steadying breath. Gritted his teeth. He couldn't say these things out loud—could hardly admit them to himself. "You're forgetting, Mom," he said softly, falling back on the mask of anger that had protected him for so long, "I'm not only *your* son."

Cora jolted to her feet, glaring at her offspring. "All your life, you've been a magnet to women. I've seen them love you. I've seen them devastated when you didn't love them back, but I said to myself, 'This is his way.' Even though I felt for the girls who loved you, I would rationalize things. I would say, 'He's so handsome, he can't help breaking a few hearts along the way.' Yes, I've seen you break more than your fair share of hearts, Ryan, but yesterday was the first time I ever saw you break a spirit. It was the first day I wasn't proud to call you 'son.'"

Ryan clenched his jaw, as tightly as a vise.

"Don't you have anything redeeming to say?" Cora asked.

She leaned in toward him, looked at him closely enough to make him wonder if she'd seen the crumbling of resolve in his eyes.

Had it been that close to the surface?

Ryan cleared his throat loudly, squared his shoulders. "No, Mom," he said at last. "I guess I don't have anything redeeming to say."

Cora's face fell. She shrank back in her seat, staring at her empty plate.

Ryan ran a hand through his hair, looking at the glorious mounds of food laid out on Cora's table. Something irrevocable had happened here tonight, and though he couldn't name it, Ryan felt its very imprint on the air. That something began the moment Abrielle Lancaster arrived in Destiny Bay, and thus far it had snaked through the lives of many—not the least of whom was him— wreaking change and upheaval along the way.

It was a waste of time to wish she had never come. Maybe all he could do now was pretend that everything was just fine. And maybe if he said it loudly enough, he just might believe it.

He shoved his chair back, looked down at his mother, and wished he could be more of the person she wished him to be.

He'd hurt her enough. Not even bread pudding would fix things today.

Ryan kissed her cheek and walked out the door.

Chapter Fourteen

"Ryan said what?"

"Don't make me say it again, Ronnie," Abby said, folding her arms tightly around her.

"Ryan can be harsh, sometimes," Ronnie admitted, nodding sagely as she followed Abby outside into the gray afternoon light. "But that's bad, even for him. I'll be havin' a word with that boy, believe you me."

Abby's head was throbbing. She'd had nothing but trouble since she'd arrived in Destiny Bay. Between the White Lady, Bartholomew, the strange experiences she'd had at the cottage, the upsetting revelations about her mother and Ryan Brannigan, she was feeling completely overwhelmed. "Don't bother. I had a word with him last night. Then I slapped him."

Ronnie appeared speechless . . . but only for a moment. "Geez, you've got a couple of brass ones, girl!" She stomped on the front step, hollered, "A curse on you, Jack!" and fluffed her hair out without missing a beat, as if cursing pirates every time you left your restaurant was as natural as breathing. "You deserve a stiff drink for that Ryan business—not to mention old Barty, spying through your window and leavin' you flowers. Did I tell you I just concocted a new shooter? I'm unveiling it at next week's Chef's Table. I call it 'the Heaving Bosom,' in honor of a steamy new romance I just read, and you've just won the honor of being the first taster."

"Gee, thanks." Abby watched as Ronnie paused in front of the bar window, the reflected image one of snug, white capris, jeweled sandals, and a pink gingham shirt—undoubtedly designer, and far too low cut and tight across her ample bust. Her hair glinted shades of red, and her very full lips were a glossy pink. Abby would have described the look as Mrs. Cleaver meets *Playboy*. It was a look only Ronnie could carry off, and Abby was coming to know it as pure trademark.

Ronnie linked her arm through Abby's as they began walking toward the police station for her meeting with officer Flynn. "You sure you've got your wee bouquet?"

Abby patted her shoulder bag. "Safe and sound." She glanced at Ronnie. "Thanks for coming with me today. I need the moral support."

Ronnie's fuchsia lips pursed as she considered Abby thoughtfully. "Bart's been known to lurk outside windows, but I never heard of him leaving anything like this. It's creepy."

"My feelings exactly," Abby said. "I'm hoping Connor Flynn can put a stop to it, though." But her thoughts were far from Bart, and it was no use denying it any longer. "Part of me feels sick about slapping Ryan," she said softly, "but there's a little voice inside telling me he deserved it."

Ronnie pursed her lips. "It's a tough one to call. He was out of line, for sure." She stared pensively toward the churning, pewter sea. "It's funny about Ryan. He's known as this hard, unforgiving man. As someone you'd never want to be caught on the wrong side of, but there's another aspect to him, you know?"

Abby's stomach was tied in knots, and for some reason this revelation only seemed to pull them tighter. "What aspect would that be?" she said, refusing to entertain the notion that Ryan could possibly have another side. "The one that impales his victims on nine-foot spikes?"

"No," Ronnie said, patiently as a tormented saint. "The one that cares. I'll tell you now, there's no other man you'd rather have in your corner when the chips are down. He'd fight to the death for a friend, and I ought to know."

A twinge of jealousy pricked her—though why, she

couldn't say. Perhaps it was the memory of the years following her mother's death. She was a child—defenseless with an absent father and no mother to love and protect her. There'd been no one willing to fight to the death for *her*. "Do tell," she said, squelching the unsettling thoughts.

They turned down Brigantine Way, a stiff gust of salty air buffeting their faces and making Abby think of beach glass and seaweed.

"When I was nineteen," said Ronnie, "I got involved with this guy—he was Ryan's fleet captain. Very charming man, but he had a dark side, see.

"The first time he hit me, I told myself that it was my fault. I can be a bit difficult. He even told me as much. By the time I'd been on the receiving end of a few good blows, I was feeling them clear to my heart. He battered the soul out of me, Abby. Made me feel as if that was the best I deserved, and he was doing me a favor by teaching me the error of my ways."

Abby's insides squeezed at Ronnie's quiet admission. She wanted to shush Ronnie, to tell her that it was all right, that it was all over, but something in the set of Ronnie's shoulders made Abby hold back. This was a story her friend needed to tell.

"Anyway," Ronnie said, "one night I get a knock on my door. I was hiding out because I had a black eye—something I rarely got because he knew how to make things hurt without leaving marks, and he rarely left a bruise that wasn't hidden by clothing.

"I creep up to the door and peek through the hole, and who do you suppose was there?"

"Ryan?" Abby asked quietly, already knowing the answer.

Ronnie nodded. "He said he'd camp out in the hall if I didn't let him in. So I did."

"What did he do?" She wasn't certain she wanted the answer, wasn't certain she wanted to like Ryan, and yet she'd seen something in him, something deeper than his anger—and it had drawn her to him in a way that was as compelling as it was frightening. There was something of a vulnerable warrior within him, and Abby had no doubt that beguiling mix of contradictions had broken through many a woman's defenses.

"He got real red in the face when he saw my eye. He took me to the couch and said that he'd figured out what was going on, and that Steve—my boyfriend—had confessed the entire thing to him."

"He confessed?"

"Well, it helped that Ryan had taken him out to sea, beaten the tar outta him and held him over the ocean by the scruff of the neck until he fessed up."

Abby's eyes widened. "Yup. That would do it."

"Ryan told me that he'd personally put Steve on the ferry to the mainland with two hundred bucks in his pocket, and told him that if he ever set foot back on the island, he'd personally see to it that he disappeared."

A chill ran down Abby's spine. "Ryan would *kill* him?"

"Oh, I doubt that. It was likely a heat-of-the-moment type of comment. But he'd make his life a living hell."

But Abby wasn't so sure. There was a passion within Ryan that seemed to burn white-hot, and Abby had no doubt that he would be capable of extreme measures when someone he cared about was in danger. "What did you do when Ryan told you?"

Ronnie smiled sadly. "I screamed at him. Cried. Called him every name in the book. Told him that Steve was going to change. Hit him. Made his lip bleed."

Abby gaped. "And what did Ryan do?"

"He let me do it. He just took it, like he was taking the lumps Steve deserved—letting me hurt him, letting me fight back, letting me get it all out, so there'd be none of Steve's poison left in me. And then when I was ready, he held me while I cried, told me that I deserved better than

Steve, rocked me back and forth." Her breath was deep and slow. "I loved him that night. And I never stopped."

Abby patted Ronnie's hand as it rested in the crook of her elbow. "That was good of him. And I'm sorry it happened to you. You *do* deserve better," she said softly. "Did it work? Was Steve's poison gone?"

"Not for a long time," Ronnie said. "But Ryan was a good friend—though sadly nothing more—and he gave me a jump start."

Abby bit her lip. A new, uncomfortable idea was niggling at her consciousness. If Ryan was that loyal to Ronnie, imagine how he would have defended his mother, if he'd had the opportunity. Perhaps all Ryan was doing was fighting back against the last tie to the abusers of his mother—and if that were the case, who could blame him? She shook her head minutely. Empathy for Ryan Brannigan was the last thing she wanted to feel . . . but like it or not, there it was.

"Ryan's had a hard go of it, though you'd never hear him admit it. First there was his father—whom you now know all about—and then his wife . . ."

"He was *married?*" Abby's cheeks flushed—the words had come out so loudly that Ronnie looked at her with an expression bordering on comical. She tried to smile but her lips felt tight and stiff. It disturbed her that Ryan had been married. *Why?*

"Yes, he was married—and a right piece of work she was, let me tell you. She's moved now. Wouldn't have the nerve to show her face in town after what she did to him."

"What *did* she do?" Abby asked, suddenly wishing she'd had a chance to sample the Heaving Bosom before they'd left The Surfside.

"What did she do?" Ronnie stared at her as if she'd just sprouted an extra head. "She left him, Abs. She up and left the man! How could she *do* that? He's God's gift, that man is, and she *left* him."

"Sometimes marriages break up," Abby said reasonably.

Ronnie gawked at her. "Maybe so, but a man like Ryan—a man who was born into heartbreak—you gotta love him fierce, or not at all. That's the only decent way of it, Abby. You gotta love him enough that every hurt he ever had doesn't matter anymore. You gotta love him enough that he dares to love you back. You've gotta love him *that much*, or bow out. It doesn't take a genius to see that Ryan's never been loved that way before. He hasn't had the rough edges of his heart smoothed over yet. Only true love can do that, Abby, and *that* woman wasn't capable of drawing it out of him."

Abby stared at Ronnie, momentarily shocked by the swell of protectiveness her friend's words had stirred within her. In her mind's eye, she could imagine the boy he had been—a child robbed of his father's love and protection. It wasn't, in fact, much different from how she had been all those years ago—and still was—for wasn't there yet the ghost of the abandoned child secreted away in her heart, looking for the love that was snatched so cruelly from her? And wouldn't she be willing to bet that the ghost of an abandoned child also hid within the heart of Ryan Brannigan?

Suddenly, she saw her mother in a whole new light, and it distorted the perfect image Abby had created of her.

"I feel terrible that my mother took his father."

She couldn't believe this woman she'd thought of as angelic had stolen a man from his child's cradle, stolen him from the wedding altar, from Cora. She raked her fingers through her hair, brought them back up to rub her temples. "I came here thinking—no, knowing—that I would learn about my mother's past. I didn't expect to hate the things I learned. How do I process this?"

"Coming here was a gamble, Abby. You had to know that."

Abby nodded.

"There's something I've been wondering about," Ronnie said cautiously. "I mean, I learned something about your mom, and I'm not sure if I ought to tell you or not."

Abby's shoulders slumped. They came to a halt in front of O'Donnell's Post and Petrol. "I'm not gonna like it, am I?"

"No."

She considered—but only for a second. Abby squared her shoulders. "Tell me."

"Right," said Ronnie, with a firm nod of the head. "Well, it seems the pregnant woman Douglas abandoned—whom we now know to be Cora—encountered your ma on the street and gave her a right talkin' to. Asked where her sense of decency was, then apparently—and this is according to my Aunty Jane, who was right there buying her newspaper at the time—your ma said she couldn't leave Douglas, that she loved him more than life itself and he loved her. Apparently she was right teary-eyed over the whole thing. Then, it seems your ma offered Cora money—said to use it to help with the baby, whom we now know to be Ryan.

"Well, Cora got herself in a fine snit, said no way would she take money from a so-and-so, and that Celeste ought to tell that man she loved so much to get his sorry self to work and support his child." Ronnie shook her head, seemingly agog. "I'm told it was a right brouhaha, is what."

Abby couldn't take her eyes off Ronnie's face, couldn't breathe, couldn't think. "What am I supposed to say to that?" she asked at last, her voice hardly more than a whisper, tears teetering on her lashes. "What can I possibly say, Ronnie?" The idea of running away from Destiny Bay was looking more attractive by the minute. She didn't want to know these things, didn't want them to be true.

Ronnie grasped her hand. "Listen, you came here for knowledge, didn't you?"

"Yeah."

"Well, you got it. Don't judge your ma, Abby. Just look

at the facts. Only the facts can lead you to the truth of what happened to your mother."

Abby started walking again. The police station had come into view, and Abby stared at it as if it were a beacon in a shifting sea. "I found something out, myself," she said at last.

"Oh? And what's that?"

Abby tucked her trembling fingers into her pockets. "The O'Donnells told me that my mother was scorned, called names, robbed . . . and she had a stalker."

"No!"

Abby nodded. "And if that wasn't enough, something even worse happened."

"Lord help the girl," she said, shaking her head. "What happened?"

"I don't know," she said, shoulders falling. "The O'Donnells didn't even know. But according to them, she just 'faded away.'"

"Come again?"

"My grandmother was the only person who'd ever talk to me about my mother, and she described a very similar thing," Abby said, staring at the age-old cobbles beneath her feet. "She said one minute, my mother was engaged in everything around her, and the next, it was like she'd vanished inside of herself. She was like a ghost," she said, echoing the image Mavis had placed in her head. "Whatever happened to make her that way happened here, on this island, and I'm going to find out what."

"That was a long time ago, Abby," Ronnie said.

"Well, if there's one thing I know about people on this island, it's that they have long memories."

Ronnie folded her arms and nodded. "Yeah. Until someone starts asking questions. These people *invented* the code of silence."

"There's more," Abby said, biting her lip. "I mean, it might be nothing, or it might be something."

"You mean more than the footprints in the dirt beneath your bedroom window that may or may not have been left by Simon Gorham, the fact that Old Bart's been peeking in at you, your coming to blows with Ryan, and the flowers Bart left for you? I couldn't imagine that would be *everything*," she said, her eyebrow lifted eloquently.

"Yes," Abby said. "More than all that."

"Saints preserve us. Hang on," Ronnie said dramatically. She fished in her purse and withdrew a silver flask, and after offering Abby a swig—which she refused—downed a healthy portion, herself. "Okay, I'm good."

Abby couldn't help grinning. She considered blurting it out for all of half a second, then reached for Ronnie's flask, wincing as she downed a stinging mouthful.

She wiped her tearing eyes. "I saw the Lady," she said at last.

"What lady?"

Abby gave her a knowing look.

Ronnie gasped aloud, her thickly lashed eyes widening. "You mean the *White Lady*? I've lived on this island all my life, and I've never so much as caught a glimpse of her!"

"Obviously, *you're* not on a collision course with disaster."

"Pah!" exclaimed Ronnie, throwing up her hands. "You don't believe that old wives tale? Everyone knows The Lady lived at your cottage. Perhaps she was just out for a stroll?"

Abby stared at her, incredulous. "I saw a bloody ghost, Ronnie! Right about now, I'd be willing to think anything. I don't even believe in ghosts! How is it possible to see something you don't believe in? I'm trying to convince myself that she was just a manifestation of my subconscious; you know, a way for it to tell me—my consciousness, that is—that things just weren't right. What do you think? I mean, Cora had just told me about the White Lady and her connection with danger . . ." An ominous chill raced through her. "Of course! That's all it is, right?"

"You're babbling. There are worse things than seeing a ghost, Abby, like being stalked, so calm down and focus." Ronnie strode a little faster. "You need to get this situation under control. *Now.* I can think of two things that will make that happen. Number one," she said, grasping the door of the police station and pulling it open, "is talking to the police, which we're about to do. If they don't take Old Bart seriously, you can bet they'll jump to action when they hear that you've seen the White Lady."

"What?" Abby asked, stunned. "They'd act on a ghost sighting faster than a stalker?"

"This is Destiny Bay, luv. We follow the beat of our own drummer. You've got some real leverage with the White Lady on your side."

Abby rolled her eyes. "So what's the second thing?"

"You'll find out," Ronnie said with a wink. She strode into the police station as if she owned the place. "Hey, Miss Warner," she said brightly. "Let Deputy Flynn know that Ronnie Morgan and Abby Lancaster are here to see him."

Chapter Fifteen

Abby watched Connor Flynn turn the bouquet that Bartholomew had left for her over in his gloved fingers. He slipped the wilted flowers into a clear, plastic bag and placed them on his desk.

She sat at a chair he had pulled up to his desk, tucked neatly between twin stalagmites of case files and books that erupted from the floor. Carefully, so as not to jar the overflowing in-box, she rested her elbow on the worn veneer of his desk. Above his head, a thin, wooden frame evidenced that somewhere beneath the fluttery deluge of thumbtacks and notes, there was, in fact, a corkboard.

In the midst of it all, a comical bobble-head police officer held a sign that read: NERVE CENTER. If this was to be believed, the nerve center was in dire need of some Valium.

"Well," he said at last, lacing his fingers behind his head and leaning back in his chair. "I admit it's sure not a pleasant thing to come home to. And you say these flowers are significant why?" he asked, frowning.

"Rosemary and forget-me-nots are both suggestive of remembrance," she said, leaning forward and pointing through the bag. "My mother lived here before, and I've heard through the grapevine that she had a stalker. Everyone says I look exactly like her. Wouldn't it be reasonable to suppose that same stalker could have taken an interest in me?"

"I suppose it's possible."

Abby hurried on, intent on wiping the skepticism from his voice. "I mentioned the painting that I'd discovered of my mother, right? Well, honeysuckles figure very prominently in that very painting. And look at what it's bound with," she said. "Those strands are definitely human hair, Officer Flynn. Just look at the color. It's the exact same shade as my mother's was. Don't you get how creepy this is?"

"Creepy is one word for it, but I think maybe you're reading too much into this, Miss Lancaster."

"I am not!" she said loudly. Faces turned toward her, some with narrowed eyes, others with expressions of unmasked curiosity. She cleared her throat self-consciously.

"And how can you be certain it was Bart who left them?"

"Who else could have done it?" she asked wearily. Her spirits were sinking as quickly as her energy level.

"Can you think of anyone else who might want to scare you or run you out of town?" he asked, eyes intent upon her.

Had he heard about her run-in with Ryan last night? *Stupid question.* She was forgetting that she was in Destiny Bay, where gossip traveled faster than the speed of light. "Well," she said cautiously, "I've had a few words with Ryan Brannigan. He's got a chip on his shoulder the size of Baltimore, and he's convinced I put it there. I'd say he wants me out of town." But was he responsible for the threatening bouquet? Somehow, she doubted it.

"You know," she said, her wheels turning faster, "I got a really bad vibe from the bartender at Rum Runner's. Johnny something-or-other."

Connor nodded sagely. "You got anything more for me than your 'bad vibe'?"

She felt instantly foolish. "No," she said, shoulders sagging. "Listen, it couldn't be anyone other than Bartholomew. I mean, if it looks like a duck and quacks like a duck, it's generally a duck."

Connor looked up as the woman who was sitting at the front desk when Abby and Ronnie arrived approached in a cloud of L'air du Temps. She smiled nervously toward Abby. "Deputy Flynn, I just thought I ought to let you know that Sheriff called, and he's on his way down."

Connor's expression was instantly guarded. "Thank you, Julie. Did you mention that Miss Lancaster was here?"

"I'm afraid so," she said apologetically. "It was out before I even realized I'd said it! I'm sorry, Deputy."

Connor nodded and smiled tightly at Julie Warner, who turned and scurried back to her desk. He grasped Abby's elbow and gently urged her to her feet. "I'll tell you what, I'll have me another chat with Old Bart. You can rest easy that we're taking this threat against your person very seriously. Now you do your part by leaving the police work to us and taking proper care."

Was she imagining it, or was he rushing her out of the police station? "I, uh, also wanted to mention that the more I think about that warning sign on Cragan Cliff

Road, the more I think it was sawed off deliberately to do me harm."

He nodded absently. "I can see how you'd think that, but let's go on the assumption that it was random vandalism, which it likely was. I don't want you getting worked up. The sign's already been replaced, in case you haven't noticed."

She had, but it was small consolation.

"Now, you just be sure to keep your doors and windows locked. Don't settle into any predictable routines—"

"Don't take candy from strangers, don't walk down dark alleys . . . I follow you. Thank you for your help, Deputy Flynn," she said hurriedly. He was nudging her toward the doorway so quickly, she was almost tripping over herself.

"That's right." He smiled kindly toward her. "I'll be sure to keep you posted on any progress."

Abby took in the sight of his perfectly pressed uniform, neatly combed hair, and shining badge. There was something authoritative about him that calmed her even as it gave her concern. Was he just placating her? And why was he rushing her out?

She kept her silence, realizing that it would do her little good to argue. It was obvious he wouldn't be dissuaded.

They met Ronnie in the lobby as she strode back into the station. "Wow!" she said brightly. "Perfect timing! I take it you folks are all finished up here?"

"All done," Connor said, his voice assuring. "Now you ladies take care. You still have my number, right, Abrielle?"

She nodded with a weak smile. "Thanks," she said, and let Ronnie bustle her out of the station.

"I've been hard at work, my friend," Ronnie said, grinning infectiously as they pulled up outside Artist's Cottage. "I borrowed the spare key from Cora. 'Solution number two' is ready and waiting!"

"Oh, this I can't wait to see." Abby slipped her key in the lock and opened the door.

Her brow lifted at the improbable scene that greeted her inside the cottage. Candles glimmered from every horizontal surface, throwing wavering light onto the ceiling and echoing the unnerving effect of the dark, stormy sky outside. Her nostrils caught the scent of something pungent and spicy, then a plume of white smoke caught her eye. *Incense.*

"Ronnie, what on earth are you up to?"

"Follow me." She led the way to the living room floor. The coffee table had been removed, and in its place sat a Ouija board, surrounded by a large circle of salt.

"Oh, you cannot be serious."

"I'm dead serious, girl."

"I told you," Abby said incredulously, "I didn't actually *see* a White Lady—or any other color lady for that matter! It was a manifestation of my subconscious."

Ronnie dismissed her with an impatient hmph. "Don't tell me you believe that psychobabble?"

"Well, when stacked against the scientific reasoning of a Ouija board, how can mere human psychology compare?"

"Now you're talking." Ronnie tossed a few pillows onto the floor. She sat upon one and motioned for Abby to do the same. "Now, since the White Lady has appeared to you, I thought perhaps we ought to have a chat with her, find out who she is and see if she has anything she wants to say. Why are you moving your lips like that?"

"I'm invoking Saint Jude, Patron Saint of Idiocy."

"Saints preserve us, girl! Jude is the Patron Saint of lost causes. *Protestants*," she muttered under her breath. "Now, we place our fingers like so, and ask it questions."

"I know how it works," Abby said wearily. "Our subconscious allows our fingers to move the gadget around, revealing exactly what we want to hear."

"Again with the subconscious! Will you get a grip, Abby . . . it's the *spirits*—provided you haven't offended them."

Abby sank onto her crossed legs, her gauzy skirt puffing around her in a fine imitation of the white dress worn by the lady on the rocks. A rippling shiver traced her spine, drawing her shoulders into its all-too-perceptible cadence.

"Ooh, spooked out, are we?"

Abby ignored the comment and placed her fingers on the arrow. "Shall we get on with it, then?"

Ronnie sighed dramatically and let her eyelids flutter shut. Abby would have chuckled if the darkened room hadn't been wavering in the candlelight, if the wind wasn't whispering around the eaves of the cottage, if the entire place didn't seem so suddenly, irrevocably, creepy.

"Oh, White Lady of Abandon Bluff," she intoned, "we call across the veil of time and death, and ask that you speak to us now."

Abby wanted to chuckle, but somehow, couldn't. There was a change in the atmosphere, finite and yet unmistakable, as Ronnie spoke.

Abby shivered involuntarily, eyes straining into the murky darkness of the room. A swath of goose bumps trickled over her flesh, calling each tiny hair to attention.

"We respectfully wish to ask questions of you. Will you converse with us, White Lady?"

Abby's indrawn breath was deep and disbelieving as the device beneath her fingers began to vibrate infinitesimally. Slowly, it drifted across the board, landing, at last, on the word, *yes.*

"Stop doing that, Ronnie."

Ronnie cracked a satisfied smile. "*I'm* not doing anything, Abs." She adjusted herself on the pillow, eyes fluttering shut again. "White Lady, what is it that you'd like to communicate to Abby?"

The arrow sprang into action, darting to *D*, then *A*, followed by *N-G-E-R*.

Abby snatched back her hands as if she'd been stung. "Ronnie! Enough already!" She began rising, stopping only when Ronnie's hand gripped her arm. Her eyes flashed intently.

"Don't you want to discover what the White Lady knows, Abby? What if she knows something about your mother . . . something that no one else knows?"

Abby paused, staring down at the board and wondering why such foolishness so unnerved her. She dropped back down, repositioned her fingers, and sighed loudly.

Ronnie paused long enough to spare her a withering glance. "White Lady—"

"My turn," interrupted Abby. She ignored the heaving in her belly, and took a breath to speak. "Okay, White Lady. Do you know why I'm here?"

The whining of the wind through the branches outside seemed to call a warning to her heart. Abby was gripped with the terrifying impression that if she were to lift her head and look through the window, she'd see the ghostly face of the White Lady staring back at her.

She began to tremble. Fear snaked through her body as the object beneath her fingers began to vibrate. Her breath came short, and then the pointer sprang into action.

S-E-C-R-E-T-S

It was all she could do not to race out of the room, for she felt certain—absolutely certain—that she and Ronnie were no longer alone.

Ronnie gave her a nudge.

Abby summoned her courage and asked, "Do you know about my mother?"

The pointer darted out from beneath her fingers and came to an abrupt halt over the word, *Yes.*

"Did you do that?" Abby whispered to Ronnie. "Please tell me you did that."

But Ronnie looked as terrified as Abby felt. She shook her head slowly from side to side, eyes as big as quarters in the dim light. "Ask something else."

"Do you know what changed my mother?"

Yes.

Abby was petrified. She forced her fear down in order to ask the question she knew she must. "What changed her?"

D-A-N-G-E-R

"What caused the danger?"

L-O-V-E

"Love?" she repeated, frowning. "Could it be that simple? By *danger* do you think she means heartbreak?"

"Simple?" Ronnie hissed, gaping. "Jeez girl, have you ever *been* in love?"

Had she? She'd *thought* she had, once, a long time ago—as much as it was possible for her to love—but had she really?

"Okay, my turn." Ronnie cleared her throat. "White Lady, is Abby in danger?"

As it had before, the pointer sprang into action.

Yes.

Both women looked at each other, terror streaking between them. "From what?" Abby asked, her voice little more than a whisper.

L-O-V-E

"This ghost has a one-track mind," Abby said, trying hard to make light of a situation that was suddenly not.

"White Lady, what can Abby do to protect herself?"

L-O-V-E

"That makes no sense!" she said, straining for bravado when all she really wanted to do was hide under the bedsheets and recite every prayer she'd ever been taught. "I'm in danger because of love, and yet in order to protect myself I have to love."

She let her eyes flit to the light switch, gratified beyond words that no White Lady floated there, and darted toward it. She flicked it on and the room was bathed in yellowy light, making every lit candle suddenly insignificant.

She stared down at Ronnie. "This was a bad idea. I'm done."

"Yeah," Ronnie said softly, looking up at Abby with the unmistakable glint of fear in her eyes. "Me, too."

Chapter Sixteen

The rustling of paper beneath his elbow made him grimace, and Ryan squeezed his eyes closed.

Yes, Abby had been on the forefront of his mind since that catastrophe of a lunch yesterday at his mother's house, but did he *have* to draw her?

Ryan didn't want to see it—the extraordinary face that would stare back at him the instant he opened his eyes— the face that rested on the desk before him, captured on a piece of paper by the restless meanderings of his own hand.

That was the thing that disturbed him most. It was not so much the fact that he had *drawn* her—artists, he knew, were compelled to re-create beauty, and her face had beckoned his traitorous artist's blood since he'd first laid eyes on her—but the fact that she had come so easily from his pencil. It was the fact that she had been waiting inside him so silently that he hadn't even felt his hand twitch with resistance.

Somewhere between hashing out a supply issue with a vendor and staring into the churning sky that loomed beyond the panes of glass, she had slipped from the dark place where he kept his hidden compulsion to create. He had looked at the formerly blank piece of paper that had rested on his desk, and there she was.

Of course, in a distracted, subconscious way, he knew his pencil was moving over the blank expanse, knew he was sketching her face. It wasn't until a moment ago when he actually *looked* at the lines of her—the shadows that hinted of loss, the eyes that seemed to hold countless secrets—that a serpentine wisp of unease slithered from a coil in his belly and swayed hypnotically to the realization that she had been nestled there in his dark place, without his even knowing.

Slowly, he opened his eyes.

Damn. She was still there.

Damn. She was still beautiful enough to make his heart thump, beautiful enough to make his eyes sting. And he had seen his share of beauty—heck, he had *had* his share of beauties—but somehow, she was different.

For the first time, he found himself incapable of saying her name, incapable of even thinking it.

Ryan lurched in his chair, roused by a thud on his door.

"It's getting busy out here, boss." Johnny Mackenzie poked his head around the door, letting The Proclaimers' "Five Hundred Miles" spill into the shadowy office. "Any chance of you helping behind the bar?"

"Yeah. I'll be out in a bit, Johnny. How's that hand?"

Johnny flexed the bandaged appendage experimentally, barely wincing as he did so. "On the mend."

"Did you fill out an accident report yet?"

"Nah, I'll get to it tonight, promise."

"You do that. Mind explaining to me how a barman with twenty years experience cut himself on a glass?"

"Just careless, I guess." Johnny winked. "That Abrielle Lancaster walked by, and my brain turned to mush."

Ryan hoped his face wasn't as pale as it suddenly felt.

A smile that really wasn't a smile lifted the corners of Ryan's mouth as the door shut behind Johnny. Long before

Ryan became the unwilling heartthrob of the island, a younger Johnny had gleefully held the title, and not a woman in Destiny Bay had been safe from his charms. They still flocked to him, truth be told. Ryan was glad for it. Johnny had always appreciated sidelong glances in a way Ryan never had.

Ryan looked back down at the portrait he had drawn of Abby, willing himself to crumple it, toss it, forget it.

Instead, he lifted the blotter, slipped the picture beneath and rose from his desk.

He opened his office door, turned off the light, and left her in the place she had come from.

It was two o'clock, and she was still in her jammies. Today, however, she decided that she wasn't even going to feel guilty about it.

She'd had an incredibly exhausting weekend. Between the mysterious footprints, Bart popping up in her window, the White Lady, the tight-lipped islanders, learning the upsetting truth about her mother, the Ouija board and her confrontation with Ryan, she was emotionally drained. What she needed was a concrete reason to stay on this island, a solid lead into her mother's history.

The telephone jangled loudly, making her jump.

"Hello?"

"Hello, Abby: It's Mavis O'Donnell, dear. Franklin thought I should visit the gallery in Destiny Bay—he remembered they have a hefty collection of McAllister paintings on view, though he was certain there were none of your mother. I'm not so sure myself. Saw one this morning I think you should have a look at."

Abby's breath caught in her throat. "Really? Oh, thank you so much, Mavis. I'll check it out as soon as I can."

"Oh, no problem, deary. I just thought you'd like to know. The owner's closing up for a few days, but I'm sure he'd be happy to take you on a guided tour when he gets back."

A few days? Abby's heart sank, but just a little. She wasn't about to let that tiny snag get her down. She promised to stop by for another visit soon and closed her telephone.

"Thank you, Mom," she whispered. Abby rested her hand on her cheek, wishing it was her mother's hand that touched her.

There was a new lightness of spirit that had her on her feet and heading to the kitchen. She hadn't had her Earl Grey yet, and she was suddenly famished.

She walked by the front door, barely glancing through the window, when a flutter of white caught her eye.

"Oh no," she whispered, her voice only a breath. She knew before she placed her hand on the doorknob, before she pulled it open and grasped the note that rose and fell on the salty breeze, that something was very, very wrong.

A tack held the note fast. She reached to tear it from the door just as the sun came out from behind a cloud to glint on a bit of metal. It was a ring, dangling from the tack and glittering in the sunlight.

It couldn't be . . .

Her heartbeat fluttered beneath her sternum.

Lightly, Abby's fingers brushed the gold—as if she were frightened the ring would crumble beneath her touch.

The sound of her breath was all around her as she lifted the ring from the nail, turned it over in her hand. Her heartbeat stopped fluttering, and started thudding.

In her trembling palm shimmered the ruby and diamond ring that her mother—and every previous Rutherford woman—had worn in her formal portrait. Every Rutherford woman except her. By the time she sat for her first portrait at age eighteen, the ring had long been lost, recompensed by insurance, and duly mourned by the family.

Now, Abby had no doubt where the ring had been lost, for there it lay, as vivid as a brilliant drop of blood in the palm of her trembling hand.

Her fingers closed tightly over the ring.

With the other hand, she grasped the note—which was written on Rum Runner letterhead—and tugged.

It ripped down the center, but not so terribly as to destroy the writing. Jagged, smeared, reddish brown in color, the words glared up at her like a primordial scream:

Welcome home, my lovely Celeste.

Chapter Seventeen

The ring was back in the family at last. She should be happy. She should be *delighted* . . . but the queasy feeling in her stomach refused to subside even for a minute.

Why she should feel so distressed over the incident was beyond her. True, it was a twisted and frightening prank, but at least she knew who had done it, and that person was about to get an almighty earful.

Abby clutched the ring tightly as she slammed her car door and stormed through Rum Runner's rear parking lot.

Ryan Brannigan. *That's* who'd done this. No one wanted her off the island as badly as he did, and he was obviously willing to stoop to frightening her as a tool to get her to leave.

But how did he get his hands on the ring?

Well, that was obvious, wasn't it? After her mother had lost the ring, it must have been pawned. Then, Ryan gained possession of it—perhaps he bought it or perhaps someone had used it to pay off their tab. Who knew?

All that mattered was that she was about to prove Ryan couldn't scare her off this island.

She burst into the main room, glaring at the man behind the bar. "Where is he?"

Johnny Mac's gaze shot up from the perfect head on the ale he was pouring. He opened his mouth to speak, then, seeming to think better of it, closed it promptly.

Abby stormed over to the bar, gripped the brass rail and leaned in as close as her small frame would allow. "Where is he?"

"Uh, he's, well—" Johnny's eyes shifted furtively toward the door of Ryan Brannigan's office. "He's busy," he said at last, squaring his shoulders.

"Not too busy to speak with me, I hope?" she said, smiling icily toward the brewmaster.

He slipped from behind the bar with a dexterity that defied his large stature. "Now, Abrielle, I don't think it's a good idea for you to go back there," he said, hands lifted in a gesture that bade her halt.

To Abby, it looked more like a signal of surrender. She pressed forward, ignoring his attempts to thwart her. "Get out of my way."

His eyes narrowed, raked her from head to foot. Abby resisted the urge to squirm beneath the gaze that rested so coldly upon her. Something in their depths wormed into the heart of her; something dark and disturbing that made her skin prickle and her heart squeeze a little too tightly in her chest.

Johnny looked her up and down, matched her posture, and said, over his own folded arms and puffing chest, "No."

She was suddenly afraid, though she wasn't sure why.

"I'm coming through," she said, relieved to sound braver than she felt. "Don't make me lay you flat in the process."

Johnny blinked in surprise. A slow grin crept over his face; his shoulders relaxed. "Why Miss Lancaster, are you coming on to me?"

"Only on *this* island," she said through her teeth, "do they grow men arrogant enough to interpret a threat of bodily harm as a come-on."

Johnny chuckled as she shoved her way past him. "Honey, you can't have been many places."

Abby ignored the teasing tone in the brewmaster's voice and kept her eyes intent on the oak door and the metal plaque that glinted in the dim light of the bar. The word inscribed upon it, PRIVATE, seemed like a deliberate affront.

She had had it with this man; with his pettiness, his pride, his outright rudeness.

Well, enough was enough.

The ruby ring seemed to glow with the intensity of an ember in her palm, its facets and claws digging into her gripping flesh.

She shoved against the door full force, striding through it as it thudded against the wall hard enough to rattle picture frames on the wall.

The split-second image was captured in her mind: Ryan lurching at her entry, eyes instantly alert and trained upon her with the fierceness of a startled predator. Without a perceptible movement, his muscles seemed to vibrate beneath the fabric of his shirt. His very aura seemed poised for attack.

Abby sensed his change in demeanor. She considered stepping back, but only for an instant. Her hand squeezed around the ring, reawakening her to a sense of her mission.

She stormed across the office, bearing down upon him with the momentum of a freight train, stopping at his desk only when her thighs bumped sharply against its edge.

His eyes narrowed menacingly. "Is there something I can do for you?" he asked—far too quietly.

She slapped her palm down upon his desk, felt the circulation rush through her fingers anew as they unclenched, and returned his glare with equal intensity. "Oh, I certainly hope so." Her fingers lifted, withdrew from the table, leaving the ruby to glitter like fresh-drawn blood in her wake. "Did you do this?" The voice that hissed in the air was unrecognizable as her own.

Ryan looked at the ring, then up at his accuser.

She leaned forward into the silence, arms braced on either side of the table he used as a desk. *"Did you do this?"*

Ryan leaned back in his chair, fingers tented beneath his chin. "I have no idea what you're talking about, Miss Lancaster."

"I think we're quite beyond formalities, don't you, Ryan?"

"If you say so," he said through his teeth.

Abby eyed him speculatively. "Since you're feeling so agreeable, perhaps you'll be willing to answer my next question. How did you manage to get your hands on this ring? You obviously weren't the original thief—"

"Thief?" He all but exploded out of his chair, hitting the desk with enough ferocity to jar the pens in their cup. "You march in here, slap a ring that I've never seen on my desk, and accuse me of being a thief? You've the devil's own nerve, woman!"

Abby leaned in, snatching the ring.

He glared at her across the desk, eyes a withering shade of gold. She saw the pulse in his throat—felt a similar thud in her own. She leaned closer. "You don't frighten me, Ryan Brannigan; not with your silly bouquets or notes, not even with this." She picked up the ring, holding it in front of his eyes. "I know you did this, and I know why!"

In a flash, he was over the desk, pens flying in all directions, shoes scuffing the aged finish, breath in her face.

She felt powerless to tear her eyes from his gaze, considerably rebuked by his fury, and more than a little intimidated by the fact that he strongly resembled a caged animal. The fact that she presently shared the cage in question made her consider with great care every word she thought of speaking.

For an instant, they stared at each other; two opponents in the face-off of their lives.

Quietly, as if straining against infinite tension, he sent the silence spiraling to its death. "Don't say another word, Abrielle." His voice was little more than a breath. "Don't say another word until we've both gotten ourselves under control."

He walked away from her, braced his hands on either side of the window frame, and stood for what seemed like an endless amount of time. "Tell me why you're here," he said at last. "Tell me every detail, or leave. I think I deserve to know *exactly* what it is I'm accused of."

Abby took a steadying breath. She squared her shoulders and jumped in, feet first. "You're trying to frighten me off this island." She folded her arms in front of her. "You might as well know that it isn't going to work."

He lifted an eyebrow. "I admit to *wanting* you off this island. I even admit to scheming. But I don't stoop to spooking people, Abrielle. Next I'll be accused of taking candy from babies."

She stepped closer, assured by his calmer demeanor. "Do you mean to tell me that you haven't been lurking around the cottage?"

Ryan's expression was a tie between confusion and indignation. "Again," he said, forcing the word past his teeth, "you've lost me."

"Oh, I doubt that."

"If we're ever going to get to the bottom of this, you need to start making sense. Now sit down, and start at the beginning!"

"Don't tell me to *sit* like I'm a trained poodle!"

"Have you always been this infuriating, or did you save it all up for me?"

"You flatter yourself," she said. "Though why that should surprise me, I have no idea."

Ryan pressed the tips of his fingers together, rested his chin upon them, and closed his eyes. Moments passed. Abby began to fidget.

"Please," he said at last. He looked up at her, looking suddenly more weary than wild. "Please have a seat, and tell me why you think I've stolen your ring. It is yours, isn't it?"

Abby stared at him suspiciously. *This* was a new twist. If his temper hadn't frightened her, his courtesy just might. She grasped the back of a chair opposite his desk, and after what seemed like a very long time, sat in it.

"Would you like to tell me about the ring?"

She regarded him pensively. "It belonged to my mother's family," she said at last. "The ring was given to the eldest daughter upon her eighteenth birthday, and has been worn in formal portraits since the early nineteen-hundreds." She looked down at her hands, significantly bare of any adornment. "Every daughter but me. The last Rutherford woman to wear it was my mother. According to everything I've been told, the ring was stolen shortly after she received it."

"May I?" Ryan asked, hand outstretched.

She considered a moment, then reached out and dropped the ring in his hand.

For what seemed like an eternity, he stared at her and not the ring. Then, lifting it to the light, he turned it one way and the other, letting its facets catch the sun to best advantage. "You're certain this is the actual ring that belonged to your mother?"

"I've no doubt whatsoever."

"And where did you find it?"

She exhaled slowly, wondering if she was playing right into his hands. "It was hanging from a nail on my door. Along with a note."

If this sounded at all strange to him, Abby noted that he didn't show it.

"What did the note say?"

"It said . . ." Abby bit her lip. An icy finger traced the length of her spinal column as she recalled the note. She squared her shoulders, not wanting him to see her fear if, in fact, he had written it. "It said, 'Welcome back, my lovely Celeste.'"

His answering stare was indecipherable.

"It was written in something strange."

"Such as?"

Abby glared at him, despising the fact that he was one step shy of interrogating her. "I think it was written in blood," she blurted, folding her arms over her chest.

Ryan's eyes lifted from the ring and rested on hers. "Are you certain?" he asked at last.

"I'm reasonably sure, but I would imagine only a lab test would say for certain."

His frown was thoughtful. "I want to see it."

Abby glanced up. His eyes had changed. His tone had changed. His very emanations had changed. No more predator, enraged at the assault in his own domain, but suddenly wary, concerned. His concern was almost as disconcerting as his rage.

She fished in her purse, anxious to avert her gaze from the intensity of his. She withdrew the ziplock bag into which she'd gingerly tucked the note, and passed it into his outstretched hand.

Ryan looked carefully at the note, his thumb gently circling the Rum Runner's logo at the top.

"You didn't send it, did you?" She knew the answer—she had seen it on his face already. If Ryan hadn't sent the note, the flowers, the ring, then who had? It seemed suddenly beyond Bart's mental capacity to wage such a systematic assault on her nerves. Could it be Johnny?

He looked into her face. "I've given you no reason to trust me, Abby, but on this I give you my word: I did not send you this note, and I've never seen this ring until today. I have no idea how the person who sent this got their hands on my letterhead."

"I believe you," she said at last, sighing deeply.

Ryan's face registered a fleeting look of gratification; not truly perceptible, but a flash, like when shadows change in a breeze. "You mentioned some other things . . ."

Abby felt suddenly as if someone had changed the rules and forgotten to tell her. *Why on earth does he care?* "There was an instance when the flowers outside my bedroom window were trampled, as if someone had made a habit of looking in, and I received something else. A small posy of flowers. Forget-me-nots, honeysuckle and rosemary. It was tied in long, reddish hair. A long time ago—when my mother lived here—she had long, reddish hair."

"Anything else?"

"Well, nothing really concrete," she said, shrugging. "Just this strange feeling I've had, like someone is watching me. It's silly, really."

Ryan rose from his chair and lifted a jacket from its back. "You need to report this. Now."

Abby felt the chair being tugged gently from beneath her. "Ryan, I really don't think—"

"Come on. I'll go with you. Sheriff and I go way back."

"Now, just wait a minute!"

Ryan gawked at her, startled.

"If I report this—"

"*If* you report this? I hate to put a damper on your day, but you've got a stalker, Abrielle, and a sick one, at that. You need to report this, the sooner the better."

Abby gaped up at him. "But I just talked to Deputy Flynn yesterday, and he doesn't even seem to want to give any of this a second thought. He couldn't get me out of there fast enough!"

"I'll make him listen," he said ominously.

She folded her arms over her chest. "What is going on here? You just admitted you wanted me off this island, and now you're helping me? Are you telling me you've suddenly been awakened to a sense of your civic duty?"

He grasped her arm—gently—and steered her toward the door. "You could say that."

"Let me go!" Abby shook herself free. "I don't need a protector, Ryan. I need to get to the bottom of this."

Ryan stared at her wearily. "Abby, if for no other reason than to eliminate myself as a suspect, I want to go to the police. With you. *Now*."

She huffed loudly. "Well, now that I understand your *true* motives," she said, gathering her purse and taking her sweet time about it, "I suppose it can't hurt."

Ryan rolled his eyes and opened the door, ushering her through.

They passed through the bar wordlessly, all eyes glued to them as they wove around tables and at last, exited the building. *And no wonder*, thought Abby, as she imagined the racket their shouting must have made. She'd be the talk of the town by nightfall, if she wasn't already.

The only sound between them was the crunch of gravel beneath their footfalls.

They rounded the building, intent on the parking lot at the rear of Rum Runner's.

Abby stopped, brought up short by the sight of her car. She stared at the ugly gashes that slashed each deflated tire.

"Bloody hell!" Ryan bellowed, face contorted in rage. He turned his focus toward Abby. "I suppose you're going to blame me for this as well?"

Abby glared at him, arms folded across her chest, but said nothing. She had been with him the entire time, after all.

A flash of movement snagged her attention. She turned in time to see Ryan break into a run.

"Bartholomew," he called. "Stop!"

Abby saw a flash of tattered garments as Bart vanished over the stone wall edging the parking lot. She sprinted behind Ryan, eyes intent on the humped tangle of clothing—a mound of laundry on the run.

"Wait!" she called out, waving over her head. "Please!"

The bundle of rags came to an abrupt halt. Abby stopped short, and Ryan almost toppled over the hunched form of a gaunt-looking figure she decided must be Bartholomew.

The mound shifted slightly. He turned to face Abby, grinning malevolently. "*Wait*, says she; *please*, says she," Bartholomew said, in a voice as deep as a rumble of thunder.

Abby stepped back, shivering at the palpable animosity he emanated.

Ryan stepped in front of her. "What were you doing in the parking lot, Bart?"

The face turned toward Ryan, eyes peering out from under the fleshy shelf of his brow bone. An uninterrupted swath of white eyebrow sprouted erratically above his eyes, shooting strands of ridiculously long hairs that entangled his lashes. "And what's a fine fellow like yourself interested in the likes of me for?"

"Someone slashed the tires on Miss Lancaster's vehicle. You wouldn't know anything about that, would you, Bart?"

A sneer that would have been more at home on the deck of a pirate ship revealed long, yellowed teeth. Abby grimaced as Bartholomew grinned wickedly at Ryan. "Oh, no, sir. Bartholomew Briggs don't know nothin' 'bout that." The grin widened.

Abby stepped forward. "I know you've been watching me, Mr. Briggs. Did you leave flowers at the cottage for me? Did you leave a note and a ring?"

A laugh resonated as if from the bottom of a barrel. "*Mr. Briggs*, says she!"

Ryan let out an exasperated sigh. "Did you see anything or anyone at the cottage, Bart?" he demanded.

"I see the moon, and the moon sees me," he sang, laughing heartily.

"Get hold of yourself, man!" Ryan shook him lightly, attempting to twist the bony frame toward him, to no avail. Bartholomew seemed to shift inside his clothing, and suddenly Ryan was left grasping an empty coat sleeve.

"Run, run, run, as fast as you can!" And Bartholomew slipped from Ryan's grasp as cleverly as a wet trout.

Ryan snatched after him, thrown off balance by the fact that he was holding a raggedy coat that smelled strongly of a well-used alley.

"Stop!" Abby called, but Bartholomew was gone; he had slithered over the wall and into the shifting bracken with all the litheness of the wind.

She looked down at her slashed tires, feeling her anger surge again.

"We'll take my car," Ryan said, his hand closing on her elbow and leading her away.

Chapter Eighteen

Sheriff Harris Flynn dragged his hand down the length of his face, rubbing his bristly chin with his thumb and forefinger. "Now, you're absolutely certain you didn't *inadvertently* pack the ring along with your belongings, and then transport it along with your luggage here to Destiny Bay?" He was a huge man, about fifty pounds overweight, with a face the unhealthy red of a man on the brink of a blood-pressure meltdown. "You're sure about that, right?"

Abby felt something menacing rippling off his skin and pooling around her. She was unaccountably nervous around this man, and she wished she'd been able to talk about the ring to Connor.

"Sheriff Flynn, I've told you, no one in my family has seen the ring in over thirty years. The insurance claim was settled long before I was born."

He narrowed his eyes at her, and Abby tried to conceal her shudder. Was this why Deputy Flynn had rushed her out of the station the minute he heard the sheriff was on his way? If so, he obviously knew something that she didn't—and she knew it wasn't good. It amazed her that the two men were brothers.

"Then how can you be sure this is your mama's ring if you've never seen it?"

"I've seen it hundreds of times," she said, trying not to be intimidated by his aggressive posture. Flynn, seeming to sense her resolve, leaned in farther. "I told you, it's the same ring worn by four generations of Rutherford women in their portraits. I was the only one who didn't wear the ring, Sheriff, because it was no longer in our possession."

Sheriff Flynn eyed her through the bloated slits that passed for eyelids.

She watched his hand, almost willing it to pick up the pen, to start writing something, anything, to show he was at least marginally interested in doing his job. "And you're sure about that?"

The seed of realization began to take root in her mind. Abby's heart thudded against her rib cage as the weedlike growth burst into flourishing being in the fertile soils of her understanding. Sheriff Flynn didn't believe her.

"Are you suggesting," she asked, almost too astounded to verbalize her thoughts, "that I brought the very evidence that would convict my family of insurance fraud to Destiny Bay, hung it on a nail along with a nasty note, and then raced down here to tell you all about it?"

Flynn lifted his brows. "Are *you* suggesting you did?"

An icy calm flooded through her. There was something more . . . something she should be putting together.

Her eyes flitted to the glass through which she could see Ryan, leaning on a desk. Connor Flynn was seated before him. The two men were chatting amicably together, completely unaware of the fact that as they spoke, this horrid sheriff was actually doing his best to build a case against *her*! Oh, she would throttle Ryan for *this* brilliant idea.

Then it came to her.

"Sheriff Flynn," she asked, "how long have you been in law enforcement?"

He frowned at her over the laminated table, then leaned forward challengingly. "Since long before you were thought of, if you're questioning my know-how."

"Oh, I wouldn't dream of it," she said, squaring her shoulders slightly. "Did you, by chance, know my mother?"

"I was here even before the great Celeste thought of placing foot on our island," he said sourly. "Yes, can you believe it? There was actually life here before your mama arrived."

Abby swallowed. She had all she needed. "Am I free to leave?" she asked, hoping she didn't sound as nervous as she felt.

He stared at her for what seemed like a small eternity. "You're free to leave."

Abby rose, grasped her purse, and with as much dignity as she could muster, walked out of the room.

From the reflection in the glass, she could see that Harris Flynn was watching her departure.

"How did it go?" Ryan asked, jumping to his feet.

"You wouldn't believe me if I told you. Deputy?" she asked, turning her attention at once to Connor Flynn.

He rose from his seat, nodding. "Yes?"

"I forgot to ask your brother something—I wonder if you can answer a question for me? I hate to bother the sheriff with something so small."

"Sure, I'll help you if I can."

"Years ago—when my mother lived here—she reported a theft. Do you recall what the item or items in question were?"

"Yes, ma'am. It was a ruby ring. Had some nice gold work around it. Family heirloom, if I remember right."

Abby whirled and faced the sheriff, who now stood in

the threshold of the door, glaring out at her. "You knew!" she said, barely above a whisper.

Sheriff Flynn sauntered arrogantly into the room. "You got something else you need to say?"

"You knew!" she said louder. "You were here before my mother set foot on this island, you said so yourself!"

Ryan caught her elbow and squeezed gently. "Abrielle, maybe we should talk outside—"

"Is this entire island in cahoots against my family?" she shouted at him. "What kind of backward place is this?"

Ryan abruptly dropped his grasp.

"No, let her go on, Ryan. I'd like to hear what the lady has to say." Sheriff Flynn hooked his thumbs into his belt loops and rocked back on his heels. "As you were saying?"

"You knew my mother's ring had been stolen, and you discounted it. You didn't even listen to her, did you?"

Sheriff Flynn grinned smugly. "You want to hear my version of events? Well, here it is: maybe you grew up hearing all about the backwoods police officers who discovered your mama's claims couldn't hold water. Maybe you got a little bitter, dug up the ring she found when she got back to millionaires' row, and brought it to Destiny Bay to vindicate your dear departed mama, like any good daughter would."

"Wait a minute, you said '*claims*.' What other claims did my mother make?"

"Why don't *you* tell *me*?"

It was too much. Abby felt tears spring to her eyes. Just as quickly, she blinked them away. "You said my mother made claims. What were the other claims?"

He leaned back on a desk, folding his arms over his barrel of a chest. "Can't say as I recall. That was a long time ago, after all. Some things are best left in the past, where they belong."

Abby snatched the note, holding it in front of him.

"Well, maybe you'll be more interested in listening to my claims. What about the bouquet that was left for me? What about Bart peeking in my windows? What about this note? The ink looks peculiar, don't you think? Like it could be blood? I want it sent to a lab."

Flynn glared at his her. "You want lab tests, you're paying for them. And you can submit your own blood, first."

"Fine," she said, "point me to the nearest syringe. My mother was right about the ring, and now some psycho wants to play head games with *me*!"

Flynn's hand came down on the desk, hard. "Your mother was a troublemaker!"

"Let's go, Abby." Ryan's grasp on her elbow was firm and insistent.

Abby shot him a look fit to wither a rose. She stormed out of the office and burst through the door into the brisk ocean breeze.

"Abrielle!"

Abby kept walking, hugging her arms closely around herself to ward off the sudden chill her plummeting adrenaline had left in its wake.

"Abrielle, will you stop?"

Ryan loped up behind her, took hold of her shoulders. "What happened?" he asked, searching her face.

She struggled to break free, to no avail.

"Abrielle," he said quietly, in a tone that made it clear he was serious. Abby stopped fighting him.

"He didn't believe her!" she said, feeling the stinging threat of tears. "My mother was a victim on this island, and not even the police would help her!

"They called her names, they closed ranks against her, they turned their backs when she needed help, and now there are people who seem determined to do the same thing to me! What is the matter with you people?"

This time, she did break free. She ran the length of Brigantine Way, turned onto Peddler's Lane and stopped at last by a telephone pole, leaning her back against it as she chased her racing breath.

A car motor sounded behind her. Abby squeezed her eyes shut, realizing that the car was stopping beside her.

"Hey, Abby girl, what are you doing out here?"

Abby heaved a sigh of relief and looked into the lowered window of Ronnie Morgan's Volkswagen. "You're a sight for sore eyes, Ronnie. As a matter of fact, I'm looking for a ride back home."

Chapter Nineteen

Ryan counted the seconds off in his head. He'd knocked at least ten seconds ago, and though he knew Abby was inside the cottage, she hadn't yet come to the door.

He braced his hands upon the door frame, struck with the realization that he would wait as long as he had to, even if it was all night. *What is happening to me?*

Guilt. That's what it was.

He'd hurt Abby badly when he told her the truth about her mother. He'd been harsh about it. Too harsh. Then, he'd dragged her down to the police station to report these strange happenings . . . a decision that had led to yet another festering revelation about Celeste.

If he'd understood Abby correctly, Celeste had gone to the police for help and they had refused her. Now, he was no fan of Celeste Rutherford, but ignoring the victimization of a young woman? That was plain wrong.

He shifted uncomfortably.

Hadn't he done the same thing to Abby? Hadn't he, in fact, actively participated in her victimization? Granted, it wasn't to the extent of Celeste's experience, but he had been outrageously rude to her, he had engaged her in a shouting match at Rum Runner's and, when she first arrived, he had gone out of his way to let her know that he had his eye on her . . . what kind of a brute behaved that way?

It made his stomach sour to think about it—how he'd let his bitterness and hatred consume him, devour his reason and cloud his judgment. He had been a class-A jerk.

The door of the cottage opened. Abby glared at him. She'd been crying, and the soft curls around her face were damp, as if she'd splashed water on her face in an attempt to compose herself.

"I've been looking all over for you."

"I can't imagine why," she said curtly, turning her back on him and walking into the small kitchen.

Ryan slipped through the door, his shoes thudding too loudly on the plank floors of the cottage. "I, uh, just wanted to let you know that Larry's Towing took your car down to the garage. They'll replace the tires first thing. I asked him to look it over for other signs of damage or tampering, just in case. Since it happened in my parking lot, I'll pay for the damage."

Abby turned toward him, arms crossed heavily over her chest. "Why?"

"What do you mean, 'why'?"

"Why?" she demanded. "Why do you care if I go to the police? Why do you care if my tires *ever* get replaced? Why do you care if I run off and never surface again? You hate Rutherford women, remember?"

Ryan felt riveted to the spot. He attempted a smile. "Last I heard, you were a Lancaster."

"Only by half."

The truth hit him squarely in the chest. He *didn't* hate her; he hadn't, in fact, hated her since he'd overheard her speaking with Cora and heard his own voice. "I don't hate you."

"You're lying."

"First I'm a thief, now I'm a liar, is it? Hate to disappoint you, but you're wrong on both counts."

"Am I?"

Damn, she is beautiful. Ryan squeezed his hands into fists, feeling the crescent-shaped sharpness of his nails digging into his palms. Things were so much simpler when he hated her. *Beautiful doesn't matter when you can't see past the fury in your own eyes.* "Yeah," he said quietly. "You're wrong."

"So why don't you tell me what's changed." Abby crossed her arms over her chest, chin lifted in challenge.

Tell her that he'd eavesdropped? That he felt for her loss in a way only another abandoned child could do? That he couldn't keep her from wandering into his dreams or that this compulsion to be near her—even though it made him crazy—was like a sickness that had crept into the heart of him and twisted with every breath?

"I can't."

"You *won't.*" She dropped her arms and walked away from him, turned on the faucet and splashed a scoop of water over her face.

He stepped toward her, suddenly very aware of the way her tousled hair touched her cheeks, of the flush of color that stained them. "I get that you're pissed, okay? You have every right to be. But here's the truth of it: I don't hate you. I tried to. I even succeeded for a while. But the simple fact of the matter is that none of this is about you." He looked up at the ceiling, hardly believing the words that were coming out of his mouth. "I know I made your life difficult. I'm sorry."

The tiny breath that escaped from her lips could almost be called a gasp. He stepped forward again. "I shouldn't have said the things I said about your mother. I had no right to speak ill of her. It won't happen again."

She tilted her head at him, considering him for a moment.

"It's the truth. Do what you like with it."

He watched the extraordinary array of emotions that crossed her features; felt the stupefying realization that every word he was saying was 100 percent true, and felt, for the first time since he'd learned she was coming, comfortable with the idea of her presence; comfortable in his own skin.

Abrielle Lancaster was the first woman who had ever had the power to make him feel otherwise.

"Can you—can *we* get past it? What I said, I mean? It's not like I expect to be pals. I just want to put out there that it was a mistake to say what I did. It'll never cross my lips again. I swear it." *Damn, she's beautiful*, he thought again. Ryan swallowed thickly, stunned by the fact that he actually cared what she thought; that he wanted her to believe him.

She swiped at a tear that teetered on her lashes. "I'm sorry," she said of the tear, "I'm a mess. I've been on a roller coaster since I got here." She cleared her throat and looked up at him. "I can get past it, Ryan. I can. And I accept your apology. Can you accept mine?"

"You want to apologize to *me*? What for?"

"I slapped you," she said, eyes wide. "I . . . I was insufferably rude. You told me about something terrible my mother did to you, and I didn't care. I want you to know that that's not like me. I was shocked. I know that's no excuse, but there it is."

Ryan nodded slowly, rocked back on his heels. "Okay. I accept your apology."

"For what it's worth," she added quickly, "I'm sure my mother didn't know Cora was pregnant when she fell in love with Douglas. At least I *hope* she didn't."

Ryan shrugged, jamming his hands into his pockets.

Abby cocked her head at him, a curious expression on her face. "You look strange."

His breath escaped in a barely suppressed explosion. "You don't know the half of it." He wanted to be done with this business, and the sooner the better. "So, you're okay?"

"I'm fine." Her arms tightened around herself. "It was good of you to check in on me."

They stood, shifting, for a solid minute longer. "Is there anything else I can do for you?"

"You mean besides verbally attack me at your bar, defame my family and drag me to the town sheriff for questioning? No. I'm good."

He actually felt himself jolt.

Abby started laughing—a sound as long and loud and free as an anthem. Not until tears were beginning to roll down her cheeks did she look up, and by that time Ryan was laughing, too. Nervously, at first. Then—when feeling the sweet truth of it, the utter relief of it—he let it spiral down to the core of him and double back 'til he rocked with it, shook with it, let it join hers and fill the room with something he knew he'd remember always.

"I'm coming unhinged," she said softly. "First I'm crying, then I'm laughing. If you knew what a ride this has been, you'd get it."

"I'll take your word for it."

Abby walked to the refrigerator, still giggling, pulled out two coolers, and handed one to Ryan.

He lifted the bottle and read. "Wild-berry Fizzer? You're kidding, right?"

"Do you want to get drunk with me or not?"

He felt himself jolt. *Again.*

He shrugged, twisted the cap and downed a healthy portion of the fruity-tasting drink. "You know, this isn't all bad. You tell a soul I said that, and I'll deny it."

"Please. Like I'd admit to drinking with the likes of you," she said, winking over her shoulder.

As nimbly as a cat, she slid over the back of the sofa and nuzzled into a mound of cushions. "It's been a bloody awful day, Brannigan, I gotta tell you."

He swallowed a mouthful of his drink, nodding. "I'm with you on that," he said solemnly, wishing the laughter was back.

"Ryan," she said, picking at the label on her bottle, "I don't want you to be awkward around me—I mean, just for tonight, let's pretend we're old pals. I need to let the stuff between us be bygones." She sipped thoughtfully, staring through the window at the surging ocean. "My mom's past is just one shock after the next. There's a sociopath intent on scaring the daylights out of me, the sheriff would like to see me in the pillory . . . what I *don't* need is a nervous drinking buddy."

"So, we're drinking buddies now, are we?"

"All I'm saying is that here, now . . . what I don't need is another enemy."

"Sure that's not just your Wild-berry Fizzer talking?" he asked, feeling a rush of something that made him hopeful and disbelieving all at once; a feeling that *this could change everything,* and suddenly hoping it did.

"Yeah. I'm sure."

"Okay, I'll be your drinking buddy, Abby, only next time, *I* bring the booze."

Abby chuckled. "You got something against my Wild-berry Fizzer?"

"So much, I couldn't even begin to tell you." He looked pointedly at her. "Listen, there's another reason I came out here. I think you should move out of the cottage."

"Are you serious?"

"Completely. This place is miles from anywhere, and I don't need to point out that there's a lunatic on the island with his sights set on you. I have a vacant apartment in town, and I know for sure Mom has a couple, as well. Maybe one of them would be to your liking."

Abby's expression hardened. "If you think I'm going to go running scared because of a few tasteless pranks—"

"And what if they aren't pranks? What if whoever sent these things is very, very serious?"

"I have locks, I have a phone and a black belt in jujitsu. I can take care of myself."

Ryan blinked. "You have a black belt in jujitsu?"

"Well, not exactly," she said, blushing. "But if you could spread the word around town that I *do*, I'd be most obliged."

"I'm serious about this, Abby."

"So am I," she said, eyeing him levelly and looking as if she meant every word. "Ryan, my mother lived here. She loved it here, and I feel connected to her when I'*m* here."

"Well, I guess you'd better get used to the fact that I'll be checking on you every time I'm out this way." He didn't mention that he had a sudden urge to be out this way far, far more often.

"That's fine," she said with a shrug.

"And if one more thing happens, Abby—and I mean *one more thing*, you've got to move out."

"I agree."

Abby laughed at the surprised expression he'd been unable to hide. "Good grief, am I so contrary that a nod of agreement leaves you speechless?"

Ryan lifted a brow. "In a word: yes."

The ocean hissed along the rocks that lined the shore, saving them both from the discomfort of total silence. "Tell me something, Ryan," she said, looking over at him with a softness of expression that made his insides twist uncomfortably. "Why do they call this place 'Abandon Bluff'?" she asked. "Who was abandoned?"

Ryan stood and walked over to the window to better appreciate the view of the surging Atlantic. "Come here," he said, beckoning with his hand.

She stepped forward tentatively. "Just right here," he said, placing his hands on her shoulders and positioning her directly in front of him. He felt the stiffening of her shoulders beneath his touch, then the slow, almost deliberate relaxing that followed.

Just as he had intended, her gaze was now riveted upon the undulating sea.

Beneath the auburn sky, the water seethed with pent-up anger. Foamy crests whispered of a another storm, and colors of charcoal flashed beneath deceptively benign shades of silvery blue.

Ryan felt the mammoth surge of power as if it flowed toward him; he felt the warmth of her flesh as if his hands rested directly upon her.

"Not *who*," he said quietly, his breath lifting the delicate strands of hair that rested against the side of her face. "*What*."

Beneath his touch, her skin seemed to warm; her shoulders lifted gently with the breath that filled her ever more quickly. *Is she feeling this, too?*

"Caution," he said, his voice barely above a whisper. "Logic. Good sense. That's what's abandoned."

Ryan felt his breath quicken. His loins seemed attuned to the threatening passion of the sea, as if uniting and rising with the primordial strength that seethed beneath the undulating mass of water.

The back of her neck was so close, so fair and inviting. He could touch her right *there*, could see for himself if she was as soft as she appeared.

He closed his eyes on the thought, shaken, even as his fingertips thrummed with need.

"What else?" she whispered. "Tell me what else was abandoned here."

"Everything that makes us what we're not." He felt the shudder, then the almost imperceptible trembling that rippled over her flesh—found its echo in his.

The setting sun fell through the window in beams of gold, touched her hair with tawny light and gilded her features with silver.

The loose shirt she wore was diaphanous on her body, the light that shone through it stroking her flesh with a nimbus that made her look golden.

"Don't move," he said quietly, his voice gruff but gentle as he walked over to the table.

Abby turned her head slightly, but the rest of her remained still. She looked at him, a curious expression on her face.

He lifted a pad of paper and pencil, ripped off the first few pages and stared at her; he drank in the sight of her that was like water to a parched throat.

He touched the pencil to the page, began the sinuous, fluid line that was her spine, the graceful swell of her buttock, the long, lithe stroke of her thigh. He started on the front, his heart slamming as if he touched her very flesh, as he drew the curve of her neck, the roundness of her shoulder, and the lush fullness of her breast beneath the fabric.

He lifted his pencil, inhaled a pacing breath, and returned to her face, where striking violet eyes gazed back at him, direct and yet shy, intangible, and yet utterly alluring.

In that instant, he understood every instinct of the man who had fathered him, for he felt the same urges now; he felt them coursing through his body and igniting a firestorm in their wake.

As if she felt it, too, she met his eyes. He saw that her cheeks were beautifully flushed, that her eyes glistened as she stared at him.

The arm that held the paper fell to his side, forgotten. The pencil he dropped rolled across the floor, making a soft rumbling that seemed to echo through his chest.

He stepped toward her, grasped her shoulders, her exhaled gasp thrilling through his body like lightning.

"Ryan," she whispered, her eyes deep pools that seemed to drink him in.

Before he could rethink it, he pressed his mouth to hers.

He wasn't prepared for the jolt that struck him to the heart, that reached into the truth of who he was and changed it into something unfathomably deeper. She was perfect softness, perfect womanliness . . . perfect.

He felt Abby's hands gently kneading the fabric of his shirt, felt the touch become suddenly more intense as she tilted her head, opened her mouth and drew him into her.

He was drunk, and it had nothing to do with the Wildberry Fizzer.

His BlackBerry chimed shrilly, ripping through the moment as effectively as a reaper's scythe.

His initial instinct was to hurl the bloody thing against the nearest wall. Instead, he pressed the ignore button, suddenly stunned by what he—what *they*—had done. He wanted to speak, but words were like a logjam in his throat.

Abby looked up at him, smiling shyly. "You could have answered that. I don't mind."

"Naw. It was probably nothing."

She tilted her head at him. "You were drawing me, just a minute ago, I mean. Before you kissed me."

"I was," he said quietly. "I've wanted to draw you for a long time."

"Then let me pose for you," she said, the pink in her cheeks deepening.

"I'd like that." And to his surprise, he meant it. In fact, the thought of her—lying still for him as he traced her body with his hand—thrilled him as little else ever had.

"So would I." Her smile widened. "I had no idea you were an artist." Then she flushed; her smile faded. Ryan looked into her face and knew she feared she'd offended him.

With anyone else, he *would* have felt stinging resentment, but with her, he only wanted to tell her his secret truth: that he *was* an artist, and as much as he sometimes wanted to, there was no way he could deny it. "Yeah, I guess you could say I'm an artist," he admitted quietly. "The only person I could have inherited it from is my father, because Mom can't draw a straight line with a ruler."

Relief flooded her face, was light in the sound of her laughter. She picked up the paper and looked at the image. "This is beautiful. I'd love to see your work, Ryan."

He nodded toward the pencil drawing. "There you have it. The complete works of Ryan Brannigan."

"You're not serious?"

"I have a bad habit of tossing everything I draw." He couldn't believe he was admitting this. Couldn't believe that she had drawn it out of him without an ounce of effort.

"Well, that's just going to have to change," she said, sinking into the billowy pillows of the couch. "Draw me, Ryan. Let mine be the first of your pictures that you actually keep."

He thought of the picture underneath his desk blotter. Hers already was the first picture he had ever kept. "Okay," he said, a burgeoning excitement filling the full measure of him. "We'll do that. Soon."

"Ryan? Did you know it was a painting that brought me here to Destiny Bay?"

"No."

She patted the couch as she looked up at him, smiled sweetly as he accepted the invitation and sat beside her. "I found a portrait of my mother in the house where I grew up. It was painted by your father. She was lying on the banks of stone just outside the cottage. There were petals sprinkled over her body. It was a beautiful painting, Ryan. I looked at it and I knew she loved the man who painted it. Would you like to see it?"

Ryan felt his blood stop in his veins. Would he? *Should* he? "Yes," he said, before he knew that he'd spoken.

Abby took his hand and led him up the stairs to her bedroom. Hanging on the wall facing her bed was a portrait of a woman who could only be her mother, and it was extraordinary.

"She's beautiful," he said.

Abby swallowed loudly, blinked as if to rid her eyes of tears. "She's happy. Say what you will about your father, but his gift was God-given, and if you've inherited it, you *must* celebrate it. Anything less would be tragic."

For the first time in his life, Ryan felt pride in his talent. *How did that happen?* It was no longer a shameful thing, inherited from a man he despised, but a glorious, wondrous thing, filled with promise. And perhaps even healing.

A crazy, impulsive thought rushed to the center of his mind. He wanted to paint her as his father had painted her mother—there on the rocks, her naked body sprinkled with petals.

What was in that Wild-berry Fizzer? He chuckled aloud at himself, shook his head.

"What's so funny?"

He took her hand, looked into her upturned face. "Nothing. Come on, there's a place I want to show you." Gently, he tugged her from the couch. "Get your coat."

Chapter Twenty

"Are you going to tell me where we're going or not?" Abby asked as Ryan parked his truck on the corner of Victoria Lane and Brigantine Way.

"We're going to see Captain Josiah Watson's house."

"Who's he?"

He rounded the truck and opened her door. Abby's insides simmered warmly. *Could it be possible that he is a gentleman?* They got even warmer as he grasped her hand and helped her down from the truck. She was suddenly glad for the dusky light—it provided some disguise for her blushing cheeks.

"Josiah Watson was one of our more famous past residents," he said knowledgeably.

Abby nodded, tried to look as intelligent as possible—which likely wasn't very, because . . . *he was still holding her hand!* What on earth was going on here? Was it a slip of his mind? Did he not realize she had already completed a successful dismount from his monstrous Navigator?

Her head was swimming. And come to think of it, her lips still felt warm from that kiss. Something was very wrong. *Or very, very right.*

Focus, Abby, she commanded herself, forcing her brain to listen and absorb what he was saying.

". . . shipbuilding was where he made his fortune, though. He built this house and lived here with his wife, Elizabeth Watson—reputedly the most beautiful woman on the eastern seaboard."

"That's a great story," she said, hoping she was right—she'd hardly heard a word of it. "I can't wait to see the house. Is it a museum?"

"No."

"Do you know the present owner?"

Ryan seemed suddenly uncomfortable. "You could say that. *I'm* the present owner."

"Really?" Now she was intrigued. "What have you done to it? Oh, please don't tell me you've converted it into rental units—I hate when people lop up grand old houses."

Ryan stopped, looked down at her. "I haven't done anything with it. After I bought it, I found out that my father and your mother had once put down a deposit on the house. They'd wanted to live in it. Together. From what I could learn, your mother left the island shortly before the sale was final, and my father lost his deposit. I guess he didn't care much about the house if he couldn't share it with Celeste.

"After that, I couldn't get my heart into doing anything with the property. It reminded me of things I'd rather forget. It's just gathered dust for the last six years."

Abby was stunned. She looked at the house in a new light. "Ryan, do you believe that things happen for a reason?"

"I never did . . . but I'm starting to change that assumption," he said, giving her a wry smile.

"Maybe you bought that house for a reason that you don't yet understand. Maybe it was always meant to be in your hands."

He shrugged. "Could be."

He squeezed her hand—the one he was *still* holding—and smiled. A complicated smile that was sad and accepting, yet peaceful and resolved.

Together, they turned onto Victoria Lane, the hub of Destiny Bay's shopping and tourist district. It was lined with pricey boutiques, galleries, restaurants and teahouses, not to mention a gracious tourist information center and town hall.

Despite its central location, only on the rarest of occasions did vehicular traffic attempt to navigate Victoria Lane. Most local folk had come to accept the fact that driving down Victoria Lane was an exercise in frustration. It took visitors only one attempt to arrive at the same conclusion. Tourists and pedestrians walked freely down the cobblestone lane, and cars could travel only a matter of feet before being forced to give way to those who shopped leisurely or admired the local architecture.

Ryan pulled out his cell phone, started dialing. "You like lobster?"

She lifted a brow. "Is that a serious question?"

"Hey, Johnny," he said into his phone. He looked at Abby and winked. "Is Gary still in the kitchen? Yeah? Great. Can you get Cook to fix up a couple lobsters and a couple containers of coleslaw, then have Jim drop it off at the Captain's House? Tell him there's a big fat tip in it for him."

Abby grinned. "What's for dessert?" she whispered.

He covered the mouthpiece of the phone. "How do beer nuts and pretzels sound?"

"Perfect!" she said, laughing.

"Johnny, throw in some nuts and pretzels, will you? Oh, yeah, I'm also going to need candles, matches and a bottle of white wine—and don't forget plates, glasses, napkins and utensils. You got that? . . . No, I don't ask for much. Thanks, man."

He rang off, tucked the phone in his pocket and took her hand again. "Hope you're hungry."

Abby's stomach started to growl. "Starving."

They walked on. Several patrons were seated beneath the huge green-and-white striped umbrellas of a sidewalk café. They nodded and waved at her and Ryan, their eyes widening, as they took in the sight of two former archenemies, holding hands.

Across the street, the stained glass windows of the Starboard Bed and Breakfast glinted in the twilight, and flowers in the window boxes shuddered in the breeze. Their fragrance floated in the air, mingled with the aromas of garlic bread, iced coffees and ocean.

They passed the shingled homes that made the town so quaint, each with a riot of rose blooms tumbling over fences toward the cobblestones of the sidewalk. Petals floated on the breeze like butterflies, touched the skin with the fleeting grace of quiet inspiration.

"I love it here, Ryan," she said impulsively. "I've never seen a more beautiful place in all my life."

Ryan's expression was unreadable. It softened suddenly as he grasped her shoulders and turned her gently. "There it is. The house they wanted to live in."

Abby looked up at the most gorgeous house she had ever seen.

It was at least four stories high, and was complete with turrets, a verandah that wrapped around the entire front, stained glass windows, a widow's walk, and commanding double front doors.

Even as she looked more closely and noticed that the house was in need of extensive repair, she was struck with love for it; for its grace and craftsmanship, for the history that was bundled between its walls, for the care that must have been lavished upon every inch of it.

Then it struck her. This was it. This was her house of healing, of growing, of peace. Her eyes filled with tears; her breath came up short. A feeling of such intensity—of such absolute certainty—just had to be right.

She was meant to have this house; she knew it as surely as she knew the sun would rise in the morning. And she knew exactly what she was meant to do with it.

She turned to him, grasped his hands in hers. "Take me inside," she said.

Ryan guided her up the front stairs, which were littered with long-dead leaves and twigs. He fiddled with the lock. At last fitted the key, and he turned the handle.

The doors opened to reveal a grand foyer, a winding staircase, two huge arched openings that led into large, gracious rooms on either side of the foyer.

The feeling grew in depth, filling her heart with unmistakable certainty. This was her destiny; there was no other word for it.

"It's beautiful, Ryan."

"You like it?" he asked, chuckling. "It's for sale."

"I'll take it."

Ryan's expression was so comical, she would have laughed . . . but her heart was in her throat and her pulse was racing far too quickly. "I mean it, Ryan. I want this house."

"What on earth for?"

"For my mother," she blurted. "For me. For every person who needs to escape to a place that's so magical they can't imagine it exists." She grabbed his hands, knew she was talking too quickly and probably making no sense whatsoever, yet she continued. "I can't explain it, but since I've come here, I've been overcome with the feeling that I want to be part of this place—that I want to share it with others." She caught the breath she'd been chasing, felt the air go very still around them. "I want people to know that their hearts can wake up again."

"When does that happen?" he asked quietly. "When do hearts wake up?"

Abby looked up at him, saw the pain etched in his face, and her heart caught. They were not so different, he and she. She took his hand, held it in the warmth of her own. Her eyes felt suddenly warm with tears. She looked down at the hand she held, turned it over in hers and traced the lines she saw in his palms, wondering if this one meant he'd been abandoned by his father, if that one meant he'd never quite unburdened himself of the pain. "I guess it's different for everyone," she said softly, her thumb rubbing a callus on his hand that spoke to her of work so intense and so focused that perhaps its main purpose had been to help him forget his wounded heart, and material that was nothing more than a providential by-product. Now, she did look up at him. The pain was still there, deep in the shadows of his eyes, but there was also something more; something that made her body thrill just to be near him. "My heart started waking up when I arrived in Destiny Bay."

"Funny," he said, his lips suddenly very, very close. "So did mine." His eyes seemed somehow deeper in color, his mouth somehow wider and softer.

He was going to kiss her again. He was going to put his mouth on hers, and . . .

A thunderous thumping sounded from the door.

"Dinner's here," he said gruffly, sounding deeply resentful, and went to open the door.

Abby leaned back against the wall, feeling delightfully stuffed. Around them were the littered shells of unfortunate lobsters, empty coleslaw containers, and a half-consumed bottle of wine. She closed her eyes contentedly. "That was delicious."

"Next time, we'll order the strip steak. It's one of the few items our chef does better than The Surfside chef." Ryan handed her a drink.

Next time? Abby looked up at him. Something had definitely changed during the course of the evening, and changed for the better. "That sounds nice." She sipped from her glass, never taking her eyes from him. "I'm glad you brought me here, Ryan. And please excuse my outburst earlier this evening—but I do mean to buy this house from you. *And* I'm going to get a great deal. It's only fair to let you know."

"Thanks for the heads-up," he said dryly.

She looked around the bare walls. "This is a good house. I can feel it. There's a lot of healing that's going to happen inside these walls."

His expression was guarded as he looked into his glass, swirled the amber contents slowly in its bowl. "That would be nice," he said at last. "And the captain would approve. His wife—whom he loved very much—died in childbirth. Her son never knew her. It feels right that this place should be about reclaiming life."

"It does, doesn't it?"

She settled back against the wall, reached across the distance between them and grasped his hand, ignoring the jolt she felt in his fingers. She softened her grasp, stroked the flesh of his hand with her thumb.

"Do you hear that?" she asked, listening to the surge of the bay outside the house, her heart thudding in response to the sound of the gurgling surf and the simple magnificence of a rush of tide. She closed her eyes, almost hearing it carving gullies around stones embedded in the sand. "Have you ever heard anything more magnificent?"

Ryan's smile was suddenly indulgent. "Nothing."

"When I was a kid, Gran and I would spend the entire summer on the cape. Dad would come up on the weekends.

"I would fall asleep to the sound of the ocean every night. My grandmother would sing Kipling's "Seal Lullaby" to me. She changed a word or two—you know, so that it sounded as if it were written for a child instead of a seal." She looked up at him through her lashes, suddenly shy that she'd revealed such a tender memory.

His hand softened in hers. She felt as if he were finally holding hers, instead of the other way around. "Sing it to me."

"Oh, I don't sing," she said, shaking her head adamantly.

"C'mon, you must sing. Everybody sings."

"Trust me. I don't sing."

"I want to hear it anyway."

She held out her glass, brow lifted. "Fill 'er up. Then I'll give it a go."

Ryan kindly obliged her, and Abby sipped a bit of courage into her veins, cleared her throat, and started singing.

"Oh! hush thee, my baby, the night is behind us,
And black are the waters that sparkled so green.
The moon o'er the combers looks downward to find us
Asleep in the hollows that rustle between.
Where billow meets billow, there soft be thy pillow;
Ah, weary wee baby, curl at thy ease!
No storm shall awake thee, nor shark overtake thee,
Asleep in the arms of the slow-swinging seas."

Abby looked up, and found him staring at her with a look of utter mystification on his face.

"Good grief," he said at last.

Abby burst out laughing. "I'm awful, aren't I?"

Ryan started laughing, too. "Well, not *awful* . . . just . . . okay, you were awful. Jeez, how does a woman who looks as beautiful as you make such terrible sounds? It's—it's unseemly."

Now she was laughing in earnest. "I warned you."

"You did, at that," he said, sounding very philosophical. "But other than the singing, the lullaby was nice. Really nice."

"Why thank you," she said, not in the least embarrassed. "I hear you, on the other hand, are known to be quite musical. Ronnie described you as the finest guitar player this side of I-don't-know-where."

Ryan shrugged. "I don't know about that, but I did take up guitar as a kid. It was the only way I could think of to channel the artistic compulsion I was feeling. Brawling only worked for so long, and it was bloody inconvenient. When it's three A.M. and you can't sleep because all you want to do is create something, you can't always run out and pick a fight . . . but you *can* pick up a guitar."

"I'd love to hear you play sometime. What's your specialty? Country, rock, heavy metal?"

"Flamenco."

Abby almost swallowed her tongue. "Flamenco?" Just when she thought this island was all out of surprises, another hit her. "What on earth made you take up flamenco?"

Ryan topped up both glasses, grinning. "You know all about our history—how the island was settled by shipwrecked seafarers, right? Well, we had a few Spanish wash up along with French, English and Scottish. If you ever go down the south side of the island, you'll see it in the coloring. Very dark folk. Anyway, there was a man up the shore who claims he's one hundred percent Spanish. Not very likely, in my opinion, but he plays guitar like he was born with it in his hands, and he was generous enough to give me lessons. Cost my mom a small fortune, but she probably thought it was well worth it. It was one of the few things I showed an interest in and it kept me out of trouble on Monday and Wednesday afternoons."

"I'm amazed. Now I *have* to hear you play."

"I'm sure we could work something out." He frowned as his phone rang, glanced hurriedly at the screen and silenced it with the press of a button. "That's Johnny. He can wait. So—" Ryan swirled the contents of his glass. "Tell me more about yourself, Abby. I know you're a great interviewer—"

"You watched my show!" she said, grinning hugely. "I can't believe it!"

Ryan cleared his throat pointedly. "Can I help what the receptionist has on the TV when I'm waiting for my truck to be serviced?"

"Oh, no. You can't help that," she said sweetly. "Now, let me see . . ." She leaned into the hollow of his shoulder, completely ignoring the instant tensing of the muscles there. "I have a knack for gardening and horses. I can skate incredibly well. I have a vivid imagination. Oh, and, I can shoot skeet better than anyone I know . . . how's that?"

"Not bad. Anything else?"

She thought for a moment. "You should see my sand castles."

"A closet architect?"

She smiled, remembering how her sand castles shone with the offerings of the tides: beach glass, shells, surf-polished stones. Remembering how she'd plucked them from sun-warmed, silver pools, and then gathered them at dusk to line her windowsill and catch the moon. Remembering how at night she'd lie beneath them, lulled into sleep by eternal whisperings of the cold, Atlantic surf.

"Penny for your thoughts."

She looked up at him, considering thoughtfully. "No."

"No?"

"There're worth more than that. How about an even exchange. Thoughts for thoughts."

Ryan lifted a brow, considering. "This is getting expensive."

"Take it or leave it," she said, reclining slightly as she felt the deal hang in the balance.

"Take it."

A satisfied smile spread over her face, then quickly melted. "When we went to the cape," she said quietly, "I'd lie in bed and sing the lullaby to myself. I'd close my eyes and imagine it was my mother singing." She let her eyes close and saw, behind the blackness of her eyelids, her little room take shape in her mind.

"When the song was over, I'd lie very still, listening to the sound of the changing tides. I'd listen so close, and lie so still that I could almost hear my mother's voice, calling to me from the sea, and every rushing wavelet that hissed on the shore was her voice saying, 'hush, hush.'

"Some nights, when the tide was high and the surf reflected in ripples of light on my bedroom ceiling, I'd pretend the shimmering rays were her fingers—stretching across the veil of death. I'd imagine that she was trying to stroke my hair until I fell asleep." Her voice trailed away like a receding tide.

"I still can't understand why she left us," she said, the walls around her heart collapsing before the onslaught of relentless grief that had pressed there for so long. Her hands began to tremble, and soon her arms were drawn into a shuddering cadence of pent-up emotion. "I was a baby! I needed her, and she left me!" Her voice was rising, her breath coming in shorter and shorter gasps. The Captain's House was a million miles away; Ryan's touch felt as though it were from another lifetime.

Ryan grasped her to his chest, rocking her gently. "I'm sorry," he said.

She took in a long, ragged breath, slowly regaining composure, slowly returning to the dusty Victorian house and the warmth of Ryan's arms around her, rocking gently. "Once, when I was about ten, I woke up to the sound of my grandmother screaming. She was having a nightmare—screaming and screaming. She wouldn't stop. I was so scared. I ran into her room, and Granddad was trying to calm her, but she was fighting him and making this awful, awful noise."

She pressed her hands over her ears, the remembered sound spiraling down to the core of her, drawing her inward and threatening to drown her in the sea of terrifying memories that tossed within her soul. "She sounded like a wounded animal," she said, sobbing. The keening wail that echoed in her heart prowled around with claws outstretched, mercilessly tearing away the years of careful distance she had placed between herself and that frightening night.

"She was calling for my mother, saying, *"Please, Celeste, please don't jump! Don't leave us, baby, don't leave us!'"* she said, tears streaming down her face. "That sound, that wounded animal sound . . . I'll never forget it."

Ryan drew her in tighter against his chest, his heartbeat sounding as unsteady as hers felt. "Go on," he said, his voice husky. "I want to hear everything."

Abby's face was slick with tears she didn't even remember shedding. She looked up at Ryan. "That was the night I realized that even someone loving you can't stop nightmares, and that someone loving you can't keep a woman from jumping out of a window. Love's not enough to keep a mother by her child's side." She wiped a tear from her cheek, looked down at the floor that swam before her gaze. "From that day forward, I was afraid of it. Love, I mean. So I never let it in."

Abby was suddenly very aware of the silence. Ryan was staring at her with an expression she found utterly unreadable.

He touched her face, drew his finger down its length. He pressed his lips to her cheek, and Abby felt him kiss away her tears; she felt him inhale her secrets and tuck them somewhere warm and safe.

His tenderness was suddenly more than she could bear, and she clung to him like a drowning person to a life raft. "Don't let me go," she whispered, and he held her tighter, stroked her back and twined his fingers in her hair.

"I won't," he said, his tone fierce and yet gentle all at once.

They sat there for a time, lulled by the eternal hiss of the sea upon the sand. Abby drank in the sound, let it fool her into believing that they were the last two people upon the earth, and that the sea wanted nothing more than to cloister and soothe them.

She closed her eyes, breathed him in, rested her hand upon the hardness of his chest.

Through the glass of the window, she could hear the sound of the sea change. The tide had turned; it was coming closer to land as if to tuck it in for the night.

Abby pulled away enough to look into Ryan's face. His eyes were warm, wounded, and looking at her as if seeing her for the first time. "You didn't forget, did you?" she asked quietly. "Thoughts for thoughts, remember?"

A shadow seemed to cross his eyes. "Yeah, I remember."

Ryan leaned back against the wall, tucking Abby neatly beneath his arm and drawing her near. "Hearing you say what you just said . . . it was tough. I've been there myself. I've been that kid who was left alone; who hears the whispers behind his back; who feels his own heart turning to stone."

Instinctively, she wanted to soothe the rising anger she heard in his voice—but something within her bade her to be still, to let him feel his fury as freely as she had felt her sadness.

"And I saw love do the same kinds of things. I saw it leave my mother brokenhearted. I saw it turn my father into a wreck of a human being." The thud of his head against the wall behind him was as resolved and certain as a death knell.

She watched as the tentacles of his pain oozed into the dimly lit room. She grasped him tighter and burrowed ever closer to him as if he were now the drowning soul, and she the savior on the life raft.

"I used to think he'd wake up and realize that I was worth more than a passing glance or a pat on the head. Used to think I deserved to be called by name in the school yard, and not '*the Artist's bastard.*'"

Abby's stomach turned at the thought, at the memory of the subtle ostracizing that she, too, had felt in the school yard. "What did you do?" she asked.

"I learned how to fight," he said with a humorless chuckle. "I took on every kid who dared look at me sideways. I think that was when my heart started turning. I decided that I wouldn't be powerless anymore," he said, his tone hardening.

Abby looked up at his face and saw that it, too, had become set and stonelike.

"I *hated* my father," he said through his teeth. "I hated what he did to my mother. I hated that he wasn't even man enough to see that we had food to eat. I hated that he was a drunk, and everyone knew it. I hated his precious art. And I *hated* that no one thought I'd amount to anything more than he did."

Ryan rose and strode toward the pillars that flanked the entryway to the living room. He placed a hand on each pillar, let his head fall low, and braced his arms against them. His back flexed in futile effort as he pushed against the pillars, and Abby was reminded of Samson, the warrior doomed to destruction because of Delilah, the woman whose love was his undoing.

The sinking in her heart was a weight in her chest that almost made her gasp. Her hand rested there, ever so lightly.

"I made myself everything he wasn't. Successful. Loyal. Honest. I even opened a bar just to prove that I wouldn't be a drunk. And when I started to draw, I destroyed everything I was compelled to create. I wouldn't let him in. Did my best to weed him out, in fact. Then you came."

Abby's spine stiffened. Was this the moment that his hatred would return?

"You came, and for the first time in my life, I was completely out of control. I hated that you could do that to me without even trying, just like your mother did to my father. I swore that I wasn't going to be that man—the man who forgets everything that ought to matter; who gets left behind to wither away and die."

Ryan strode the expanse of the room in three huge steps, coming to a crouch before her. "I swore I wouldn't be *him* . . . and never in my life have I broken a promise, Abby," he said, his voice ragged. "But here, now . . . I know that's a promise I can't keep anymore."

He grasped her shoulders, and the moon beyond the window lit his face, throwing it into stark relief. "Abby, I can't outrun who I am. I can't ignore half the blood in my veins. I can't deny the pain that's stalked me all my life . . . and neither can you."

The air in the room was electric, trilling over her flesh as she stared into his eyes.

"Before we were born, our paths crossed. I don't know what happened between my father and your mother, but it was profound enough to draw us to this night, over thirty years later."

Abby's heart was in her throat. Never had she felt such palpable intensity from another human being, and just as Ryan now understood his father, she understood her mother . . . and the inescapable attraction she had seen in her mother's eyes in the portrait that had brought her here in the first place.

Ryan stroked her face. "You talked about love hurting people, making them end their own lives, diminishing them enough to let them forget they have a child who needs holding. That's not love, Abby. That's fear."

"Do you believe that, Ryan?" she asked, searching his face, desperately needing to know if it was true.

"I didn't until now."

Abby lifted her hand and touched his face. She felt her own fear drain away—the fear that had insisted she hold life at arm's length; that had masqueraded as mistrust; that had robbed the color and joy from her life for so many years. She looked into Ryan's face and saw that he, too, seemed somehow free.

"All this fear started somewhere, Ryan," she said.

"That's what I'm here for, to find that seed of fear and destroy it."

Ryan ran his thumb over her lips. "I know, and I want that healing you talked about to start *right here*. This is the place for those hearts to wake up, Abby. This is the time."

Abby gasped, looked up at him in time to feel his mouth press against hers in a way that made her forget everything she wasn't, remember everything she was. *This* was the abandon of Abandon Bluff, and it was in her, around her, seeping into the air they inhaled in gasping breaths and transforming them both. Her heart was full in her breast, thumping out the anthem of her glorious awakening.

She put her arms around his neck, pressed her body to his, and Ryan's response was as explosive as a sunburst.

His arms were around her, his hands stroking her back and bringing her higher, deeper into their kiss.

Somewhere in the distance, his phone was ringing again. Mercifully, it stopped.

Abby drew Ryan down with her to the smooth, wooden floor of the Captain's House; she seemed to feel the countless yesterdays this house had known enfold them as their passion grew in the soft candlelight.

"Abby," he groaned . . . but the phone started ringing again.

"You'd better get that," she said, feeling unaccountably concerned, feeling that somewhere, something was very wrong. Ryan looked at her with an expression that bordered on pained. There was no mistaking that the last thing he wanted to do was talk on the phone. Still, it rang out incessantly. "Ryan, go get it."

Ryan heaved himself up, stalked across the floor and snatched the phone. "Yeah?"

Even in the dim light she could see his face blanch. She stood up, wrapped her arms around herself and walked over to him.

Ryan looked at her as if her face were the last thing he

would see before dying, as if he was trying to grasp hold of one solid, stable being before his world started spinning out of control. He slapped the phone shut and burst into action. "Help me blow out the candles!"

Immediately, she obeyed. She was gripped with panic but had no idea why. "What is it?" She snatched her coat, grabbed his, and was hot on his heels as he raced out of the house.

The sky outside was lit with an eerie glow that seemed to come from the waterfront. Ryan grabbed her hand and started running.

"What's going on?" she shouted.

"It's Brannigan Fisheries—it's on fire!"

Chapter Twenty-one

"Slow down, Ryan!" Abby gripped the door handle, foot pumping involuntarily on the nonexistent passenger-side brake pedal. She thanked the good Lord she'd insisted on coming. If she hadn't, he'd surely kill himself. "You'll be no help to anyone if you're dead!"

The Navigator cornered dangerously around the last bend, putting them in view of the blazing inferno that was Brannigan Fisheries.

Abby clapped a hand over her gaping mouth just as she heard a stifled curse from the driver's side of the truck.

Ryan jammed the vehicle in park and jumped out, sprinting down the road toward the red flash of lights, the crack and groan of timber, the withering heat that billowed from the flaming building.

"Ryan! Stop!" she screamed, kicking off her high heels and ducking her head as she raced behind him, splashing through rivers of water that coursed over the roadway.

The heat was intense. From fifty feet back, Abby felt the heat of the flames that shot out the windows, licking the darkening sky with tongues intent on devouring the world.

"Ryan!" she shouted, louder this time. He was gone—swallowed in the press of firefighters, police officers and spectators.

She was sick for him. Sick with worry that he would do something stupid; sick at the unbelievable sight of his business going up in flames. Sick.

"Stand back, stand back." Police officers were placing cones along the opposite sidewalk of Brannigan Fisheries, holding the spectators at bay.

But where had Ryan vanished to?

Frantically, Abby searched the crowd, looking for Ryan, and then seeing him at last, in the arms, in the embrace, of a woman who looked into his face with heartbreaking concern and obvious love.

Ronnie.

One A.M.

It was officially morning.

The lingering scent of smoke clung to her, along with the dampness of the firefighters' spray. She needed a bath in a big way, but the thought of dragging water to the tub made her cringe.

Instead she stood in front of the window, tea in hand.

A thick fog oozed out of the east, nestling against the coast like a fur muffler.

Abby peered down into the ambiguous billows of gray that cloaked the cottage footings. Her little house seemed eerily bereft of substructure, swaddled, as it was, up to the window sash in folds of gray fog. She at last withdrew her scrutiny. If there was, in fact, a solid foundation somewhere in the swirl of mist, she was unable to discern it.

Her entire life seemed as if its foundation had vanished

in a sea fog. What was happening to her? She had kissed Ryan Brannigan, for crying out loud . . . *and she had liked it!*

She touched her lips, closed her eyes, wishing the raspy feeling of his face would come back to her; wishing to feel the soft, demanding pressure of his mouth against hers just once more. And another fragment of her foundation seemed swallowed into the cottony mouth of the fog.

This wasn't like her—not in any way, shape or form. She was actually fantasizing about a man she had detested mere days ago. But oh, that *kiss!* She shook her head in a vain attempt to shake away the undeniable feelings that were growing within her.

The memory of his voice made her insides simmer with secret warmth as she remembered his warning . . . that logic and all of its bland counterparts were forgotten on Abandon Bluff.

Abandon Bluff indeed! *She* had certainly abandoned her logic—or it had abandoned *her.*

She raked her fingers through her hair in frustration.

Unbidden, the image of Ronnie and Ryan—bathed in the amber light of flames—appeared before her mind's eye. Ronnie had held him as he looked up at the fire, but it was the *way* she held him . . . with a certain familiarity that spoke of possession. *Is a fire of another sort beginning to kindle between Ronnie and Ryan?* It was no secret that Ronnie was crazy about Ryan, but was the emotion reciprocated? Just the thought made Abby's insides turn.

"Well, this is a fine kettle of fish," she whispered to herself.

Her head was aching—had been since the smoke of the fire twisted its way into her lungs—and the last thing she needed was to add to that incessant throbbing by confusing herself over Ryan.

Ryan. The fire.

Had they been able to salvage anything from the wreckage of the flames? She sighed quietly. It would have been impossible. Even to her untrained eye, she could tell the fire was massive; complete in its destruction.

What would he do?

Her head throbbed all the harder. She had to clear her mind, had to sleep, had to erase the deafening confusion that gonged through her soul.

She looked back at the fog, concentrating on the nothingness of it.

She was beginning to understand it; the parallel that existed between the two native forces of Destiny Bay: the people who lived here, and the fog that occasionally claimed ancient dominion.

Gray seemed not so much a color as an actual dimension for people who lived by the sea. She'd seen it shadow the thoughts of people who permitted it; infiltrate homes with its distinctive dampness. Life moved more slowly when the sky turned gray.

Somehow she knew that in this land of gray and riotous color, life could be as simple as the breeze running salty fingers through her hair; anthems could be as elemental as sandpiper's songs. Her life, however, seemed to have taken a decided turn for the complicated.

First, the mysterious footprints, then the bouquet. Now the ring, and always, the unsettling feeling of being watched.

But perhaps even more perplexing was Ryan.

Her head fell against the windowpane with a soft thud. There he was again.

How? How was it possible that she was feeling what she was feeling? And that she had shared with him the things she had shared? How was it possible that the man who had so mistreated her was suddenly her champion? How was it possible that she felt so compelled toward him—so riveted by his presence that she could scarcely take her eyes from him?

Was it some inexplicable awakening of memory she had experienced since setting foot on the island? Was she drawn to him because her mother had once loved his father?

Stranger things had happened.

She rested her head against the window frame, exhausted both physically and emotionally. In the moonlit forest beyond the glass, tendrils of fog snaked through the spindly trunks of birch and wind-crippled pine.

She had heard tell of a phenomenon called genetic memory; that sometimes, when a personally cataclysmic event occurs, it changes the chemistry of a person, intertwines with the double helix of their DNA and becomes an intangible inheritance for generations to come.

Then later, a descendant touches the rounded cheek inherited from grandma, and remembers a flash of something impossible—something that happened to another person in another time.

Maybe there *was* something to genetic memory. Maybe, just maybe, the feelings she had for Ryan were nothing more than a primordial synapse in her brain, a reminder that once, before she was even born, some of her blood had loved some of his.

She nodded her head minutely, smiling. Of course. That was all it was. And now that she had figured it out, she could finally go to bed.

Chapter Twenty-two

Ryan sat behind his desk at Rum Runner's, rubbing his aching temples. He was exhausted, but there was too much on his mind to even think about sleep.

Brannigan Fisheries packing facility was a complete loss. That fact alone put fifty people out of work, and not one of them could afford it. His fleet was undamaged, but if he had nowhere to process and pack the harvest, what would be the point of keeping men on his boats? He calculated that that left another forty people out of work.

The mantle of responsibility rested heavily upon him. These were people he'd grown up with, people he liked and respected. People with children at home.

His head pounded harder. It always made things worse when there were kids at home—kids who might go without.

A flood of memories hit the heart of him, steeling his resolve. He wouldn't do it. He would *not* put these people out of work, and no child on this island would go hungry because of him. He'd find a way to get the business operational again if it was the last thing he did.

His spirits rose just a little. Hadn't a fisheries company in Marriott's Bay been shut down when the police had learned it was a front for drug trafficking? How long ago had that been? A rough calculation placed it at about ten years ago. The equipment wouldn't be as modern as his, but it might work until he could rebuild the packing facility. Would the present owners be willing to rent it to him? It would mean that his employees would be driving over an hour to work, but at least they'd still have jobs.

He jotted a number one on his list, and beside it

wrote: *Find out who owns abandoned packing facility in Marriott's Bay. Inquire about a tour/possible rental.*

Number two was a no-brainer. His eyes almost glazed over as he looked at the fan of insurance papers spread on his desk. And about that . . . the initial suspicion was that the fire had been deliberately set. Sheriff Flynn had discovered what he believed to be traces of an accelerant, likely gasoline.

Was finding out who hated him enough to burn Brannigan Fisheries to the ground number three?

Sheriff had to be wrong. Things like that just didn't happen in Destiny Bay.

Before he began searching for the culprit—if indeed there *was* one—he'd wait to hear the official findings of the fire chief.

So number three became: *Ronnie.* He didn't want to admit it, didn't want to hurt her, but the truth was, it was happening again.

He'd felt it when Ronnie had held him as Brannigan Fisheries burned to the ground, felt it even more strongly when she went home with him and demanded he shower and eat.

Ronnie was in love with him . . . again. Or maybe still.

He dragged his hands down his face. He loved Ronnie in the comforting way of old friends, but he knew that she cared for him in a way he could never reciprocate.

And then there was Abby. His chest squeezed at the thought of her.

Abby was a woman he could love. He could lose himself to her, find himself, change cataclysmically, and though they had made major strides toward healing their past wounds, he wasn't ready for cataclysmic change.

Women of her blood and men of his were a dangerous, volatile combination. They made the kind of combustible heat that devoured everything else in their lives; that consumed them until there was nothing else left.

That was the kind of passion that made a man lose control—and if he didn't have a firm grasp on his heart and soul, then who was he? What good would he be to anyone?

Yes, he could be at peace with her, but he couldn't—especially in light of this new and unexpected catastrophe—involve himself in something that might consume him completely.

His skin prickled with heat at the thought of her; at the thought of them, together at the Captain's House. There was no doubt in his mind that if that phone call hadn't come when it did, he would have made love to her.

Even now, in the face of the fire, she was all he could think about. It made him panic, made him feel out of control and . . . there was no denying it—vulnerable.

The thought made his head throb.

The truth was, Abby had gotten under his skin, and for the life of him he couldn't figure out how she'd managed it. More tenacious women had tried their hand at it, and had failed miserably.

There had been many . . . too many. It wasn't a fact he was proud of, but his past was what it was. He'd never been able to let a woman in completely, because he knew firsthand what could happen when a man let a woman possess him, heart and soul.

He squeezed his eyes shut, rubbed his hands over his face as if to scrub away the memories of the women he hadn't been able to love: Michelle, the brilliant young attorney who'd seemed to wither when he left her; Sophia, the woman who'd wanted nothing more than to marry him, have his babies, love him forever; Angie, the poet with the tender eyes and even softer heart. Last but not least, there had been his wife, Jennifer . . . the woman who couldn't get over the fact that his heart was closed and might never open enough to satisfy her. He'd seen it in her eyes that he never loved her enough, never met her *right there*, in the place reserved for absolutes: absolute love, absolute commitment, absolutely hers.

He'd wanted to. He'd tried to. But he'd failed. He knew in the soul of him that he couldn't love in a heart-shattering sort of way. Quite frankly, he hadn't thought it was possible. For *him*, anyway.

Every one of those women had deserved better than him, but for some unfathomable reason, none of them believed it.

Now this: a face he couldn't get out of his head, a voice he heard even in his sleep, a scent that thrilled him to his bones.

What was he supposed to do about it? How could he make right the fact that he had been all over her?

But she was all over you, too, said a little voice in his head.

Things were officially out of hand.

He shoved himself out of his chair, strode across the length of the room, and glared through the window into the morning.

Something inside him was changing. Some sort of shift had occurred—an internal rift that had allowed a part of himself to slip out, and part of Abby to slip in. Something of his steely rage had vanished, something of his untouchable soul had succumbed, and at that moment, at that *precise moment* of weakness, something of her tenderness had seeped from her flesh and melted into him.

A hitch in his heart brought him up short of breath. He *had* changed, and there was nothing he could do to change back.

He'd never been on this side of the equation before. Caring this much left him feeling off-kilter, out of control, crazy with frustration.

And what about this stalker business?

Number four: *find a way to get Abby out of that cottage.*

The cottage was far too remote, far too insecure for his

liking—but he had a feeling that nothing short of eviction would budge Abby from the place.

Ryan smiled to himself, struck with a bolt of inspiration that made him want to pat himself on the back.

He grabbed the telephone book, looked up the number for Carl Watson—the contractor Cora used when work was required on any of her properties—and dialed.

He knew *exactly* how to get Abby out of that cottage, and with a smile on her face, to boot. She'd made it very clear that she wanted a bathroom, and that was just the ticket to get her safely tucked away . . . *where?*

An apartment would be almost as vulnerable as the cottage if she were there alone, and Ronnie's place was way too small. His place, he decided firmly, was out.

Of course. Cora's. Abby would be safe there.

Carl picked up his phone at last.

"Hey Carl, Ryan Brannigan here. Listen, I have a job for you up at Artist's Cottage . . . bathroom addition . . . Do you think you could get started right away? . . . Tomorrow? Yeah, that would be perfect . . . Why don't you come on down to Rum Runner's and we'll go over the details."

He hung up the phone, satisfied despite the mess he was mired in.

Ryan's chest squeezed. He couldn't, he *wouldn't* love Abrielle Lancaster.

Even though he wanted to.

History, he decided, was a damnable thing.

Chapter Twenty-three

Overnight, it seemed as if autumn had burrowed its roots into the earth, steadily eased them outward like tentacles intent on tranquilizing the last flourishes of summer. Abby had moved in with Cora temporarily, but she was eager to return to Abandon Bluff.

Despite Cora's hospitality, she still felt off-kilter because of her hasty cottage exodus.

The one thing she knew for sure was that Ryan was responsible for the contractor who'd arrived suddenly and announced he was there to begin the new bathroom addition. He'd shown her the work order and told her that she was to pack and go to Cora's house while the construction was under way.

A quick call to Cora had caught the woman completely off guard. She hadn't arranged for the renovation for another week, and had no idea why the contractor had arrived so early.

But Abby had known, just as clearly as she knew that Ryan Brannigan was a man who got exactly what he wanted, even when what he wanted was a woman out of her cottage.

She steamed a little at the thought. Really, she ought to have torn a strip off the man, but every time she worked up the ire to burst into his office, both guns blazing, the thought of hot baths, long showers, and a flushing toilet stopped her dead in her plumbing-loving tracks.

Plus, he was so busy dealing with the aftermath of the fire, the last thing he needed was a distraction from her. That *was* why he hadn't called, wasn't it?

Abby lifted the lace curtain on Mavis O'Donnell's front window and peered into the street. Mavis had invited her to dinner, but the conversation had been stilted. Why couldn't she shake off her distraction?

As if she didn't know. All she could think about was Ryan—his lips, his hands, his . . .

She bit her lip. Hard. If Ryan didn't have time for distractions, then neither did she. The days were ticking by ever more quickly, and there was no doubt in her mind that she hadn't begun to scratch the surface of her mother's experience here in Destiny Bay . . . but she'd been hopelessly distracted since her passionate encounter with Ryan. In fact, it seemed as if the entire island was conspiring to keep him at the forefront of her mind.

The sand reminded her disturbingly of his topaz eyes. The sun was the warmth of his touch, and the smell of the ocean was the scent that clung to his skin. She'd even walked by a bookstore today and seen that bloody book *He's Just Not That Into You* staring back at her.

But despite evidence to the contrary, Abby knew that he *was* that into her. She had felt something magical spring up between them.

Surely it was the inevitable fallout of the fire that kept him from calling. But what if it wasn't? Abby steeled her resolve. As soon as she left the O'Donnells', she'd call Ryan.

In the meantime, she was determined to glean more information about her mother than the tiny snippets Mavis had shared with her over dinner. She felt certain there was much more information than the old woman realized lying just below the surface of her conscious memory. She also planned to ask Mavis about the Marauder's Return, which seemed to be growing louder with each passing minute.

Outside the window, she could see the festivities for the annual celebration beginning to take shape.

Abby sat back down at the table as Franklin and Mavis reentered the kitchen. "I've been meaning to ask you about tonight . . . the Marauder's Return."

"Oh," Mavis said, shuddering, "you don't want to talk about the Marauder's Return."

Franklin winked at Abby from behind Mavis's back, making Abby grin.

"Of course I do! I know it's a celebration, but I want to know the history."

Mavis looked at her, askance. "Don't tell me you've not heard it?"

"Oh, I've heard a few versions," she said with an eloquent lift of her shoulder. "But I've lived on this island long enough to know that the only story worth betting on is yours."

Mavis patted her bouffant demurely. "Well, now, I'm not sure as I'm *that* much of an expert, but if it's history you're wantin'"—she scooped up their empty plates and set them on the counter—"that much I can surely provide."

Abby settled into her chair, ready to witness the weaving of a proper Destiny Bay yarn. There was nothing she liked better than hearing well-worn stories pulled out, shaken, and spread for her delight—and (she was quite certain) nothing the islanders enjoyed more than telling her.

"Do tell then, Mavis," said Franklin as his wife laid out teacups.

Mavis shot a marked scowl toward the window, from whence belly-deep rumblings of revelry had begun to drift. "Pure pagan is what it is!" she said, thumping the table for effect.

It worked. Abby lurched in her chair at the thud.

"When I was young, only the worst sort of a hooligan took part in The Return, but now, everyone from Doctor Thompson to the minister's cat can be found down there, flagrant as you please, reclaiming the pirate blood that no doubt runs amok in their veins," Mavis lamented, hand on her heart. "You'll stay away if you know what's good for you, Abby. It's not for the likes of you, that's for sure."

Before Abby could protest, Mavis cleared her throat pointedly. "The Marauder's Return is the anniversary of the night the ship *Defiant* ran aground, and the pirates aboard came ashore in search of a boat to commandeer and women to ravage. They found both, to the everlasting shame of Destiny Bay." Mavis squeezed her eyes shut, as if pained at the very idea. "What's become of a society that celebrates rapists and murderers?"

Abby shrank in her seat, feeling slightly abashed. "I had no idea."

"Wicked night it is. I'll be glad when it's over." Mavis sipped her tea.

"Let me wash those for you," Abby said, rising, as Mavis gathered the remnants of their dinner and carried them to the counter.

"No, you don't," she said, shooing Abby away. "You'll need to be getting home before the streets are closed. Now, I'll be sure to call you if I remember anything else about your dear ma, God rest her." Mavis's face suddenly blanched. "Oh dear," she said quietly.

Abby grasped her hand. "What is it?"

"As I was talking, I remembered something about your mother. It has to do with the celebration," she said, waving her hand toward the window, where sounds of revelry were already drifting through. She paused, as if bringing the long-ago night back into focus. "Yes, it was *definitely* the Marauder's Return. I was down to the pub with Franklin, having a nip before the festivities began. I saw Celeste and Douglas sitting at the bar. He was half in his cups, as usual, and Celeste was holding onto his arm, looking up at him as if he hung the moon. Poor misguided lass," she said with a sorrowful shake of her head.

"Yes, yes," Abby said, restraining herself from shaking the story out of Mavis's memory.

Mavis was unfazed. "I remember her plain as day, rising on her toes and whispering in his ear. Such a pretty girl she was. Anyway, she whispered a bit more, and then he gave her money to catch a cab home and said he'd be along after another pint or two, and off she went."

Mavis sat back in her seat. "I don't need to tell you that McAllister's 'pint or two' dragged on most of the night. He forgot all about your ma, who was waiting for him back at the cottage.

"I saw her at the grocery the next day. Your ma came in to buy aspirin—likely for that old sod she lived with—and that's when I first saw it."

"First saw what?" Abby asked shrilly.

"That's when I first saw your mother as a ghost."

Abby's skin prickled. "Wh-what?"

Mavis looked at her husband. The two exchanged knowing glances. "That's what we called her: 'the ghost.' It's the best word we had for what she turned into. Anyway, that's when it happened. That was when she changed; lost her spirit—the night of The Marauder's Return!"

Abby felt as if a cold hand reached into her chest and clutched her heart.

An avalanche of memories deluged her—the sound of hushed whispers when she walked by, the cold stone that marked her mother's place in Cresthaven Cemetery, the image of her grandmother's night terrors at the attic door . . . *this night* was where it all began.

Mavis's expression was pained.

Time seemed to hurtle backward. The abyss Abby had been outrunning her entire life yawned wide beneath her feet, hungering for her soul. It had never felt as close as it did right this minute.

Abby rose and rushed to the door. She needed air, fast. She grasped the door frame behind her and held on tight. "I-I have to go."

Abby broke through the back door at a run and fled down the back stairs, two at a time. Mavis called out to her, but the words were lost to the cacophony raging through her head.

Tonight, tonight. It happened tonight!

In the street, the Jolly Roger waved at every lamppost. People were suddenly everywhere, glasses held aloft as they wove through the crowd. All around her, faces were transformed by the gilding of moonlight's glow and the blush of drink. Recklessness glinted in the eyes of the young; remembrance shone from the eyes of the aged.

She leaned against the stone wall of a storefront, where she bent over at the waist and breathed slowly in and out.

What had come over her? She felt the pain and disbelief of learning about her mother's suicide as if it had happened yesterday, not years ago. She had never been so gripped by the need to escape in her entire life. But it was more than that. It was as if the mention of this night had resurrected her mother's age-old terror; as if it now coursed through Abby.

But terror over what?

She pressed her hand to her forehead, regaining an ounce of self-control. With shaking fingers, she withdrew her cell phone and dialed Ryan's number.

"Ryan Brannigan here."

"Ryan, it's Abby."

"Abby? Where are you? I can hardly hear you."

"I'm downtown," she said, stifling the quaver in her voice. "At the Marauder's Return."

"*The Marauder's Return*? Don't tell me you're there alone."

"I'm here alone, but I don't want to be. Can you come meet me? Please?" she asked, hating the pleading in her voice; the vulnerability it suggested.

"Where are you?"

Abby looked at the dubious characters surrounding her and decided that this wasn't anyplace she wanted to linger. "I can meet you on Brigantine Way, by the café."

The line was silent but for the noise in the background. "That's across town from Run Runner's," he said, almost to himself. "I'm behind the bar, but I can get to you in half an hour."

"Half an hour?" she echoed, her stomach clenching.

"The streets are closed, Abby. I'll be on foot. Don't talk to anyone, stay in well-lit areas, and *be careful*."

"I will." She closed her phone, secured her purse at her shoulder and stepped into the crowd, forcing thoughts of her mother's tragedy out of her mind. If she were to find her way across town in this crowd, she needed her wits about her.

The only route to Brigantine Way from where she was standing was by way of the waterfront.

The surge of the crowd seemed to be heading toward the docks, so Abby let it move her along. By the ceaseless momentum of hundreds of moving bodies, Abby found herself at the north end of Pirate's Landing Beach. Now, she just had to get to the south end, and she'd be right on track.

She kicked off her shoes and stuffed them in her purse. The sand was cold beneath her feet and the wind on her face was as moist as a mermaid's breath, cooling the feverish heat that streaked through her insides as she replayed Mavis's words again and again.

All around her, the party was well advanced, and the belly-deep thumping of drums seemed to rattle her sinews. Beyond her, a towering bonfire spit sparks into the black cavern of night.

She inched her way toward the water, where the crowd seemed thinner. From there, she could see that people had gathered around a raised dais, where Dermot Malone, owner of the kite shop, recited the story of the marauders' first landing on the island.

His audience leaned in raptly, murmuring in response to his story. She'd have to fight through the crowd, thick as it was, but she'd never felt so desperate to feel the strength of Ryan's arms around her.

She began slogging her way through as Dermot's words drifted out over the night sky.

". . . when at last, the alarm rang through the town," Dermot said ominously, "it was too late. A pirate stood upon the threshold of every door. The few able-bodied men who weren't fishing were cut down. The screams of women pierced the night."

Like a steadily rising tide, the crowd seemed to surge with barely suppressed offense. An answering ripple of unease swelled within her. She wanted to run, yet running would be impossible. She pressed on, determined to get through to Ryan, ignoring the angry grunts of those she was forced to shove.

"They plundered every home," said Dermot, "sending a few to their maker along the way. And many of those who lived, lived to carry the seed of pirates in their bellies."

She wanted to block out the words. Something terrible had happened to her mother on the night of the Marauder's Return, just as it had happened to those women so long ago. It *wasn't* just a story—it *wasn't* just for fun . . . didn't these people understand anything?

She leaned into a particularly thick gathering of people and pressed through, wishing she were anywhere but here.

Ghosts of the past seemed to force their ominous presence upon her, as frightening as Black Jack the pirate, and every bit as dangerous. Hair stood erect on the back of her neck. Something felt as if it were closing in on her.

Run! said the voice of her fear, but her feet churned hopelessly on the shifting granules of sand.

"Before long," said the relentless storyteller, "our forefathers returned to the carnage left by Black Jack Rawlins and his crew of villains. The strongest men of the village set off to follow the fishing boat they had escaped in, and after a struggle on the high seas the men of Destiny Bay returned victorious!"

"Death to pirates!" roared the crowd.

Abby winced at the volume, was almost overturned by the surging crowd. The mood was growing decidedly menacing. She *had* to get to safety . . . to Ryan.

"Take care when you curse a pirate and his blood," warned Dermot. "For who among us can be sure that the blood of pirates does not course through *our* veins?"

An uproar that had Abby clapping her hands to her ears rose from the crowd.

"For this, my friends, for the blood that sings in our veins at the very sight of the sea, we give the pirates this one night of freedom; we relinquish our grasp on the civil, the lawful, the passionless. Tonight, *we are pirates!*"

Chapter Twenty-four

Does she honestly think she can hide from me?

The Lover raked his fingers through his hair, feeling the strands catch on the partially scabbed A that blazed in his palm. It was red; a deep, angry red that spoke to him of her deception.

When he awoke in the dead of night with his hand throbbing and a fine, red thread weaving upward beneath the skin, he knew in the heart of him that things were going awry, that his love, his darling, had made a terrible choice.

It was poison. Of the blood. But he'd been careful. He had cleansed the flesh before he sliced, had sterilized the razor blade, and had only removed the bandage when he absolutely *had* to see the evidence of his love, the evidence of *her*, come back to him at last.

So, what was this poison?

It could mean only one thing.

The Lover opened the buttons of his shirt, let his fingers trail over the first letter he had carved into his flesh—over thirty years ago.

It was a C, for his lovely Celeste.

He had carved it the moment love took hold of his heart, had rubbed it raw on nights that he lay, yearning for her, seething that she slept in the arms of the artist, biding his time until the time was right.

Ah, yes, good things come to those who wait.

He remembered the day he felt the very chemistry of the C change; he'd felt as if the graceful curve of her blessed letter had been carved by brimstone.

Foreboding had sickened him until he retched with it, groaned with it, railed against the heavens that had brought her to him and then tortured him so mercilessly.

He had thought, for a moment, that he had offended the heavens in some way; that *this* was why they toyed with him. But then logic, sweet logic, had filled him with the calm certainty that he had done nothing wrong— reminded him that he had done only what he was born to do: love Celeste.

If someone had sinned, it certainly wasn't him. And there was only one other person it could have been. His lovely Celeste.

Wasn't history filled with stories demonstrating the treachery of women? Even deeply *beloved* women?

The Lover had stolen into the night, crept through the darkness, and had peeked into the window of her cottage.

His heart almost tore from his chest when he saw her, standing naked in front of a mirror she had carelessly propped against the wall. She was looking at herself, a small smile on her lips.

He watched her hand, graceful and deliberate, grasp a bottle of perfume, smile sleepily. She unstopped it, dabbed the crystal stopper behind her ears, on her throat, between her breasts.

This was why his wound blazed. She was readying herself for the artist.

The Lover had turned and retched in the bushes outside the window.

Then it had come to him.

It was up to him to sanctify her, to turn her heart to what was good and right, what was meant to be. No, he would not let her degrade herself as had his mother!

The smile crept onto his face, lighting his heart as if the sun shone directly into it.

He had waited long enough. The time was now.

As always when he thought of that night, The Lover simmered with the most delicious warmth.

It seemed like yesterday—and yet a million years ago—that he'd crept into the cottage and stood, watching her as she lay in her bed waiting for the artist.

Well, he had changed *her* plans, yes he had. He had entered the room and smiled at her, ignoring her crises of dismay and thinking how lovely and modest it was that she clutched the sheet over her bosom, as if he had never seen her naked body before.

He went to her and bade her to be still—which she did, clever girl. She knew better than to anger him, patient man that he'd been.

Lovingly, he had drawn her from the bed and just looked at her—so beautiful and silvery in the moonlight. She trembled with desire for him, just as he did for her, but he wouldn't have her there, in the artist's bed. He had better plans for his lovely Celeste.

He had wrapped her in the bedsheet and driven her along the winding cliffs, then grasped her hand, taking her to the pirate's cave.

Celeste had cried out beneath him, but the thundering of the cave drowned out all sound. He had held her fast, as she was so terribly shy—his sweet, gentle one—and he'd made love to her until the sun rose.

The stupid artist, who'd drunk himself into a stupor at the bar and apparently never even bothered to come home that night, was never any the wiser.

But the burning in his hand brought him back to himself; brought him back to his duty. He rubbed his thumb over his palm until it throbbed.

The poison could mean only one thing: that Abrielle was set on betraying him.

Already, she had moved from the cottage. Where, he had not yet discovered. But he would find her, oh yes, he would, his coy little flower; his treacherous love.

But he had made good use of the time she had been away. He had purchased surveillance equipment online; had spent a leisurely morning affixing tiny cameras in strategic places.

Soon, he would know all her secrets, as every good lover should.

His heart was restless. He had gone too long without sight of her.

Perhaps he would see her at The Marauder's Return, which was already fully under way, from the sound of it. He decided that he would attend, just in case.

It was the night of the Marauder's Return, after all, that he had finally felt moved to consummate his love for Celeste those many years ago. His chest warmed at the memory. The night of the Marauder's Return was special. Very special.

Ah, yes, the time was near. The fates were about to smile upon him again. He could just feel it.

Chapter Twenty-five

An unimaginable commotion filled the night, broke out on every front.

She *was* surrounded by pirates, by madness. She had to get to Ryan! Abby turned north—or toward what she thought was north—and found herself nose to nose with the dais.

"Abby, you idiot," she hissed under her breath. If she could just get off the beach and find Water Street, she could get to Brigantine Way. But where on earth *was* Water Street? Where the devil was *any* street? All she could see in any direction was people.

She closed her eyes for a moment. Surely she knew the way back . . . like a salmon, she reasoned. *There will be hell to pay if I'm not at least as intelligent as a salmon!*

She opened her eyes, dove headlong into the crowd, and started forging ahead again.

Men and women danced as if plunged into another epoch; the pulse of drums seemed to draw them into a primal dance of seduction.

Faces she recognized—and some she didn't—leered at her. A man leaned in far too close, his face bathing hers with sour-smelling moisture. "Well, if it isn't our own little TV star. Come to see how the real men play, have you?"

She shoved the drunk aside, thankful he was intoxicated to a near stupor.

Abby felt swallowed, consumed in one bite by the menacing crowd. She was ogled by men wearing eye patches, deafened by the squeals of women . . . all she could think about was reaching the safety of Ryan's arms.

Then, she felt it.

Utterly distinct from the unconscious press of the surging crowd . . . someone had touched her, had run a finger down the length of her spine.

Her breath came more quickly. The ghost of that touch wailed along her backbone like an internal siren.

She looked left and then right, confused by the flirting light that bathed the edges of faces with firelight's gold.

Another touch—unmistakably deliberate—as someone yanked her arm.

Abby shrieked. Frantically, she scanned the surging crowd. No one looked her way.

Was this ominous night going to repeat its vile history upon her?

"Not if I have anything to say about it," she said through her teeth.

Elbows out, she began to fight her way through the crowd.

"No!" Another touch. This one squeezing behind her knee tightly enough to send pain shooting up her leg. Tears sprang to her eyes, just as a hand grasped her hair and tugged.

Her head snapped backward. Both hands reached for the stinging area on her scalp, holding her hair to keep it from being ripped from her head.

She could be snatched, right here, and no one would even notice, no one would even care.

She *had* to escape . . . her safety depended on it.

Abby swallowed her fear and plunged headlong into the throng, shoving, elbowing, even punching when necessary. She ignored indignant howls as her foot came down hard on those of others.

"Abby!" a hand grasped her elbow tightly.

She swung around, ready to do battle. "Ryan!" she cried, collapsing against him. "Help me find my way out of here!"

"Come with me." He took her hand, leading her through the thickness of the crowd and cutting a swath before her.

At last, he turned and pulled her into the shadow of a building. "You weren't at Brigantine Way," he said, his face etched with worry. "What happened?"

"I couldn't get through," she said, all but sobbing.

Ryan grabbed her to his chest and held her tight. He lifted his hand, stroked her hair from her face. "You're safe now."

Am I? She held him tighter. "You didn't call," she said into the bulk of his sweater. "I told you my secrets, and you didn't call. I trusted you—and I don't trust many people."

He cupped her face. "Trust me, Abby. I heard your voice tonight. I thought of you out here alone, and everything came into focus."

Abby's breath caught in her throat when she looked up at him and saw him searching her face, her eyes, letting his gaze linger upon her lips. His thumb stroked them, followed the sinuous curve of them as he watched her mouth. His other hand found her waist and drew her closer. "Trust me."

The thrumming pulse of the night drummed in her veins, drew her heartbeat into a frenzy of desire. "Ryan," she whispered, slaking her thirst for air with a deep, intoxicating draught of his breath. Her concern vanished, replaced by something infinitely more potent.

He pressed against her in answer; a leg between hers, an arm behind her back, another cupping her neck. He drew her closer, then pressed his mouth to hers with the thirst of a man who had been wandering in a desert, drinking her in, consuming her breath, devouring her groans, claiming her every nuance of movement with his body.

Abby's memories of the last terrifying moments melted away. His presence was like a river, mighty and deep. She felt herself disappear beneath the surface, where the swift current tossed her, caressed her, made her its own. She grasped his clothing, kneading it in her hands as she moved against him, the taste of him filling her, the feet of him his body a hardness she welcomed.

"Ryan," she gasped into the sweet darkness of his mouth, wanting him so suddenly and so completely that every fear fluttered into oblivion. Ryan was hers. She felt it in her soul. She felt it in his rising passion, felt it as the walls around his heart gave way, felt it in his growing need, and she exulted with the joy of it.

Her breath caught on it, coming in little moans and filling his mouth as he devoured the sweetness of her surrender and gave the same gift back to her.

"Abby," he whispered, groaning with the sound of her name, trailing his mouth over the flesh of her neck. "I need you. Tonight."

His words landed with a soft thud in her heart. "This is too much, Ryan," she said, pulling away from him. "Too soon."

He dragged in a slow breath, his forehead against hers, his eyes closed tightly. Abby's own heart thudded in her chest as she breathed in his exhaled need, felt it slowly withdraw from her as if in regretful retreat. "You're right. It is," he admitted.

His hands fell from her waist as he pulled himself away from her.

"I'll take you home," he said roughly.

"But how can you? The road is impassable."

"Not my mother's home. Mine. We won't make it back to Mom's on foot, and we'll never get through with a vehicle."

"Oh. Of course," she said.

Ryan took her hand. He turned to her, still flushed. "Stay close to me, understand?"

They stepped into the madness, ducking through alleys, slipping between houses. After what seemed like an eternity of walking, they escaped from the crowds, the groping hands, the overpowering scent of mingled bodies and alcohol.

The moon was high; the wind on the brink of chilly. "I

can't imagine what would have happened if you hadn't found me, Ryan," she said, shuddering at the thought of where she'd be or what she'd be enduring if he hadn't come. "Someone pulled my hair. It *definitely* wasn't random."

He stopped dead in his tracks. "You're sure about that?"

"I'd bet my life on it." She watched his face intently. She needed someone to believe her as much as her own mother must have needed someone to believe in her so long ago.

A flicker of something moved behind his eyes. "Did you see who did it?"

"No."

His grasp on her hand tightened. Abby couldn't help feeling that something about tonight would change things drastically—had *already* changed things drastically—for both of them.

"I need to tell you what happened at the O'Donnells' tonight." As they walked in the darkness, Mavis's revelations poured from her heart.

"Ryan, a woman alone on a night like this is a prime target. Something happened to Mom the night of the Marauder's Return, and I don't know if it happened on the streets, or back at the cottage. I think she might have been hurt."

"Attacked?"

Abby nodded, tight-lipped.

Ryan's expression was inscrutable. "I hope you're wrong," he said at last, pulling her hand gently. "Let's get you inside. It's not much farther, now."

They approached a long, low Cape Cod. Weathered shingles reflected the moonlight, and substantial white trim glowed softly. The entire house looked framed against the shifting, sparkling sea that glinted beneath the stars.

"This is yours?" she asked, surprised. "Ryan, it's beautiful. I've admired this house ever since I first saw it."

"Thanks." Ryan let her in with a twist of his key. "I'll

start a fire," he said, extending a hand to lead her into the living room. "It's a little chilly."

Abby stepped into the room and saw a magnificent stone fireplace, a bank of floor-to-ceiling windows and a view of the moonlit sea that made her heart skip a beat.

Ryan crouched in front of the fireplace, crumpling paper and stacking it with kindling. He struck a match and held it to the edge of the paper, letting it dance along the edge and grow in amber brilliance.

The fire crackled warmly, and Ryan sat down beside her. "I was way out of line tonight. Kissing you, I mean. I never would have done it if I'd known you were already upset."

She looked him squarely in the face. "Don't apologize. Besides, if I'd wanted you to stop, I would have said so."

"Are you sorry I *did* stop?"

"Yes," she said, barely recognizing the breathless voice as her own, barely able to keep from shivering as goose bumps rose on her flesh. She reached across the miniscule, unending distance between them, touched his face. "I want to forget *that* touch. I only want to think of yours."

He pulled her hand to his lips and kissed the palm. His tongue touched the mound of flesh beneath her thumb, his mouth closed over it, sucking gently.

Ryan closed, then opened, his eyes. In them, Abby saw the color of the sea in storms. It thrilled her, frightened her, made her forget the hands that had been so unwelcome and think only of his, holding hers.

He looked at her with an intensity that threatened to pry every truth from her heart, and the truth was, from the moment Abby had first seen him, she had been captivated—her yearning was rooted in something she didn't understand and could no longer suppress.

Ryan breathed it in—the very truth of her—and Abby felt herself slipping inside him along with her secrets. With an unsteady breath, she took him deeper still into the rich soils of her heart.

She would be open to him this night, she knew, as she had never been before. The moment swelled and simmered. She sensed it quiver all around her, felt her heart vibrate beneath its weight. She felt the whine of tension and knew the moment was about to rupture into something magnificent.

As light as breath, his lips touched hers. Behind her closed eyelids, she felt an explosion of light that rushed to the core of her, scattering every remembrance of her life as it had been, singing through her veins an anthem of new possibilities.

She grasped his shoulders and pulled him deeper into the kiss, felt his fingers splayed on her back and opened her mouth wider.

At last he was hers, completely. She felt his pleasure as he tasted her, drew her lip into his mouth and flicked his tongue over the silky, swollen flesh.

She pressed closer to him, needing him to feel the beating of her heart, needing to feel the beating of his.

He responded with a force that shocked her—tasting the secret folds of her mouth, breathing himself into her with a longing so fierce that it left her breathless.

As if she were weightless, he lifted her from the couch, her legs dangling over his arms.

She felt the room disappear behind her, felt the jerking roughness of stairs beneath her, felt the brush of a foreign hallway, the thud of foot against door, shoving it open.

The softness of a mattress gave beneath her weight as he placed her upon his bed, lowering her by degrees, as if unwilling to relinquish his hold. The scent of him was all around her, within her; the feel of him was all hard planes of muscle flexing beneath the cable knit of his sweater. In that moment, she could believe that wild, seafaring blood pumped through his veins.

Ryan dropped his head to kiss her, blotting out the light

and yet magically unfurling it within her in one swift motion.

He lowered his torso onto hers as their bodies began to move together as one. His hands stroked her, lifted her toward him, glided over the bareness of her back in a hypnotic, fluid motion that was so like the sea, she felt buoyant.

Abby gasped beneath him, wanting nothing more than to consume him, to draw him inside her. There was nothing between them of bitterness, of hatred, of age-old resentment. There was only a blind, consuming need, the likes of which Abby could scarcely understand.

"Abby," he whispered. He looked down at her, stroking her face with his hand. "I can't, Abby," he said softly, his voice sounding as if it had been dragged over broken glass. "*We* can't."

She blinked at him. "What are you talking about?"

"I don't want you regretting anything."

She narrowed her eyes at him. "I'm quite capable of deciding what I will and will not regret, Ryan."

He rose slowly from the bed and pulled a blanket onto her. "You were right, what you said tonight. This is too much too soon."

Abby felt a pang of jealousy. "Is this about Ronnie?"

"Ronnie?" he asked, sounding genuinely baffled. "No, it's about you and me."

She took his hand, lifted it to her heart, pressed it there. "Feel this, Ryan. Feel *me*." Her heart raced in her chest, fluttering beneath his hand like a captive butterfly, longing to be set free. "I want to be with you, Ryan. I want *you*. If you have something going on with Ronnie, please tell me. I swear, I wouldn't dream of interfering. But if you don't— if you can truly say that you never will—then what do we have to lose?" She paused, chased the breath that seemed determined to outrun her.

"Ryan, you and I, we could have something amazing. Don't ask me how I know that, because I couldn't tell you, but I feel it, Ryan, deep in a place I've never let another man. Don't ask me to turn my back on that. Don't you turn *yours* on it."

Understanding was unfurling relentlessly within him. All of a sudden, he understood his father's fascination for Celeste, and his torment upon losing her. He understood it all as if he carried the memory in his blood. He understood it because now, it *was* him.

He looked down at Abby, rubbed his hand over his swollen mouth and drew it across his burning face to distract himself from the other, much more disquieting flame that kindled brighter with every indrawn breath.

He'd never wanted a woman as badly as he did her. He looked into her trusting, upturned face; he remembered the women before her that he had hurt so badly. Did he want that for her? Was he capable of caring without destroying? And would loving her destroy him as loving had destroyed his father?

He felt as if he stood on a precipice, overlooking a future that was shrouded in uncertainty. Loving Abby would mean leaping into the chasm of chance, submitting himself to the pull and tug of fate.

Something within him had awakened. Something long dormant, fiercely demanding, and as restless as a caged animal. He knew what it was; he knew it intimately, for this was not the first time it had whispered warnings to him.

It was not pirate blood. No, lust and hedonism were not new to him, and certainly didn't unsettle him. Those, he could understand.

It was the blood of the artist.

He felt it now, demanding a quenching that could come only from that rare, exquisite union of muse and master. It rose to an aching crescendo within him—the throbbing need to touch, to consume, to be absorbed by her perfection, her luminescent beauty.

He felt Abby draw her fingertips down the length of his cheek, leaving trails of invisible fire in their wake. He looked down at her, his heart hammering as their eyes met. If he had it in his blood to want her this much, there was no question that he had it in his blood to love her . . . and loving her would be more than a little dangerous, more than a little magnificent.

He cupped her face in his hands, straining against the fierceness that threatened to consume him. "No," he said, answering her at last. "I won't turn my back on that."

Her eyes glistened with a fervency that he felt to his core. "Neither will I."

He kissed her, deeply, madly, felt the walls around his heart crumble and the warmth of her desire slip in. "You were meant to be mine, Abby," he swore. "I can't breathe without thinking of you; I can't sleep without dreaming of you. It's like I woke up the day you arrived, and realized I was only half here; I realized that everything I never knew I wanted was right in front of me," he said, grasping her face. "I don't know why, 'cause God knows, I don't deserve it—don't deserve *you*—but I want you, just the same."

Abby drew away from him, returning the fierceness of his gaze. "You can't have me without making peace with the past, Ryan, because like it or not, that's where we started. That's where this passion began." When she kissed him, Ryan felt the timeless ghost of the past rise within him, flow around them—eddy and pool in the hollows created by old resentments and erode their edges until they were gentled into something impossibly alluring. "We started with Douglas and Celeste," she said. "And part of their love beats in our hearts."

He grabbed her to his chest, wanting to draw her light into the dark places of his soul, and she was right there with him, accepting the deluge of long-denied passion that thundered over them both.

She was exactly as he'd imagined, from the way she touched his fevered skin to the aching, almost frantic need she stirred within him.

Her hands were all over him . . . delicately tracing the lines of his body, then kneading his flesh almost ravenously. Her need matched his own as they threw off their clothes, tumbling over each other in greedy abandon, matching pleasure for pleasure, pain for pain.

He sank into her, and they rolled over the bed in a tangle of sheets, knocking a bedside table and sending coins, a watch, and a lamp skittering in all directions, but he was oblivious to everything except Abby: her hands, her mouth, her body, the raggedness of her breath.

She was his, at last. Completely and irrevocably. And with that realization, a wild pleasure shuddered through him, echoed in her own trembling release.

Afterward, Abby touched his chest, distanced them minutely. Her face was soft and lovely in the dim light. "Douglas and Celeste—they've come full circle in us," she said quietly. "Tell me you can let it go, Ryan. That's the only way this will work."

Ryan inhaled slowly, tentatively—searched his soul for the answer even as he searched her eyes and saw the treasure that she was; he saw the possibilities that waited in her wide-open heart. Could he possibly let the past go? Was he even *capable* of letting it go?

He understood, now—in a way he hadn't until he looked into Abby's face and gave voice to the dark and secret truth of what she did to him—that regardless of their shared history, he simply didn't have the strength to overcome the sudden, exquisite ache of wanting her. In fact, he didn't *want* to overcome it.

The truth was, that for the first time since love had left his spirit as shattered as his parents' union, he felt ready to live in spite of the dangers loving brings—ready to *love* in spite of it.

There's no way on this green earth I'm letting her walk away. Part of him had come back to life since knowing her and was pounding at the door of his heart.

An unimaginable warmth filled the breadth of his chest, purled through his being—and the answer was there, illuminated by the hope he saw in her eyes. Yes, he could let it go. In fact, he already had.

Chapter Twenty-six

"I must say, Abby," said Ronnie as they walked toward Rum Runner's. "I've been looking forward to tonight all week. Speaking of which, you've been awfully hard to get hold of. Where've you been, anyway?"

Where've I been? Abby's stomach tightened at the thought of telling Ronnie about her budding relationship with Ryan, but tell her she must . . . this much she'd resolved before leaving the warmth and comfort of Ryan's house to meet Ronnie for their prearranged evening out.

There was no doubt in Abby's mind that Ronnie would take the news badly. Even so, keeping the truth from her friend was out of the question.

Reluctantly, Abby relinquished her comfortable spot on cloud nine, giving herself over to the tug of responsibility. As she did so, a pang of guilt hit her square in the chest. She couldn't shake the feeling that in falling for Ryan, she'd betrayed Ronnie. Ronnie, after all, had loved Ryan since they were teens, and Abby had known as much.

A gust of wind ruffled the trim of the awning they walked beneath, bringing with it the bracing scent of salt, sea and sand. Abby inhaled deeply. She wanted nothing more than to air out her soul, let it snap in the breeze, bleach in the sun; let rough grains of sand slough the dingy stain of betrayal from her heart.

"Hellooo, in there." Ronnie waved her hand in front of Abby's eyes. "Are you awake, Abby?"

"I'm sorry, Ron," she said, feeling miserable on so many levels, it made her stomach clench. "Ronnie, I have to be honest with you about something."

"Can honesty wait, Abby?" Ronnie picked up her pace, trotting over the cobblestones en route to the downtown core of Destiny Bay. "There's a crew in town from that Australian ship, and they're headed to Rum Runner's tonight. I thought I'd introduce myself to the first mate."

The first mate? "Just wait a minute here," Abby said. "I thought you had your sights set on Ryan?"

The smile melted from Ronnie's face. "I'm crazy about Ryan. He's not crazy about me. You do the math."

Ronnie had given her just the opening she needed. Abby took a deep breath. "Ronnie, I'm in love with Ryan."

Ronnie stopped walking. Abby stopped breathing. The wind stopped blowing.

"It's true, Ronnie," Abby said, her voice straining past the lump in her throat.

An extraordinary array of emotions flitted over Ronnie's features: disbelief, rage, hurt . . . Abby saw them all, and a few she couldn't even identify.

Ronnie brought her hands up to her hair, grabbed two fistfuls and held on tight. Her breath was heavy and fast; her eyes blazed with anger. From between her forearms, she stared at Abby as if she were a ghost. "You—you *love* him? You—*what?*" Her hands were rubbing her forehead as she broke into a frantic pace, looking at Abby occasionally, as if to make certain this wasn't a bad dream.

The wind was back, colder, darker. Ronnie whirled on her, her face a contorted mask of rage. "How?" she gasped.

"How do you go from friend to traitor in . . . how long did it take, Abby? How long before you fell hook, line and sinker for the man I love?"

Abby's mouth jawed up and down wordlessly. When at last she could muster words, she spoke. "I'm so sorry, Ronnie. I mean, I'm *not* sorry that I got together with Ryan; I *can't* be sorry about that, but I'm sorry that I hurt you."

"Well, that kind of sorry doesn't count!" Ronnie shouted, heedless of passersby who turned and stared. "You just don't understand what you've done. You don't get it at all! He was the first man I ever loved. I practically beat my head against a wall for fifteen bloody years to get him. And here you waltz onto our island and grab him up like he's a berry, ripe for the picking! What makes you so special that not even the invincible Ryan Brannigan can resist you? Have you inherited your mother's gift for stealin' away the hearts of men?"

Abby felt as if she'd been struck. She looked into the sky to keep from crying. *This is so much worse than I thought it would be!* And far above, clouds scudded across the silvery moon like clippers on the wind. "This is between you and me. Please don't bring my mother into this."

"Why? Because she's off-limits?" Ronnie let out a cry. "Well, guess what? So was Ryan!"

"You said yourself that he doesn't love you," Abby shot back, feeling anger of her own now. "Do you expect him to stay celibate for the rest of his life?"

"No, but nor do I expect a friend to set her claws in him. It would have been different if someone else had happened into his life, but not a *friend*, Abby. Never a friend."

Abby's indignation puddled around her ankles. Ronnie was right. It was a terrible thing to do to a friend. Truth was like a weight in her belly. "Ronnie," she said, tears brimming. "What can I say to you?" She reached for Ronnie's hand, but was rewarded with a glare that could freeze water. "What can I *do*?" she asked, even though she knew there was nothing she could do to soothe Ronnie, nothing she could say to take the pain away. There was only the truth, and the hope that in time, it would be easier for her to accept.

Ronnie looked down at the slick cobblestones, her hair falling across her face. "Part of me wants to hurt you like you've hurt me," she said, and the anger in Ronnie's voice was suddenly tempered by something worn and weary; something so sad it made Abby's breath catch. "But the strangest thing is that another part of me wants to hold your hand and feel for you." Ronnie's eyes hardened again. "'Cause there's nothing I could do to you that will hurt you as much as Ryan can. *And will.*"

Abby let Ronnie's words sift through the air and anoint her with understanding: Ronnie fully expected their affair to end badly. Well, Abby wouldn't let that happen.

"It's funny, aye—how fate is?" Ronnie said acidly, arms tight across her chest. "You're so like your ma, it's scary. Taking what's not yours, flaunting your conquest for all to see. What makes this especially wrong is the fact that you've seen the results of your mother's actions, and yet you choose to follow in her footsteps anyway!"

Ronnie was in such pure, palpable pain, Abby couldn't even pretend to be angry. Her own stomach wrenched violently; she seemed to absorb some of Ronnie's torment and recoil at its bitterness. "I'm sorry," she said again, and the words were laden with absolute honesty, absolute sorrow for the injury she'd done to Ronnie.

"I need to be alone," Ronnie said through a sob. "Please, don't follow me." She turned and ran down the cobblestone street, sorrow streaming behind her like the tails of ropes that bound her to a man who would never be hers.

When the sound of Ronnie's footfalls at last became more distant, Abby let out a breath she hadn't realized she'd been holding. Hand on her chest, she chased the air that seemed pitifully insufficient to fill the gaping emptiness in her chest; the emptiness that sprang into being at Ronnie's loss and suddenly dulled the luster of Abby's joy in finding love.

Ryan. She'd give anything to have his arms around her *right now;* to hear him tell her she wasn't as cruel as she believed herself to be. More than anything, she needed to feel the twin of her desire echoed in his touch; she needed his strength to stare down every whisperer who claimed that she and Ryan would always be haunted by the specter of their shared history.

There would always be people who—like Ronnie— would be intent on pointing out the fact that she had snatched Ryan away from someone better suited, just as her mother had done with Ryan's father.

Yes, there would always be doubters. How long would she and Ryan be able to withstand having the past thrown in their faces? What if she finally, *finally* let herself love completely, and the past became too much for Ryan? What if he turned his back on her? How would she ever recover?

"She is *not* going to do this to me!" she said through her teeth, forcing the fear from her mind. Her head was aching and her stomach tight. She had to see Ryan, had to be in his presence when she asked herself if she dared risk it— because loving Ryan would be the biggest risk of her life.

With tears in her eyes, she made her way toward Rum Runner's.

Raucous sounds from the bar spilled into the street— along with a staggering drunk or two. Abby turned just in time to see Bartholomew Briggs receive a hearty thump on the back from a bouncer twice his size.

"Go on with ya, Bartholomew! Come back when you're a little steadier on your feet." In helpful demonstration of the bouncer's assertion, Bartholomew promptly fell face-first into the street.

Abby gasped, torn between the impulse to ran to his aid, and the voice of logic that told her to run, altogether.

Tentatively, she took a step forward. She might be feeling unsteady herself, but at least she wasn't face-first on the street.

"Hold up there, miss," called the bouncer. "Old Bart's like a rubber ball. Bounces up in a second or two. He's got the stomach of a dandy, though. I'd stay back, if I were you."

Bartholomew rolled laboriously onto his back and stared into the sky. His lips moved as if in supplication to the spinning stars, then fell still as his eyes rested at last upon Abby's face.

A trembling finger rose, pointed directly at her. "Leave! If you know what's good for you, lass, you'll leave!" He turned his head and began retching. "The devil's comin' for you! He'll have you like he had your ma! Leave, leave!" he hollered between gags.

Abby's knees went weak. She reached out, found the hood of a car and leaned in to support herself. *The devil's coming? He'd have her like he had her mother?* The ground seemed to spin out from beneath her, the stars overhead seemed to sway. She had to get to Ryan—had to get to safety.

Too late, she saw a singing, stumbling, drinking crowd of sailors coming right for her. She scrambled to get out of their way, but was snatched around the waist by a burly seaman, twirled into the heaving center of their jovial midst and moved by sheer forward momentum along with the crew. When she was finally plunked back down by the well-meaning, beer-soaked bunch, it was smack-dab in the middle of Rum Runner's.

"Perfect," she said to herself, regaining her balance.

She forced through the undulating crowd, secretly glad for the press of people. They held her upright when her still-trembling knees threatened to deposit her flat on her butt.

A glance around the room revealed that Ryan was

nowhere in sight. She skirted the bar and made her way toward Ryan's office.

The door was unlocked, and as she slipped inside, she saw him reclining in his chair, his guitar on his lap.

"Hey!" he said, brightening.

She drank in the sight of him, the light in his eyes when he saw her, and that quickly, she was reassured. "You promised to play me a song," she said, looking at his guitar. Talking about her encounter with Ronnie—dampening the perfect sight of him—was the last thing she wanted to do. Ronnie could wait.

"Well, I didn't actually *promise*," he said teasingly. "I tend not to play for people."

"Play for *me*," she said, walking into the room, holding his eyes with hers and breathing in his scent. "I need you to."

A wordless exchange passed between them, a moment hanging in eternity. Her chest was hollow as she watched him position the instrument. The revelry beyond the confines of his office was suddenly a million miles away.

Ryan's eyes met hers, locked there and forbade her to look away. "This means something," he said quietly. "Me playing for you, I mean."

"I know," she whispered.

Ryan plucked a few strings tunelessly. Finally, he lifted his head and looked into her face.

A deluge of notes tumbled from the strings—a bull-fighter's fanfare, an echo of galloping hooves and crackling fires.

Abby's insides seemed to simmer within her. She swallowed loudly, never taking her eyes from him for a moment. The room was silent, expectant.

Ryan closed his eyes and placed his hand against the wood of his guitar. The fingers twitched, as if feeling the echo of a thousand plucked strings. His hand moved slowly, deliberately, and at last freed the first, quivering note into the anticipating silence.

The stillness vibrated—pierced by the shard of music—and then another stirred in its wake, sending ripples of sound that lapped against her flesh. Three more rising notes simmered with pent-up emotion; then, a slow, haunted chord thrummed deeply beneath the rest.

Abby's flesh prickled from head to foot, stroked by the whisper of invitation she heard in the sound—and by the richer, humming suggestions that rested in the silences.

His fingers touched the strings again, teasing, as a lover would. Again, the music rose to them, drawn by the inexplicable bond between captive and liberator. His hand lifted and cupped as if cradling the sound that vibrated beneath it—then thudded against the amber grain of his guitar, silencing the trembling notes with brutal finality.

Ryan caught her eyes and held them.

Breath caught in her throat as she sensed his fingers start to move. Without taking his eyes from hers, he strummed and pulled, vibration building upon vibration as his fingers tumbled over the strings in a fervent need to express. Higher and faster rose the fevered pitch of the music.

When she dared not look at him a moment longer, she closed her eyes and felt every shiver of his music—bare, carnal, unforgiving, tripping along her flesh. It tugged at her, enveloped her, threatened to ply every untruth from her heart.

Oh, yes. He is infinitely, infinitely worth the risk.

Abby opened her eyes, saw that his were now closed; the muscles around them tightened as his head tossed and his shoulders leaned into the music.

Finally, as if sensing the twin tensions of the strings *and* Abby, his music stopped. Ryan at last opened his eyes.

Abby couldn't speak. Her skin felt as if it were lit from within, as if she had been skillfully and thoroughly loved. "That *did* mean something," she said breathlessly.

He was walking toward her, and though she knew he

couldn't have known about the silent conclusion she had arrived at—that he was worth the risk of her heart and more—she couldn't help thinking that he looked oddly as if he'd come to the same conclusion, that *she* was worth the risk of *his* heart.

She looked at him for a sweet, endless moment, and he at her. He was perfectly still, touching her with his eyes in a way that thoroughly disconcerted her. He swept them over and through her, bringing her own to meet his. The scent of him was warm in her lungs—a woodsy smell, mingled with sea air. She took a bracing gulp of the sweet-smelling stuff.

"C'mon." He took her hand in his. "We're leaving."

And Abby knew she was already gone.

Chapter Twenty-seven

The autumn air outside Rum Runner's was crisp and welcoming after the simmering intensity of Ryan's music.

His hand was warm and substantial around hers, giving her the extra measure of security she so desperately needed. "Thank you," she said, looking up at the lines of his profile. "That was incredible."

He looked down at her. Smiled. "Just well practiced."

"You're too modest." She remembered what he had said that night in the Captain's House, about how music had become the outlet he'd needed during the long, sleepless nights of his youth. "You were born with the talent to create, Ryan, and whether you do it with music or with paint, I don't think it matters. The point is, you're an artist." She felt the uneasy tightening of his hand around hers, but she wouldn't let him go. "And it was your gift that got you through."

"And what got you through?" he asked, looking at the thick spangling of stars that twinkled overhead.

Abby thought back. She'd had her own share of youthful sleepless nights, and had survived them by telling herself that she wasn't the first kid to endure the suicide of a parent, and sadly, she wouldn't be the last. "Telling myself that I wasn't alone. Losing myself in a book. That's where the idea for *Write Away* came from."

Ryan nodded approvingly, swinging her hand in time to their footfalls. "You know, I think I just figured out why I'm crazy about you."

Abby lifted a brow. "Do tell."

"I didn't have a choice," he said, leading her down Peg Leg Lane. "You see, a good many women have tried mighty hard to pin me down—"

"I take back what I said about your being modest."

Ryan chuckled. "But then you came along, and I didn't have a clue how to withstand a woman who was as strong as I was."

Abby pulled him to a stop beneath the shadow of a sprawling oak tree. Above them, the branches rattled and scratched amongst themselves, as if leaning in to better appreciate the goings-on beneath the shifting shadows they made. "So you settled upon the old adage: if you can't beat 'em, join 'em?"

The eyes that looked into hers were warm and mirthful. "Essentially, yes."

She rose onto her toes and planted a noisy kiss on his mouth. *Oh yes, he is so, so worth the risk.*

"You make me laugh, Brannigan," she said, smiling. "Immodesty and all, you make me laugh."

He kissed her, this time deeply and soundly, melting the smile from her lips and sending a scorching heat through her body. "Want to guess what you make me?" he asked huskily.

Abby grinned again, but an unexpected gust from

the sea made her shiver involuntarily. The image of Bartholomew burst into her mind. She shivered again, but this time, not from the cold, as she remembered his threats about the devil that was coming for her. "First, I have something to tell you. And where are we going, anyway—back to the Captain's House?"

"No," he said, linking his hands behind her waist and pulling her tight against his length. "I'm taking you to a place my father took your mother. I can't tell you what you really want to know about her, but I can show the places I know she's been. I don't know if that's any help to you—"

"Of course it is! Where is this place?"

"You wouldn't believe me if I told you—that's why I'm going to show you. Now, what did you want to tell me?"

Abby tried very hard to concentrate—which was a feat, considering the feelings elicited by his body pressing against hers. "I ran into Bartholomew Briggs tonight."

"And?"

Abby couldn't bring herself to say it—to make his raving real. Why should his words frighten her so deeply? Bartholomew was a madman and everyone knew it. "He, uh . . . he said that if I knew what was good for me, I'd leave. He said that the devil was going to come for me, like he came for my mother."

Even in the dim light afforded by the street lamp, she could see him blanch. The expression was fleeting, but she had seen it in his eyes: *fear.* "Don't tell me you believe him, Ryan?" she asked, hearing the panic in her own voice.

He took her into his arms. "No, no, I don't believe him, Abby. Bart's crazy, you know that. He only said that to you because you were the first person he saw. He'd have said it to the telephone pole if you hadn't been there."

"Are you sure?" Oh, she wanted him to be—she didn't want to leave Destiny Bay, not now that she'd found him.

His kiss on the top of her head was firm. "Yes, I'm sure."

"Good. There's one more thing."

Ryan frowned. "I'm not going to like it, am I?"

She took his hand again, started walking. "I told Ronnie about you and me," she said, biting her lip. "I hope you're not angry."

Ryan's face clouded. "Not angry, no. I should have done it myself." He took her hand and resumed walking. "How'd she take it?"

"Not well," she said, wondering to whom she should nominate herself for Understatement of the Year award. "I'm pretty sure she hates me."

"She'll be upset for a while, but she'll get over it."

"I doubt that," she said miserably.

"Ronnie's a forgiving person. Trust me on that."

"If you say so."

"I say so. Now, tell me, have you found any new information about your mother?"

"Not yet, but tomorrow I'm going to the gallery to have a look at some paintings. I was told that my mother may figure in one of them. Other than that, I've come up against a wall of silence."

Ryan shrugged. "Maybe that will crumble now as people realize that you know about Cora and Douglas and the part your mom played in their relationship." He said it without a hint of resentment, Abby noticed, and she squeezed his hand.

"You mean that all this time, people were keeping their mouths shut because they didn't want to hurt Cora by dredging up her past?"

"Yup. We do things like that for each other, here in Destiny Bay. We watch out for strangers," he said with a wink.

"That's sweet. A pain in the butt if you happen to *be* the stranger—"

Ryan chuckled.

"—but sweet, nonetheless." She stopped, linked her arms around his back. "Now, where *are* you taking me?"

Ryan's answering grin bordered on devilish. "Captain Jack's pirate cave."

"*What?*"

"You *can't* come to Destiny Bay and not visit Captain Jack's cave. Your mom even went."

"My mother went to a pirate's cave?" she asked incredulously.

"I know for a fact she was there at least once."

"Okay," Abby said at last. "But if we encounter any plundering pirates, it's on your head."

"The only plundering pirate you'll be encountering is me."

"Aye-aye, captain," she said, meeting his lips and suddenly wondering how Webster would define the word *plunder*. Funny . . . she'd never thought of the word in such delightful terms before.

Abby looked down—and instantly regretted it. Lit by the full moon, the ocean that surged beneath them was menacing, and far, too far away.

According to Ryan, who now walked slightly ahead of her on the path, this was the way to the pirate cave. Abby could see why—there was no doubt in her mind that whatever Captain Jack had put in his pirate cave, it would have been safe up here.

They walked in silence along the rocky inclines, dips and peaks that edged the heightening cliffs, choosing footholds seconds before leaping onto their precarious surfaces. Ryan led as though he had been born climbing, moving fluidly over the jagged profusion of lichen-edged stone.

The path—a narrow thread tracing the ascending curvature of the cliffs—was near enough to the edge to allow them both a spectacular view. Rising from the thundering surf at the base of the cliffs were gracefully curved stones, too numerous to count.

Ryan pulled her closer and pointed toward what appeared to be a darkened slash in the stone. "Over there. See?"

Abby looked more closely. "Is that the cave?"

"Yup."

Ryan led her over and slipped through the opening. Abby made certain that she was close on his heels. She emerged on the other side of the opening in a tunnel of stone.

They began inching down the slick decline of moss-covered stone, searching for dry footholds as they progressed. Conversation was forgotten, their steps slowed, as they peered down toward the darkened cave floor, both falling into a similar pattern of cautious, halting steps.

"Catch the rope," he said, then reached up and gripped an aged length of twisted hemp that was suspended near the top of the cave wall.

Abby gladly followed suit.

The rope ran the length of the cavern, and though it was enshrouded in several varieties of slime, she felt a great relief holding the substantial thickness of it in her hand.

The smell of the ocean was intensified, as were the earthy aromas of moist, green mosses and perpetually damp soil. With every breath, their cloying scents and warm, salty moisture filled her lungs.

Ryan's labored breath echoed her own as they descended farther into the ever-darkening tunnel. New aromas rose around them, seemingly stirred with each footfall. The scents were far less earthy and familiar and were heavy with the carnality of dark, moist places.

"What *is* this place?"

"You're about to find out." Ryan disappeared through a narrow opening.

She froze in her tracks, then let out a held breath as his hand reemerged.

She bit her lip in effort as she shimmied, feetfirst, through a narrow opening that revealed a shaft of welcoming light. Her heart beat faster as she squeezed through the oblong tear in the stones, and at last, lowered herself onto a ledge of rock beneath.

She looked around in amazement.

They stood on a ledge of stone maybe twelve feet square that seemingly jutted into space. Around her feet, spent candles slouched in glossy puddles of wax. Ryan lit the tallest of them.

The rich, mineral walls of the massive cavern surrounding them glistened with moisture. It dripped from a kaleidoscope of shapes that loomed eerily in the cave's muted light.

Water lapped at the bowed, seaward opening of the cave, and reached halfway to its apex. Beneath them surged the rising tide. The dark watermark of high tide reached a place about four feet beneath the shelf of rock supporting them.

"Wow," she whispered.

Ryan grinned smugly. "Brace yourself," he said.

"What do you mean, *'brace yourself'*?"

Ryan turned to watch the glistening water rise and obliterate the opening of the cave.

The water swelled, a slow, immense undulation that climbed the posterior wall of the cave. Then another swelling could be heard.

Curiosity overcame her apprehension. She watched the water as it was seemingly sucked through the back of the cave, and unraveled the mystery of it as a thunderous boom reverberated through the stone walls and echoed somewhere in the base of her abdomen.

Her eyes shot open in simultaneous shock and delight. "There's another cave!" she shouted over the amplified rush of water.

"Just behind this one, in fact," he said.

The flow was receding, leaving its glistening mark on the reddish walls.

"That other cave—is that where Captain Jack hid his treasure?"

Ryan frowned. "I didn't say he kept his treasure here. I don't even know if he ever *came* here—it's just a legend, about this being his cave."

"But I thought—" A tingling rushed over her skin. Abby felt suddenly feverish. No, it wasn't Ryan who had mentioned treasure in relation to the cave. It had been her mother. "How could I have forgotten?"

"Are you okay?" Ryan asked, rubbing her arms. "You look like you've seen a ghost."

"Remembered one, more like." She looked up at Ryan and took a deep breath. "It all came back to me just this second. My mother kept a diary. I found it years ago. There were only two or three entries, but the last one was a story, of sorts, of a secret cave where pirates once hid their treasure. In the story, a poor young artist takes his love there, because she was *his* treasure, and promised her that one day, he would crown her with jewels fit to make pirates mad with envy. But the lady dies before he can keep his promise, so he paints a portrait of her there." Abby swallowed loudly. The cave felt suddenly haunted, as if the pirate, the painter and the lady had crept from the sea to hear her tale. She clutched Ryan tighter, and he pulled her into the folds of his jacket. "He painted the finest jewels on earth onto his lady—the silver of the moon on her skin, the glow of the sea in her eyes, the gold of the sun in her hair. And after he, too, had died, the portrait was hung on the wall of the finest palace, a testament to the love they shared."

Ryan's eyes were intent upon hers, his expression guarded. He grasped her shoulders and turned her gently toward the cave wall.

Abby looked over her shoulder, searched his face, then turned her attention to the rough stone, where a rash of explicit graffiti was scrawled.

"Who's Helen?" she asked, staring at the praises paid to her upon the wall.

"Uh, she was regarded as a tutor, of sorts."

"I see," she said. "*Your* tutor?"

Ryan cleared his throat loudly. "Uh, sort of," he said, rocking back on his heels.

Abby gaped at a very explicit illustration. "And is this artistry *your* homage to Helen?"

"I like to think I can draw better than *that*," he said. "That was left by another admirer, I'm afraid."

"She had a few, I see."

Ryan shifted her slightly. "Forget Helen. Look over there." He pointed up higher.

Abby gasped. "Ryan," she said, shaking her head.

There, slightly above a large declivity in the rock was written in aged script:

Douglas
Celeste
Evermore

She reached out, let her fingers touch the faded words. "She did come here."

"*They* came here. They probably made love here."

Abby shivered.

Beneath the precipice, swirling whorls of unbridled ocean surged beneath them. Ever so lightly, Ryan nudged a pebble with his foot, watched it tumble over the edge and slip into the rising swell of ocean. Hungry for the falling stone, the sea rose in lazy invitation, swallowing the pebble soundlessly, eternally.

Yes, her mother had been here with the artist. Abby could almost feel her presence.

The cave greedily siphoned another mouthful of sea, then shuddered in response to the roar from the antechamber. The ripple of sound echoed down her spinal column.

Ryan pulled her closer.

Slowly, defiantly, her flesh began to ripen to his nearness—like the sun, coaxing crimson velvet from the milder tones of yellow in a tender, summer peach. With great deliberateness, she opened her eyes, almost wincing as her body seemed to turn in on itself and relish the shimmering warmth that radiated from him.

Her spine quivered involuntarily, drawing her body into the cadence of a shiver that whispered one word: *Ryan*.

"You are so incredibly beautiful," he said, barely audible over the returning rush of the sea.

She wondered, pointlessly, if it was his presence, or the magnificence of their surroundings that made her shiver, for every hair on her body stood erect; every inch of flesh was excruciatingly, alarmingly, alive.

"You know," Ryan said, "I watched you at Ronnie's party that first night. For a long time."

"Did you really?"

"I did." He lifted a lock of her hair and let it sift through his fingers like sand. "You were beautiful."

He grasped her hand, drawing her close enough to smell the warmth rising from his flesh. It was salty and male and utterly delicious.

Her cheek brushed against the smooth, bronze skin of his throat. Her flesh came away damp with the glistening veil of perspiration that was beaded on his skin.

"When I left you that night, I picked up a shell," he whispered. "I rolled it in my hands, tasted the salt it left on my fingers. I found the soft, pinkish caverns inside, and I thought of your skin." He stroked her cheek, light as a petal. "Right here," he said, and dipped his head to hers, brushing his lips across the sun-kissed flesh near the bridge of her nose. "They're two of a color."

"Ryan," she gasped, knowing, and yet not knowing what to say.

He lifted a length of her hair amidst his fingers, brought it to his face and inhaled, his eyes never leaving her face until they closed.

Strands of her hair entangled his lashes; breath caught in her throat as she felt the caress of tiny shivers, trickling like silver raindrops over her skin.

Abby stared into his face, searching the shadows that dwelt there and the shards of tiger gold that lit his eyes. They were fierce with an honesty she had never before seen there, with a desperation that thrilled her even as it frightened her.

"It's still hard to believe that this is happening," she said softly.

"*Believe* it," he said, his words breathy and ragged, his hands cupping her face. "Believe *me*."

And Abby felt the truth of their connection in every thud of her heart.

"Do you trust me, Abby?"

The sound of her heartbeat pulsed in her ears with the rising of tide as his question hung between them . . . *do you trust me?*

"I'm getting there," she said honestly.

He tilted her face up to his, his breath caressing her as his eyes searched hers. His hands circled her back, pressing her more deeply against his body. With each exhaling breath, she was molded more precisely into him.

"I want you, Abby. I've known it from the first moment I saw you."

She shook her head, feeling suddenly afraid, suddenly gripped by the familiar fears that had demanded she hold love at arm's length. Her mother's story of doomed love seemed to fill the cave with misgiving, seemed to make every pitfall of love all too real. "No. No, you didn't."

"I did," he said insistently. "I just wouldn't believe it. I didn't want to believe that I could be so completely out of control of my emotions. I didn't want to believe words like 'surrender' were in my vocabulary."

"And are they?" she asked quietly.

"You tell me." Then, in a motion as natural as the rising tide that surged beneath them, he pressed his lips to hers. He whispered her name against her lips as they parted in answer to his tongue.

With an exquisite gentleness, he removed the barriers between them, first her clothes, then his. She heard her sharp intake of breath fall softly against the moistness of his throat; she felt his fingers knot in her hair.

He cradled her head and explored each and every secret place of mouth and neck and breasts—as gently as if plying open the petals of a rose.

The sea's heady incense caressed them as Ryan washed through her like the tide, surging through her veins like an aged and potent wine, dissolving every fear in her mind, reminding her of what she really, truly wanted.

She was breathless at the taste of him—pure male and salt and warmth.

"Say it, Abrielle." He caught her face in his hands, searching her eyes. "Say you trust me. I want to hear the words on your tongue." The demand was not softened by the quiet of his voice, for the desire in his eyes was anything but questioning. They penetrated her own, seeming to strip her heart of pretense, to strip it of fear.

The tragic love story was just that—a story. This was real.

The cave worked a spell upon her, anointing their bodies with its salty moisture, filling their lungs with earthy aromas that awoke the need to be purely, achingly human.

"Yes," she breathed, unable to tear her eyes from his

gaze. "I trust you." The words tore at her heart even as they filled it with relief. "Do you trust *me*? Will you promise me your heart, Ryan?"

Ryan's silent answer simmered dangerously through his flesh and scorched her own with sudden certainty. He grasped her arms, lifting her closer to his face. Beneath his fingers, she felt the tender flesh darken in protest—she would wear the evidence of his desire within hours—and yet it seemed to thrum in warm, defiant pleasure.

"You have my heart, Abby, I swear it," he said fiercely. He drew her closer, so that his words were spelled out upon her lips. "You have everything."

Abby clung to him fiercely, her breath meeting his in the moist air between them, yet his eyes did not stir. His body was still but for the rise and fall of his chest. "And you, Abby? What do you offer in return?"

She spread her fingers wide over the front of his chest. His heart beat strongly beneath them, seeming to echo the rhythm of hers.

Slowly, she pressed her body into his, wrapped her legs around his waist so that he could join them in the most intimate way of all. She tilted her head, touching her lips to the bronzed hollow of his throat. "What you get is all of me."

His flesh trembled beneath the touch of her mouth, sending a twin cadence through her being.

"Ryan!" She caught what air she could before her mouth was devoured in a kiss that answered every silenced need, that whispered of luscious, dark places she'd never imagined she possessed.

Abby met his kiss with identical fervency. A burning swath of flesh tingled across her cheek in response to the rasp of his unshaven skin.

She yielded entirely to the pressure of his body within hers as they lured each other into a rhythm as old as the sea, and nearly as powerful.

Ryan locked her fingers between his, spreading her arms wide and pressing her back against the wet cave wall. She was open to him, completely, as he devoured her mouth again with his.

His every touch spoke of passionate surrender, and demanded the same of her. She cried out beneath him, aching for more.

He must have felt it, too, for the quality of their touching intensified.

"Abrielle," he groaned, stroking her face.

And then he said nothing more, but traced the shape of her lips with the tip of his tongue. She touched hers to his, and tasted infinite longing there.

She savored it breathlessly, drawing him into her mouth and sighing her pleasure into the warmth of his. There was no doubt in her mind that many people had been drugged by the atmosphere of this cave, had made love on this precipice. She was also certain that her mother and the artist had been counted among them.

He took her then, driving her over the precipice to a surrender so sweet, Abby knew she was gone for good.

"I knew you'd be worth the wait," he said once he'd recovered his breath. With his finger, he drew a strand of hair from her face, tucking it behind her ear. "Treasures always are."

She couldn't speak, so she only looked up at him, and all around them, the cave thundered.

Chapter Twenty-eight

The day of her visit to the gallery had come at last—and not a moment too soon. She desperately needed to feel that she was making some progress in the search for her mother's past, because she'd come to an impasse.

But her trip to Destiny Bay had been far from a failure. She'd found Ryan, after all . . . and she'd opened her heart, along with his.

A quiet thrill pierced her belly at the thought of him, at the memory of the pirate's cave. She'd fallen in love, plain and simple.

Abby stood beneath the storefront awning of Extraordinaire, enjoying the sweet aroma of Belgian chocolate wafting enticingly into the street. She knew the scent well, having become one of Delia Larsen's most loyal customers. She recognized also the metallic aroma of the butcher shop that mingled with it in a sickeningly sweet whorl of scent. Overlying them both was the thickness of the air, heavy with rain.

This was what she was beginning to expect from Destiny Bay: the enticing, the lovely, the charming—all underscored by the startlingly discordant.

As thrilled as she was about Ryan, she couldn't deny that there was still something amiss in Destiny Bay. Number one, she hadn't been able to get in touch with Ronnie since their confrontation on the street in front of Rum Runner's. Number two . . . the stalker.

He hadn't left her any disturbing tokens recently, but Abby felt certain that he was still out there, and still obsessed.

A splash of rain jerked her back to reality. She ran her

fingers over the supple leather of her shoulder bag, felt the
swells and groves of its contents and noted the columnar
shape of her umbrella. She would need it.

As if in silent agreement, the swiftly darkening sky let
fall the first smattering drops of what promised to be
nothing short of a torrential downpour.

Abby scurried across the street to the West Shore
Gallery.

"Good morning, Abby!" The gallery owner swooped
down upon her, helped her off with her coat, and swung it
over a hanger with a flourish. He was short, stout, and
dressed from head to foot in black. His reddish, thinning
hair was spiked and stiff with gel, and intelligent gray eyes
peeked out from behind trendy glasses. "I was thrilled to
get your call, darling. *Thrilled!* I've been waiting to have
you in my gallery since I first learned you were coming to
Destiny Bay."

"I'm glad to be here, Kyle," she said. "I so appreciate
your opening early for me."

"Anything for art's sake," he said pleasantly. "Now,
would you like to go straight to the McAllister Room, or
would you prefer the grand tour?"

"I'd like to go straight there," she said. "But I'd be happy
to see the entire collection before I leave."

Kyle brightened. "Oh, that would be no trouble at all."
He snatched a fuchsia feather duster from a pedestal, eyes
wide with chagrin at the sight if it, and tucked it under his
arm. "I'll take you to the McAllister Room now."

Abby walked with Kyle through the rooms of paintings,
sculpture and folk art. She recognized the McAllister
Room as soon as she set foot in the place. Color-splashed
canvases filled the room; glimpses of ocean, air and land
were an invitation in and of themselves.

"I'll leave you so that you can fully enjoy the art," Kyle
said softly. "McAllister is best appreciated in silence."

"Thank you," she said as she sat quietly on a bench. Her

purse slipped down the length of her arm, landing on the floor with a dull thud.

Directly in front of her was a painting that captured a spindly scrub pine leaning over the ocean as if trying to sweep foam from the waves. To the left of that was a stylized version of the view from her living room window.

Abby took her time, breathing in the man's talent, wondering at the train wreck of his life, the pity of his death, and the sad fact that his body was not discovered or even missed—if rumor was to be believed—until weeks after he'd died, when the snow finally melted from Cragan Cliff.

Poor Ryan. Poor Cora. Poor everyone that man ever touched.

"No pretty lady on the rocks—gone she is," came a tremulous whisper. "Gone they *both* are; the artist and his muse." Bartholomew Briggs stood on the threshold of the door, kneading his grimy cap and staring forlornly at the collected work of Douglas McAllister.

Abby looked up slowly, her heart hammering in her chest. Part of her wanted to run, but he looked so harmless, so lost. There was something different about him that she couldn't put her finger on—something that made loss emanate from his flesh like an advancing fog. Nothing about him was frightening. Perhaps this would be the best possible time to talk to him, to express how she'd felt when he'd frightened her. Perhaps she might even learn if he was the one behind the note, the flowers and the ring.

"Bartholomew," she said gently, so as not to startle him, "please, come in." She slid down the bench, glancing toward the door and hoping that Kyle Gibbons would not choose this moment to make an appearance.

The shelf of Bartholomew's brow lifted as his gaze at last fell upon her. "Ye'r like her."

Abby knew exactly whom he was talking about. "She

was my mother," she said softly. "Did you know her, Bartholomew?"

Bartholomew answered with an indecipherable grumbling from the back of his throat. His nod was nearly imperceptible, and he made no move to approach Abby or the bench she patted encouragingly.

"Tell me about the pretty lady on the rocks."

Bartholomew cast her a sidelong gaze, lips trembling within the nest of gray bristles that sprouted around them. "She's gone. Pretty lady's gone away," he sang quietly as he inched deeper into the room, clasping his hands behind his back.

Abby rose and slowly approached him. "Did you see her on the rocks, Bartholomew? The pretty lady?"

His mouth split in a toothy grin that nudged leathery folds of skin up to his eyes. Abby stepped back, not sure if she was repulsed or fascinated by the man's extraordinarily grotesque features.

"I see her now," he said cryptically.

Abby let her gaze follow the direction of his watery eyes.

She ran to the wall, only inches away from the paintings, searching frantically from frame to frame, seeing nothing— no one—that resembled her mother.

She spun to face him. "Where?" she asked. "*Where* do you see her, Bartholomew?"

The grin was back—toothy and foul-breathed. "I sees her everywhere," he said. "She's there," he said, pointing to a picture of an ocean storm. "There's the color of her eyes. I see her right in front of me." He looked Abby up and down, his expression bordering on leering.

Abby's heart sank. The man wasn't in his right mind. What did that make *her* for pinning hopes on him? "Great," she said quietly. She picked up her purse, hitched it on her shoulder, and made for the door. She'd come back another time, when it was quieter.

"Leavin', without so much as a good-bye to your mother?"

"I'll be seeing you, Bartholomew."

Her heels made muffled thuds on the floor as she walked toward the door.

Then, she saw it. It was a small painting, and the plaque beneath it read: NUDE WOMAN BATHING.

She stood directly in front of the picture, hands braced on either side.

"Ah," came the knowing sigh from behind her, then, a wheezy chuckle. "Found her, did you?"

"Mother."

It was her, thigh deep in ocean water that eddied around her legs. One hip thrust forward, eyes shut, hands smoothing water-slick hair down her back. Abby's eyes searched the background.

"Where is this?" she asked—more to herself than anyone else.

"It's the pirate's cave."

Abby jumped at the sound of his whisper, so close to her ear.

He was right, of course. She saw the shelf of stone that shot out into the well of the cave just slightly over her mother's shoulder.

"How on earth did they get down there? It must be deadly," she said, remembering the churning current.

"Ah, you've been to the pirate's cave, 'ave you?" Bartholomew was grinning in a way that made Abby squirm.

She didn't have to answer in the affirmative to let him know the truth of it, and that much she knew for sure. She felt her cheeks flush. She squared her shoulders. "How did you know about this painting?"

"Bartholomew has eyes that see, and ears that hear," he said, his voice heavy with secrets. "Bartholomew is a tree; Bartholomew is a stone. No one sees Bartholomew, but he sees all."

"I see you," Abby said, "and I know you know things.

Things about my mother. Tell me, Bartholomew—tell me about her." She reached out, grasped his fingers in hers, felt the electric-sharp jolt of his body as their skin met.

"There's secrets in the cave," he said. "Best you don't go near the place. Best you don't take the lower entrance and wade into the water, like your ma did, No, no. Best you don't do that."

"What lower entrance?" she asked frantically. She was losing him—she could see his eyes were beginning to go soft and distant. "What secrets?" she pleaded, grabbing his shoulders and shaking urgently.

"Run away, little girl!" he sang out, his voice discordantly shrill in the small room.

"Bartholomew Briggs!" Kyle Gibbons stood in the door, hands fisted on hips. "How many times have I told you not to come in here?"

Bartholomew turned an icy-cold grin on the owner, stretched his neck forward and hissed at the man.

"Out!" Kyle barked, his finger pointing the way. "Don't make me call the sheriff, Bartholomew. Out!"

Bartholomew lumbered past Kyle, a hump of tattered layers, muttering wildly. "Yo, ho, ho, and a bottle of rum! That's what the pirates sang, oh yes, it was."

Abby heard the thudding of Kyle's feet against the rugs, the indignant slam of the door as Bartholomew exited.

Another succession of thuds, and Kyle reappeared in the doorway. "I'm so sorry, Abby! I've told that man a hundred times to stay out of here! Honestly, I don't know how he manages to get past me."

Abby placed a soothing hand on his elbow. "Think nothing of it, Kyle. He seems harmless."

"Yes, well," Kyle said, sounding as if he were agreeing more to be polite than for any other reason.

"Tell me, Kyle, are any of the McAllister works for sale?"

"Oh no. They're all owned by an avid collector."

"May I ask the name of the collector?"

"You may, but I'm not at liberty to tell." Kyle winked delightedly. "It's a matter of the utmost confidentiality."

"I see." Abby peered more closely at the painting of her mother. "And is this the only one with this woman in it?"

"Lovely, isn't she? It's the only one *I* know of." Kyle looked from the painting to Abby, eyes widening. He slapped his hand to his chest. "Oh, it couldn't be . . . it is! Oh, Abby, this is too much! It's your mother, isn't it?"

Her cheeks blushed furiously. It was one thing to look at the picture herself—but to have her mother's naked body looked upon by strangers . . . she forced back the hand that rose to cover her mother's flesh. "I believe it is," she said quietly. "Kyle, I understand that you're unable to disclose the name of the owner, but perhaps you could contact him yourself and express my interest in this painting. Naturally, I'd offer you a handsome bonus for your trouble."

"Oh, of course I could!" He grasped her by the elbow and the two made way toward the door. "Give me a day or two, hmm?"

"I'd be so appreciative." She looked out into the street, where the sun now glinted in puddles. "Interesting weather you folks have here," she said with a lifted brow.

"Oh, you know what we say. If you don't like the weather, just wait a minute."

Abby air-kissed his cheeks and Kyle chuckled delightedly. "Oh, I just love city folk!"

"And *I* love that painting," she said pointedly. "In fact, I think I might go explore the lower entrance of the pirate's cave where this was painted."

Kyle blanched. "Oh, Abby, what on earth put that notion into your head? You'd be killed for sure!"

"What? I've been there before and I survived just fine, thank you very much."

"Through the upper entrance, I'll wager. Abby, *no one*

goes into the lower entrance of the pirate's cave. People have been killed there. They call it Devil's Throat, and not many who've ventured there have lived to tell about it."

"Devil's Throat?" she asked, blanching. "Why Devil's Throat?"

Kyle linked his elbow with hers, leaning down conspiratorially. "Well, about twenty years ago, a few college kids who came home for the summer decided to go in through the lower entrance. They swam for a bit, but then the tide started to rise. Of the five kids who went in, only two came out. The other three bodies were never found. One of the survivors said the current was so wicked that it felt like he was being gargled by Old Scratch, himself."

"Hence, Devil's Throat."

Kyle nodded sagely. "You can't go down there, Abby. You just can't. There's nothing there to see, anyway."

Abby's shoulders slumped. Another dead end.

"And who in their right mind would suggest you explore that place?"

"Well, no one *exactly* suggested it."

"No one *exactly?*"

"It was Bartholomew, okay?"

Kyle gaped. "Bartholomew? You accepted tourist information from Bartholomew—the town lunatic?"

"He showed me the painting of my mother and told me there were secrets in the cave."

"Well, you can trust me that what you saw in that painting is artistic license. No one, including McAllister, would have been foolish enough to venture down into Devil's Throat."

Chapter Twenty-nine

The Lover crouched in the closet behind a rack of outdated clothing that smelled old and neglected. It had been difficult, prying his way into Cora's house, but he knew it would be worth it.

Cora, he knew, snored lightly down the hall in her own room. He'd discovered that Abby had been staying here since abandoning Artist's Cottage.

But there was that one night he couldn't account for . . . he couldn't bear to think where Abrielle might have been or whom she might have been with. If he thought too hard, he might come up with the answer, and then he'd have to punish her. And she was too lovely to punish. Yet.

Yes, there was still time to sway her to him, and he vowed with every fiber of his being that he would try his hardest. He *refused* to believe that she couldn't be saved—that she was as lost a cause as his mother had been.

His thoughts stilled as he heard the floorboards creak. Breathlessly, he parted the garments he crouched behind, affording himself a view through the cracked-open door.

Abrielle had just entered, wearing decidedly modest pajamas consisting of pale green pants and a matching tee shirt. She had a cup of tea in her hand, which she placed on the bedside table beside her book—a weighty thing entitled *The History and Lore of Saint Cecelia Island.* Yawn. He could think of much better things she could do with her time.

The thought made him dizzy with lust. Oh, yes, she would be his . . . and the things she would do to him!

He closed his eyes tightly, forcing his mind back to the matter at hand. Accomplishing his goal would require precision timing and more than a little luck. He conjured the image of his lovely Celeste in his mind and invoked her loving spirit. *Prevail upon your daughter, my darling. Make her mine, as you once were.*

As if in answer, Abby padded out of the room.

He waited just long enough to be certain she was gone. Sure enough, he heard the bathroom door close and the faucet turn on with a squeak.

Silently, The Lover slipped from his hiding place and crept into the softly lit room. From his pocket, he withdrew a small vial of white powder, opened it, and poured the contents into the steaming tea. He stirred it quickly, his ears attuned to any sound in the hall.

The powder dissolved completely in the tea. Just enough Rohypnol to make her groggy, compliant and forgetful. Getting his hands on it had been as easy as taking candy from a baby—or at least from the college kid he'd caught trying to slip it into a blonde's drink down at Rum Runner's. He'd always known those packages he swiped off the kid would come in handy.

The Lover sidled back into the closet just as Abby entered the room, yawning hugely.

She slipped into the bed, smiling softly to herself— could it be she knew what was coming? He grinned at the thought. Yes, he had always been particularly adept at pleasing women.

Drink up, my precious, he thought as she brought the teacup to her lips and sipped contentedly. *Yes, that's it.*

The Lover missed Celeste so much it hurt. He couldn't help thinking of her as he watched her daughter sip the drugged tea.

When would that Rohypnol kick in?

As quietly as possible, he slid down the wall and crouched at its base.

As much as he had tried to resist of late, that night kept coming back to him—the night his lovely Celeste died.

He had been there. He'd seen her body lying on the ground. Her head bent at an impossible angle, beautiful hair splayed upon the flagstone terrace like a halo.

His terror had been palpable, gargantuan; a creature mutating millisecond by millisecond until it filled him with paralyzing anguish.

Weeping, he had lain beside her, cradled her in his arms, kissed her mouth, touched her soft skin, until at last, the sun rose. Then he had watched over her from the shelter of the bushes until she was discovered by the cook, whose scream was a black serpent, slithering from the heart of her and twining with his own snakelike grief that coiled and swayed in the sky above all Regency Park, above all the world.

It was too much to think about, and so, he dared another peek at Abrielle.

She was slumped against her pillows, the tea spilt over the yellow comforter.

He emerged from the closet and stared down at her, his heart breaking with love.

He touched her cheek, and it was as soft as he'd known it would be.

No, tonight he would not make love to her as he had planned. He would just hold her, the way he had held his lovely Celeste all those years ago.

The Lover stripped off his clothing and slid into bed beside Abrielle. Gently, he removed her clothing, too. He held her soft, naked body against him, cradled her in his arms, kissed her mouth, touched her smooth skin, until at last, the wicked, hateful sun began to rise.

Chapter Thirty

Abby drove down the cobblestone streets of the town, mind wandering as she made her way toward Cora's, where a lunch of seafood chowder awaited her.

She'd spent the morning with the O'Donnells, but had learned little else about her mother. It was probably just as well, she thought. Her head was aching so badly and her mind so fuzzy that she likely wouldn't have absorbed anything, anyway.

For the life of her, she couldn't figure out why she felt this way. Emotional exhaustion was the only plausible answer she could come up with, because she'd never been so wiped out that she fell asleep with her tea still in her hand, and she had absolutely no recollection of taking off her pajamas. She blushed. What if Cora had walked in?

This business about Bart had her mind in knots.

What did Bartholomew know about the pirate's cave and the portrait that had been painted in it? Had he spied on the painter and his muse, possibly even witnessed their lovemaking? With the booming of the surf, it would be easy enough to lurk unnoticed just outside the narrow opening to the cave.

Abby bit her fingernail, considering. *The next time I see Bart,* she decided, *I'm going to try to talk to him.*

Abby was beginning to feel that somewhere inside his spectacularly convoluted mind, he knew something about her mother. Maybe he didn't even *know* that he knew.

Abby was beginning to think that old Bart knew more about this island than anyone gave him credit for. What had he said to her at the gallery?

"Bartholomew has eyes that see, and ears that hear," he had

said, his voice heavy with secrets. *"Bartholomew is a tree; Bartholomew is a stone. No one sees Bartholomew, but he sees all."*

Yes, she had to get to know him, to lure out the secrets he likely didn't even know he kept. She'd buy him coffee, she'd build his trust. But first, she'd talk to him about the cave. Were there really secrets in it, or was that only the ramblings of a disturbed old man?

In front of the French Pastry Shoppe, a white-faced mime did his best imitation of a man trapped in a box and unable to escape into the delectably aromatic bakery. Abby barely spared him a passing glance, for just there, on the periphery of her vision, she could have sworn she'd seen the familiar hump of tatters and rags that was Bartholomew Briggs.

She swerved into a parking spot, jammed the car into park, and leapt from the vehicle.

All that was visible of the strange man was the tail of his coat as he disappeared into an alley. Abby glanced both ways and raced across the street—hand held up to hold back the meager noonday traffic.

"Bartholomew! Bartholomew, wait!"

Still, he retreated into the darkness of the alley, as if he hadn't heard her.

Abby picked up her pace, scampered around the dining tables that dotted a sidewalk café, wove around a man sweeping his store steps and she ducked into the alley.

She stopped short as her eyes adjusted to the shadowy gloom.

In contrast to the charming streets that were trademark Destiny Bay, the alley could have been in any town. Dingy, dirty, hemmed in on either side by brick and smelling strongly of garbage, it was the last place she'd imagined finding herself. Or anyone else, for that matter.

She wrinkled her nose and started forward, peeking around industrial Dumpsters and calling out cautiously. "Bartholomew?"

Like a startled pheasant, a mound of raggedy clothing erupted at her feet, darting into the depths of the alley. Abby lurched back. *I shouldn't follow any farther, I really shouldn't . . .*

She broke into a run, calling his name and closing the gap between them with every stride. Finally, she grabbed his arm and pulled.

Bartholomew spun toward her, and Abby looked into a face so remarkably homely she could scarcely tear her eyes away.

"Oh," he crooned, eyes glinting like shards of glass amidst the leather folds of his face. "'Tis the pretty miss, coming to see Bartholomew, eh?"

Abby winced at the foulness of breath that wafted onto her face, sweet with decay. "Bartholomew, when we were at the gallery you told me there were secrets in the cave. Do you remember that?"

Bartholomew's grin revealed a row of rotting teeth. "Too pretty to be chasin' after Barty, she is; too pretty for the likes of me."

Again, she grabbed his greasy coat. "Focus, Bartholomew. What do you know about the cave?"

Bartholomew turned away, trundled deeper into the alley, muttering all the while.

Abby dropped her arms to her side, exasperation fueling an audible sigh, and loped after the lumbering figure of Bartholomew.

The light cut at her sharply, and Abby lifted her hand to shield her eyes from the daylight into which they had both emerged.

As far as she could tell, she had been led into a vehicle demolition site. Wrecked cars had been stacked ten high, creating a maze into which her reluctant tour guide seemed intent on vanishing.

"I want an answer, Bartholomew," she said, arms folded

across her chest. "Are you the one who's been spying on me, leaving me threatening notes?"

Fast enough to make her lurch, Bartholomew whirled, charged toward her. Abby took a step back, feeling suddenly very fearful.

The eyes she looked into were no longer glazed, no longer wandering. "If I was trying to hurt you, do you think you ought to be here with me . . . far from anyone who'd hear you scream?"

Abby swallowed and stepped back, eyes scanning the wreckage around her for an escape route.

Bright, focused eyes the color of coal glared into hers. He stepped toward her, his posture threatening and his tone icy. "Better watch out or you'll come face-to-face with what waits for you in the shadows."

A flush of fear crept up her throat, stained her cheeks crimson. "What are you talking about?"

"Well," he said, so softly that she had to lean in close to hear, "since you're too daft to be fittingly frightened, you'll likely find out soon, won't you?"

Abby's reply caught in her throat. She stepped back, recoiling from the unmistakably menacing tone of his voice. Her eyes darted around frantically. She was trapped, physically hampered by the barrier of wrecks, and emotionally pinioned by his terrifying suggestion.

Breath exploded from her lungs when she heard the sound of tires on gravel, saw a flash of white, and then a cruiser creep into her line of sight.

She waved her arms, almost crumpling with relief. "Over here!"

A single wail of the siren was enough to make Bartholomew jolt. Abby watched in disbelief as he smiled sidelong at her. Then, the lucid expression melted from his features.

All at once, he was the town vagrant again. He turned

slowly, looked at the car with eyes gone distant and mouth hanging slack.

"Don't you be bothering the ladies, Bart." Connor Flynn leaned out of the window of his cruiser, words directed to Bartholomew, but eyes intent on Abby. "You ought to know that puts Sheriff in a right foul mood. You okay, Miss Lancaster?"

"I . . . I'm fine." She glanced back at Bartholomew, saw the familiar vague expression resume as he blinked at her. "Thank you, Deputy Flynn. I'll, uh, just be on my way."

"Warned her, I did. Warned her 'bout that old devil, comin' to get her . . ." Bartholomew's voice trailed after his shuffling frame, as he disappeared behind a tower of crushed vehicles.

A snakelike tendril of apprehension slithered down her spine.

Flynn watched the man's retreat with a peculiar expression on his face. He turned to Abby. "You know, it seems to me that if you suspect Bart's behind all this business up at the cottage, you'd want to steer clear of him."

"You're right," she said, chafing her arms with her hands. "I thought for a moment that he could be reasoned with, but clearly I was way off."

His lifted his brows. "I'd say. Now, technically speaking, I'm not supposed to give people rides in my squad car, but under the circumstances I could make an exception."

Abby managed a smile. "Thank you, but no. I'm just parked up there," she said, motioning toward the alley. She turned to leave, then remembered something she'd wanted to discuss with him.

"Deputy Flynn? I was wondering," she said. "Did you ever run a lab test on that note I left with you? I've been waiting to submit my blood for analysis, but I haven't heard anything."

Connor's face clouded. "Well, now, about that. Seems we can't find that note anywhere."

Abby gaped. "You *lost* it?"

"I'm sure it's not lost, just misplaced," he said soothingly. "It'll turn up, don't you worry."

"Right." She turned to leave, not at all surprised by this latest turn of events. Sheriff Flynn was behind the disappearance of that note—she'd be willing to bet on it.

"You sure you don't want a lift? I'd be happy to take you to your car."

Right about now, the last thing she wanted was another close encounter with a Destiny Bay man. "I'm sure. But if you could just keep your eye on me until I'm through the alley, I'd really appreciate it."

Connor tipped his head. "I'd be happy to."

Just try not to lose me, she almost said, but thought better of it.

"Thanks." Abby glanced back over her shoulder as she retreated. To her utter relief, the cruiser stayed in place, Deputy Flynn watching her make her way into the alley and head toward the haven of her car. Somewhere amidst the wrecks, Bartholomew still shuffled, still muttered. Or did he?

She looked around at the rusted hulks of forgotten vehicles, the relics of another age. Looked at all the places a person could hide . . . or could be hidden. She rubbed her arms to ward off the chill of unease that had settled there.

Abby closed her eyes, attempting to ward off a thought that was just too unsettling for words.

What if Bart wasn't actually the incompetent everyone thought he was? What if he was very, very sane?

That, she decided, would be a dangerous situation, indeed.

Ryan was right. And so was the White Lady.

There was no doubt she was in danger.

Abby hadn't been able to concentrate on anything but

the realization that her safety had been jeopardized, and it was looking more and more like Bartholomew Briggs was the culprit. Even keeping her mind on Cora's delectable seafood chowder had been an effort.

A rustling from the hallway closet snagged her attention, bringing her firmly into the here and now.

Cora poked her head back into the kitchen. "Here it is," she said triumphantly, walking into the kitchen with both arms hidden behind her back and what looked like an anticipatory smile on her face.

"Cora, you really shouldn't have brought me a gift," Abby said in protest. "You're already too kind."

"Nonsense! Besides, it's not like I went out shopping. This is something I've owned for a while, and I think that you ought to have it." She pulled the painting, *Nude Woman by Candlelight*, from behind her back.

Abby gaped in confusion at the painting. "Cora, how did you get this? Kyle told me the owner was a closely guarded secret."

Cora's smile was soft. "I'm the owner, Abby. At least I was. Now it's yours."

Abby looked from Cora to the painting. "I don't understand. You own *all* of them?"

"Yes. I do. And they'll be Ryan's one day. Whether or not he wants them."

"You're giving him his father."

Cora sighed sadly. "I pray he'll soften to the idea of it one day. Douglas was what he was, and unrepentant along with it. Complete, utter failure as a father, a lover, a friend, but, by the heavens, *he was an artist*," she said quietly, fiercely, eyes glistening. "And he was my son's father. Two qualities that redeem him in the face of every other failure."

Abby touched Cora's arm, squeezing gently. "He'll thank you one day, Cora. I'm sure of it." She pulled Cora into an embrace that hinted at a child's longing for a mother; that answered Cora's generosity and spoke a volume more. "And I'll thank you *now*."

"You're welcome, luv. Here," she said, patting Abby's arm, "put that down and come help me clean up these dishes."

Reluctantly, she set the painting aside—promising herself a good long examination of it as soon as she was alone—and followed Cora to the sink.

"Cora," she said, forcing out the words, "I have to talk to you about Bart."

She told Cora everything: about the gallery, about the alley, about the terrifying transformation that took place right before her eyes.

Cora frowned. She plunged her hands into the iridescent bubbles and emerged with a sudsy plate. She rinsed it under a stream of water, then handed it to Abby. "Old Bart's always been a little off, you realize—even when he was young. Are you sure he appeared lucid?"

Abby dried the plate and shelved it with the others. "I'm telling you, Cora, it would be hard to imagine anyone *more* lucid. It was the eyes," she said, grasping a bowl and running her cloth over it. She shivered minutely. "They were like ice. So cold, so focused . . . he looked right into my heart, saw everything I feared and spoke it aloud."

"You mean the business about something waiting in the shadows?"

Abby lifted a brow. "Something waiting in the shadows isn't enough?"

"Oh, I didn't mean that, deary," Cora said quickly, arm scrubbing at a pot. "All I meant was that he could have said those words to anyone, see. He's *always* imagined things lurking in shadows, around corners, in closets . . . drove his mom and dad batty with his imaginings, he did."

Abby accepted the pot, ran her cloth over its surface thoughtfully. "What if he was right?"

"What if he's just crazy?" Cora answered, just as quickly.

"Mentally ill, Cora."

"Quite right. Mentally ill, it is."

Abby bit her lip, understanding Cora's reasoning, yet unsettled in her heart. "So, when he said those words, it was simply coincidence that I may actually *have* someone lurking in my shadows?"

Cora frowned at the idea. "So it seems." She reached into the depths of the sink, pulled the stopper, and dried her hands as the water drained. "I think it's time you gave up the cottage, Abby, just for a bit. I know you'd hoped to move back in this weekend, but I'd really rather you didn't. I've a nice little apartment on Musket Lane, right next to my cousin Dotty's son, Reginald. He's a big man, aye? He'd be able to put a right clobberin' on anyone who's got designs on you."

"I think you're right," she said sadly.

"Oh, I *am* glad to hear it. I've been fair concerned over this stalker business, Abby. I know Ryan will be more than happy to help you move." Cora handed her another plate. "Speaking of Ryan . . . Mavis mentioned that she's seen him about town. With you," she added, sounding far too smug.

"She did, did she?"

"Well, her and half the folk in town. Don't keep me in suspense, deary—have you nabbed that son of mine?"

Abby threw her head back and laughed. "Cora, you are the most startlingly direct woman I've ever met!"

"And *you* the most evasive."

Abby looked at Cora, felt her cheeks blushing warmly and her heart beating happily. "I want to make him happy. I want that so much it shocks me."

"That's what they call 'love,' deary." Cora's eyes were intent on the bubbles in the sink. "And, so I don't start boo-hooing, let's have a change of subject, eh?

"It bothers me that you're being deliberately frightened,

Abby. Even if it *is* only by Bartholomew Briggs. I've always considered the possibility that one day, his harmless ramblings and oddities could take a darker turn. It seems," she said quietly, "that they finally have."

Chapter Thirty-one

Ryan hung up the phone with a satisfied smile. The packing plant in Marriot's Bay was his. An appointment with his lawyer to discuss the details of the lease was in order, but for now, the workday was done.

He shrugged on his jacket with a smile, not even able to recall the last time he'd been anxious to leave work for the day. Sure, there was a mountain of paperwork fit to keep him at his desk for another several hours, but he had more pressing matters to attend.

He grabbed the bouquet of roses he'd purchased on his lunch hour and grinned down at them. Abby would love them. They were the softest pink the florist had—*perfectly delicate*, she'd said as she wrapped them. Something about them reminded him of Abby.

"You leaving?" asked Johnny Mac as he passed. "But it's only four o'clock." His eyes fell to the flowers and glinted knowingly. "I *see*. Got yourself a little action, eh?"

"The only action you need to concern yourself with is table seven," he said, trying to sound stern but failing. Jeez, his work ethic was going to hell in a handbasket. "Their glasses are empty."

He walked into the sunlight, realizing, suddenly, that there was a spring in his step. He did his best to rectify it before anyone noticed and loped around the back of the bar toward the parking lot.

He stopped suddenly, a chill clutching the back of his

neck. A piece of white paper secured beneath his windshield wiper fluttered in the wind.

He snatched the paper, glaring at it for a split second before the words sank into his mind and clutched his heart like a vise. Adrenaline surged through his limbs in answer to the instinctive call to fight or flight.

Touch her again, and she will die

As if in a dream, he heard the back door of Rum Runner's screech open, heard Johnny Mac making yet another wisecrack as he lumbered to the trash bin and tossed in a bag.

"Abby," Ryan said, more to himself than to Johnny.

"Oh," said Johnny, wiping his hands down his pant legs. "So that's where the action is."

Fight or flight?

Ignoring Johnny, Ryan slid behind the wheel and jammed his foot on the gas.

Fight. *Definitely* fight.

Ryan burst into his mother's house, breath tight in his chest. "Where is she?"

Cora all but swallowed her teacup. "Wh-what? Who?"

"Abby!" he said as he raced into the living room, searching for signs of her. "I need to talk to her. Where is she?"

In what he could only describe as a typical response to his heightened state, Cora seemed to sink purposefully into her seat and draw calmness around her like a blanket. "Whatever are you on about, son?"

Ryan fell to a crouch before her, grasped her shoulders and squeezed as gently as he could—which he feared was not very gentle at all. "Work with me, Mom," he said, his heart threatening to jump out of his chest. "Where's Abby?"

"Well, I imagine she's back at the cottage packing up,"

she said placidly. "I've finally convinced her to move into town where she'll be safer. What is all the fuss about?"

Ryan grabbed the now-rumpled paper out of his pocket and tossed it onto her lap. He strode across the room, raking his fingers through his hair.

"Oh no," she gasped.

"Yeah, that was my thought, exactly." Struck with sudden inspiration, Ryan pulled his wallet from his pocket and withdrew his Visa. "I'm heading up to the cottage. Get on the phone and book her a ticket home."

"Wh-what?" Cora stammered, following him to the door. "But, but—"

"But nothing. She needs to be safe, Mom, and that means she needs to get *out* of here."

He turned to leave, but was stopped by her hand on his sleeve. "I think you should know she had an encounter with Bart today. He scared her."

Resolve was a solid stone in his belly.

"Make the call, Mom."

Chapter Thirty-two

Abby rubbed her hand over her heart—where a pang of remorse still resonated. She'd known for a while that the only safe and reasonable thing to do was pack up the better part of her belongings and lock up the cottage. She wouldn't even get to enjoy the lovely new bathroom addition that had been completed that very morning.

From the moment she'd arrived on the island, had set up her home in the cottage, she had felt a long-festering wound beginning to heal. She'd sensed the internal resurrection of dormant dreams, found solace in the tranquil beauty of the forest.

Now fear marred the tranquility.

Gulls wheeled over the inlet, calling a melancholy omen to her heart. Nothing was as it seemed. Bartholomew Briggs was truly a frightening character—she was almost certain now that he was the culprit behind the notes, the ring and the unsettling feeling she'd had of being watched. He'd said it himself: *Bartholomew is a stone: Bartholomew is a tree. No one sees Bartholomew, but Bartholomew sees all.*

Abby shivered at the memory. Bartholomew certainly fit the profile of a stalker.

She looked over the list of possible suspects she had begun to compile. The criteria was admittedly broad. To make the list, the person had to be male, had to have been of a certain age when her mother lived in Destiny Bay, and had to have had contact with her since she'd arrived.

At the top of the list was Bartholomew, followed by Sheriff Flynn and Johnny Mac. *Who else?* she wondered. Not that it mattered. The police had absolutely no interest in her situation, and the fact that the sheriff was on her list probably narrowed her chances of enlisting his help considerably.

Abby forced herself to place the list back on the table and resume her packing. She had to finish up and get out of the cottage—the sooner the better.

The sound of footsteps coming down the verandah stopped her in her tracks. Abby's heart hammered in her chest. She scurried to the corner of the room and snatched the toilet plunger—a parting gift left by the contractor—and held it high over her head.

Breathlessly, she peered through the window that overlooked the verandah . . . and saw the top of someone's head approaching the door.

The door opened. "Abby?"

Abby slumped against the wall in relief, let the plunger fall from her grasp, and sucked in a great lungful of breath. "Ryan, you scared me! I thought you were—*you know.*"

Ryan bent down, grasped the plunger and examined the rubber cup. "So you brandished your toilet plunger in order to, what . . . shove *you know* down the nearest drainpipe?"

"I could have knocked him off balance."

"Or, more likely, you could have knocked *yourself* off balance and found yourself in a less than ideal position."

Abby deflated. She looked Ryan in the eye, felt her defenses switch to high alert when she saw the color of his face. He looked positively ill. "Ryan?" She placed her hand on his forehead. "You look awful. Something's wrong."

"Come sit down, Abby." Ryan took her hand. "There's something I have to tell you."

Abby shook her head. "I'm not going to like it, am I?"

"No."

She followed him to the living room, allowed him to steer her to the couch, then sank into its plush depths.

Ryan took her hands. "I'm not showing you this to frighten you, Abby—I want you to understand that. I'm showing it to you because you need to understand how serious this situation is, because I don't think you get it."

"I *do* get it, Ryan."

"Do you really?" he asked, sounding more than a little ticked off. "Because here you are at the cottage—the last place you should be without me." His face was mottled with red, his eyes beginning to blaze. "And Mom told me that you had an encounter with Bartholomew, when you know you ought to stay clear of him!"

Abby sank to her seat. "I'm sorry, Ryan."

"Is that what you're going to say when they're wheeling you into the emergency room—or worse? That you're *sorry?*"

"Don't shout at me!"

He yanked a folded note out of his pocket, tossed it onto her lap.

Before she even opened it, she knew it was bad. Her fingers vibrated with the knowledge. "What is it?"

"Open it."

She did, feeling as if the contents within might explode in her face. Abby looked at the words on the paper, felt her world spin out from beneath her.

She dropped the note, clapped her hand over her mouth. Her body started trembling, her eyes misting with tears. "What—what is this?"

"It's a death threat, Abby," he said, taking her into his arms. "This man wants to kill you."

"*I'll die* if you touch me again? Who *is* this person?" Abby demanded. Her body was shaking uncontrollably, torn between terror and rage. "What right does he have to frighten me? I've never done a thing to him!"

"Shh," Ryan said, rocking her gently. He stared up at the ceiling as if an answer to this impossible situation were somewhere up there. "Pack your bags, Abby. I'm putting you on the first plane out of here."

She broke away, gaping at him. "I'm not going!"

"You're leaving, Abby."

She grabbed his arms. "No! I'm not leaving you!"

"It's just for a while."

Abby thought she might vomit. She sank back on the couch, her body shaking. "This man has to be caught, Ryan. I can't just run away—what's to stop him from following me?" Her voice had risen substantially, making her sound on the verge of hysterics.

Ryan's eyes were a brooding topaz. He grasped her shoulders, looked into her face with a raw expression that hinted at the torment he bore. Abby stroked his cheek, almost expecting her hand to come away singed from the emotion that simmered beneath the surface. "I won't let that happen, Abby. I'm going to find him, myself."

Tears welled up in her eyes. After all this, she wasn't going to lose him. "Ryan," she said, "you can't do that—he'll hurt you!"

The face that looked back at her was tormented,

ravaged by a new reality that he surely didn't wish to face. "Better me than you."

Abby pressed her mouth to his, drank in his honor and his honesty and the man that he was. "I won't let him take you from me. I'll find him, and then I'll have you back, Abby," he swore. "You're *mine*—destiny has made it so, and damn him for thinking he can undo it."

She watched his hand, rising—as if through water—to touch hers. "I *am* yours. I always will be."

Ryan grabbed her to him, kissed her tenderly, wildly. His kiss felt like coming home. It washed through her being with the relentless, sweet intensity of wine against a summer's thirst. The sound of his groan spiraled downward, wrapped her heart in tendrils of desire—made it purely, achingly, his.

Her hands entangled in the thickness of his hair. It slipped like silk through her fingers, filling them with a lushness that she gripped in urgency, drawing his mouth yet closer to her.

"Ryan," she said, inching her mouth toward his, "I don't want to let you go. I love you."

The fever of needing him was stronger than anything she'd ever known. Abby abandoned every fear she harbored and trusted only in the truth of the moment. She took him, without question, to the rich soils of her heart, and laid her soul bare to his tender gaze.

"I love you," he promised back, touching her body in a way that defied the gravity of his hands. They were weightless, yet somehow all consuming. Their coaxing strokes shaped her body to his will, touched her every place at once, seemed to transcend flesh, and caress her very soul.

The full, lush pressure of his lips stirred an inextinguishable fire in her veins, consuming her with a passion so intense that she cried out beneath him. Every breath was his name and every heartbeat begged for more.

He kissed one eyelid, then the other, then kissed her

mouth again, this time longer, drawing the essence of her to the surface.

Abby felt an unfathomable stillness in the core of her being while around it smoldered the burgeoning need for him—all of him. Not just his body, but a revelation of him—as he had coaxed from her.

"Ryan," she finally whispered, "how is it that you have this power over me?"

He drew her close into his embrace. "I could ask you the same."

"Don't let me go," she whispered, wrapping her arms around him, memorizing his scent, his taste, breathing him in. *For even when you do, I'll be yours,* said her heart, but soundlessly—for her voice was drowned in the flood of impossible remembrance that surged from her blood, her bones, the part of her that always was and ever would be.

His eyes held hers as his finger traced the outline of her cheek, his touch seeing so much more than vision would allow. He followed the curves of her face, her neck, the shape of her head through the tousle of hair. He traced her arm and lifted her hands into the light that fell across his eyes. Gently, he turned her hand, watching the light cast beams through her fingers. Then, without speaking, he brought her fingers to his face.

She knew instinctively how to touch him, knew what the curve of his lips would feel like beneath her searching thumb, knew the rasp of his unshaven chin.

She closed her eyes to feel him completely, to let his warmth, his breath, be hers. He filled her every fiber of being with his presence; something of him would always be inside her—*had* always been inside her—secreted in the very most tender corner of her heart.

"I don't want this to be over. We've only just started things."

Ryan touched his lips to her mouth, drank her in. "I'll

give you more," he said quietly. "The day will come when I take you home with me. Keep you warm, keep you safe."

Abandon Bluff seeped into her bones, peeled the blindness from her eyes, let her see the man—the *real* man—who looked into her face with such bare, unrelenting honesty.

She held his gaze as if clinging to a lifeline, felt the cord sing with acute and marvelous tension, felt their mingled breath strum it, felt its bone-deep vibration, and felt changed because of it.

She closed her eyes against the intensity of it, opened them a moment later to see his, softer now.

He brushed his lips against hers, eyes squeezing with an unutterable emotion. "That day *will* come, Abby, I promise. But for now . . . you have to go."

Tears flowed in earnest down her cheeks. The quiet of the cottage was a blanket, cloistering and warm around them in the twilight hour. Abby felt an extraordinary sadness settle around her, bloom within her. She took his face in her hands. "I'm going to hold you to that."

He kissed her, then—an unmistakable kiss good-bye— and broke her heart with his tenderness.

Chapter Thirty-three

The Lover rewound the surveillance tape again, staring at the grainy image of his love . . . in the arms of Ryan Brannigan.

It couldn't be true—yet here it was, in black and white. She was in love with the artist's son. She was *seducing* the artist's son!

He rubbed at the scabbed flesh that burned like an

ember in his palm, that foretold the embrace of brimstone awaiting the woman whose initial was seared into his cupped hand. Oh, she would burn for this, would pay for her sins *and* her mother's!

The tape played on, displaying the two lovers, closer now, curled into the depths of the couch.

Was no one able to learn from the sins of the past other than he? Was everyone so blind, so innately stupid, that they would cheerfully hurtle down the path of destruction, willing to trade their everlasting souls for a moment of earthly satisfaction?

Well, he would mete out punishment, as he had done so many years ago.

Still, he remembered that night with satisfaction—the night he had punished the artist and sent his soul to the damnation that awaited him.

That night, so many years ago, he had followed the pitiful, staggering drunk artist up the road, through the cemetery, and up, up, up to Cragan Cliff—the place where he had once laid his filthy hands on lovely Celeste, the place she had groaned beneath him under the full moon as The Lover watched, seething, in the shelter of the bracken.

The earth was blanketed with snow, sparkling beneath the moonlight, and the artist had sat on a boulder, looked out to sea, muttered incomprehensibly into the still night air. The gauzy plumes of breath were the only indication that he did, in fact, speak, and the ripe, oval tears on his cheek hinted that old Douglas missed Celeste almost as much as he did.

Almost, but not quite.

The Lover had stepped into the wash of moonlight that pooled on the new-fallen snow.

Douglas had turned, hadn't even bothered to wipe away his tears, weakling that he was. He had greeted The Lover with a small nod, as if finding him here were the most natural thing on earth . . . as if he didn't fear meeting Celeste's avenger here, in the dark, far from anyone who would hear his cries. Douglas trusted him—as did everyone else—never imagining that he held life and death in his hands.

Fool.

It had taken very little effort to overpower Douglas, and The Lover had enjoyed his helpless struggle down to every last twitch, had gloried in the long-awaited revenge of watching the life fade from the artist's bulging eyes as he squeezed the man's surprisingly fragile throat.

Dead fool.

After, he had dragged the body far off the path, buried it in a shallow grave of frozen leaves, twigs, and finally, snow.

He had sat on the same boulder the artist sat upon, looking out over the wintry sea, watching his breath stir the still, night air, dreaming of his lovely Celeste.

He let the memory of that night fade; he thought, instead, of the night he'd first made love to Celeste. He had explained to her in no uncertain terms that if she stayed with the artist, he would be forced to destroy the man. She had left the artist shortly thereafter; then, she left the island.

His heart squeezed painfully at the memory. He looked back up to see that the television screen was blank, the film of Abrielle and Ryan—the two sinners—played out to its horrible end.

The Lover seethed. He would make the artist's son pay, and he would cleanse beauty as only love could. She would be his . . . if not in this life, then surely in the next.

The Lover lifted his gun and peered into the barrel. It was pristinely clean. He placed it on the table beside a glinting, sharpened knife. Both fitting instruments for the offering of sacrifice.

He smiled grimly.

Sometimes, only sacrifice would impart the cleansing

needed. He thought of Abby's face, thought of the word *sacrifice*, thought of its root in the word *sacred*.

It was his duty, as The Lover, to sanctify Abrielle by this act of ultimate love, to send her to her maker before she sinned against the love he had offered her yet again.

Foolish girl. Just like her mother, she was. Just like *his* mother.

Well, this time, there would be no weakness on his part. He would cleanse her by the act of sacrifice, even if it meant breaking his own heart.

He would save her; he would scour her soul with the pains of sacrifice; he would cleanse it in the flow of crimson blood.

This was love, he thought fiercely, as a tear for his imminent loss trickled over his cheek. *This* was sacrifice.

This was also something else, something dark and vengeful and filled with the indignation he'd felt when his mother had abandoned him, leaving him to an unknown fate. Even after she'd gone, she still called him her lovey-boy, still teased him with her promises, with her assurances that good things come to those who wait.

He had been a child, unable to execute the dreamed-of revenge of every scorned saint and lover. If he'd been able, he would have punished her as he was now forced to punish Abrielle.

Only Celeste had been true to the end. He remembered the first time he saw her, looking so much like his long-dead mother that it brought his breath up short. Yes, she had lost her way with Douglas McAllister for a time, but eventually she had sent her daughter to him as an offering of her regret.

But like his mother, Abrielle had failed him.

Soon, both she and Ryan would know that if *he* couldn't have her, no one would.

He sat down slowly into the depths of his armchair, his

hand resting on a small plaque his mother had given his father back in the days when she was still faithful and true. It said:

> *"Entreat me not to leave thee, or to return from following after thee: for whither thou goest, I will go; and where thou lodgest, I will lodge . . . where thou diest, I will die, and there will I be buried."*

Was he ready to die when Abrielle did? Was he ready to go down in a blaze of sacrificial flames?

He breathed in the certainty offered by his mother's pledge.

Yes. He was ready. This was his destiny.

Chapter Thirty-four

Abby was standing in Cora's living room, knee-deep in luggage.

Since yesterday, Ryan had left her only long enough to sign a lease agreement for the packing facility in Marriott's Bay, and had insisted that Cora stay with her the entire time he was gone.

At any other time, Abby would have thought the entire thing overkill, but today she was glad of the company. The note that Ryan had received had frightened her more than she cared to admit.

She was also devastated to be leaving the island without an answer to her quest.

The entire thing *had* been a fool's errand. She had learned a few things about her mother, but had failed to produce the key to her tragic end. She had learned how to love at last, but in a bitter twist of irony, had had love snatched from her grasp.

She glanced at her watch. Her plane was leaving in the morning—less than ten hours away, now.

Where was Ryan? He'd been gone long enough, and she wanted him home, with his arms around her.

Distractedly, she picked up her cell phone. She *had* to see Ronnie before she left, but Ronnie hadn't been answering her phone. This time, Abby tried her at the restaurant.

Rose, the hostess at the Surfside, answered her call. "I only saw Ronnie once today," she replied when questioned, "and that was when she rushed in to grab her paperwork. She said she was going back out to the cottage to talk to you about something, but that was over three hours ago."

Abby frowned into the phone. "Did she seem upset?"

"No, just anxious to see you. She heard from Cora that you were leaving the island, and she wanted to put things right between the two of you."

"Thank you, Rose. If you hear from her, please let her know I really need to talk to her. I'm going back home— just for a while—and I really, really want to say good-bye."

"Oh? Well, we'll be sad to see you leave, Abby. I'll be sure to let Ronnie know when I see her."

The phone went dead in her ear. Abby folded her phone and placed it on the nearest box. Something didn't feel right.

She had stopped by Ronnie's apartment earlier, but the windows had been dark, with her afternoon newspaper still resting, unopened, on the doorstep.

Would she have gone to the cottage and simply waited for Abby?

She glanced at her watch. It was seven o'clock, and very dark. That possibility didn't seem likely.

So where was she?

Her phone vibrated in her hand—perhaps it was Ronnie? But the text message on the screen was from Ryan.

Meet me at the cottage. Very important. See you soon.
Love Ryan

Well, that was strange. Ryan had expressly forbidden her to leave Cora's house. She tried his phone, but got no answer. Maybe he was in an area with poor reception—perhaps that was why he'd chosen to text instead of call?

She walked into the den. Cora was fast asleep on the big leather chair. She looked so peaceful, it seemed a shame to wake her—and why should she?

Quickly, she snatched a sheet from the pad on the counter, letting out a small yelp as the paper sliced neatly into the flesh of her finger. She frowned at the cut, thankful it was such a clean one. Blood had always troubled her, but she could certainly handle the small amount that the slice produced.

She scrawled a note to Cora explaining where she'd gone and why, jumped into her car, and headed for the cottage.

She pressed aggressively on the gas pedal, and the tires spat out gravel as she rounded turn after turn.

At last, her headlights caught the glint of a vehicle in the driveway. *Ronnie's VW?* So Ronnie *had* come to the cottage to speak with her after all. But Rose had said Ronnie had left to come here over three hours ago. Surely she hadn't been waiting at the cottage all that time. Abby pulled into the drive, hopped from her car and eyed the Volkswagon.

"Okay," she said to herself, her stomach tightening involuntarily. "Ronnie's here, but where's Ryan?"

Something didn't feel right. She thought back to Ryan's adamant insistence that she remain at Cora's house—that she not be without companionship at any time. Why, then, had he sent her a message to meet him at the cottage?

She dialed his cell phone number again.

"*. . . the person you are trying to reach is out of range . . .*"

Small hairs on the back of her neck were beginning to stand on end. Of course he was out of range. He was in Marriot's Bay, for crying out loud, and she'd been an idiot to come out here.

But what about Ronnie . . . Where on earth was she?

Reluctantly, Abby turned back toward the cottage. If somehow Ronnie had found a way inside, she'd ask her to come back with her to Cora's and they'd have a nice cup of tea—try to work past the Ryan situation. She locked the car, dropped her keys into her purse and started walking.

In the darkness, the path to the verandah was treacherous. Humped tree roots, stones, and tufts of grass made her extra cautious, but caution wasn't enough.

With a gasp, she sprawled over the ground, sending the contents of her purse flying.

Springing into action, she fumbled around in the dark. She ferreted out a lipstick, a pack of gum, her mirror and a tiny penlight . . . but no keys.

There was a flashlight in the cottage, but she couldn't get in without her keys—nor could she get the car going without them!

"Ronnie?" she called, hoping against hope to hear Ronnie's voice.

Nothing.

To prevent another fall, she turned on the penlight and slid her feet across the ground toward the verandah. Rounding the corner expecting to find Ronnie, she found . . .

No one.

She rose on her tiptoes and peeked through the window. The cottage was dark and empty.

Abby squinted into the pitiful beam of light emitted by

her penlight. She took a step forward, and paused immediately. There was a slick sort of stickiness beneath her foot: a mild adherent that seemed to fix her shoe to the planks of the deck.

She squatted, shone her flashlight down onto a pool of near-black liquid that spread over the decking.

A surge of adrenaline seized her heart in a viselike grip. She slapped her hand over her gaping mouth to stifle the scream that clawed at her throat.

She was instantly terrified.

Blood . . . it's blood!

Was this another attempt of the stalker to frighten her, or was this something much more deadly?

The possibility spread through her veins like an injection of ice water.

Her eyes darted over the shifting boughs of evergreens, knowing that the blackness of their shadows was a perfect place in which the predator might hide. He could be watching her right now, and she'd never know.

As quickly as a lightning strike, she was racing down the length of the verandah, breath coming in gasps, hell-bent on her vehicle. Then, as deafening as a peal of thunder came the realization that her keys were missing, and . . .

Ronnie's car is in the driveway, but Ronnie is nowhere to be found.

Her heart was an immovable lump in her throat—constricting her cries, strangling her breath—as the shrillness of theories colliding with instincts sounded in her head. She teetered on her feet, weak-kneed, staring at the two vehicles—one a symbol of her helplessness, the other, a harbinger of doom.

She had to find her keys and get out of here, but she also needed to protect herself.

Without a second's hesitation, Abby snatched a rock from the ground and threw it at the car window with all her might, wincing at the explosion of shattering glass.

She reached in the resulting hole and pulled the trunk release, then raced to the rear of the car. The tire iron—which was standard equipment in her rental car—would be her weapon of protection.

Now, to find her keys.

But what if Ronnie is here somewhere and needs help?

The primal hoot of an owl rent the stillness of the night. Abby screamed as if the hand of evil had reached into her throat, clutched the heart of her terror, and torn it free.

Terrified, she dropped back down to her knees, and with the light thrown from the open trunk, she found her cell phone.

She clutched it, and with trembling hands, dialed 9-1-1.

"Deputy Flynn speaking."

"Deputy! This is Abby Lancaster. I'm up at the cottage, and I need help!"

"Calm down, now, Miss Lancaster. Tell me what's wrong."

Another wave of fear washed over her, nearly smothering her with its weight. "Just get up here, please!"

"I'm on my way, I'm on my way—talk to me, Miss Lancaster . . . what's going on up there?"

"Ronnie," she cried, almost choking on her panic, "she's not here, but her car is."

"Ronnie's a big girl. She can take care of herself, miss."

"You don't understand. I found blood, Flynn . . . did you hear me? Lots of blood!"

The shrill sound of his siren pierced the conversation. "All right, now, listen here, Miss Lancaster," he said. "If that's the case, I want you to drive yourself to a safe place till I get up there."

"There *is* no safe place! It's dark, I've lost my car keys—I'm stuck here!"

"Just stay on the line. I'm coming up Reynold's Pass right now."

"Okay, okay," she said quietly, gasping for breath, sinking down the wall of the cottage. She landed in a squat at its base, penlight trained on the black expanse that yawned before her.

"You still there?" Flynn was all business, his voice edgy with the adrenaline of danger. "I'm turning up Crawford Lane right now, Abrielle. I oughta be there in about ten minutes."

"Okay," she said again. "You don't suppose Ronnie's been hurt, do you?"

"Hurt? Oh, I doubt that. Probably a reasonable explanation, is what I'm thinking."

"You're right," she said. "There just has to be." *Then why is my gut telling me otherwise?*

"Did you call anyone else, Abrielle? Ambulance, Ryan, anyone?"

"Just you," she said, wishing Ryan could hear her thoughts, could feel her panic and come to her aid. "I left a note for Cora so she'd know where I was, but I didn't call an ambulance." The panic was rising again. "Should I have? Oh, what a stupid question—of course I should have!"

"Just calm down. I can do that from my console here in the car."

Abby's heart lurched. She had heard something . . . something like the snapping of branches from the area of the dock. "Ronnie?" she called timidly. "Is that you?"

Nothing.

"Ronnie!" she screamed, hating the frightened sound of her voice.

"I sure hope you're someplace safe, Miss Lancaster!" The voice on the other end was panicked—but the tone paled compared to what Abby was feeling.

Abby ignored the pleading voice, focusing instead on the vicinity of the sound she had heard. She swept her light toward the side of the cottage.

Nothing.

"Miss Lan—"

"Shhh, Connor; be quiet! I heard something."

"Then get out of there!"

"It might be Ronnie!"

Slowly, she rose from her crouched position, lifted the trembling penlight, and hooked her phone onto her belt loop.

Training her light toward the water, tire iron held aloft, she walked slowly into the night.

To her fear-quickened ears, every footfall against the weathered grain of the dock was a resonating thud in her ears. Every breath was as ragged as if drawn over glass.

Her grip on the tire iron was slick with sweat, and she grasped it more tightly.

"Ron? You're scaring me."

The right sweep of the inlet yielded nothing. She trained her light on the left-hand shore, sweeping it over stones, the ghostly white trunks of birch and . . .

Just between the spindly trunks, she saw a shifting column of white. The White Lady.

"No." The word were scarcely more than a whisper. "Connor, I'm hanging up now. I'm going to call Ryan. Get here fast."

"Don't you do that, Abrielle! Don't you hang up this phone—"

Abby hung up on Connor. She *needed* Ryan. She dialed his number.

"Hello?"

"Ryan!" she cried, tears of relief springing to her eyes. "I need you. I'm at the cottage, and something has happened to Ronnie!"

"Why did you leave the house?" he asked, panic evident in his voice.

"You sent me a text message . . . but you didn't. I figured that out already. I need you, please hurry."

"Are you okay? Have you called the police?"

"Connor's on his way."

"So am I. Don't hang up, Abby."

She walked slowly down the length of the dock, hearing the sounds of the night all around her. "I won't," she whispered into the phone.

The clouds shifted above her, sending a beam of moonlight to the earth. There, draped across the rocks, was the body of a woman.

Abby began to tremble; her breath began to snag on something immovable that suddenly burgeoned in her throat. *"No!"*

"Abby, what is it? Get to safety! Get in your car—drive!"

But she could hardly hear him over the beating of her heart.

Abby leapt onto the rocks that rimmed the shore; she stumbled into the water. "Ronnie!" she screamed, wading through the surf, climbing onto a jetty of stones that pierced the inlet.

She jumped from stone to stone, eyes intent on the whitish glow that had first caught her attention: a delicate foot, toes trailing in the water. She fell to her knees, unable to understand what she was seeing.

It was her mother, in the painting . . . but it wasn't!

Abby's blood was an ocean at storm, raging in her head as she dragged one breath, then another, past the tightening constraints of her esophagus. Her phone fell from her grasp into the lapping ocean.

When at last she could, she stumbled forward, hand outstretched to grasp the pale, lifeless one of her friend.

Ronnie sat on the stones, naked body arranged in a perfect likeness of the portrait that had first brought Abby here . . . except for the gash that streaked across her throat.

She didn't know how long she stood there, screaming, or when she first understood that the sound of the siren had stopped, and a vehicle door had opened and shut.

The splash and swish of approach was upon her before she realized that she wasn't alone with the body of her friend.

"Holy saints, preserve us!" Connor's voice sounded as if it had been dragged over sandpaper. He collapsed beside Abby, genuflecting at the sight of Ronnie.

A voice, unrecognizable as her own, seemed to tear her heart from its moorings. Abby collapsed, waist deep in the water that was clouded with Ronnie's blood. She reached up and began sobbing, certain she would never stop. "Hurry, Ryan," she sobbed.

Connor grabbed her by the shoulders and shook her gently. "Get hold of yourself, Abrielle. Did you get through to Ryan?"

"I—yes. He's on his way."

Connor's mouth hardened. "What I don't need," he said coldly, "is another civilian corrupting my crime scene." He circled behind Abby, slipped his hands under her arms and began hoisting her up. "Sit here, Abrielle. Don't, and I mean *do not* touch anything."

He deposited her on a rock, drew his pistol with one hand, and pressed the radio at his shoulder. "Dispatch, this is Flynn. I need backup here at Abandon Bluff, and I need it fast. You get Sheriff and Wright out of bed and put a call out to Marriott County. We're gonna need their expertise."

His voice was a million miles away, swallowed by the quiet lap of the sea, drowned in crimson tendrils of blood.

Abby saw her hand rise, like a disembodied thing, and touch Ronnie's arm. She had a desperate desire to cover her, to spare her the indignity of Connor's eyes, of the worse, more glaring investigation that would follow.

She squeezed her eyes shut at the thought.

How . . . how on earth could this have happened? A tear slipped over the roundness of her cheekbone. *Surely this is a bad dream.*

Flynn's weapon glinted wickedly in the moonlight

despite the trembling of his grasp. He walked slowly, legs swishing through the water, weapon panning back and forth at the shore and light piercing the blackness of the forest.

Abby rocked back and forth on the rock, arms gripped around her body; every exhalation was a hum of disbelief, every breath in a gust of withering heat.

"Halt!" Connor suddenly croaked, pistol and wide-eyed gaze fixed upon the shifting bracken. "Bartholomew, you come on out with your hands raised. No one else has to get hurt!"

Abby leapt from the stones, was immersed to her waist in the water as her eyes darted frantically and at last caught the whitish glow of Bartholomew's face.

The madness of the full, rising moon caught him amidst the blackness of shifting bracken, slid down the knife edge of his nose, and disappeared in the darkness of his mouth.

"Come out, now, Bartholomew . . . you don't want to make things worse than they are." Connor's gun was trembling almost as much as his voice.

Abby felt her sensibilities awaken, felt a renewed fear for both their safeties emerge. She held her breath, watched in abject terror as Bartholomew's gaze shifted from Flynn to her.

She watched the corners of his mouth lift. Then quickly, he was swallowed by the springing motion of branches.

"He's getting away!" she cried, then shrieked at the piercing sound of a fired bullet.

Connor's gun darted wildly, his eyes following suit. "I can't see him! Bart, you come on out now!"

A moment passed—a moment strung so tightly that Abby felt the hairs on her body rise to meet its tension.

Connor's gun lowered a little. "He's gone," he said, more to himself than to her.

Abby was silent.

"You need to come with me, Miss Lancaster."

"No. I want to stay with her."

He nudged her upward. "Come on, now, miss. I'm sure you don't want to be here. There's nothing you can do for her, now."

He was right, of course. Abby let herself be lifted, then turned to touch her friend one last time. Her hand squeezed around Ronnie's wrist. "I'm so sorry, Ronnie."

Then, she felt something flutter beneath the touch of her fingertips. For the second time that night, her blood all but stopped in her veins. "No! Wait," she said, shaking free of Connor's grasp. "I felt something in Ronnie's wrist. It was a pulse, Connor, I swear it!"

She fell to her knees before Ronnie, grasping her wrist with new urgency. "Come on, come on. Do it again for me, Ron!"

Connor stood in transfixed silence.

"There!" she shrieked. "She's alive!"

Connor all but threw her into the ocean in the struggle to reach a hand to the macabre mess of Ronnie's throat. He pressed, eyes closed in concentration.

Another set of lights pulled into the driveway. Abby's heart soared with relief when she saw that it was Ryan.

Connor saw, too, and broke into a run toward his cruiser, presumably to fetch his first-aid kit.

Ryan tore out of his vehicle and bypassed Connor in his rush to get to Abby. He sloshed through the shallows, intent upon her. "Abby, what the—" Ryan grabbed her, then let her go as his arms fell slackly to his sides.

Abby looked up and saw his face—horror stricken, disbelieving—as he stared at Ronnie. His jaw moved soundlessly up and down. He looked down at Abby, touching her face as if to make sure she was alive, then reached out and touched Ronnie's leg.

Abby clutched Ryan's sweater, staring at Connor as he

administered what first aid he could, pressing a hand to her heart.

"She's alive?" asked Ryan.

Connor's tone was grim. "Just barely."

Ryan's expression hardened, his eyes flashed. "Who did this?"

"Can't say for sure without an investigation, but—"

"It was Bart!" Abby blurted, clutching Ryan. "*He* did this! I saw him disappear into the woods with my own eyes." She looked frantically between the two men. "You've got to find him!"

"We'll find him," said Ryan, as he lifted his head at the sound of approaching sirens. "He'll pay for this."

Chapter Thirty-five

Abby had arrived at the hospital by way of the same ambulance that brought Ronnie.

In an act of sheer brute force, Ryan had grabbed the EMT by the sleeve, threatened him with bodily harm if he dared deny Abby a lift in the safety of his ambulance, and seated her in the back. The red-faced EMT opened his mouth as if to censure Ryan's behavior, but seeing his face, apparently thought better of it. Abby didn't blame him one bit.

It had been a harrowing ride, to say the least.

She slumped against the wall, closed her eyes, and—still wet from the lake, still reeking with the blood of her friend—prayed.

The prayer didn't last long, just a simple, heartfelt "Please." Every time she closed her eyes, horrific images burst upon the theater of her mind: images of the sticky deck, of Ronnie, of Ryan's face looking between her and Ronnie as if trying to decide which of the two needed him more.

Abby's heart thudded painfully in her chest, exuding rivers of anguish to the far reaches of her body and soul.

All this has come about because of me.

If she hadn't been so desperate for answers to questions that didn't even matter, then the evil that lurked on the island wouldn't have been awakened. If she'd only gotten on with her life and accepted that her past couldn't be changed, Ryan and Cora's lives wouldn't have been turned upside down. If she'd been wise and taken what lessons she could from her mother's tragedy, she wouldn't have come to Destiny Bay in the first place, and Ronnie wouldn't have been attacked and very nearly killed.

If, if, if.

She thought of the life she had left behind—the life that seemed, in retrospect, perfectly livable, if lonely. Then she thought of the life she'd traded it for. A life of chaos and uncertainty, of fault and terror, of friends, fighting for their very lives because of her.

And then there was Ryan, who was probably combing the woods for a crazed would-be murderer at this very moment.

She slid down the wall, grasping her heaving stomach. She was going to be sick. She was going to cause even more of a stir in an already frantic emergency room! Her gaze darted around and rested upon a wastepaper basket. She grabbed it and vomited into it as discreetly as possible.

She wanted nothing more than to rewind time, to change her choices . . . and barring that, to simply disappear.

Yes, Ryan was right in saying she had to leave Destiny Bay—had been tactful not to say she shouldn't have come in the first place.

He deserved so much more.

She had dared to love, and this was the pain that resulted. She'd known what to expect from love, and yet she'd jumped into Ryan's arms, ruined a friendship and quite possibly ruined another person's life.

She had no right to Ryan's love after the pain she'd caused him, and no right to Ronnie's friendship after what had befallen *her*.

With the thought of her friend, Abby's gaze returned to the glassed-in trauma room that teemed with controlled chaos. Ronnie was in there, fighting for every breath.

Because of me.

Abby's stomach threatened to revolt again. She expressly forbade it, pressing her hand there in an attempt to calm the internal storm.

She needed to make amends, but how? How to take this impossible situation and make it right?

Maybe she never could. But maybe she was on to something . . . maybe the best she could do for everyone involved would be to simply disappear.

Finally . . . an aspect of this madness she could control.

An hour—which seemed more like a lifetime—passed, and still no sign of Ryan.

Ronnie, though critical, had been stabilized.

"Please," Abby prayed in whispered tones. "Please keep him safe. And *please* don't take Ronnie."

"Did you say something?" asked the nurse who led her down the hall.

"No. Nothing."

"There's a right ballyhoo kicking up out there," said the nurse as she nodded toward the window.

Abby recognized her attempts to distract, but beyond glancing at the tossing trees outside the window, she could scarcely muster a response.

"They say there's a hurricane a-comin'. Only a category one, mind, but still a good night to be inside, says I."

Unless you're in a hospital bed, rubbing shoulders with death.

The nurse showed her Ronnie's door. "Just buzz if you need anything."

Abby walked into the room. She knew—with a flimsy, secondhand sort of knowledge—that Ronnie was dangerously near death.

In that moment, her quality of knowledge changed.

To know with the mind is one thing. To know with the eyes and heart is an entirely different matter. Abby understood in an instant that it's *that* sort of knowing that can change the very landscape of the soul.

She felt her own landscape shift. She walked toward the bed as if the floor were littered with mines, allowing herself to touch nothing, to hear only the low-pitched hum of hospital circuitry in her ears. She smelled her own fear—tasted the cottony dryness that filled her mouth.

When she could walk no farther, she stopped by Ronnie's bed and looked down at her.

A woman, unrecognizable as Ronnie, lay unconscious.

Abby crumpled to the floor. This was *her* doing. If she'd only stayed a lifetime away from Destiny Bay!

She might not be able to change the past, but she could see to it that the future was safer for everyone. She would not hurt her friend anymore. The least she could do was bow out of the race for Ryan's heart—surely Ronnie deserved him more than she did. Surely his life would be better with a woman like Ronnie.

Abby understood now, as she never had before, that to her, love would only ever mean pain—pain she could no longer endure. She would leave Destiny Bay, as Ryan had asked, but she would not be coming back as he thought.

When at last she could, she rose, smoothed her rumpled clothing and sat in the chair beside the bed.

With each turning of her thoughts, the very real possibility of Ronnie's death darkened her heart. With each subsequent step toward utter blackness, a singularly aloof portion of her mind withdrew another fragment of the emotional presence she desperately needed.

She squeezed Ronnie's hand, marveling at the curse her love had brought to her friend.

This was where it had to end. The quest was finished. There was no great secret that had led her to the island. There was no reason beyond depression for her mother's suicide. There was no great call to love.

But there *was* destiny . . . only she had misunderstood. She had thought that destiny was bringing her to healing, when in fact, destiny's purpose had been to teach her that love was a very dangerous thing, and that fear had a very real purpose.

This time, she promised to believe it.

And what of Ryan? Was he still out searching for Bartholomew? What would happen to Ryan if he found him?

Panic scorched through her at the thought. Ryan had strength, youth and vigor on his side. But Bartholomew had his madness. He was without guilt, inhibition or rationale.

He was possessed.

"Of all the insensitive, loutish ideas!"

Abby's head snapped up at the sound of Cora's voice.

"I can't believe you expect her to go back up there! . . . No, you listen to me, Connor Flynn, I've known you since you were a lad, and—Abby!" Cora all but dropped her phone as she stopped outside the door of Ronnie's room. "I've been looking over God's green acre for you, luv!"

Abby glanced at Cora's cell phone. "You're not supposed to use those in here."

Cora waved her objection away. "Just a minute, dear." Then, phone back at her ear, she said, "I'll speak with *you* later, Connor—and that fool brother of yours, sheriff or not. I'll have some words for him."

Cora wore an expression of outright dismay. "That was Connor Flynn on the phone. It seems the police are insisting that you revisit the crime scene in order to go over things with him."

Abby joined Cora in the hall, shutting Ronnie's door behind her. "I can't, Cora . . . I can't go back there!"

She stroked Abby's hand. "I know, dear, but it's just for a wee bit, Abby. And you'll be there with the police."

"Oh, *that's* comforting."

"I'll come with you two, if you like."

Abby bit her lip. It was time to put everything to rest, and if that meant going back to the cottage, then that's what she'd have to do. She steeled her resolve. "No. I need you to stay here and keep your eye on Ronnie." She grasped Cora's hand tightly, feeling bone tired and urgent, all at once. "I dropped my cell phone in all the confusion—when I saw Ronnie . . ." I'm sure it's here somewhere, She was babbling and couldn't help it. "Listen, I'll call you from the cottage phone as soon as I get there. I need you to be here in case anything changes with Ronnie."

"I can do that. And if it's any consolation, Sheriff Flynn will have a piece of my mind on this matter, believe you me. He hasn't heard the last of this business, dragging you down to that forsaken place, right on the heels of poor Ronnie's attack."

Abby dragged her hands down her face. "I doubt that they're *trying* to be insensitive. They have to gather all possible evidence before pressing forward with an arrest, I suppose."

"So, you think they'll arrest Bartholomew?"

"Yes," she said quietly. "We both saw him, crouching in the bushes."

"Sometimes, even when the expected happens, it still leaves you reeling," said Cora.

Abby managed a weak nod, then looked up.

"Bartholomew didn't go *in* the cottage, as far as I could see. It looked as if the . . . the struggle," she said, "occurred on the verandah."

Cora bit her lip. "Nonetheless, Deputy Flynn wants you there to go over your version of events . . . at the scene," she added bitterly.

"Then I guess I should get going."

"Wait," Cora said, looking at Abby with a pained expression. "Whatever possessed you, lass, to go to the cottage in the first place?"

"Ryan sent me a message telling me to meet him there."

Cora shook her head. "Oh, no. He'd never do that."

Looking back, Abby knew it, too. Ryan never would have endangered her by asking her to leave the safety of Cora's house. Someone else had sent her the text message. Someone who knew Ryan's number and had entered it into the computer from which the message was sent, effectively making it look like the text was from him.

"Cora, there's something I didn't tell the police," she said.

"What's that?"

"The painting of my mother that I told you about—the one that brought me here in the first place . . ."

"Yes?"

Abby took a slow, bracing breath, willing herself not to faint. "Ronnie . . . she looked just like that."

Cora's normally ruddy complexion was suddenly ashen. "Abby, are you sure?"

"I'm positive. I thought, for one ridiculous moment, that I was seeing my mother's ghost." Abby reached into her pocket, withdrew a dried honeysuckle blossom and let it fall to the table. "I found this on her . . . on her stomach. There were more."

"Abby, you've got to tell the police. There's obviously some connection between the painting and Ronnie's attack."

"I know that."

They stared at each other in charged silence, each weighing thoughts too heavy for words.

"Well, here's what *I* know, and I don't mind saying it," Cora said, suddenly brusque. "That attack, m'dear, had nothing to do with Ronnie, God bless her. That attack was meant for you."

Abby felt the full weight of Cora's declaration. It was true.

The sound of approaching footsteps was a welcome distraction.

"Abby!" Ryan rounded the corner, froze on the spot, then strode the distance between them in a few, massive strides. He opened his arms and grasped her to his chest.

He smelled like forest and ocean. Abby wrapped her arms around him despite the screaming protests in her head. She had to touch him—just once more.

But how, how can I ever let him go?

"I'll let you two have a moment," said Cora, who quietly vanished around the corner.

"Abby," Ryan whispered into her hair, rubbing his hands through the chocolaty strands, "Thank God you're all right. Let me take you home."

Home. When he said it, it sounded so right. *But* said the quiet voice of reason within her . . . *you made your choice. You chose to let him go. And it was the right choice.*

Impossibly, she found the strength to place her hands on his chest and push him away. "No. It's over, Ryan. I was a fool to think that I could do this—that I could love you. It's over. *Over.*"

Ryan stared at her, his eyes intense, bewildered. "What are you talking about?"

She turned to run, blinking madly to obliterate the tears in her eyes. "I have to go."

"Oh no, you don't—"

"Don't you see?" she said, whirling on him. "This is all my fault! Love is poison to me, and I'm poison to you and to Ronnie and to my mother. I'm poison to everyone I touch." She struggled against his grip on her arm. "Let me go!"

He pulled her closer. "You are *not* walking away from me!"

"I am," she swore through her tears, trying, but failing, to extricate herself from his grasp. "I'm doing what's right, Ryan, and you can't stop me. I'm staying in town until Ronnie is able to hear me tell her how sorry I am, and then I'm leaving this island. For good."

Pain, disbelief, anger—she saw them streak over his face like a runaway fire. "I never took you for a coward," he said through his teeth.

She *did* succeed in breaking free this time, but only because he let her. "What's cowardly about doing the right thing?"

"Nothing," he said, looking at her disdainfully. "But there's nothing 'right' about running away."

"Don't you see? I'm running *to* something. I'm running to the *truth*. It may not be the truth I'd hoped to find, but at least I'll be the only one who gets hurt when I get there."

"But you'll be *alone*, Abby. Is that what you want?"

"Yes." *No. But it's what I need. It's what you need.*

Ryan whirled, clenching his fists until the knuckles turned white.

Abby squeezed her eyes shut, felt her heart turn in on itself and begin the familiar, deliberate process of deconstructing hope, of building walls with the rubble that was left in teetering piles around it.

"You know, you expect life to be this perfectly ordered experience that doesn't offend anyone or hurt anyone— most especially *you*—" he said, turning back to look at her. "Well, I've got news for you. Life isn't tidy or polite. It doesn't follow anyone's rules. Sometimes it's cold and it's messy. It breaks your heart and it marches on whether you want it to or not. But sometimes, Abby—" He caught her shoulders, looked into her face with such exquisite longing as to make her want to reconsider everything she'd just said. "*Sometimes* it's sweet and it's beautiful. And sometimes, even after it breaks your heart, it lets you wake up at that perfect moment—right between heartbeats— when nothing at all hurts, just to let you know that even sadness passes."

He cupped her face in his hands and tilted it up, forcing her to look into his eyes.

"Life is all that, Abby, and I ought to know, 'cause I've lived on both sides—but most of all it's *worth* it . . . every messy, magnificent, heartbreaking, glorious moment. *Don't* say no to that, Abby. Don't make me watch you turn your back on it—not when you've just begun learning to live— because I'm *not* stepping back into the fog I was in before I met you."

Abby looked at him and felt her heart break—heard the soul cry of every molecule in her body as it seized at the thought of walking away from him.

But she walked away anyway.

"Good-bye, Abby," he said.

One sentence, one moment—made extraordinary in a multitude of notorious moments now forever engraved in her memory.

"Good-bye."

Chapter Thirty-six

Hurricane or not, Abby was going to that bloody crime scene for Connor Flynn. She'd do whatever she had to do to keep her mind off running back to Ryan and falling into his arms.

She pressed harder on the gas pedal, blinking away the blinding tears.

If only I'd never come to this bloody island!

She thumped the steering wheel in futility. She wanted nothing more than to go home and forget that Destiny Bay even existed. Forgetting Ryan would be a horse of an entirely different color . . . but she had little choice except to try.

And there was another piece of this tragic puzzle. She had finally learned how . . . *remembered* how to love—and it was all for naught.

"Better to have loved and lost," she said aloud, and felt the floodgates open. Shakespeare, she decided, was a complete moron.

By the time she arrived at the cottage, charcoal thunderheads rested their cheeks against the heaving bosom of the sea.

The hurricane was whipping against the shore, intent on walloping Abandon Bluff and leaving devastation in its wake.

Clouds scudded across the full moon and waves tossed beneath. Abby took it all in uneasily.

Her unease retreated minutely when she saw the whitish blur of a police car pulled over on the side of the road. However grudgingly, she had to admit that the vigilance of the police force in the face of such unaccustomed violence was a boon to her heart.

Abby jumped out of the car and raced toward the door, noting the crime scene tape that draped the entry. The sky was about to open, and she wanted no part of the downpour, nor did she want to catch sight of the bloodied planks that creaked beneath her feet. She steered her eyes toward the lock and key and let herself into the cottage. Once inside, her purse slid down the length of her arm and fell where she stood. She flicked the light switch—to no avail.

No power.

"Oh, you've *got* to be kidding," she said, barely stifling a groan. "Hello?"

Nothing.

"Where is that Flynn?" she muttered to herself as she gathered several pillar candles. Perhaps he was checking the perimeter of the house?

Outside, the attitude of the rain turned decidedly aggressive. Flynn had better get in soon, or he'd be soaked to the skin. Within minutes, rain was battering the coast with an all-out fury, scarring the sand with its violent assault. Drop after massive drop chased rivulets of water down the pane of the living room window.

Abby watched, transfixed, then turned back to the matter at hand. First one, then the other candle pierced the darkness. The cottage was all shadows.

Abby rubbed her arms, determined to overcome the chill that had settled upon her flesh like a cloak.

She decided that she'd give Flynn five minutes to show his face, and then she was out of there. She didn't want to admit that she was more than a little nervous, more than a little afraid.

"Three more minutes, Flynn," she whispered, watching the candle flames grow in brightness as ice pellets hissed against the windowpane. She sank into a heap on the floor, watching the storm grow in intensity.

Bartholomew Briggs. She never would have guessed he was capable of such evil, not in a million years! Lunacy, yes, but *evil*?

A clap of thunder rumbled across the arch of sky.

"One-one-thousand, two-one-thousand, three-one-thousand . . ." A tracery of lightning cut a jagged swath into the blackness, leaving her momentarily night-blind in its wake.

Another rip in the blackness, and the sky was lit by a brightness that rivaled that of noonday.

She screeched, scuttling backward on the palms of her hands and her feet until her body hit the couch behind her.

An image was seemingly burned into her retina: the shape of a body, backlit, hands pressed against the windowpane. Strands of rain-soaked hair were indelibly imprinted in her memory.

Had she actually seen it? Was there actually someone out there other than Flynn?

The floor beneath her palms resonated in symphony with the thunder overhead.

Timidly, she began to count. "One-one-thousand," she whispered, training her eyes on the black sheen that was the window, "two-one-thousand . . ."

The tiny hairs on her arm stood at attention, vibrating in the split second before the lightning cracked.

A ghost of a figure scampered on the periphery of her vision. She *had* seen it!

"Flynn!" she screamed at the top of her voice.

There was no doubt in her mind that the figure she had just seen outside the window was Bartholomew Briggs. Had he hurt Flynn? Was she now defenseless against Bartholomew?

She snatched every ounce of bravado she could muster, leapt to her feet, and dashed across the room. She locked the front door; then, she wrenched open the cupboard and grabbed the flashlight she'd always kept there. She flicked the flashlight on, almost crying out with relief when a beam of light sliced the darkness.

A small yelp escaped her lips as the thunder churned again.

She had to call for help.

Abby extended her arm toward the telephone, never for a moment letting her eyes leave the scene through the window. She lifted the phone from its cradle and placed it to her ear.

Silence.

Had someone cut the telephone lines?

The sickening thud of her heart all but ripped a cry from her throat. Something was very, very wrong; she felt it in the tiny hairs that stood erect on her body, the creeping of her flesh . . . the deadness of the telephone line.

The phone dangled like a hanged man from its swaying cord. If only she had her cell phone.

She inched toward the window, breath heaving, heart racing, and trained the beam of light into the darkness. A yellowish glow illuminated the verandah, shone from raindrops, and paled against a flash of lightning.

She craned her neck, searching the yard for evidence of the trespasser she knew she had seen.

Nothing.

A surge of fear engulfed her as she realized precisely how stupid she had been to come out here alone.

Where the devil is Connor Flynn? Her mind raced at lightning speed. The chances of getting to the car before being intercepted by Bartholomew were slim. If she was detected and pursued, could she possibly outrun him?

Her skin flushed with terror. Bartholomew had eluded the police and had come back for her, and Connor Flynn should be inside by now, yet there was no sign of him. Visions of Ronnie, lying naked and bloody on the shore flashed relentlessly in her mind. She knew what

Bartholomew was capable of, and that knowledge made her weak with fear . . . Had he hurt Connor?

Her heart seemed to pause in her chest as she glanced across the water and noted several homes dotting the opposite shore were all well lit in the darkness. All had power except hers.

"How could you be so stupid?" she whispered aloud. She slid down the wall, crouching in a corner and trembling, wondering what she should do.

Abby's cry was a whimper in the darkness. She had to find a weapon, fast.

She fell forward onto her hands and knees, prepared to slink across the room and retrieve a knife from the cutlery drawer. The biggest, most menacing one she could find.

And then, another sound. A creak—this time, from *inside* the cottage.

Awareness tiptoed over her flesh, leaving goose bumps in its wake as she remembered the window behind the stairway.

Without knowing how she knew, she was certain she was no longer alone in the house and that someone had crept through the back window.

She held back the sob that threatened to rip from her throat, inching herself forward, eye trained on the cutlery drawer and mind focused on the carving knife that rested within.

Another creak.

Her heart froze in her chest. She inched forward again, heart now pounding with terror.

Forget the knife. She had to get to the car! Her breath hissed in the charged stillness of the cottage, as if the only part of her body capable of movement was her heaving lungs.

And then, she heard it.

A sound: soft, commanding.

She closed her eyelids over the tears that sprang beneath them, terror thrumming beneath her skin like an animal that prowled to be loosed.

She turned slowly toward the darkened corner by the stairway—the place from which the sound had come.

She saw him then, as if his voice had caused him to materialize.

"Celeste," he whispered, the word saturated with undisguised longing.

"Who are you?" she said, her trembling voice barely registering.

She saw the core of blackness shift and move from behind the stairs. "Only who I've *always* been. You'd have recognized me if you'd tried."

The voice reverberated down her spine and lifted the hair on the back of her neck. She had heard that voice before, and it *wasn't* the voice of Bartholomew Briggs.

Her eyes made a panicked dart toward the door as she wondered if she could make it back to the car. As if sensing her thoughts, the figure bolted at her, slamming her against the wall where she was pinned, helpless.

"Connor?" she gasped, staring up at the mad, blazing eyes that looked down at her. Confusion collided with disbelief. This wasn't right—Connor wasn't the man who had stalked her, who had hurt Ronnie . . . *was he?* Surely this was a joke; surely this would all make sense in the morning. "Connor, please," she whimpered, "what on earth are you doing?"

Connor spun her around with a dexterity that belied his form, twisting her arm painfully behind her. His breath was moist on her neck as he inhaled deeply. "I've waited so long for this, my lovely Celeste." His tongue touched the skin behind her ear, drew upward with unhurried pleasure.

Unimaginable terror streaked through her, seemed to light her psyche with the screaming red that warned of deadly danger.

How can this be? Abby's brain had come to a terror-stricken halt. Nothing was making any sense; nothing seemed real. All this time it was Connor who had been stalking her.

And Connor had just called her Celeste.

"Connor," she said, pleading, "it's me. It's Abrielle Lancaster!"

He heaved against her back, pinning her more ruthlessly to the wall. Abby gasped with pain, feeling as if her arm were about to twist in two.

"Celeste," he said, his voice sounding heavy with wanting, "I knew you'd come back to me."

Abby felt his expression change, felt his cheek lift as with a slow, evil smile. He pushed his tongue into her ear before he spoke, sighing as if savoring something perfectly delicious.

"I knew you'd come. Good things come to those who wait."

Chapter Thirty-seven

"Connor, listen to me; it's *Abby!*"

A growl of anger rattled in his throat. He yanked her from the wall and shoved. Abby stumbled to the floor, knocking her shoulder on the corner of the table and sprawling onto her back.

Connor glared down at her. "I know who you are," he said menacingly. "You are my future, my past, my *everything* . . . and then you abandoned me." He kicked the table, sending it halfway across the room. "Tell me your name!"

She winced at the sound, crying in earnest, suddenly incapable of separating the sound of her sobs from the rain, his breathing, her own beating heart. They all collided within her. "Abrielle," she sobbed.

He erupted with a primordial sounding yell that sent her spirit spiraling in on itself. "Tell me your name!" he roared, droplets of spittle raining down upon her.

Abby gasped, knowing she had only one chance of survival. "C-Celeste," she said quietly, not believing her own voice.

He knelt before her, crowding her view with his face. His smile was slow and ice-cold. "Now that's better." He tilted his head closer, whispered, "I knew you'd remember. The night of the Marauder's Return, how I took you to the cave. Everything we did there. How I made you scream with pleasure."

Abby wanted to gag. This was the secret Bart had been talking about. Connor Flynn had not only stalked her mother. He'd raped her. Was he going to rape again? "Connor, please—"

His face came closer. Abby saw a glazed sort of fearlessness there. "That's it," he said. "Ask me." He lifted a length of her hair, pressed it to his lips. His eyes closed blissfully. "*Beg me.*"

"Please!"

"Do you remember the last time you begged me, Celeste?"

Her flesh crawled with sudden awareness. He actually seemed to think she was her mother. Perhaps her only hope for survival was to play into his madness—to *become* Celeste.

Abby turned a searching eye inward, scrabbling together every ounce of strength she could find in order to rise above her fear and use her one bargaining chip to her advantage—and that chip was the fact that Connor was insanely in love with Celeste.

"No, Connor," she answered, praying she sounded sweetly penitent. *Should I touch him?* Abby extended her trembling fingers and touched the cuff of his sleeve. "I don't remember the last time I begged you. But I want to . . . can you help me?"

Connor looked down at her fingers. His eyes were as cold as death, and yet Abby could see that something had penetrated that icy detachment—he was softening.

An answering chuckle resonated from the back of his throat. "Shy Celeste. Such a lady. You know, that's what I always loved about you." The smile melted from his lips. "So like my mother. Until she left me."

The glint in his eyes looked suddenly dangerous as he spoke of his mother. For her own safety, she *had* to change the subject. "Tell me what happened the last time we were together."

It worked. The anger faded. Connor stared at her, eyes hooded and almost drugged. The sleepy, blissful smile that spread over his face struck her to the heart with debilitating fear.

"Don't you remember, my sweet?" he asked dreamily. "I came to look after you in your fine brick house. I hid in the attic, made a peephole right over your bed. I watched over your baby when you slept. I gave up everything to come to you."

The dreamy expression faded from his face. "I didn't mean for you to fall, my lovely. I didn't mean to leave that window open. I was waiting for you when you came up that night. If only you hadn't played hard to get, hadn't tried to push me away, you never would have fallen through that window."

Abby couldn't speak, couldn't think. He'd been in Regency Park? He'd been there the night her mother died? "My mother didn't kill herself?" she asked, stunned. No, of course she didn't—he'd just admitted as much. He'd been waiting for her in the attic. He'd tried to rape her again, and she had fought back. That's why her mother had died!

"You murdered her!" she shouted.

His fist shot out. Abby gasped in shock as the sickening thud hit her belly, leaving her winded, gasping frantically for breath. On the periphery of her vision, she saw him rise, saw him fumble with his belt buckle.

No, no! she thought silently, eyes darting as she searched for something, anything, to use as a weapon against him.

She knew it all then, as he flipped her onto her belly and bound her wrists with his belt, knew that his vile, wretched hands had groped her mother's flesh as they now did hers, knew his foul breath had bathed her face with the same rancid lust.

A million thoughts converged in her head: his eyes upon her, watching from the forest, imbuing the darkness with his secret, quivering pulse.

With clinical detachment, she recalled how Connor had known immediately about her mother's ruby ring when she'd questioned him at the police station how he'd conveniently lost the note that was destined for the lab; how he'd tried to coax her into his petrol vehicle when she had followed Bartholomew into the wrecks; how he'd been undeniably angry when she had called Ryan at Ronnie's crime scene . . . because he'd wanted her there alone.

And it had been he and not the sheriff who had instructed her—through Cora—to go back to the cottage in order to go over the scene.

And all this time, Bart had been warning her against the devil waiting in the shadows. If only she'd needed his warning.

"Help!" she screamed, twisting beneath him. "Someone help me!"

A fist came down on the back of her head, slamming her cheek into the floor. Pain exploded behind her eyes, leaving her groaning—but she knew that above all, she must not give in to the shock that threatened.

"Celeste loved me. Just like my mother did . . . and *you* will."

She felt his fury as he turned her face up, straddled her, yanked on her shirtfront with unabashed rage. Abby cowered at the sound of ripping fabric, saw her creamy flesh glow in the darkness of the cottage. An instinctive urge made her want to shield her skin from his view, but that was impossible. All that mattered was getting away.

"I showed her," said Connor. "Showed her what love was all about. When I was through, she understood that I wouldn't let another man touch a woman of mine. She left the artist at my bidding. She would have left your father at my bidding, had she not died. And you'll leave Ryan Brannigan, because after tonight, there won't be a Ryan Brannigan to love!"

"It was you," she said, sobbing. "You did it all. You tried to kill Ronnie!"

His face barely registered a response. "That was for you, my lovely. An image to remind you of who you really are. Didn't she look pretty, posed like my lovely Celeste?"

The blood drained from her face. He was going to kill her.

Abby tried to scream but couldn't.

He pinned her wrists painfully against the rough carpet. "I can't let you be wanton like your mother—like *my* mother. Not when I love you so much. It's better you die. It's better that I make you pure."

"My mother didn't love you, Connor," she dared. "She left you! She could never love you!"

The transformation of his expression was horrifying. "It was *his* fault! It was the artist's fault that Celeste left!"

Connor grabbed her by the shoulders and thumped her onto the floor. Pain resonated from her bound wrists, and she writhed with the shock of it. He bent down, drew his tongue over her cheek. "She loved me. She gave herself to me. And she was sweet like honey."

"You're a sick rapist!" she screamed, forcing the words past the strangulating lump in her throat.

His hand descended so quickly, she couldn't dodge it. It collided with the side of her face. She cowered into her shoulders, aching for a more substantial protection from him, but there was nothing. Connor Flynn would destroy her as he'd destroyed her mother.

With the sound of cracking wood, the front door was thrown open.

"Abby!"

She tried to turn to the sound of the voice . . . of *Ryan's* voice . . . but she was pinned too securely.

Ryan burst into the room, colliding shoulder to shoulder with Connor. They fell to the ground, rolling in a spectacular tangle of rage. Abby scooted backward, digging her heels into the floor until she thudded against the couch.

In the dimness, she couldn't make out who was winning the fight—but she heard it just fine. The sickening thud of skin and bone, the jarring collision of body and floor, the panting of breath . . . then, silence.

"Ryan?" she gasped. "Ryan are you—"

"I'm okay," he said, rounding the coffee table and lowering himself beside her. He was dripping wet, and blood oozed from a gash on his forehead. He leaned her forward and began working on her bonds.

"How did you know to come?" she cried, arms jerking as he tugged to free her.

"I decided I wasn't going to let you walk away."

"Is Connor . . ."

"Out cold." Ryan grabbed her to him as her bonds finally broke free. "Let's get out of here before he comes to—and before the hurricane tears this cottage to shreds."

The cottage shuddered in response just as an ear-splitting crack yanked a cry from her throat.

Above her, Ryan's body bucked violently. His face froze

in a grotesque grimace, and he collapsed in slow motion, landing upon her with a crushing weight.

Abby shrieked in disbelief. "Ryan!" She struggled beneath his weight, then stopped abruptly as he started to groan.

The realization slammed into her: Ryan had been shot!

"Ryan!" she whimpered, stroking his hair almost frantically. First her mother, then Ronnie, now Ryan. This monster was determined to destroy everyone she loved.

Well, she wouldn't have it. Not while there was breath in her lungs . . . and not while her hands were unbound. At least now she had a fighting chance.

She held Ryan against her, realizing in a shattering instant that she could never, *would* never give him up— she'd been crazy to think it possible—and she would overcome both the fury of the hurricane and the evil of Connor Flynn just to call Ryan hers. "This is *not* the end of us, Ryan," she swore under her breath as she watched Connor rise before them. "I'm going to lead him away. You do your best to get out of here, understand?"

Ryan's breath was ragged against the side of her face. "Don't do it, Abby."

Her heart twisted in her chest. "Would you rather watch him rape me?"

Ryan was silent. He shook his head minutely. "Run," he said, the word dying on his lips as he sagged against her.

A black shadow stretched across them both as Connor stepped closer. Abby clutched Ryan tightly to her, peered over his shoulder, and into the eyes of pure evil. She shoved Ryan gently aside and placed herself between the two men. "Let him go," she said. "It's not him you want. It's me. I'm yours, Connor. Just call an ambulance, and I'm yours."

She was as calm as she had ever been, her thoughts ordering themselves in tidy succession, her mind preparing for the worst. She could do it, for Ryan. She breathed him in, exhaled a prayer for his safety, and concentrated very hard on the sound of his breathing. It was shallow. Too shallow.

"Connor," she asked, trying with all she had to sound seductive, "don't you want me?"

His gaze was icy as he looked down upon her. He drew back his leg and kicked, sending Ryan aside in a groaning heap.

"Don't touch him!" she shrieked as she scuttled across the floor to Ryan's side. Connor raised a finger in warning.

"Don't *you* touch him. You touch him, he dies."

Abby's hand trembled with the need to comfort Ryan, yet she held it in place at her chest. Any move she made toward him would be answered with punishment upon Ryan. She could see it in Connor's eyes.

"Now," he said, "come with me."

She stared at his outstretched hand, her entire body recoiling in revulsion. It came with every labored pulse, and slowly overwhelmed her body in its smothering embrace. At last, she reached for him.

"Ahh," he said quietly. "That's more like it."

His face was twisted in strange delight. "Come, Celeste," he said, drawing her toward the bedroom. "Come back to the portrait that started it all."

She stifled a cry of terror and followed obediently.

"I came to her while she slept. Before she was fully awake, I had her wrapped in the sheet so I could take her to the cave. I taught her to love me that night. Then she left me," he said, despondently. "But you came back, Celeste. I always knew you would."

"Of course I did," she said, voice quavering as her eyes searched the darkened stairwell frantically.

There. Hanging on the wall in the upper hallway, glinting with menacing light was a brass bed warmer—a long-handled device once filled with hot coals and placed in a cold bed. It looked very much like a frying pan. A very *lethal* frying pan.

A bone-deep terror burgeoned within her as she mounted the last few stairs. She could smell him, hear his breath, sense his eager nearness, and her body revolted against it all with a nausea that threatened to overtake her.

She gripped the banister tightly, gaze riveted upon the bed warmer with a fixation that propelled her onward despite what would await her at the top of the stairs if she failed . . . but she must not fail!

Her lips spoke a silent prayer for Ryan, for them both, as she mounted the last step. One false move, and she and Ryan would both be dead.

With a cry that tore from her throat, she lunged at the wall, grasped the long, wooden handle, and pulled with a knowledge that her very life was hanging in the balance.

She reeled on him, warmer held high, throat raw with a wail she had no conscious realization of making, and swung with all her might.

Connor's eyes sprang open, his hand reached reflexively for his weapon. It was rising, rising in the surreal slow motion of the moment, grasped in his hand and aiming at her.

Abby kept swinging, prayed that her arm, the warmer, would move faster—would make crucial contact with her attacker.

The impact was jarring. Her arm dropped; the warmer clanged to the floor. Both she and Connor stared into each other's eyes in stunned paralysis as he teetered and swayed on the topmost step.

Silently—in the endless, spiraling moment—she pleaded with him to fall, begged him not to make her strike again.

Please, her mouth shaped soundlessly, as she watched in fascinated horror the trickle of blood that wound its way down the side of his face, as her breath filled the tiny landing with the scent of her fear.

He swayed again. "Celeste," he groaned, reaching toward

her, then toppled backward down the stairs, his body thudding grotesquely on each wooden step, until at last his body lay inert at the bottom.

Abby shrieked, slapped her hand over her mouth, then bounded down the stairs. She leapt over Connor's slumped form, eyes frantically searching the living room for Ryan.

"Ryan!"

She skidded around the sofa as if she were on roller skates, and saw . . . nothing.

"Ryan?"

The front door creaked on its hinges, swinging in the building wind. Abby stared at it, straining to make sense of what had happened

Had Ryan escaped? Had he made it to the car?

She had to find him! She lurched toward the door, only to feel Connor's grasp on her arm.

She thudded down painfully on her belly, rolled over and saw Connor looming above her, his face contorted with rage.

"No!" she grabbed the couch leg, reared back and kicked with all her might.

Connor bucked, hand grasping his groin.

It was the split second she needed. Abby scrambled to her feet and ran to the side door. If Ryan had gone toward the car and had not made it—if he had collapsed on the front lawn or verandah—she needed to draw Connor as far away from him as possible.

Her best refuge was one of the cottages across the lake. Could she make it that far?

Her head was pounding, her face stinging, her heart thudding as if trying to leap from her chest.

She burst from the cottage and turned her tear-blind eyes to the cliffs, ignoring the urge that bade her to search out Ryan. His only hope was if she could lead Connor away from him.

Her ankles turned and twisted underneath her as she

plunged into the dark woods, felt the lashings of alders on her skin. She welcomed the stinging pain, for fear, she knew, could be her best ally.

Connor was crashing through the woods at her heels. Abby ran faster, driven by her desire to live.

A stiff gust from the promised nor'easter raced up the cliff side, siphoning ice crystals into the air. They glistened and spun with scalpellike precision, exposing the bare aggression at the core of treacherous wind.

Abby burst through the iron gate that led into Hill Top Cemetery.

The light of the full moon was sufficient to illuminate the path before her. Now and again, it would emerge from its cloak of clouds, and the entire, rain-soaked hill would mirror its pearly geography. Abby didn't know whether she ought to curse it or welcome it. She needed light to see . . . but so did Connor.

Humps of granite marking the tombs of the dead seemed to lean toward her. Abby gagged on her own terror, wondering if she would soon join the silent throng that slept beneath her feet.

A large, black shadow loomed before her, and Abby raced to the sarcophagus that created it. She crouched behind it, gasping for breath, eyes darting from monument to tombstone, heart pleading for release.

"Celeste," came the taunting voice. "Hide-and-seek is for children."

She squeezed her eyes shut, straining to decipher the location of his voice in the tossing wind.

On hands and knees, she crept toward the corner of the sarcophagus, peering into the blackness.

Connor was nowhere to be seen.

As if drawn by an otherworldly force, she crouched and ran past the shadowy humps of monuments and gravestones; past the magnificent, marble tombs with rain-soaked effigies peering into the heavens; past the oldest of the stones, where yellow lichen crawled deep into the recesses afforded by inscriptions. She stopped at last, huddling beside a massive hunk of granite. The words made her heart pause in her chest.

Here lies Douglas McAllister
Who loved Celeste

Abby began shaking. "Mom," she whispered raggedly, "help me, please."

She looked up toward the dark shelter of the tree line. There, moving fluidly over the earth, gown still as moonlight in the raging wind, was the White Lady. She turned to look at Abby.

Abby's racing heartbeat came to a stop. She looked into a face that could have been her own.

"Mom," she whispered, stunned to her core. Her eyes flooded with tears as she looked into her mother's face.

The White Lady—forever after to be known as Celeste in Abby's heart—smiled.

A surge of recognition, of love, of peace flooded her soul. She lifted her hand as if to reach across time and space, as if to touch the woman who looked at her so gently. "Help me," Abby mouthed, staring at her mother. And in an instant, the peace she saw in her mother's face filled her heart. Instinctively, she knew that her mother would do all she could to help.

Would it be enough?

"Come out, come out, wherever you are!"

Her heart lurched anew at the sound of Connor's voice. A voracious wind encircled her, whipping her hair into the cadence of its howl. She grasped the strands that would surely be visible in the moonlight, and held them to her head with both hands.

"Celeste!" he cried, matching the wind in fury.

Abby cowered by the headstone, trembling as she reached from the shadows and grasped a glass urn that rested on a neighboring stone. Slowly, she pulled her arm back into the darkness. From where she crouched, she could see him lurking, peeking behind stones, gun lifted and ready.

She grasped the wilted flowers that sprouted from the urn, lifted them free, and placed them silently on the ground. If he got close enough, and if she were fast enough, a piece of broken glass would make a fine weapon.

A tendril of hope twisted through her veins. Her fingers twitched with it. *This is not the night that I die.*

Abby lurched at a rustling behind her, screamed as the shadows seemed to converge, gather speed, and take form in the hurtling body of Connor Flynn.

"No!" she shrieked, sprawling forward on her belly and smashing the urn against the stone.

He had found her!

She jabbed at his arm with the sliver of glass that was left of the urn. Still, he pulled her closer.

"You're mine!" he roared.

"Rot in hell!" she cried.

Connor was too strong. He pushed her to the earth, closed his hands around her neck.

Her strength was waning; her heart was sick with thoughts of Ryan and what had become of him.

Surrender began to wash over her like a bloodred tide. Connor's hands on her throat, his face filling up the whole of her vision.

She peered into the sky over his shoulder, felt her circle of awareness shrink into a pinprick of light that was the moon overhead. She would watch it, would center her spirit there until the last moment.

Her blood was a thundering tide in her ears, soothing her, drowning her.

She bucked beneath him, felt the futility of it even as she forced herself to fight him this last time. She twisted, her eyes darting as blackness crept in along the edges of her vision.

Abby closed her eyes, flailed out in desperation, and felt a shard of glass pierce her hand. She was fading, fading, but could still feel the glass with her fingertips. She grasped it, squeezed her hand around it, felt the sharp edges cut into her flesh.

The glass was slick in her grip, warm with the blood that coated it.

Help me, she entreated the heavens, her mother, anyone who could feel her terror. Then, with her last ounce of strength, she plunged the glass dagger into the throat of Connor Flynn.

His face froze above her, his eyes piercing her with a zeal that made her weak with terror.

Blood was a river of warm fury, sluicing over her hand, down her wrist.

She watched his eyes widen, felt his grasp on her throat loosen.

"*Why?*" he asked, the words lost in a sickening gurgle.

Abby stared in horror at the shard protruding from his flesh. She bucked beneath him, struggled out from his weakening body, and dragged herself to the headstone of Douglas McAllister.

Her throat throbbed as breath filled it with choking intensity. She gagged on it, cried with it, swallowed it whole and thanked God for it as a slow realization came over her: *she was alive*.

Rain was hitting her face, and *she was alive!*

She cried out with relief, turned to her side, and retched into the grass.

When at last she could, she looked at Connor Flynn. The sound of his dying was all around her, all within her, as he lay on the earth and breathed in his last breath.

"Please let Ryan be safe," she prayed, and felt consciousness drift from her body.

It wasn't a dream, was her first conscious thought.

She was soaked and shivering. Connor lay dead only feet away from her. Her throat throbbed with every breath.

A nightmare, maybe—but not a dream. She was painfully awake.

How long had she been here? And where was Ryan? She had no idea where he was or what had happened to him.

Tears slipped over her cheeks as she forced herself to her knees, refusing to look at Connor's slumped body.

In the near distance, a twig snapped sharply. Someone was coming, and she couldn't even lift her head to see who it was.

"You all right?"

Only her eyes moved. Abby looked at the shadow that stood above her.

A length of wood dangled from Bartholomew's hand as he turned his attention to the inert form of Connor Flynn. He eyed the man disgustedly. "Bugger's pinned his dirty dealings on me for the last time," he said, water spewing from his lips as he spoke into the slicing rain.

She blinked, trembling all over as she drew herself toward a tombstone and leaned in for support. "Bartholomew," she said, gripping her shirt together over her chest for what meager shelter it provided. "I—I don't understand. Did you know it was him all along?"

"Told you there was a devil waitin' for you. Tried to scare you off before he could get you." He spat in the direction of Connor Flynn, face contorted in a mask of perfect distain. "You shoulda listened."

Abby squeezed her eyes shut—the better to contain the fragmenting of her emotions. All this time, Bartholomew had been trying to frighten her away from the island and the menacing threat that Connor presented. In his own twisted way, he had been trying to help.

"How did you know it was him?" she asked, unable to speak her stalker's name.

A snaggle-toothed grin pierced the darkness. "Bartholomew is a tree. Bartholomew is a stone. No one sees Bartholomew—not even the devil—but Bartholomew sees all."

"Why didn't you turn him in?"

"Folks these days don't believe in the wisdom of trees and stones," he said, the smile slowly giving way to the madness that was now familiar to her. Bartholomew looked up at the moon, tilted his head at the glowing orb as if only it could understand him. "No one believes Bartholomew."

Abby was starting to shake uncontrollably. She had to get back to Ryan. "I believe you, Bartholomew. I believe you know where Ryan is."

"Cora's boy is safe. I lugged him into the woods myself."

She stumbled to her feet, legs trembling as if she were a newborn foal. "Thank you," she said, eyes blind to the rain, to the slumped figure of Connor Flynn, the bedraggled one of Bartholomew Briggs; her body ignored the stabbing pain that cried to her from every limb and joint. "He needs my help."

"Yep," he said, as if she had just commented on the weather. "You best run along home, now."

Abby stared up at the figure he presented, and stumbled into the night.

Chapter Thirty-eight

Abby stood in the chill of the morgue and tried only to feel gratitude for the fact that Ryan was safe and healing, and that she was alive to rejoice with him.

Still, the body lying on the slab of stainless steel seemed to mock her efforts.

She traced the edge of her jaw with her fingers—knew that the flesh her fingers rested upon was the putrid yellow of waning bruises! She knew also that it could have been *her* lying on that slab, and not Connor Flynn.

Her hand fell to her throat as she remembered the sickening moment she had found Ronnie on the rocks. Then it fell lower, to her heart. It lurched in her chest as she recalled every millisecond of Ryan's shooting—the scent of gunpowder, the scent of blood, the scent of her own fear.

Thank God he's all right.

For the thousandth time, she uttered another prayer of gratitude for Bartholomew Briggs—town lunatic and outright savior of Ryan's life—and now, celebrated hero of Destiny Bay.

During her police interviews, she had learned that shortly after hiding Ryan in the woods and then racing to her aid in the cemetery, Bartholomew had run to the home of Simon Gorham—the man who watched over the cottage for Cora—and convinced him to call 9-1-1.

By the time Abby made it back to her cottage and found Ryan—limp and bleeding amidst the blackberry bushes— she could already hear the screeching whine of sirens.

Even here and now, the memory of that sound seemed to bring it all back to her.

The terror was still too close to the surface, threatening to bubble up and overtake her at any moment. She felt hollow, fragile as an egg, and considerably disconcerted by the fact that she stared down at her would-be murderer while standing beside his older brother.

Sheriff Flynn shifted on his feet. He clutched his hat in his hand as he frowned down at Connor, an expression of mingled sorrow and mystification on his face.

Abby moved her mouth to speak, but what on earth could she say to him? It wasn't as if she was without compassion for the sheriff, but Connor would have killed her if she hadn't grabbed the shard of glass and . . .

She shuddered involuntarily, squeezing her eyes shut at the memory.

"I'm sorry, Sheriff Flynn."

Flynn jolted. It was as if he'd forgotten that she stood right beside him.

Funny, because it was he who'd brought her here in the first place. Granted, *she'd* made the somewhat unorthodox request, citing closure as her reason to see Connor Flynn.

"I wouldn't have done it if there'd been any other way." She forced herself to look up at him, forced herself to see the shadows beneath his eyes and his haggard, disheveled appearance. "He *was* going to kill me." She'd told him all this in her statement, and had been informed by a younger officer that the evidence found in the cemetery and cottage supported her claims . . . yet she felt compelled to speak.

The corners of his mouth dipped lower in seeming contemplation. "Yes. I know he was."

An oppressive silence fell over the room. Abby looked up at the sheriff. "You knew."

His expression was transformed before her eyes. A crimson flush stole up from his collar, mottled his cheeks. All disbelief seemed to fade from his features as he looked down at her.

"Why did he do this, Sheriff?"

His head fell forward, started rocking back and forth. When he looked back up, his face was calmer, if still quite flushed. "He was only eight when our mama left."

Abby's spine stiffened involuntarily. "Go on," she said with some caution.

"We were better off without her, see, but Connor never understood that." The sheriff stared at the white-painted cinder block that was the wall as if calling a memory to life upon the blank canvas it presented. "The day she left, Connor latched onto her leg and held on tight. He didn't want her to go. Mom was trying to shake herself free of him, and I was tugging on his waist, and we were all . . ." He squeezed his eyes shut tightly. "We were all crying."

He looked suddenly smaller, and his white-knuckled grasp trembled on the lip of the steel table upon which Connor lay. "She ran off with some hack from Marriot's Bay—her hometown.

"Connor'd pray every night that she'd come home. She never did," he said with a philosophical lift of his shoulder. "Once in a while she'd call, and when Connor would ask when she was coming home, she'd just say that good things come to those who wait."

Ice water coursed though her veins. *That's what he said to me. Good things come to those who wait.*

Abby thought back to the evening she'd shared with Ryan at the Captain's House; that night when she understood the awful legacy that fear thrust upon her, upon Ryan, upon Celeste. At that moment, she'd realized that all that fear had started somewhere, and all she'd wanted to do was find the bitter seed and destroy it.

Now, in hearing the sheriff's confessions, she had found the seed. But how to destroy it?

Sheriff dragged his hand over his face. "The fella she ran off with, he was a real piece of work. He knocked Mama around something awful 'til he finally beat her to death in a drunken rage. Connor was twelve when she died."

"I'm so sorry," she whispered, her lips feeling stiff and cold, her heart beginning to understand at least some of what had driven this boy—this man—to madness.

Sheriff lifted his shoulder, let it drop. "Her landlord dropped by a box of her belongings and there was a diary inside. Connor took it. He read that thing 'til it was good and worn, and though I never saw the words for myself, Connor told me that Mama wrote a promise she'd return to her boys one day." The sheriff exhaled slowly. "Our mama had long red hair. Just like *your* mama's. And she was right pretty."

It was starting to make sense to her.

Sheriff rubbed his nose. "She'd tickle his bare belly with her hair, and he'd laugh like there was no tomorrow. He always believed she'd come back to him. Even after she'd already died."

"So when my mother came to Destiny Bay . . ."

"A part of him must have seen that hair and decided that Celeste Rutherford was his destiny."

"Did you know your brother was stalking her?"

Sheriff shrugged. "Never knew for sure."

"But you suspected it?"

"You gotta understand that I was brand new on the force. The sheriff at the time—that was our daddy—had me parked at my desk knee-deep in paper work. He wouldn't let me anywhere *near* that case."

"So it's likely he suspected Connor?"

"I s'pose. If he did—and I said *if*—Dad musta decided to handle it privately so's to spare the family any embarrassment. Besides, Connor was all of nineteen at the time. Dad likely figured that between your ma and that artist friend of hers, they could keep a nineteen-year-old kid at bay."

"And if not, they deserved what they got?" she asked acidly.

"That's not what I mean to say." Sheriff sniffed loudly.

"It's all a sorry mess, is what, and it never should have come to this."

"No, it shouldn't have." Abby bit back the stinging tirade that clawed at her esophagus. She wanted to scream at him, to punish him, to have his badge on a silver platter. All this could have been prevented, and *would* have been, if he'd just opened his eyes to the poison that lurked within his own family. "It's true what I said in my statement—my mother didn't commit suicide. He really was there. He attacked her and she fell through that window."

Flynn nodded. "I believe you. I don't want to, but I do. There was this time way back when he just disappeared. We had no clue where he'd gone. When he finally came home, he offered no explanation at all." He squeezed his eyes shut. Shook his head slowly.

Tragedy was thick in the room, and Abby needed to get out soon. "Sheriff Flynn?"

"Yeah?"

"I'd like some time alone with Connor."

Flynn looked at her as there were a third eye in the center of her forehead. "Why?" he asked, eyes narrowing.

"I'm not planning any mischief, if that's what you're worried about. I just want to . . ." What *did* she want to do? She gripped her clutch purse tightly. "I . . . I need to say good-bye."

Flynn nodded minutely, turned his back on her, and strode toward the door. "You got five minutes."

She forced her gaze upon Connor.

He *had* meant to kill her.

Technically, he had failed, but had he succeeded in some more insidious way?

For what seemed like the thousandth time, she wondered if Connor had killed her on some deeper, unseen level, had killed the very heart of her. She wondered if she would ever *feel* again. Ever trust again . . . ever sleep again.

She stood, staring at the man who had consumed her imagination with thoughts of terror, the man who had seemed undefeatable.

Now, lying on steel—his skin bluish and wiped clean of blood—he seemed significantly cut down to size.

How had he done it? How had this man, so common in measure, twisted her life, and that of her mother's?

"I'm not going to let you win." she said to him. "I had a life . . . I *have* a life, and I won't let you take it with you."

She stepped closer, watching him, hawklike, as though he would lurch into being and snatch everything that was left of her.

She bit her lip and tucked her hand into the crook of her other arm.

Abby looked at him, and understood—with a bone-chilling clarity—that she could choose one of two routes.

One, she could allow time and fear to eventually plunge her into the darkness that now threatened to bloom within her. She shivered at the thought, imagined the specter of her fears twining 'round her, sucking her under.

Or, she could let it go.

She wasn't entirely certain how that was done, but it had to be possible. It simply had to be.

Abby waited for the eureka moment to come, listening to the sound of her breath fill the room, watching his bluish eyelids; but all that came was a quote, remembered: ". . . *and a great and strong wind rent the mountains . . . and after the wind, an earthquake . . . and after the earthquake, a fire, and after the fire, a still small voice.*"

And the still, small voice—that sounded almost exactly like her mother's—said, "*Abrielle, it's over, and you have won. For both of us. Let it go.*"

Abby blinked and looked around the room; it was empty but for her and Connor Flynn. She had heard the voice, hadn't she? And then she knew this: of course, she had.

She had heard her mother's voice from the only place it

could have come from: from her heart, her soul, from the part of her mother that beat daily in her veins, that weighed every battle of her heart, for her mother was yet alive. Her mother was alive within her, now and forever.

"Eureka," she whispered, and walked out of the room.

She drove straight to Ryan's, suddenly filled to overflowing with anticipation for their future. No, Connor couldn't take her joy if she wouldn't let him.

A note tacked on his front door read: *I'm up at the cliff.* Abby rolled her eyes. "Nice to see he's following doctor's orders and resting."

Still, she was glad for the fresh air.

She was following the footsteps that led toward the edge of the forest. The scent of autumn was rich in the forest. She stepped into the soothing shadows that cloaked the earth in a blanket of slumber. Wind-ravaged heather caught the last vestige of light, reflecting amethyst, charcoal and deep, bluish gray.

"Abby!"

She was snatched into a crushing bear hug—enveloped in Ryan's arms, and just as quickly released with a grunt.

"Be careful!" she said, gripping his forearms and studying his face. "Are you hurt?"

Ryan lifted a brow. "Oh, fine, aside from a bullet hole in my side."

Abby touched his face, felt the stubble on his jaw, saw the shadows beneath his eyes and the raw glint that lit them from within. He was a mess, pure and simple. Abby thought that she'd never seen him look quite so handsome. She forced a weak smile. "Don't talk about it—please. I can't stand to remember you on the floor, bleeding . . ." She suppressed a shiver.

"It's over now," he said softly. "Nothing left but healing."

He embraced her again, this time with greater care. She felt dizzy at the scent of forest that clung to his skin. She wrapped her arms around him, then breathed—just breathed—the scent of his hair, his skin, his touch. "I'm so sorry this happened to you. It's all my fault."

"It's over, Abby. *All* of it."

"No," she whispered, smiling. "It's just begun."

The supple leather beneath her hands hinted at the muscular frame it cloaked. She held tighter, grateful to her bones for the innate strength of him.

"I love you, Ryan," she said, marveling in the feel of the words on her tongue. She buried her lips in his neck as she clung to him. The wind tossed around them, and whipped her hair into a frenzied halo. She felt his hands smoothing the strands, felt the warmth of his face touch her own.

It was neither day nor night as she turned to the east, looked into the wind with her face upturned and with words of promise still warm on her tongue. The earth and sea rolled out before her—their terrible beauty a living thing that could destroy as well as heal in one magnificent instant of contradiction. The sky glowed opalescent, touched hill with tawny light, hid valley in violet darkness—seemed to glow in quiet celebration and will a small portion of its strength into her open soul.

Tears filled her eyes as she witnessed twilight's magical passage into night. She would carry this picture with her always—the colors that breathed a promise to her soul.

She turned, looked into Ryan's eyes, and he into hers. It was a timeless moment, perfected by the surety and peace that filled her. His soul seemed to call out to her heart, to awaken every dream she had harbored of love and of beauty. She felt her heart rise to his invitation, felt his promise to fulfill each of those dreams, and felt her silent acceptance. And in that moment, she had found her destiny.

A tear escaped her eye as she wished the moment would never end, and yet, she recognized an intensity that could burn as well as exalt. *Don't look away*, his eyes said.

And she—knowing that it was hardly possible to turn from him—held fast his gaze, met the clear, topaz oasis of honesty amidst the firestorm of emotion that seemed to swirl around and within them.

You are mine, his eyes spoke again—in a language beyond words, a prose ignorant of untruths and incapable of deceit. *And, you are mine,* she promised. *Forever.*

Abby looked out to the sea, felt her heart grow still as she saw the White Lady—her mother—drifting silently toward the waves, a gentle smile on her lips. In defiance of time and space, Abby had found her.

Without knowing how she sensed it, Abby knew that this was the last time she would see her, and that by finding her own peace, she had in turn given peace to her mother.

Bye, she mouthed silently.

For now, replied the voice in her heart, the voice of her mother, and the White Lady vanished into the shimmering mist of the sea.

Ryan grasped her tighter. If he'd seen her mother's ghost, he hadn't let on. "Stay here," he said. "Stay with me in Destiny Bay."

She blinked a tear from her eye before she turned to face him.

"I will," she whispered into the wind. "Forever."

For centuries they have walked among us—vampires, shape-shifters, the Celtic Sidhe, demons, and other magical beings. Their battle to reign supreme is constant, but one force holds them in check, a race of powerful woarriors known as the

IMMORTALS

The USA Today *Bestselling Series Continues*

Immortals: *THE REDEEMING*
Coming September 2008

Immortals: *THE CROSSING*
Coming October 2008

Immortals: *THE HAUNTING*
Coming November 2008

Immortals: *THE RECKONING*
Coming Spring 2009

TRIPLE EXPOSURE

"[Thompson] more than holds her own in territory blazed by Tami Hoag and Tess Gerritsen."

—*Publishers Weekly*

COLLEEN THOMPSON

Better than anyone, photographer Rachel Carson knows the camera can lie. That's how lurid altered photos of her appeared on the Internet, starting a downward spiral that ended with her shooting a nineteen-year-old stalker in self-defense. Fleeing the press and the threats of an un-identified female caller, she retreats to her remote home-town in the Texas desert. In Marfa, where mysterious lights hover in the night sky, folks are used to the unexplainable, and a person's secrets are off-limits. But recluse Zeke Pike takes that philosophy even further than Rachel herself. In her viewfinder Zeke's male sensuality is highlighted, his unexpressed longing for human contact revealed. Through a soft-focus lens, she sees a future for them beyond their red-hot affair, never guessing their relationship will expose the lovers to more danger than either can imagine.

AVAILABLE AUGUST 2008!
ISBN 13: 978-0-8439-6143-0

JUDITH E. FRENCH

SUPER KILLERS

Human monsters. They torture and terrify, then terminate innocent lives. For pleasure. And always there is a pattern, a signature that sets their crimes apart.

BLOOD SPORT

Agent Jillian Maxwell is sure she's identified one of the worst ever. Twenty-three unsolved murders in two years. A trail of bodies with slashed throats, dumped by the sea. Her distractingly hot new partner disputes her theory, but Jillian's instincts tell her she's closing in on her quarry. The postcards she's received before each strike hold the key; she knows the scene of the next murder—Ocean City, Maryland. Despite "Cowboy" Reed Donovan's objections, she'll go undercover to draw out the perp. Only too late, she realizes there's more than one player in this deadly game, and she's been set up to be the latest loser.

ISBN 13: 978-0-505-52757-8

CHRISTIE CRAIG

"is a must-read."
—Nationally Bestselling Author Nina Bangs

Katie Ray was about to marry a man she didn't love—and who didn't love her. Even losing her $8,000 engagement ring wasn't enough of a sign to call things off. What did it take? Being locked in the closet with a sexy PI, and being witness to murder.

Carl Hades had been hired by an elite Houston wedding planner to investigate some missing brides. When those brides turned up dead, Carl saw where the whole situation was headed: just like Katie's wedding ring and her ceremony, right down the toilet. Because, while the gorgeous redhead was suddenly and delightfully available, he had a feeling she was next in line to die....

Weddings Can Be Murder

ISBN 13: 978-0-505-52731-8

New York Times Bestselling Author

Marjorie M. Liu

Lannes Hannelore is one of a dying race born to protect mankind against demonic forces. And while those who look upon him see a beautiful man, this illusion is nothing but a prison. His existence is one of pure isolation, hiding in plain sight, with brief solace found in simple pleasures: stretching his wings on a stormy night, long late drives on empty highways, the deep soul of sad songs. But when Lannes finds a young woman covered in blood—desperate and alone, with no memory or past—he will be drawn into a mystery that makes him question all he knows. And though it goes against his nature and everything he fears, Lannes will risk his heart, his secrets, and his very soul, in order to save someone who could be the love of his life…or the end of it.

A Dirk & Steele Novel

THE Wild Road

ISBN 13: 978-0-8439-5939-0

☐ **YES!**

Sign me up for the Love Spell Book Club and send my REE BOOKS! If I choose to stay in the club, I will pay only $8.50* each month, a savings of $6.48!

AME: _____

DDRESS: _____

ELEPHONE: _____

MAIL: _____

☐ I want to pay by credit card.

☐ VISA   ☐ MasterCard.   ☐ DISC●VER

CCOUNT #: _____

XPIRATION DATE: _____

IGNATURE: _____

Mail this page along with $2.00 shipping and handling to:
Love Spell Book Club
PO Box 6640
Wayne, PA 19087
Or fax (must include credit card information) to:
610-995-9274

You can also sign up online at **www.dorchesterpub.com**.
Plus $2.00 for shipping. Offer open to residents of the U.S. and Canada only. Canadian residents please call 1-800-481-9191 for pricing information.
If under 18, a parent or guardian must sign. Terms, prices and conditions subject to change. Subscription subject to acceptance. Dorchester Publishing reserves the right to reject any order or cancel any subscription.